The War Between Heaven and Hell Begins Now

"These angels can be vindictive and cruel, more human than you might expect and oozing supernatural abilities. . . . If you think you have the guts to take on this novel pick it up."
—*Boulder Examiner*

"A dark, bold story."
—*Lexington Literature Examiner*

"This book is one of the best debut novels seen in a long time. Benulis writes a no-holds-barred tale of destruction, love, power, and friendship. Everything you thought you knew about God, the Devil, angels and demons will be wiped away and replaced with a world so terribly beautiful that you will find yourself gazing out into the night sky, hoping against hope that magic is real. Her characters have depth and 3-dimensional personalities, while her scenery, complete with candlelight and stained-glass windows, emphasizes the primal battles that humans go through on a daily basis."
—*Tulsa Books Examiner*

"With the first installment in her trilogy, Benulis uses lush descriptions and larger than life characters to tell the story of a battle between Heaven and Hell. . . . She proves herself as a force to be reckoned with. . . . I will definitely be on the lookout for the next installment in her book of Raziel series so I can grab it up and pour over each page."
—*Suspense Magazine*

"This plot is original in every way, and it resembles nothing that I have ever read before."
—*Wilkes Beacon*

ARCHON

THE BOOKS OF RAZIEL

SABRINA BENULIS

HARPER Voyager
An Imprint of HarperCollins Publishers

ARCHON. Copyright © 2012 by Sabrina Benulis. All rights reserved. Printed in the United States of America. No part of this book may be used or reproduced in any manner whatsoever without written permission except in the case of brief quotations embodied in critical articles and reviews. For information, address HarperCollins Publishers, 195 Broadway, New York, NY 10007.

HarperCollins books may be purchased for educational, business, or sales promotional use. For information, please e-mail the Special Markets Department at SPsales@harpercollins.com.

A hardcover edition of this book was originally published in 2012 by Harper Voyager, an imprint of HarperCollins Publishers.

FIRST HARPER VOYAGER PAPERBACK EDITION PUBLISHED 2012.

Designed by Paula Russell Szafranski

Library of Congress Cataloging-in-Publication Data has been applied for.

ISBN 978-0-06-211690-1

16 17 18 19   OV/RRD   10 9 8 7 6 5 4 3 2

*For all those who encouraged
me to fly toward my dreams:
Let's soar.*

ACKNOWLEDGMENTS

Thank you to God. You made everything possible for me, whether by arranging one amazing coincidence after another, blessing me with this crazy talent to create crazy worlds, or throwing people into my life who couldn't help but encourage that talent. Not to mention angels. Did I mention I really like Your angels?

Thank you to my husband, Mike, and to my Mom and Dad, Gary and Sharon Naples. Your patience in listening to me babble about imaginary people, places, and things was more valuable than you can ever know. But what meant more was your belief in what I could accomplish. Through it all, what I wanted most was for you to be proud and happy, and I pray I can make you feel that way forever. You'll have to bear with me as I keep trying and hopefully keep succeeding.

Thank you to my family and my steadfast friends, each and every one of you. Of course I didn't forget you! Please know that your excitement for me and your overall support helped me through some of the toughest times. I wanted to entertain you and whisk you away to a faraway place. Now you'll have to fess up and tell me if the magic worked.

Sincere thanks to my agent, Ann Behar, and my editor, Diana Gill. Your risk taking and vision shaped my novel into what it is today and I'm endlessly grateful for all of your hard work and dedication. Novels are never the work of just one person, and in this case that is most certainly true. If you hadn't poured your time and effort into this project, where would I be now?

A heartfelt thanks to my friends and fellow classmates at Seton Hill University's Writing Popular Fiction program, especially my mentor, Timons Esaias. Poor souls, you had to read an amateur version of something that resembled this book. But somehow I managed to enchant you and make you believe in it, and that, I learned, is what real writing is all about.

And last, but not least, thank you to my cockatiel, Caesar. Because of you I fell in love with all things with wings.

That reminds me—thank you to the Birds, both those in Heaven and on Earth. It's easy to reach for the stars when you have guides to show you the way.

ARCHON

Blood on Her head,
Blood on Her hands.
Death for Her servant,
Eye that commands.
Heaven and starlight,
Or Hellfire and fear.
The choice is Hers.
The Ruin looms near.

Zero

Israfel rather enjoyed the sight of the human stumbling into his nest.

Angels were fond of freshness and youth, and though he'd expected a girl, maybe even a woman, this turn of events was undeniably interesting. Here was an opportunity to be relished; a beautiful thing, weak and fragile as glass. The young man was slender, but also tall and well-built, ringlets of brown hair spilling against the base of his strong neck. He'd hesitated, one hand resting on the door handle. Now he leaned forward, scanning the church's insides, breathing softly.

"Yes?" Israfel peered from behind a column.

The human gasped. His hand slipped, snapping the handle back into place.

It was a typical reaction. Any angel could be beautiful, but Israfel knew he painted a far more imposing picture than most. His figure bordered on ambiguous, his blue eyes were larger than a human's, ringed with stylized circles of kohl, and the hair that framed them shimmered whiter than the stars. A single word from his lips and the universe stilled to listen. This wasn't the first time he'd left someone with nothing to say.

"Your name then?" he said more gently.

The human shut the double doors, their handles latching with a *click*.

Slowly, he crept closer, too enthralled not to get a better look. But his journey stopped at a mildew-covered pew, and he steadied himself with a hand on its armrest. "My name is—Brendan," he whispered. "Brendan Mathers."

"My name is Israfel." He glided out into the open, still feigning shyness.

Silence lingered between them, rain pattering against the church's outer walls, droning steadily as it dampened old buttresses and statues. The building was small compared to others in the city, but sadly abandoned to time and the elements. Holes speckled the lower ceiling, some revealing the towers sparkling against the night sky, others allowing the breeze to bluster raindrops into puddles near Israfel's feet. Mold splotched the altar, darkened spots of the walls, stained paintings, and obscured once-intricate tapestries.

Brendan, though, was oblivious to it all. "Israfel . . ." he whispered again. "You are aware this part of the Academy is off-limits to civilians and students?"

"You were listening to me sing, weren't you?"

Brendan swallowed, his voice cracking. "That has nothing to do with the fact that you're in a restricted area and—"

"We both know I'm not a student."

Israfel allowed his toes to catch the light, their tiny scales glistening like diamond dust.

Thunder, too faint for human ears, rumbled out in the distance. Another storm was arriving fast, threatening to saturate the church. Israfel made a show of brushing dirt from his feet and stepped gracefully toward the altar at the end of the aisle, its odor of rotten wood stale and thick. A single, long glide would have shortened the journey, but this was hardly the time to reveal his wings. "It was a pleasure to meet you, Brendan. Perhaps we'll cross paths again sometime in the future."

Brendan's footsteps echoed from behind.

Israfel paused, forcing back a smile. "Is there anything else? I am leaving after all."

"You—" Brendan sounded as if he'd been slapped. "You're not going to leave by yourself? Are you? Let me escort you home." He averted his eyes. "You don't look like someone who's been in Luz for long—and the city can be dangerous at night."

"Then you probably won't be happy to see where I live." Israfel looked over his shoulder. "In fact, you just might evict me."

He continued strolling to the right of the altar, toward a doorway with wooden molding warped and blackened by moisture. Brendan moved to follow him, peeking up at the skyline through the nearest hole in the ceiling. The storm's fringes were rolling inland already, their clouds dyed lethal shades of purple and black. "You never answered my question," he said, trailing after Israfel again. "Do you even know that you're on Academy grounds? The barbed-wire fence should have been warning enough."

"I could say the same for you."

Israfel ascended the flight of stairs, his airy steps suddenly interrupted by creaks and groans. Darkness surrounded them, and he traced his fingers along the window that paralleled the staircase, allowing its smooth surface to guide him upward. The first hints of the downpour spat against the glass, glazing a view of broken turrets and curled shingles. Brendan slowed as they passed, his voice hushed.

"You live in the rectory?"

The path ended, cut off by a pitted door.

Israfel pushed it open, spilling warm light from his room onto the landing. His chamber was somewhat dull for an angel nest, any hope at elegance destroyed by the cobwebs waving from the ceiling. But what humans lacked in maintenance he'd made up for in thievery. The carvings circling the windows and door frames were the perfect place to hang mirrors, broken or cracked. Musty velvet cushions and small end tables lay scattered throughout the room, mixing with Israfel's hasty collection of jewels and brushes and musical trinkets. Luckily, the candlelight could only reach so far, hiding some of the garbage.

"Perhaps you should wait out the rain." Israfel picked up a crystal bottle within reach, unplugging the stopper and savoring the nectar inside.

A drop escaped, trickling down his throat, wetting his collarbone.

"That is," he said as he licked his bottom lip, "unless you're going to kick me out of my nest."

Brendan was staring openly now.

Israfel turned away from him, rearranging another set of decanters on the table. Eventually he settled into the loveseat, offering his crystal bottle, swishing the small portion of nectar sparkling inside. Brendan took the hint and sat next to him, fastidiously plucking at his black coat. Its contours were slim and sharply cut, but the fabric remained buttoned down to his ankles. More sweat beaded his forehead, gathering in a thin line above his collar. The young man ran a shaky hand through his curls, blinking only to find Israfel gazing into his eyes.

"Well," Israfel said, "go ahead and ask."

Brendan's handsome face paled. "Ask you what?"

"All right. I'll answer." He placed the bottle in Brendan's hands. "I'm male. Now why don't you have a drink? Where I come from, it would be a great honor for you to share my glass."

The young man took the decanter, examining it with a slight frown. Then he raised the rim to his lips, sipped, and sipped again, unaware that some of the nectar was dribbling down his chin. "You're a—male," Brendan said, surfacing for air. "A man . . ." He laughed nervously but choked down his last mouthful and set the bottle on the floor, looking like he'd been wounded somehow.

Israfel bit his lip, trying to contain his amusement.

Rain had matted the fine feathers of his hair, and he gathered them into a short rope near his chest, stroking the strands down to their tips.

Brendan remained silent, staring down into his lap.

Every now and then his glance flicked back to Israfel, taking in his long neck, his tapering fingers.

"So now you must tell me something about yourself." Israfel shifted closer. "Perhaps you have an interesting family . . ."

"My family." Brendan's expression hazed over. He slumped lazily into the couch cushions, shut his eyes to the candlelight and the broken ceiling lamp. Sweat dampened the hair around his ears, shone across his temples. "All I have left is a sister. Angela."

Lightning flashed outside, brightening the walls of the room to silver, briefly revealing piles of feathers that had drifted near its corners. But Brendan wasn't paying attention, and the thunder followed soon afterward, slightly drowning out his voice.

"I'm told she's arriving here soon."

Brendan sighed, his broad shoulders rising and falling heavily. In one swift movement, he unclasped the hooks holding his collar closed.

"Her and the hundreds of other blood heads that show up every semester."

"I see." Israfel clenched his fingers into the couch's armrest, fighting off a round of painful cramps and a wave of nausea, his newest smile tight and perceptibly forced. Already. He'd timed the last injection to keep him going for hours, but either his ailments were getting worse, or the hours of singing were finally taking their toll. Well, it was obvious now that he didn't have much longer to wait. According to Brendan, Luz was the right city after all. Perhaps he should take this opportunity and indulge himself for a change.

Human souls were rumored to be quite sweet.

"You said you wanted me to leave this place." He slid a hand over Brendan's. "But what do you *really* want, Brendan? Why are you *really* here?"

The young man looked at him, at his fingers, pale. "I don't know what you're getting at."

Yet the thirst was there, gleaming behind his eyes. His lips parted, voiceless.

A second passed where they regarded each other.

"I—" Brendan slid nearer, tentatively touching Israfel's arm, breathing hard. He was shaking all over; visibly disturbed by the idea of whatever he thought or felt. But then he reached out again, delicately stroking the length of Israfel's neck, looking like he expected the dream to be over at any second. His fingers were chill and much damper than before. "You're saying that you would sing it for me—" His voice choked away. "The song I've been hearing until now?"

"If you're willing."

Brendan went rigid, his eyes wide. "I'm—willing."

"All right then . . ."

So Israfel began softly, his tone soothing and warm. Such shyness deserved a gentle beginning. But after a short time, Israfel subtly switched to a longer series of verses, his tone pure, yet with each note more powerful than the last. The room throbbed with their closeness, with a new heat. Brendan's body relaxed, his tension dissipated, and Israfel's lilting voice reached out for his Beloved and back again, until the universe seemed to gather around them, tight and suffocating. Even with his eyes closed, he saw the stars, the water, the beauty of their dawn. A flashing, living past.

When he opened them again, Brendan was gone.

Or at least his mind had left him, swallowed inside Israfel's own dreams. As a human, Brendan couldn't understand an angel's song, or the significance of the words and images Israfel conjured. But he could feel that significance, and it had drawn him into a fog of illusions. Sights and sounds that would steer his soul until the day he died.

Israfel reached the climax of the final refrain.

Brendan collapsed into the couch, moaning like he'd been mortally injured. He struggled to sit up but failed, sinking deeper into the cushions. Glazed eyes, a shivering body, a weakening constitution. He was the image of a blossoming enchantment, all his strength dissolved by that final release.

"What . . . did you do to me?" Brendan spoke with increasing difficulty. "I thought you were an—"

A small door swung open.

The singing had alerted Israfel's Thrones, Rakir and Nunkir, and their suspicious glares met Brendan so that he froze instantly. The black-haired Rakir emerged first, the angel's thin wings arched high above the floor, his figure tall and menacing. His twin, Nunkir, glided behind like the light to her brother's darkness, her long, silver hair tied in matching braids. Both angels radiated deadly protectiveness, and Brendan sucked in a sharp gasp as Nunkir leaned in close enough to touch him, the tiny jewels on her wings chinking together.

Israfel slid a finger beneath Brendan's chin, turning the young man's ashen face back to the light. Humans were so weak. Yet Raziel had chosen to become one of them—a red-haired girl Israfel could snap in two like a twig. And he might never understand why or for what reason.

Thunder boomed through the building.

The storm whipped more rain against the windows. All the candles burned out but one.

"I've heard that humans can be fascinating," Israfel said.

Rakir and Nunkir moved to either side of the loveseat, their wings surrounding Brendan in a feathered prison.

Yes, he might never understand. But—

"Now we can see what the fuss is all about."

One

_____

That this Person will meet with these angels, there can be no doubt.
But meetings take place both in the imagination and reality.

—ST. IMWALD, LETTERS TO THE HOLY FATHER

"That's an incredible painting. The lines, the textures, the brush-strokes. One would swear you've been doing this for fifty years. Can I ask how much you're willing to sell it for? I could give you one thousand dollars—"

"It's not for sale." Angela stood from her bench, nodding politely at the group of appraisers to her right. One of them—a stout, middle-aged man wearing an expensive suit—had paused in front of her darker work: an abstract of acrylic on canvas, the figure portrayed in its center more a conglomeration of shadows and smoke than a person. A bone pale face had been sketched amid the gray, its crimson eyes intended to shock the viewer as much as they had shocked Angela. It had been easier than she'd thought to evoke sensations of sickliness and dread through art, coming down to little more than mixing the right colors and matching them to the images already in her head. Really, it was more practice than talent. She'd painted the darker angel so many times, most of the features outlined themselves by now. "In fact, none of them are for sale. I just couldn't bring myself to choose, even if I had to part with a single work."

"A true shame," the stout man said, turning from her to another picture.

This time it was the more beautiful angel of the two. Not her best representation, but the watercolors had a strange way of conveying the soft loveliness in the angel's wings, his eyes.

"And to think," he was saying, "that such skills will be hidden away at this school. The Academy is a little too protective of you blood heads." The man snorted, adjusting his tie. "Not all of us believe the Vatican prophecy, you know. The world is sorely lacking in common sense nowadays. Every time I step foot in this city, I feel like I've been thrown back to the Middle Ages."

Angela pretended not to hear, greeting another visitor to her exhibit with an outstretched hand. Surprisingly enough, the young woman took it, giving her a firm shake.

"Well, I wish you luck," the appraiser said, his shadow uncovering one of her brightest paintings as he and his group meandered off to the left.

The young woman looked like she was pushing sixteen, but her blouse matched Angela's, its embroidered tree symbol circled by thirteen stars—the mark of a college freshman. She strolled over to the uncovered picture immediately, one hand settled on her hip as she bent down, inspecting, judging. The second her finger stretched toward a raised band of paint, Angela pushed her hand aside, shaking her head. "You really shouldn't touch them. It can cause damage."

"Sorry." The young woman folded her arms and raised an eyebrow, looking more curious than mad. She was short, and her Academy skirt swung well below her knees, making her look too small for her clothing. Otherwise, she was plain and unremarkable. Brown hair yanked up into a messy bun, some of the tresses loose and frizzy. Bloodshot eyes that were a muddy hazel. Her boots looked like they had been through a few wars, most of their leather stitched with red thread. "You're really more assertive than you look," she said to Angela, examining the painting again. "Good for you, not selling your picture to those dolts. He wasn't offering you enough anyway."

"It had nothing to do with money," Angela said, sitting back down. She pulled up her tights, her arm gloves, trying not to appear awkward and freakish.

It wouldn't make any real difference. Blood heads got attention wherever they went. And if you were a blood head who never bared your arms and legs, even when you wore a short skirt and a ruffled blouse, that only made you ten times more interesting. The granite Exhibit Hall was so stuffed with students, teachers, Vatican novices, priests, appraisers, and proud parents, every other someone was noticing Angela at every other moment. She was probably just as fascinating, if not more so, than the paintings that had gotten her locked away for two years.

"Yeah, you're right." The woman waved her hand. "Only geniuses and richers come to this academy after all. Oh, and blood heads."

"That had nothing to do with it either."

"So it was a matter of talent, huh?" She stood back, still judging. "Yeah, well, you do have some. Although I can't understand why you paint the pictures with the dark gray angel completely in the abstract. I feel kind of cheated."

"It has to do with what I see." Angela pointed at the architecture surrounding them; a vaulted cathedral ceiling of stone, its upper crevices riddled with peering statues and grimacing faces carved into the rock. A few of the walls were so tall, their highest corners faded into a vast network of shade and darkness. It was easy to imagine that real monsters might live up there, hiding, analyzing the thousands of people that milled across the tiles below, waiting for individuals to separate themselves from the main herd and get lost in the innumerable halls and corridors that made up the Academy's largest student center. "Look at that." Angela pointed at the statue of an angel with swanlike wings, his hand grasping a lantern meant to light part of the room below. Unfortunately, the candle inside was sputtering to nothing. "See how clear and defined his features are. You can see everything. The expression. The folds in his robe. The nails on his toes."

Now she pointed at the window behind them, its lead panes streaked with heavy rain.

Barely discernible through the blur of water and wind, another angel statue leaned out from the gable, his palm lifted high, as if to catch the drops that had worn it down to a flattened disc. Thunder shivered the glass, and an intense flash of lightning highlighted the ghastly flaws in his features.

"But over here, it's different. I know this is an angel, but everything about him is blurred, and dark, and changeable." Angela indicated the pictures of the gray angel. "So the painting comes out like this."

"You seem to like this one—with the bronze wings," the young woman said. She was inspecting the nearest image of the beautiful angel, awed as Angela was always awed by his proud eyes and perfect pink lips. Often he appeared dressed in a red coat that dazzled her with its silver thread, or wearing jeweled barrettes in his hair, or carrying a lyre made of crystal. "But I don't get the wings on the ears," she continued. "Was that your idea?"

"Like I said"—Angela couldn't stop her sigh—"I just paint what I see."

But even more often, he would walk into her dreams and leave without saying a word.

"It's like you know them personally." The girl sat down next to Angela on the bench, crossing her legs and rifling through her bag. Her hand reemerged with a sack of cheddar chips, and she offered some crumbs, generous. "You actually look an awful lot like them. You've got big eyes, has anyone told you that before?"

"They certainly have," Angela said, taking a handful of food. "Thanks. I'm Angela Mathers, by the way."

"Nina Willis." Nina drew in her legs, finally realizing she was going to trip someone. "I hope you don't mind if I sit here for a minute. I've been looking for a bench for about an hour. So are you in the university classes?"

"You could say that. I just arrived in Luz three days ago, actually. I haven't even had a chance to open a book yet." Angela stood up, bowing to a passing group of Vatican novices, a few of them eyeballing her longer than she felt comfortable with.

There was a tall one at the end of their gang, so strikingly pale that his skin resembled paper, his eyes a vivid and penetrating amber color. Like the others he wore the long dark coat of a novice, but his hair was as striking as his face, the strands pitch-black except for a chunk dyed fire engine red.

When he left with the others, Angela felt it wouldn't be for long. "Despite what you said about me being a blood head, I actually got into the Academy because of my art. And because my parents are dead. They never let me get out much." She continued to stare after the novice with the black hair. "Though I didn't always disagree with that. Sometimes I feel like I'm really the one on display, not the pictures."

Nina shrugged off the comment, shifting aside to let a couple examine Angela's best self-portrait. The painting wasn't perfect, but it captured her large blue eyes and angular face rather well. She was reclining on her parents' old parlor room sofa, her fine blood-red hair covering half her body like a poker-straight curtain. That was before the burns, the scars, and the need to cover herself almost head to toe in fabric.

The couple made sure to remark on that before turning to the neighboring booth.

"Are you talking about the novices?" Nina said. "Don't pay any attention to them. They're just all tightwads about blood heads lately because of the murders near the Academy. They think the sororities and fraternities are getting out of hand again, dabbling in all kinds of occult stuff. I think they're giving Stephanie and her lackeys too much credit."

"Stephanie?"

"Stephanie Walsh." Nina stared down at her shoes, a chip half raised to her lips. Her voice hushed drastically. "I'm actually surprised you haven't met her yet. She has a habit of meeting new blood heads, absorbing them into her sorority, then controlling their lives for three more years after that. I guess you could say she's the queen bee here at Westwood, keeping tabs on everyone who's anyone—and even people like me, who aren't. You're pretty popular already, so I'm sure she's going to make it a point to meet you. Just so you know."

Popular? The only place Angela had ever been popular was in the psych ward at the institution. There, her long hair and scars had made her more intriguing than a supermodel. But anywhere else, she was a freak, a monster, a danger, the possible fulfillment of a prophecy that meant death and destruction on a staggering scale.

A century had passed on Earth since the Vatican chose to reveal its ominous conclusion: The dark messiah it had long feared—the silencer of all people, things, and hopes—would be a human with red hair. The One, who would forevermore be known as "the Ruin," had been prophesied as having blood on his head and blood on his hands. From that day onward, children born with red hair were detested, shunned, or, in the saddest cases like Angela's, abused. It wasn't until the Vatican established its island city off the coast of the American continent that those now termed "blood heads," especially blood heads with supernatural prowess, seemed to find their place.

Only in Luz were blood heads accepted and encouraged to discover what kind of powers or special abilities they might possess, even though sometimes it was hard to figure out whether the Vatican officials feared or admired that unique fourth of their student body. Were they protecting people like Angela? Or were they merely gathering them together like rats into a trap, ready to poison them once they'd found the Ruin they were looking for? This place was full of contradictions like that. From the first day Angela entered Luz, she'd been overwhelmed by its sense of backward elegance and almost topsy-turvy culture. While the supernatural was welcomed—though always under strict control—technology couldn't survive. Electricity gave way to candlelight, modern building materials to stone, wood, and elaborate tile-work, most of it decaying beneath acid rain and neglect. From the coast where her parents' house had burned to the ground, Angela would stare out at the ocean, gazing at the city that sat like a lonely lump of crags, turrets, and oddly twisted spires, its iron support beams lashed by waves taller than trees. Luz was a city on stilts, its grandest buildings built on top of others, all of it looking ready to crash into the sea at any time.

Luz, the city of lights. The Vatican's wonder of the world that was now a world of its own. So many candles burned here that the Academy twinkled at night, covered in a million artificial stars.

"Believe me," Nina said, wagging a finger at her, "when you're pretty, and different, and you're the talk of the school, Stephanie takes notice."

"Why are we assuming that people think this about me?" Angela said, a crisper clip edging into her voice.

"Is your brother really Brendan Mathers?"

Angela slumped, her tone cooling to a hiss. "What does he have to do with it?"

"So it is true." Nina smirked. "Sorry, but I had to check you out. He and Stephanie are an item, you know. That alone makes you ripe for gossip."

"That's impossible. He took vows."

Nina was laughing now. "Yeah. He did, didn't he? But would that stop you if some red-headed succubus was throwing herself on your lap? He's still human, after all." She crumpled her chip bag and stood, wiping her hands on her skirt. "But prophecy or not, Stephanie's a blood head with some real power. A witch. You'd be smart to stay on her good side. Hell, even the Academy faculty stay on her good side."

"Well, thanks for the warning, but I doubt she's going to take any notice of me like you said. I'm not the only blood head entering the university this semester. Besides, Brendan probably wouldn't have talked about me much. I'm more of an embarrassment than a real conversation point."

"That's fine." Nina stooped down to snatch up her bag. "Just don't be too surprised when it happens."

"Where are you going?" Angela stood alongside of her, casually scanning the hallway for the novice with the pale skin.

"Oh, just back to my dorm. I've got some reading to do before lights out. Thought I might steal a smoke in the bathroom on the way. Care to join me?"

No. He mustn't have been half as interested in her as he seemed. All thoughts of a forbidden romance aside, it would be nice to question someone about her brother. Learn where he lived and what classes he oversaw as a teacher's aide. Hopefully, *without* this Stephanie finding out. Angela pushed the hair from her eyes, trying to peer through the crowd.

"Hello?"

A cigarette dangled in front of her face.

"No thanks." Angela swatted it away, still trying to see. A ripple was passing through the large bunches of people, the students pulling back from either side of the exhibits to let a band of blood heads pass through. There were ten of them, but the woman at their head was obviously the leader, her heeled boots clicking across the tile with measured precision. Her skirt was at least two inches too short, and she wore a black overcoat over her blouse, its breast pocket embroidered with a five-pointed star surrounded by a circle. A pentacle. With every step, her thick ponytail swung side to side, shining beneath the wall sconces.

She stopped for a second, whispering to one of her friends—another blood head with layered hair and thigh-high tights. Then they both caught sight of Angela and strolled toward her fast.

"Shit." Nina's voice sounded like an ominous gong in Angela's ear. "We're done for."

Before anything more could be said, the ten students were ringing Angela's exhibit, silent and oddly forbidding. The lights in the room began to flicker.

"Well, hello," the leader said to Nina.

Nina kept her mouth shut.

"So I guess you couldn't stay away from an opportunity like this. Not that I blame you anymore. You see," she said and smiled at Angela, "Nina here has a fascination with angels, demons, spirits. She even says she talks to them. In her sleep, or something." The leader laughed gently. "She tends to gravitate toward new blood heads who don't know any better, eventually wearing them down with a million useless, overly imaginative questions." She glanced at Nina. "Right?"

"Who are you?" Angela said, trying to ignore Nina's strange silence. This had to be Stephanie. But it took more than a funny symbol on her coat to make her a witch. And right now, she couldn't be more mediocre. "Why are you here?"

"Why am I here?" She laughed again, some of her friends joining in. They all looked the same: heavy makeup and red eye shadow. More like bad mannequins than people. "I'm here to welcome you to Westwood, of course. I'm Stephanie Walsh, head of the Pentacle Sorority on the campus. I make it my personal responsibility to meet every new blood head who steps onto Academy grounds."

"That's nice of you, but I'm not too keen on sororities. Or being recruited."

"Oh, that's fine. But you might want to reconsider your opinion."

"Why is that?" Angela said, aware that her eyes were narrowing to slits. The girl with the thigh-high tights was poking at her favorite picture, tracing the line of the angel's long neck with a finger.

Stephanie nudged Tights sharply with an elbow, snapping her back into position. "Because you might find life to be a little easier here at the Academy when you have sisters to lean on. Otherwise, it can be hard." She glanced at Nina, a frown twitching on her mouth. "You don't want to start off on the wrong foot, acquainting yourself with people who don't have your best interests at heart."

"So you're saying that if I don't join your sorority, I should prepare to be miserable?"

"I'm only trying to help." Stephanie stretched out a hand, and the blood head with the thigh-highs handed her a paper. She offered it to Angela. "If you change your mind, our house is in the Western District of the campus, close to the Tree. We have group nights every Tuesday and Thursday where we initiate new members if they decide to join."

"This Thursday is Halloween," Nina said, muttering.

Stephanie lifted an eyebrow. "So it is."

She turned and headed for the exit at the far end of the hallway, the other blood heads gathering behind her. Angela crumpled the paper, tossing it on the floor when they were out of view. "She's crazy if she thinks I'm going to spend my college years handing her papers."

"Thank God." Nina ruffled her hair, messing it even more. "I thought you were going to cave."

"Why would I have done that?"

"So many people said the same thing. Until they met Stephanie face-to-face. The one in the thigh-high tights, Lyrica Pengold—she was stupid enough to spread rumors about her. Then her hair began falling out. Now she's Stephanie's most devoted slave and has hair that would make a shampoo commercial jealous."

Angela let the matter rest, keeping her thoughts to herself while she opened her portfolio case and began taking down the paintings, one by one. The exhibit had an hour to go yet, but she felt sick, and exhausted, and really didn't want anything to do with people until tomorrow. She wasn't used to so much attention, good or bad, and the strangeness of it all had left her in a daze. Almost forgetting that Nina was still present, she picked up her favorite picture—a gorgeous oil portrait that focused on the beautiful angel's sapphire eyes—and snuck a kiss on the edge of the canvas.

This was all for him anyway. Her last hope at finding a reason to live.

"Hey, Angela, I'm going to go now." Nina's voice seemed to come out of nowhere.

"Leaving so soon?" A male voice joined her. "And after I made the time to take a closer look at your exhibit."

Wonderful. More people.

Angela slipped the last painting into its case and turned around with a fake smile at the ready. But then it became a real one. The novice with the pale skin and honey-colored eyes was standing across from her, his long coat swishing as he swayed slightly, stealing a quick peek before she zipped up the case. He was even more handsome up close, and a flattering shelf of bangs hung carelessly in his eyes. It was a portion of these that he'd dyed such a shocking red.

"They allow that—even though you're a novice?" Angela nodded at his hair.

"Not everyone in the Vatican is as backward as the authorities in Luz, Miss—what's your name?"

"Angela Mathers."

"Pretty. It suits your work."

Nina had been a step away from leaving again. Now she sat back down and busied herself with a book, glancing at the novice whenever he wasn't looking.

"Anyway," he continued, "I'm sorry to bother you. I can see you're packing up for the night."

"Oh, it's no problem. I wasn't intending to leave so soon; I just . . ." Angela sighed. "It's been a long day."

"Would you like me to help you back to your room? I'm also heading in that direction."

Nina was trying harder than ever not to appear engrossed with the conversation. But she was also turning the book's pages much too quickly.

"No, that's all right." Besides, didn't it occur to him that it might not be a good idea to be seen alone with her? Angela felt her cheeks starting to go red. She'd planned on asking him about Brendan, but now the thought of how and why was the furthest thing from her mind. It would be great to have a meaningful relationship with a person who either wasn't part of her dreams, or hadn't taken a vow of celibacy. But dating a priest in training certainly wouldn't start things off on the right foot. "Thanks for offering though. Maybe next time."

"Of course. Maybe next time." He wandered away from the exhibit, gradually vanishing into the crowd.

The instant he was out of sight, Nina tossed her book aside and grabbed Angela's arm. "Do you know who that was?"

"Should I?" Angela blinked, partially blinded by a nearby flash of lightning.

"His name is Kim, and he's off-limits. *Don't* get involved."

"You know, he was the one who forgot about the whole vow of celibacy thing—"

"He's involved with Stephanie," Nina hissed.

Angela hoisted her own bag onto a shoulder, careful not to snag her arm gloves. "What? You said that Brendan is Stephanie's boyfriend!"

Something she still found hard to believe.

"Yeah. The official one. The show-off boyfriend." Nina pointed down the hallway, at wherever Kim had disappeared to. "He's the real thing. And if you like guys and you go to the Academy, it's the one reason you might wish you were in her shoes for a change. So listen to me this time and stay away from him."

"And if he approaches me instead?"

Nina rolled her eyes and grabbed Angela's smallest portfolio. "I can only warn you once." She took a deep breath. "Now tell me where you live and I'll help you cart your stuff. At least I won't be flirting with you along the way."

"On the east side of campus. Near the ocean."

"Good. Let's go."

Angela picked up the rest of her belongings, dragging her largest painting in a portfolio on wheels, sidestepping the dwindling crowd. The second she looked up again, there was Lyrica, standing a few feet away, a curious expression on her face. She must have lingered behind Stephanie, maybe to spy on Angela, maybe to get a moment to herself. But it was obvious she'd also seen everything that had taken place with Kim. Lyrica lifted her eyebrows, amused. Then she sauntered away to the exit.

Already, I'm under some kind of microscope.

Already, Angela was wishing the fire had worked.

The next storm swept in off the coast after dinner hours.

Luz vanished behind a screen of silver, raindrops battering mercilessly against old stone edifices, spouting in vast sluices from gutters that hung hundreds of feet above Angela's dormitory. She'd been situated on the upper floor of an old mansion, half of its foundation angling perilously over the sea, the other half facing toward the center of the Academy where she could revel in the view of a hundred or more towers, most of them connected to one another by vast bridges of stone, or at the very peak, thick tunnels of carefully sealed glass. Candles flickered through countless windows, yellow eyes that glared out toward the sea.

The surf was breaking hundreds of feet below her building, and still it sounded almost as loud as the thunder. Angela must have fallen asleep without realizing it, because when a particularly loud *boom* shivered through the walls, she jolted in her seat, shocked to find the book she'd been reading was now lying on the floor.

She picked it up and set it back on the mantelpiece above the fireplace. The flames had muffled to a mass of burning cinders.

Angela stared at them, bitter inside.

Fire wasn't enough. Or bullets. Or knives.

She rolled down one of her arm gloves, examining the grotesque patches of skin, most of them slightly raised and dark with scar tissue. Her legs had fared better, but not by much. When Angela set the blaze months ago, her arms had, of course, been nearest to the fire, but after passing out, she'd survived to find horrendous burns striping her legs to midthigh. The disappointment of seeing those wounds almost equaled her disappointment at being alive. She'd planned on waking up wrapped in the wings of her angel, not trapped for weeks in an infirmary.

Now you're here in Luz, wasting your time so you can apologize to a brother who probably wishes you'd succeeded too.

It was hard to kill yourself when someone or something you couldn't see was protecting you. At least, Angela had come to the conclusion that the supernatural was looking out for her after she tried stabbing herself, and the knife blade snapped when it met her skin.

Ten separate times.

Then there were the guns. All in perfect working order. All either misfiring or refusing to fire when the moment arrived. Nooses held tight until she slipped them around her neck. Then they unraveled and dropped to the floor. If Angela tried to suffocate, she'd simply black out and wake up to find herself breathing again. If she tried drowning, the effect was usually the same. Fire had been one of her last resorts, and that had ended the most disastrously of all, killing her family instead. That left two options: jumping off a building, or getting someone else to kill her. The latter choice usually either wouldn't be fair or wouldn't be right. Encouraging serial killers wasn't the morally sound way to rid the planet of your existence. And most people didn't want to be a murderer, even an accidental one.

And jumping off a building?

It never hurt to try. She'd just never been keen on surviving as a lump of shattered bones.

Angela turned from the grate, strolling over to the enormous bay window overlooking the highest street. Two of the windows had upper panes made of stained glass, their intricate designs adding a splash of brightness in the otherwise drab den. But they were also made solid from top to bottom, lacking a latch. Only the middle window was completely clear and tall as the ceiling, its lower half already cocked open half an inch.

She climbed over a large couch, its upholstery a disgusting mélange of flowers and crushed red velvet. The bay seat was behind it, but most of the wood had blackened from the moisture. Below, though, the porch roof stretched out into the night, slippery with rain and old shingles.

It must have been a fifty-foot drop to the cobblestones beneath. Maybe more.

Angela leaned on the opened pane, forcing the space to widen with her elbows.

The rain was dying off into a drizzle, but the farther parts of Luz remained wrapped beneath a thick blanket of fog and low clouds. Brief flickers of lightning crossed the sky like a strobe light. Angela reached out to test the roofing, finding it even more slippery than it looked. She took a second to kick off her boots before climbing out of the window and onto the shingles. A sharp breeze whipped some of her hair into her mouth, and then plastered it, wet and slick, to the side of her neck. Water soaked into her socks.

The sound of voices filtered up from the street. Angela rose to her feet, steadying herself with one hand on the window frame, half blind until she caught her hair with the other.

Two women stood in front of the dormitory, talking in voices too low to hear their conversation, but animatedly enough that it would be hard not to take any interest. One of the women was definitely a student, though her skirt and blouse lacked the Tree symbol. She was tall, with an elegant way of clasping her hands, her hair a flowing mass of chestnut that had frizzed to a mat in the rain. Her skin had the creamy look of porcelain, and instead of boots she wore pretty slippers that were an expensive-looking silver.

But the other woman, though she had a perfect face and a figure to envy, had an unnerving hardness in her eyes—very large, very dark eyes, now that Angela looked closer—and a nasty twist to her mouth when she talked. She'd protected herself from the rain in a lengthy hooded cloak, but the hood was down right now, exposing her hair.

Long, thin, blond braids, maybe hundreds of them, had been gathered up into a ponytail that must have been heavier than coiled rope. Their color was a surprising contrast against the woman's copper skin. Maybe she was from overseas somewhere. That would probably explain the strange tattoo curling upward along her neck.

She spat more words at the polite young woman and vanished into the rain.

Angela waited for the other woman to leave before sliding down the roof any farther.

Then she was at the edge, peering down into the street and a great puddle of water. The cobblestones shone back at her beneath the light of a hanging streetlamp—its sconce surprisingly fitted with a bulb instead of a candle. And the stones continued to shine tantalizingly back at her, smooth and beckoning. Offering death, possible oblivion, or most disappointingly, broken bones.

This really would be the last time. If she failed, then it was either murder, or the real reason she'd come to the Academy in the first place—fulfillment.

Angela tensed the muscles in her legs, preparing to jump.

What if you just survive in a bunch of little pieces? You didn't think about that.

"Are you looking for something?"

The voice of the student with the silver slippers. Apparently, she hadn't left. Instead she was suddenly standing in the middle of the street, a little to the left, gazing up at the porch roof and Angela, who teetered on its edge.

"You're not going to jump?" the young woman said, her voice soft, but also carrying itself across the gap between them. "Are you?"

Damn it. Now what do I do?

Yes, Angela could still jump, but it wouldn't be very nice to splatter herself all over the student's shoes. Or for her to see it happen. So she backed away, edging for the window again, trying not to twist her ankle or slide off the roof and bang into the gutter. "I—um—I was leaning out the window and I dropped a ring. I think it fell into the gutter."

The student stared back at her. Her expression was at once sympathetic and too smart for the lie. But she smiled, her tone still gentle. "I'm sorry about that. Perhaps you'll come across it again. Are you the new student in this dormitory?"

"This dormitory?" Angela pointed back at the building.

The student nodded.

"I thought I *was* the only student in this dormitory."

The young woman shook her head. "I live in the private apartment below the library. But perhaps I'll move up a floor or two and give you some company. Would you mind?"

Angela had inspected that apartment when she'd arrived, and it was so bare and drafty, she hadn't considered anyone might be staying in it. A few blankets and pieces of junk scattered here and there weren't enough to convince her. It was hard to believe someone would actually even choose it unless they were punishing themselves. "Oh—no. That's fine."

"All right then. I'll start moving my things upstairs tomorrow evening. What's your name?"

"Angela."

"Angela," the student repeated. She was gazing upward with the same delicate face, but her eyes widened a little, and her smile appeared more genuine the second time around. "Well, good night, Angela. And if you were in fact planning to jump, I hope you'll rethink things and stay alive for a while yet. Death, and the mess it makes, tends to inconvenience people."

She left, her footsteps tapping lightly across the sagging porch. Then the door creaked open, shutting closed again with a *click*.

I don't know how she did it, but I actually feel stupid.

Angela knelt on the shingles, her knees scraping across tar. Carefully, she stood up again and peered into Luz, picking out a bridge here or a tower there, half wishing that she could just spy an angel soaring through the fog, his great wings whipping away clouds or rolling the air beneath them like the thunder of the sea. The rain was picking up again, slanting sideways so that it needled into her eyes. Angela pulled herself up near the window frame and lifted a foot to slip back inside the den.

Something peppered the porch roof. She spun around, startled.

A few shingles had been scraped off the upper gables, and now they sat in a sad pile, their edges curled with water. Was someone standing on the roof above, looking down at her, like she had been looking down at the street?

She tried to focus on one of the turrets, but the rain made it difficult to see. There was a statue near the highest apartment window, perched mysteriously on the very edge of its lower eaves, right above the dropped shingles. It resembled a gargoyle, or some other kind of stylized devil, its face both pretty and terrible, peering back at her, its wings sickle shaped and arched tightly against a thin back.

The eyes seemed to reflect the poor light of the alley below.

Or maybe they were glowing—a hypnotic phosphorescent yellow.

Angela stared back into them a moment longer than was probably necessary, but finally crawled back inside the den, slammed the window shut, and locked the latch in place. Her hair was dripping onto the musty hardwood floor, and her socks felt like wet rags weighing down her feet. Ironically thirsty, she padded down the rickety stairs into the parlor and swung around a devotional statue, entering the kitchen. The light was still on from when she'd had a snack—

There's something new you can try. Starving yourself.

No. That was too prolonged. Quick and relatively painless would be much nicer.

Angela got a glass, filling it with water from the sink. Then she pulled out one of the chairs and picked up an Academy newspaper lying on the table. Drops from her hair plopped onto the front page, smearing some of the ink. The paper was from a week ago, its headline printed in a large, attention-grabbing font. There was a picture of a dead body, half covered by a blood-soaked sheet.

MURDERS CONTINUE: VATICAN DENIES
OCCULT CONNECTIONS

Eastern District, Luz—After a week of relative silence citywide, the murders continue in Luz, their seemingly occult connections vehemently denied by Vatican officials at the Academy and abroad. Theories abound on both sides, officials suggesting that a human serial killer might be loose in the city, but with a small percentage of others pointing to the animalistic savagery and brazen continuance of the murders as proof of a possible zoological, or even supernatural, origin. Vatican authorities residing in Westwood Academy have another, even more controversial theory, some blaming the high population of blood head students at the school, and their sometimes strictly censured dabbling in the arcane arts . . .

Angela sipped the remaining water in her glass, engrossed and instantly sick. Could Vatican authorities actually be right? Would Stephanie and her friends actually harvest body parts for their midnight rituals?

Nina did call her a witch. But that girl's definitely got a screw loose herself.

> *... yet the signs of teeth marks, missing organs, and the predatory efficiency of the woman's torn throat cannot be denied. Residents in the Academy's Eastern District on the east sea cliff of Luz are being strictly warned to stay indoors in the late hours of the night and during hours of heavy rain and black cloud cover, as these conditions seem most suited to the killer's habits . . .*

Well, that absolutely didn't sound right. She couldn't imagine Stephanie deliberately getting her hair wet, even if it was to glean ingredients for a potion that could dry, curl, and shine it in a minute flat. Angela pushed the paper back into the center of the table, her thoughts wandering back to the creepy devil perched on the top of the dormitory.

Maybe if it had been real, she wouldn't have had to worry about who might kill her or why. She would be the only student in school wandering out in the rain and early hours of the morning, hoping that something sinister would swoop down and cut off her head.

Instead she'd have to work to find her angel. Wherever he was.

She glanced out the kitchen window, gazing across an expanse of slate roof tile. Amazingly enough, the same creepy devil statue had been set on the far side, near to the chimney with the kink in its middle. She didn't remember seeing it there before, but then again, didn't remember trying to notice either. It had the same, intense expression on its face, all hunger and watchful evil, staring back at her. The ears were long and pointed, pressed back against a head that had been painted with black hair. The skin must have been carved from marble.

But it didn't move or climb closer to eat her alive. Just like every other statue in Luz.

"You're pretty disappointing," Angela said out loud.

She shut the blinds with a *snap*.

Two

What is the essence of life?
Without which substance do we meet death?
For despite the dark future the Ruin brings,
Her crown is made of that precious crimson.
—CARDINAL DEMIAN YATES, *Translations of the Prophecy*

The cigarette flared in the darkness of Angela's room, but quickly dulled down to a delicate spot of orange, its tip floating around in the shade as Nina moved from the corner of her bed to the dressers and back again. She seemed fascinated by Angela's doll collection, which wasn't the most expensive or even the largest that could be found in the city, but certainly the most diverse. Angela had never quite understood her own obsession with dolls. It was kind of like her obsession with the angels, except instead of being fueled by dreams, it festered in that part of her preferring ceramic people to real ones. Artificial humans could be life-sized or small enough to fit in your pocket. You could dress them in the latest fashions, or force them to wear costumes that would make a showgirl jealous. But best of all, they were friends that would never judge you for things like blood-red hair and the scars on your legs. They didn't care. They didn't have hearts.

They sat in their orderly rows, deaf, blind, and beautiful. Forever.

"You have no idea how much this freaked me out when you opened the door." Nina picked up the doll of a pretty woman jester, her curled hair gathered beneath the traditional three-pronged hat. She examined its feet, the jingling bells, and then set it back next to a shepherdess that was at least fifty years old; a hand-me-down given to Angela by her cousin. "And if you're smart, you'll never let anyone else see this fright fest. God, Angie, it's messed up."

But she was grinning.

"You should make one of Stephanie and stick pins in its knuckles."

"Not really my style," Angela said. "It'd be better to draw her in a gray purgatory somewhere. I don't think I dislike her enough yet to choose some circle of hell."

"I could ask if they have room for her there," Nina said, her eyes sparkling.

Angela sighed. Stephanie had hinted that Nina was ultimately more interested in communicating with spirits than with other human beings.

But she wasn't a blood head. The odds of her being able to do it at all were slim to none. Wishful thinking, probably.

"I don't know if you need to. I could just paint her in some Academy tower, locked up in a circle of wet bricks, her hair growing longer but never drying out. In the end, Luz isn't much different than purgatory, is it?"

Angela walked over to a window and pulled the curtains back, revealing a late-morning vista that could have been mistaken for a late-evening apocalypse. The sun tended to hide itself in Luz. Was it the position of the city relative to the winds and the tides? Was it the latitude? The chimney smoke? The pollution from the iron ships entering through the coastal supports? As the city grew, each building settled on top of the lesser architecture of its ancestors, the light sallowed more and more, its golden slivers less frequent amid the mists and the fog. Finally, the weekly forecast stalemated into storms, rain, or a monotonous sleet in the winter months—a foul time period where no one visited Luz, and nobody left. The city of lights, it was said, might have been cursed by the large number of blood heads living there. But they weren't leaving any time soon. So, while they entered the school one after the other, the storms became more violent and the lightning developed into a plague, and people used the degrees of darkness to determine the hours of the day and the passing of the seasons.

Right now, it was early fall. Without the trees to say so, most students had only their calendars and the amount of rain in the streets to go by. The Academy Tree was one of the last of its species in Luz. The Vatican needed more space for housing than for giant weeds.

"You'll get used to it after a while." Nina took a long drag on her cigarette, tapping the ashes into a cup near Angela's bed. "I'm surprised you like the sun anyway. Who does? It's hot, and bright, and yellow, and it makes people shade off into a second-class tan. There's nothing like that corpse-white hue."

"Then I guess I am going to be popular for a change. I used to get tans all the time back home, and everyone said I'd end up marrying 'beneath my family's expectations.' The more I liked that, the more they thought I was deranged. So then they sent me to the institution and I forgot what the sun was all about. I didn't miss it so much until I got back home."

"Are you?" Nina said. She lay down on the bed, flat on her stomach, a hand still lifting the cigarette to her lips.

Angela swept aside her hair, sitting down on the floor.

Dolls surrounded them from floor to ceiling, crowding the old bookshelves and storage cabinets, their glass eyes cold and scintillating. While most of her paintings remained hidden away in their portfolio cases, two of them hung on the walls, portals to either a dream or a nightmare, whichever happened to suit her fancy at the moment. She felt a kinship to both of them, one day aching for perfect beauty, and the next, for a grayness that wiped away her soul.

"Am I what?" she said, tugging on an arm glove.

"Deranged."

What did she want to hear, anyway? But Nina was intent on the question, mouth set in a line of excited fear. As if she were watching a horror movie and couldn't tear her eyes away.

"Well," Angela said, lifting one of her hands, "Some people think I am."

She slipped off the glove, allowing her scars and knife slashes to get some air. Nina locked on them without a sound, balancing the cigarette on her fingers, letting its ashes dribble onto the floor. Like she'd forgotten the world. "You sick bitch," she said, awed.

"You sound like my parents." Angela ran a finger along a particularly large burn. "My diagnosis was pretty grim from the beginning, you know. My brother was born during a freak storm that nearly swept away the hospital. I was born a few seconds after him, apparently tearing parts of Erianna to shreds on the way out. My mother," she said, glancing at Nina, seeing there was need for explanation. "She could never have any more children after us. It was a miracle she even survived. And she and Marcus never let me forget it. They didn't kill me outright. I was part of the Mathers family, and that wasn't how they did things. Instead, they took a more passive route. Long years of no friends and a lot of harsh homeschooling. Some of the scars are from that."

Nina opened her mouth, maybe to ask which ones. Then she simply said nothing.

"The paintings are what got me sent to the mental institution. I believed the angels were real—I still do—and I tried to kill myself a few times to get it over with. Because I wanted to be with people or beings that I really understood and cared for. At the institution they taught me how to make human friends and feel okay about the opposite sex, and I had a few brave boyfriends here and there when I got out. But I always wanted to be with him," she said, pointing at the beautiful angel and his overly large, proud eyes, "and I kept trying. It's simply my bad luck that I can't kill myself and wake up in Heaven or Hell somewhere, staring back at him."

"Why not?" Nina said, whispering.

"Because it doesn't work." Angela waved at a drawer in the end table near the bed. "Open that and give me the pocketknife inside, next to the notebook."

Nina obeyed, tossing the closed knife at Angela.

She caught it with one hand. "Now," she said, snapping the knife open, "watch carefully."

"Wait a second," Nina said, "you're not going to actually—"

"I mean it. Keep watching."

Angela pointed the blade's tip at her heart and pulled her hand back, lifting it higher than she really needed to. Drama would help get the point across.

"Shit—" Nina sat up from the bed, looking like she was either going to scream or lunge for the knife. The cigarette dropped from her fingers to the floor. Her arms shook like twigs in the wind. "What the hell are you going to do—Angela—*no*—"

Angela brought the knife down against her chest, merciless.

Maybe I'll get really lucky. Maybe I'll do it this time.

The blade sank into her skin a half inch deep. A second later it broke with a loud *twang*, the handle flying onto the bed next to Nina, the rest of the blade dropping out of Angela's skin and clattering to the hardwood floor, its once sleek metal now jagged at the edges. Warm blood pooled from the cut, soaking into her shirt. Nina stared at the knife on the bed like it was a demon crawling for her own throat. When she decided to look at Angela again, her face was even whiter than a cadaver's.

"You sick bitch," she said again, her lips almost slack. She began laughing. "I thought you were going to dye me red. You sick, lucky, lucky . . ."

She slid off the bed, stamping out the light of the fallen cigarette.

"Don't even bother," Angela said. She dabbed at the cut with the arm glove. "It's not as deep as it looks. It never is."

"How the heck—"

"Maybe there is a real angel, protecting me. That's the only reason I can figure." Angela leaned back, resting her elbows on the floor. More blood blossomed on her breast like a flower. "That's why I have the burns. I got frustrated and tried fire, but I must have just fallen unconscious, and the blaze killed my family instead of me. All I got out of it was some freaky scar tissue."

She lifted another arm, a leg.

"You didn't go to jail? Even if it was an accident—"

"My family had good connections, good lawyers." Angela shook her head. "And a reputation to uphold. My relatives just wanted me out of the picture, maybe so that Brendan could continue with his education, or maybe because they were afraid of me. But no matter what, it was an ironic way to get my freedom back."

Nina played with her skirt, looking unsure of herself.

"Are you sad?" she eventually whispered. "I mean—that your parents died because of . . ."

Angela hushed along with her. "Because of me?"

Sad.

No. She'd murdered her guilt the second it became clear that nothing about her past could ever be changed. For better or for worse, her failure to die had erased the other lives that had made hers a nightmare. But even though that chapter of her life had ended as painfully as it began, it was finally over. The morning Angela awoke in the emergency ward, she almost felt resurrected. The possibilities for her future, limited as they might have been, somehow seemed endless.

"They were the ones who beat me when I cried. By the time they were gone—I promised myself whatever tears I had left wouldn't go to waste."

Nina nodded, suddenly more confident in the face of Angela's confession. She rubbed a few tendrils of frizzy hair from her forehead. "I can't say I don't admire you for that. Most people would do what you said: wall themselves up and cry." She sighed heavily. "Luz is a hell of a place to start over, though. You could have gone anywhere—"

"I came here to apologize to my brother. But also to see if there was a way I could find *him*." Angela stood, walking over to the dazzling portrait next to her dressing mirror, brushing the curl of her angel's bronze wings with a finger. "If that's even possible. I'm a blood head, but besides dreams and lacking the ability to kill myself, I don't have any other powers that I'm aware of. I was hoping that maybe the priests could help me. It's a long shot, but the Vatican is the worldwide authority on angels, aren't they? I've been thinking that somebody could recognize these two. Tell me who they are and why I dream about them. Or even help me see them somehow. Which reminds me—"

Angela stooped down and picked up the broken knife blade, handing it to Nina.

"I've been going over this in my head since last night—and if you came to visit, I thought I'd ask—could you do it? Could you . . . kill me?"

Nina focused on her feet, half biting her lip. "God. What makes you think I'd say yes?"

"I don't know."

A lie. Kind of.

"And what makes you think I won't go to the school counselors and tell them about this? That I won't get you kicked out of the Academy? Or"—Nina's face darkened, a wicked light brightening her eyes—"sent back to that institution?"

Angela shrugged. Good questions, but she had an answer for most of them. "Because I know you're a lot like me. Because I could tell them that you're a nut who believes she's talking to spirits, and then suggest that we both end up in an institution together. Though I'd probably be the only one to survive it. And not even by my own choice."

Nina examined her, cautious. More respectful. "What makes you think that I'd even be successful?"

"Other people can hurt me. Pretty badly if they want to. My parents have, my tutor did. But they never went far enough, like they knew that keeping me alive was more of a punishment." She fiddled with the knife blade for a second longer, handing it to Nina again. "I want someone to do me a favor, and I don't want it to be someone who gets off on violence and guts. That's like prostituting myself. And just so you know, I won't hold it against you. You can have all of my belongings. Everything. I want to get the hell out of here."

"Come on, Angela. What's in it for me? For anyone who's actually sane? Really?"

"Money. That's all I've got."

Nina traced a line of thread on the bedspread, as if pondering all the possibilities that could be had in murdering a blood head. Then she sighed, her shoulders rising and falling. "This is messed up. As much as the thought of being rich might tempt me, it's not enough to murder someone. Anyone. Not even you—no offense." She took the broken knife blade and tossed it into the trash bin next to Angela's desk. Between the blood and the humidity, it wouldn't take long to rust. "Looks like you're going to have to stick it out for a while longer. I'm not too keen on my conscience torturing me, or the police locking me up for sixty years. Though it is brave of you," she said, sliding to the edge of the bed, "to ask me in the first place. Sorry. I don't have the stomach to kill other people or myself. I'm not that—crazy."

Angela slumped, her head cradled by a hand. "Great. Well, thanks anyway." She peered between her fingers. "Let me guess? We're not friends anymore? You're scared to death of me?"

Nina reached for the jester doll and displaced it from the shelf again. She took off its hat, jingling the bells. "I didn't say that."

"Were we even friends to begin with?"

"Either way, it's too late now." Nina picked at the doll's hair, another cautious glaze coming over her eyes. Rain began pattering gently against the window. "So you said that angels are real."

That's why you came in the first place. Stephanie isn't a complete liar after all.

Angela touched the painting again. The angel had an expression of wounded pride, his heavy-lidded eyes gazing back at her almost in contempt. Even the lines of his lips were so engrained in her by now, she barely had a thought process as she drew them. The art had become automatic. Full of life, yet ultimately lifeless.

It was time for more. "Why else would I have those dreams? Sometimes I feel like they're memories. Not necessarily mine. They have that kind of nonsensical quality to them. Always images that mean nothing in particular, like seeing the angels drink or sleep. Scenes from a movie reel I never watched."

"Oh."

"You're disappointed?" Angela allowed an edge of annoyance in her voice.

"Um—" Nina paused. "No. Not like you think. I don't see angels, and I'm not a blood head, so there's no controlling them or summoning them myself. But—"

She paused again, clutching the jester doll.

Angela waited for her to rediscover her nerves, but soon she couldn't help it anymore. "Not every blood head can do stuff like that. I think the prophecy is mostly crap."

"Do you?" Nina's voice shook a little. She was looking down at her feet, searching for something again. Maybe the sanity they'd lost tonight. Most people didn't ask a new friend to kill them or reveal that their dreams were a step from reality. "I've heard voices—and seen people—for a year now. Women. Men. Children. Everyone you can imagine. Most of the time, their voices all blend together, like they're shouting at me. And they usually talk about terrible things I don't understand, keeping me from sleeping most of the night." She ran a hand through her hair, tearing out some strands from her bun, as if stressing the real cause of her bloodshot eyes and frazzled appearance. "But lately, I've been able to hear them more clearly, and I've figured out that they're waiting for someone. To let them out of wherever they've been locked up for so long."

This time, Angela felt an odd shiver of fear. Death didn't scare her, yet the dead did.

How strange.

"That's—"

"Crazy?" Nina said. She plucked at the doll's clothes.

"That's why you came here to visit. Isn't it?" Angela folded her arms, pacing toward the window. "To find out if I could hear or see the same things?"

Nina went silent for a while, and the rain continued, gentle, droning.

Angela stared at her own reflection in the glare on the glass, startled to find that her eyes looked larger, warped by the optical illusion. And in that illusion, she was standing in front of the ominous, black clouds, and their lightning and rain was part of her fine hair, now tangled by a sharp and relentless wind. Her forehead held a crown of fallen stars—candles, flickering in some nearby windows.

"They've been saying that She's coming," Nina said at last.

The words sounded too soft. Whispers that were more like shadows.

"You're talking about the blood head in the prophecy," Angela said. "So it's a woman? I guess you should tell the priests. They'd be grateful."

"No. They'd cut out my voice box."

"So they know already?"

"Some of them." Nina left the bed and pressed a hand against the glass next to Angela. Maybe she could also feel the sudden cold out there, leeching through the pane. "There have been rumors that this bad weather, the killer in the city, the unstable sea—that it's all an omen that She's finally coming and the darkness in the world is welcoming the Ruin. That it's on the move. Which means people like you and me will continue to suffer, seeing and hearing all sorts of nightmares. We're just symptoms of the world's sickness. Get it?"

"So . . . the priests know this. Is that why the Academy humors witches and blood heads?" Angela couldn't bear the idea that her suspicions were correct. If Nina wasn't lying, and if the dead were complaining, and if she was dreaming of angels and unable to die, then maybe the Ruin really was coming into Her dark heritage. Maybe the Vatican was simply waiting for Her to make the move that would define Her once and for all—hopefully at the Academy—and then stamp Her flat before everything got out of hand.

But would it really be so easy? Someone like Stephanie, a person used to privilege, wouldn't go down without a fight.

Then again, neither would I.

"Is that," Angela said, "why Kim is dating Stephanie? Sleeping with the enemy. That kind of thing?"

"You don't think she's the One?" Nina said, horrified yet again.

It was doubtful, but— "Maybe I should ask him."

Nina rounded on her fast. "You'd have to be a fricking moron, Angela. He's not like the other novices. If we're right, he'd probably cut out your tongue just to shut you up."

"So? What do I care about that?"

They stared at each other.

Nina was the first to speak again. "Talking about this stuff is one thing. Acting on it's another. I told you. Don't go near him. Stephanie will have your head."

"Then she already wants it. That Lyrica Pengold saw us talking."

"Oh, God. Don't. Don't do it. He might even use you just to piss Stephanie off. Their relationship isn't exactly ideal—"

The thump on the door startled them both.

"Hold on a second," Angela said, walking over to the door and grasping the knob. It rattled as she turned it, echoing the irritable twist of her wrist. "Who is it—"

A dead rat lay at the threshold of the door, its throat torn open. Blood, maybe even redder than the blood on her blouse, drooled from the hole near its head, seeping between the floor boards. Angela realized she was still staring at it as the student with the silver slippers stepped out of the shadows and in front of the doorway. She was holding a box, stuffed with fabrics and sewing materials. Either she hadn't seen the rat—

Or she killed it.

"My belongings," she said to Angela, setting the box down on the floor. She glanced at the rat, impassive. "How messy."

A soft scuttling sound echoed from the rafters in the hallway.

Angela poked her head out of the door, peering up into the musty gloom. The student looked up with her, but there was no one above them. No one that could be seen, anyway. Only shadows, and an old drapery swaying beneath a draft. What sounded like breathing could just as easily have been wind, entering through spaces in the roof. Angela ushered her inside, shutting the door behind them, sick of feeling watched and hunted by everyone. Even invisible fears and creepy statues.

"I'm afraid," the student was saying, "I interrupted someone's dinner."

"It was an animal that did that?"

"Did what?" Nina turned from the window, looking sick to her stomach. As if she already knew.

The student rearranged the curls of her hair, silent for a moment. When she spoke, her voice was softer. "They were rather quick. It's easy to mistake what you see on evenings like these. Though I would suggest"—she picked up her belongings again—"that you both stay indoors a little longer."

She moved to leave, but Angela grabbed her by the wrist.

Before the young woman could argue with her, more noise whispered through the hallway. It was faint, but it reminded Angela of a predator's hiss, cool with frustration. Vaguely familiar.

"What is it?" Angela said. "A cat in the building?"

The student let go of the knob, seeming to resign herself to staying for a while.

Angela left her and picked up the broken knife handle left on the bed, pitching it into the trash bin to rest in peace with its other half. "My mother had a cat. Pearl. She caught mice in the basement and left them at my parents' bedroom door. Like a gift, to show what a great hunter she was."

"Yes," the student said, gently turning the door lock with a free hand.

But she didn't look very convinced.

"I suppose that is a way of showing affection."

Three

Angela was wrapped deep within the embrace of her newest dream.

Sleep had come, the world vanishing with it, taking her to a better tableau of illusions.

There he was, the beautiful angel with the bronze wings, almost as distinct as in her portraits. She could have been wrong, of course. "He" could just as easily have been a "she," and that probably made more sense considering his delicate features and poised mannerisms, the gentle way he could blink those large eyes. But there was an authority in his steps that always made her think otherwise, and his face commanded her to simply watch. Not listen or understand.

As usual, he had nothing to say to her.

His was one in a pair of eternally voiceless recordings, whisking in and out of her mind, intruding when she expected them least. Tonight the angel with the bronze wings leaned over a round desk made of glass, writing with a pen in some kind of blocky script— all circles, interconnected lines, and angles. He wore a form-fitting ivory coat, its fabric pristine even compared to the gleam of his feathers. Rubies dangled from chains woven through his hair.

Angela opened her invisible mouth to speak. To call to him.

He looked up from the desk, setting down the pen. He was turning his head, his winged ears fluttering gently.

He saw her.

No.

He was looking past her at someone else. Someone who liter-

ally walked through her invisible body to stand in front of him, her unearthly silver dress reflecting all the light. A young woman with flowing curls of hair, tall, mild-mannered, her hands clasped modestly above the knee, had arrived to confront him. But the angel straightened immediately, and he was not only taller than this new person but distinctly unhappy. Those pink lips pursed into a tightly controlled frown.

The woman pointed behind him—to a gray figure in the distance—but he shouted at her and dismissed her with a wave of the hand, surprisingly angry.

Then she was stepping aside, facing Angela with the distinct sense that they saw each other. They were suddenly in front of a gigantic staircase of light, each step clearer than diamond.

But most astonishingly of all, Angela knew who she was looking at.

Four

Grant, we beseech Thee, that the One who is destined to bring Iniquity will perish in the eternal flames. Oh, God, help us in our hour of greatest need. When the Ruin approaches, be not far from your children. Amen.

—CLOSING HYMN, FRESHMAN INTRODUCTORY CEREMONY

The student with the chestnut hair was named Sophia.

She had no living relatives, Angela learned. No personal belongings that amounted to anything valuable. The more they had talked, the more she became a mystery, and the night ended with her dancing in and out of Angela's dreams as elegantly as the bronze-winged angel, her outfit suddenly an exotic dress of silver taffeta. But Sophia was a real, live, flesh-and-blood human being who could speak when she was spoken to, responding to a person's feelings with practiced delicacy. The angels, of course, were always moving out of Angela's reach, never truly glancing at her when she questioned them. Impolite and impressively untouchable.

Meanwhile, in the background, Sophia listened, smiled, and genuinely cared.

It had only been a day, and Angela feared she was developing a terrible infatuation with her, not understanding why until she awakened and noticed one of the dolls on her dresser. It was a Victorian-era miniature with a china complexion and vacant gray eyes. Her curls dropped to her waist in a waterfall of chestnut, their shorter

44 ~ SABRINA BENULIS

strands snagged behind a black velvet headband. Nearby, like a blur in the corner of Angela's vision, Sophia sat on the opposite bed, her own gray eyes lingering on the even grayer rain, its drops slanting onto the rooftops and framing the city with morning fog. Curls dribbled down her back, shiny and tempting, their ends gathered with a thin black ribbon. She'd folded her hands, settling them on top of her lap, looking like she was waiting for someone to pick her up and dress her. She'd never gone back to her own room after all, probably too frightened to leave after finding the rat at the door.

It was hard to blame her.

She turned to Angela again, smiling in that gentle way.

No. Sophia was prettier than the doll. Just as quiet, but definitely prettier.

"Will you be trying to kill yourself today?" she said, her tone matter-of-fact.

The words were like a sharp knife, cutting through Angela's leftover dreams. All too quickly the dazzling stairway, the light, even her beautiful angel, seemed like ridiculous details. So wrong in such a dreary world.

Angela sank back into the sheets, her skin sticky from the humidity. Winter couldn't come fast enough. "I don't think so," she said after a minute had passed. "There are a few things I have to do around here first."

"Oh? I was hoping you would say that." Sophia left the bed and glided over to Angela's desk, picking up a folder stuffed with papers, one of them Stephanie's sorority invitation. But instead she pulled out a letter printed with font in an expensive signature-style script. The school seal had been embossed in gold leaf at the top, its large Tree glittering beneath the wall sconce that guttered above Angela's desk. Most of the dorm's chandelier candles had already melted to stumps, their wicks burned into little ash piles. "Today is the official introductory ceremony for incoming students. I was afraid I'd be attending it alone, but perhaps we can go together?"

She looked back to Angela, hopeful.

"Do the novices attend?"

"They preside."

Angela kept silent for a little while, listening to the creaks and groans of the attic floorboards. Now that Sophia had moved upstairs, the lower levels of the mansion were cavernously empty. Any leftover noise probably came from the wood, expanding or contracting in the wet weather.

Probably.

"I guess I'll go," she said at last. "My classes don't start until tomorrow anyway. It would be better than wandering around the city with nothing to do."

"Wandering in Luz alone"—Sophia was staring out the window again—"is not recommended, you know."

"Because of the serial killer?"

Sophia put the folder back on the desk. "There are less sensational ways to die on this island. More people fall through the ocean grates on the city's lowest tiers, or ignore the signs near the bridges and topple into chasms when the lamps are close to burning out. Of course, that's in the areas without electricity. Most of the Academy streets have lamps with bulbs."

"They should set up fences around the chasms. Barbed wire would keep people out."

"Not everyone is afraid of barbed wire." Sophia shook her head, curls bouncing. "Some even think of it as an invitation."

"True. I know I certainly would."

It was just her luck that drowning never worked out. She'd likely take all that trouble to jump, then merely float in the chill sea until somebody fished her out, her brain slipping in and out of unconsciousness. The air would be salty and thick with brine, but not suffocating or foul enough to murder her. She might as well stay in the bedroom, pretending that she'd already gone through the process.

Angela sniffed, wrinkling her nose.

A sour odor seeped throughout the dorm.

It had to be the blood. Blood on the broken knife in the trash bin. Blood staining the blouse she'd thrown on top of it. But mostly the smell of blood from that damned rat lying outside the door. Nina had left, and Angela still hadn't bothered to dispose of the corpse, hoping that the cat would do it for her and lick up any remnants. She slid out of bed, looking for the towel she'd dropped next to the dresser the other night. Her floor-length pajamas thankfully hid the scars on her arms and legs, but the lace scratched at her feet when she walked, irritating new, tender skin. "Let me get rid of this rat outside, and I'll get dressed. If we're going to go to the ceremony, we should get there early. I'd like to find a seat where I can see but not be seen."

"Oh, the rat?" Sophia said over her shoulder. She busied herself making the bed, straightening its silver-and-red comforter. "It's gone. Since very early this morning."

"Really?" Angela dropped the towel, immediately aiming for her dresser where she kept her tights and arm gloves. Those would—absolutely had to—go on first. "Thanks. I don't like dead animals, especially throwing them out. I'm always afraid of contracting mites."

Not a virus, though. Or bacteria. Angela, very disappointingly, couldn't get sick.

Even when she deliberately tried.

"Oh, no, I didn't touch it."

Angela tugged open her bureau doors, grasping another blouse with the opulent Tree symbol. Her black-and-red skirt hung next to it, the gold buttons near the pocket snatching at the light. "So the cat came back sometime before this morning?"

"In a manner of speaking."

Sophia was waiting again, her hands folded atop her lap, her skirt neatly spread on either side of her legs. She had such a delicate, porcelain appearance, Angela didn't want to believe she was anything else than a doll, a gift from the heavens to crown the collection ringing the room. Nina was an interesting person, and she had a few things in common with Angela, but she still had a very solid presence that grated after a few hours. Sophia blended much better with Angela's paintings and artificial friends, like a precious coincidence that never stopped presenting itself. She imposed on Angela's desire to be alone, but with the tact of a butterfly on a rose. It was like they'd been friends for years.

"This might sound odd," Angela said as she stopped to peer into a mirror, disgusted by the knots in her hair, "but I was surprised to learn you didn't have a roommate. I saw you talking to another student yesterday; some woman with blond braids. I thought maybe you lived in the same house."

"She's a member of the Pentacle Sorority," Sophia said softly.

No way. That means—

"Are you?"

A brief pause. Then, "Yes."

Goddamn it.

"So Stephanie sent you to spy on me?" Angela snapped, sounding more angry than she felt. It wasn't easy to get mad at Sophia. Her disposition softened you somehow. Which must have been why Stephanie chose her. To entice Angela into dropping her guard even further.

And there I was giving her the benefit of a doubt.

"She didn't send me," Sophia said, lifting her hand. A golden ring, its red stone engraved with a gold pentagram, sparkled on a finger. "Don't pay attention to this, all right? It's a coincidence that we're in the same house. Stephanie has nothing to do with rooming students together."

"Yeah, well according to Nina, she only pulls every other string on this campus."

"It's true." Her voice shook, genuinely upset.

"Why don't you stay in their house anyway? Why are you on your own?"

"A punishment. I'm being punished."

"For what?"

Sophia averted her eyes, her pretty mouth sealing shut. Angela was almost finished pulling up her tights by the time that whispery voice made itself heard again. "I can't tell you why. It's forbidden."

"Then tell me this. Are you friends with her or not? You're not a blood head. Neither is that blonde. You both had to ingratiate yourself with her somehow."

"Like I said, I'm suffering through a punishment. The one you call 'the blonde' is in charge of that. It's a fallacy that you have to be a blood head to join the sorority. That's only the inner circle—the tier with privileges. A lot of students aren't aware of that. Even those who've been here for years."

Strangely enough, what Sophia said made sense. And instantly, so did the strange tension between Nina and Stephanie. In essence, Nina was bitter. Really, it wasn't difficult to assume she'd also attempted to join the sorority, only to be cast aside like yesterday's news. And if she'd told Angela the truth yesterday about hearing dead people moan and groan, then she'd also be a perfect candidate to join the lower tier. Instead, she'd been passed over, as if her abilities were defective at best.

"I'm not friends with Stephanie Walsh," Sophia continued, "or with the blond woman you saw talking to me in the street. They can punish me. But my will is my own."

She said the last words so strongly, a shiver crawled up Angela's arms.

"What do you know about Lyrica Pengold? Or Brendan Mathers? Anything?"

Sophia frowned slightly, the expression full of polite contempt. "I'm kept from knowing too much about Stephanie's personal affairs. Those names mean as much to me as they do to you and Nina Willis. Maybe less."

"So you can't tell me what's going on in the Pentacle Sorority's house?"

"I can tell you that Lyrica is the real underling to watch out for. Usually. Don't be alarmed to find her spying on you or trailing you between classes."

"I was more annoyed than shocked yesterday."

"Good."

Angela grabbed her clothes, hiding behind the dressing screen and its painting of extinct peacocks. What a sight they must have been, with their tails more gaudy than an opulent Vatican mansion, decked in iridescent purples and greens. She was slowly growing used to the gold scattered throughout the building, usually found in the form of tarnished brass. Her family had been rich but always preferred silver. "Never mind. I guess we should go to this ceremony together anyway. It's not your fault if Stephanie's punishing you—likely for something stupid. But if you cause me trouble of any kind"—Angela stuck her head out from behind the screen for a second—"you'll pay dearly. I can tell you that much."

Even if I am weakened by your smiles. Why do you have to be so damned nice?

"What if you pay dearly for *befriending me*?" Sophia was sitting in the same position when Angela stepped out again. She barely acknowledged the sight of her tights and gloves, not even questioning them with her eyes, as if she understood why they existed in the first place. "There are stipulations in the sorority that apply to other students. I don't have to reveal them to you."

"I'm not really afraid of Stephanie. Not the version I saw of her anyway." Angela slipped on a boot, lacing the leather until it cinched tight below her knees. "What I am afraid of is that she and everyone else will end up making my search ten times harder than it has to be. That I'll be slowed down."

"What are you searching for?"

Angela stopped tying her boots. There were a lot of answers she could give. Brendan. Kim. Her angels. Death. But each one also required a longer explanation than she felt like giving. Especially when it might find its way back to Stephanie's curious ears. "For my sanity," she ended up saying.

But that was probably too late by now.

"When you turned that lock last night," she continued, "it was like being in the institution all over again. They always made sure we couldn't get out of our rooms at night. And that no one else could get in. I'm not too keen on stray cats inside the building, but I wouldn't have cared if it was hunting a mouse in the bedroom either."

Sophia left her seat, reaching for the ceremony pamphlet. "The lock was for peace of mind. Not to act as any kind of barrier." Her eyes were cold and opaque in the gloom of the room. "It would have held, but only for so long."

"What—is this a super cat we're talking about?"

"I never said it was a cat."

An awkward silence drifted between them. Angela finished lacing her boots and stood, ready to leave the room, but not quite so ready to open the door. Now it seemed like nothing more than a sliver of wood positioned in front of a crushing and invisible menace. There was no cat? What, then? Angela would have heard a dog days earlier, and foxes and weasels were extinct on the island. Maybe a raccoon? "If the lock couldn't keep it out—"

That's right. Not a cat now. An 'it.'

"—what did?"

"The light," Sophia whispered. She pointed to the chandelier swinging above them, its brass half gray with tarnish. "The candles that I lit, when you finally fell asleep."

The introductory ceremony had been scheduled for an hour after breakfast, during a time when downpours were common. That way, so the thinking went, the students would stay indoors and attend, rather than meandering back to their dormitories in the fairer weather. But in a stroke of irony the sky broke open, and instead of water, dreary sunshine descended on the city with rays of sickly yellow. The light looked like it had aged somehow, pent up behind a screen of clouds for days, and Luz aged beneath it, all of its flaws newly glaring and raw.

Angela had decided to sit in an apse of the church, hoping to be screened by darkness.

Yet the sunlight glowed through the stained-glass window, haloing her and Sophia with red and purple. Everyone else who'd bothered to come—and there weren't many—sat in relative obscurity, half hidden by pillars, or shadowed over by a large statue meant to hold two flickering chandeliers. Now, it was too late to get up and change her seat, joining them. The novices were deep in the middle of a boring ritual, their Latin prayers and monologues utterly alien to her, and the moment she stood up to escape, she was sure a hundred heads would turn and take notice of the transgression. One of those heads would be Kim's. He stood behind his older peers, reciting the prayers with a tormented expression, and he glanced at Angela every once in a while, his amber eyes dull like the sunlight.

She did little to acknowledge him, merely nodding and slumping deeper into the pew.

Brendan, oddly enough, was nowhere to be found. For a person who adhered to rules like a fly to honey, he was behaving more than out of character.

He probably did what you can't and finally ended it all. Are these ceremonies supposed to be this boring?

She leaned over toward Sophia. "Please tell me this is almost over."

"Five more minutes," Sophia said. She was also watching Kim, maybe because he was watching Angela. She certainly didn't have a lovesick glitter in her eye like some of the other students. "You should consider yourself lucky," she said with a teasing smile. "The Masses tend to last two hours."

"They have Masses here?"

"Oh no. Not here. Unless there is a special feast day to celebrate, this building isn't used as an actual church anymore. It's more like an auditorium or gathering hall. When it isn't a holiday, daily Mass takes place in one of the chapels spread across the campus. There are about twenty of them. Those nearest to the Bell Tower are the most popular."

"You're talking about normal Masses, right?"

Sophia stared straight ahead as she spoke, her hands clasped delicately on her lap. "What would give you an impression otherwise?"

"The rumors I've heard. The newspaper articles. The Bell Tower is in the Eastern District of the Academy, isn't it? Where they're finding the dead bodies? All this craziness about monsters, killers, and occult conspiracies—it really gives more weight to what people on the Continent say about this place. That it's cursed. That all this 'holier than thou' stuff is an act." Angela nodded at the altar, at the novices lined two by two in their orderly rows, like clones covered head to toe in black. At least Kim's chunk of crimson hair added some color. "What are they saying right now, anyway?"

"It's a prayer meant to call down the blessing of God on the new students. And also, a petition for protection from the Ruin. Some believe, though, that their prayers are only making everything worse." Sophia's whisper was barely audible. ". . . they're asking that the Ruin perish in the eternal flames reserved for the wicked in Hell . . ."

"I always found it funny that they assume Hell is on fire."

"Only parts," Sophia said, even less audibly.

Then she remained silent for the duration of the ceremony, barely moving until the novices chanted in unison, giving the final blessing for everyone to leave. After the students stood, stretching and chatting, the novices filed away off the altar, entering a side room to the right, Kim lingering behind to glance back first at a window and then at Angela before following them into the shadows. Angela would either have to wait to speak with him, hoping that he might approach her in front of too many curious students, or she would have to confront him one-on-one in some dark little corner before he left the church. Neither option was ideal. But if she wanted to find Brendan—or pry into Stephanie's secrets—she didn't have much of a choice. The opportunity was slipping away fast.

"Angela," Sophia said, tapping her on the shoulder, "I'm going to go back to the dormitory."

"You don't have any classes today?"

"I never have any classes."

Angela stared back at her. "What—"

"The punishment," Sophia said, as if that could explain everything. She glared at someone standing behind Angela, a little to her left.

Kim stepped out into the open, his hair streaked through with more color in the warm light of the window. His voice was smooth, the essence of a gentleman. "Have we met?" he was saying to Sophia. "I don't remember saying anything to deserve that kind of look."

Sophia glared at him a second longer. "Good day to you," she said, bowing slightly.

The glance she shared with Angela was brief, almost admonishing, before she joined a mass of students leaving the church down the middle of the aisle.

"*Have* you met?" Angela took another seat, this time beneath a carving that depicted a sea serpent with thousands of scales, its massive coils wrapped around an island with trees and waterfalls. The church echoed away into a strange silence, punctured here and there by the rumbles of thunder slowly bearing down on the city. The sunlight was already fading. "Or do you just have a bad reputation?"

"You're rather straightforward," Kim said, sitting across from her.

He's not stupid enough to sit right next to me. But he's interested enough to talk.

"More like cautious. I've been told not to speak with you. You're Stephanie Walsh's property after all."

"Only when I feel like it," Kim said, running a hand through his bangs. His other hand rested on the back of the pew, tapping the wood. "I was surprised to see you here, especially if you don't want me to take any notice of you. Are you trying to make Stephanie mad?"

"Are you?"

"I simply do what I like. At the time, I liked your paintings. If that's made life any more difficult for you, I'm sorry."

"Your love triangle is making life difficult for me. As I'm sure you know, Brendan Mathers is my brother. Apparently, he's also

Stephanie's official boyfriend, vow of celibacy or not." She paused, relishing the cool breeze floating through the open doors. The blush on her cheeks could have been from embarrassment or the mere idea that they were alone. But either way, it made her warm. She clicked the heels of her boots together, choosing to stare at them, at their ragged laces. Anywhere but at Kim. He was gazing back at her intently, as if he knew exactly what information she wanted out of him and why. "By association, I'm already involved, so if you wouldn't mind, try to keep your eyes from wandering too much. Especially in my direction. I'm sure you can imagine what it would be like for me—caught between the two of them or needing to explain myself to the priests. I'm attracting enough attention already."

Kim regarded her for a moment, his gaze even more intense. His eyes were such a strange color, peering back at her like yellow suns behind a web of hair. "Is that all you have to say to me? Usually I'm the one lecturing students, not the other way around."

It's now or never.

Angela looked up at him again, still startled by the paleness of his skin, how it had sapped to an even more chalky shade now that the light was leaving them. Was he really a novice? Or maybe the better question was: Why had he bothered to take vows at all? Brendan's choice was somewhat understandable. His entire life had been regimented by the Mathers family, so the transition into Vatican life was a preordained affair. But Kim looked and acted completely at odds with the priesthood. Surely the Academy officials knew about his relationship with Stephanie. Did they fear him for some reason? Or like Angela suspected, was he a spy, dating Stephanie to determine how risky she was to Earth's well-being?

"I didn't expect to see you here," she finally said. "But I was hoping you could help me out."

Kim had been glancing at the windows again. Now he stood, his long coat brushing the floor tiles. "Would you mind if we discussed this on the way to my next teaching session?"

There was a new tremor in his voice. Maybe he was nervous too. The two of them alone—it was like engaging in a secret tryst, something forbidden. Stephanie's territory was being painfully invaded. But this was the price Angela would have to pay to understand who and what she was dealing with. Finding Brendan would be a bonus.

"That's fine," Angela said, also peering at the windows, "as long as nobody sees us."

"We'll take one of the back alleyways," Kim said, and then his mouth settled into a hard line. As if they were about to walk into a war zone of some kind. "Follow me."

She trailed behind him, and they both left the church only to emerge in the middle of a depressing drizzle. Water slimed the cobblestones along the street, dripping from the gray moss that crusted parts of the brick-hewn towers to their right. The church courtyard was ringed by taller but much less impressive buildings, and sometimes, through their golden portholes, Angela saw students milling back and forth in narrow hallways or caught the flutter of thick draperies, their velvet half exposed to the wind. The thunder had swerved away somewhere to the west, booming like faraway drums. They passed very few people, most of them other novices, one of those a woman with rain-soaked hair. She questioned Kim with her eyes until he stopped to bow and wave her away.

Then they slipped into the alleyway. Open sewage must have been flowing through a groove in the roadway. At least, that's what it smelled like. The second Angela and Kim sidled away from it, he grabbed her hand and pulled her beneath a soggy canopy. They continued walking beneath it together, heading east.

A large crow screeched overhead, quickly dropping onto the street ahead of them.

Kim's mouth set even harder, but he soon found his humor again. "I wouldn't suggest taking this path on a dark night."

Or with a stranger like you?

Not that Angela had the inhibitions of normal people anymore.

If anything, she was begging to be murdered. But Kim was probably too much of a gentleman to either allow that or even do it himself. No sense asking. "Even before I found out that you and Stephanie were an item"—it was difficult to hide the eager curiosity in her tone—"I thought I'd ask you about my brother. Brendan. Do you know where he lives here, at the Academy?"

The crow screeched, strutting nearer.

Kim fiddled with something in his pocket, never taking his eyes off the bird. "Of all the things for you to say . . . Why don't you go to the registrar and make your inquiries? Why would I care about where he lives?"

Maybe because you're making him look like a fool, sleeping with his girlfriend.

Didn't these priests in training have any kind of loyalty to one another?

"Because you're a novice too. Don't you guys all hang out together? Bond, drink, and share stories?" Maybe even more than that. Luz was full of rumors and most of them revolved around the Vatican, the overall creepiness of the city, or even worse, the backward morality you could find in the most unlikely places. So far, Angela had avoided the parties for incoming students, trying to keep what was left of her innocence intact. "I was hoping to at least give him a message. The registrar turned me away. Since I left the institution—"

Kim glanced at her, raising an eyebrow.

"It's a long story." She turned away from him to watch the crow. In the short second he'd looked away, it had flown nearer to them, landing on a rickety gutter. "But anyway, I can't just find out where he lives. My parents made sure to sign restraining papers to prevent that."

"So you're insane," Kim said, whistling between his teeth. He found the crow again, seeming to lock it in place with his words.

"You sound impressed."

"I am. Your naïveté is off the charts. Most of the female students know better than to walk with me alone in a dark alleyway.

Most people in general know not to bother with me at all." He turned on her, quicker than thought, pinning her back against a brick wall that scratched and tugged at her skirt. Kim's hands met the wall on either side of her head, and he leaned in close, his honey-colored eyes catlike in the dark. Angela's heart hammered, a thin trickle of sweat touching her blouse collar. His mouth was so close, its breath warmed her neck. "Haven't you heard the news? What if I'm the serial killer that's been murdering people in the city? What if I'm going to cut your throat this very second?"

The crow screeched in the background, frantic. Warning Angela away.

Even a bird had better survival instincts than she did. She grabbed Kim's collar, pulling him closer. "Then do me a favor and get it over with."

He stared at her. Perhaps trying to gauge how serious she was.

A second later, he let go, stepping away from her and back into his smooth, gentlemanly persona as if there'd never been a change. Too bad. She was hoping he'd actually follow through on the threat. Unless he was holding back simply to spite her. "Brendan," he said gently, running a hand through his bangs again, "has been missing for at least a week. We were under the assumption he took a vacation at the start of the semester."

"So you do know him?"

"Not very well. I'm somewhat of an outcast in his social circle. I can't imagine then"—he sounded satisfied with himself—"why his girlfriend would cheat on him with me."

"Just like I can't imagine why the Vatican tolerates her witch sorority. That is, if what I'm hearing is true."

Kim was silent for a short while, but at last he approached her more slowly, reaching out to touch her long hair. Angela let him examine it, softened both by his attractive eyes, and the delight of knowing that—at least in Luz—she might actually be a step above a typical beauty like Stephanie in desirability. Dating Kim was still a bad idea. And it was hard to figure out why she felt so guilty about this when Stephanie was also two-timing Brendan. Maybe it was because, despite being called a witch, the girl seemed somewhat normal. But there was always the chance that if Angela played the game well enough, Kim would give her information about Stephanie that could prove useful in the future. If Nina was telling the truth about her, it never hurt to threaten blackmail when the situation turned foul. "Are you sure you want to do this?" Angela said. "I might be insane, just like you said. I could be even crazier than a serial killer. It's not smart to get involved with someone like me."

"You said keep my eyes to myself," Kim replied, "not my hands." He tugged on the lock of her hair and let it slip through his fingers. "Stephanie told me you refused her invitation to join the sorority." He shook his head. "That wasn't very smart either, now was it?"

"Is that why you're interested in me? Because I said no?"

"Your paintings helped," he said, his tone cool. "I'd planned on asking you that night—if I walked you back to your dormitory— what your source of inspiration happened to be? Certainly no one you know?"

He was interrogating her. Perhaps just like he interrogated Stephanie whenever he got a chance. The only difference was that he and Angela weren't in a bed. Yet. "Is there really any way of knowing them?" she said, taking the chance. "Angels, I mean?"

"Perhaps." His smile laughed at her. "Although I'm not about to tell you here. I'll be late for my class if you don't let me go. Student teachers are bound by the general rules of the Academy." He tapped his wrist, sighing. "There are penalties, none of them very fun."

"Then why don't you come to my dormitory tomorrow night?"

"Alone?" His face was even more handsome in the dim light, the shadows hollowing out the sharp angles of his cheekbones. "That's not a smart thing to do either, Miss Angela Mathers. We could get into trouble, you and I. What would your friend think? I don't believe she's very fond of me."

Whether he was talking about Sophia or Nina, it didn't really matter anymore. Angela had made up her mind. "I'll make sure that nobody bothers us."

Kim examined her for the last time. Then, apparently deciding to take a chance himself, he took her hand and gave it a light kiss. "And I'll make sure that you don't regret it."

His lips were as cool as his voice and soft.

"Now why don't you follow me until we're safely indoors?"

Angela strolled behind him, slightly aware of the crow dancing straight ahead, wings flapping. She was feeling sick inside, and a little queasy at how easily their little rendezvous had been planned. They were going to talk—that was all—but already it seemed defined as something taboo. Kim's looks weren't helping either. He was finely built, with a delicate nose and thin lips, and his eyes and skin contrasted artistically with the inky mess of his hair. His voice promised secrecy and savory things. How many female students—how many blood heads—did he investigate like this on a regular basis? Stephanie might have been the prime candidate to be the Ruin, but she could hear the priests granting Kim a special kind of dispensation to determine how well that theory held. They'd probably schooled him to be clever and charming.

"Are you keeping up?" he said, pausing to wait for her.

She caught up to him, watching him fiddle more with whatever was in his coat pocket. This time he pulled out a strip of paper. Its edges had curled in the humid air, slightly obscuring the Latin words written along its length, but Angela recognized a prayer of some kind. Kim tossed the paper at the crow, muttering something under his breath, his voice taking on that shaky, nervous quality she remembered hearing before they'd left the church.

The bird spiraled up and away, screeching in a fury.

It wasn't until they turned the corner of the street that they saw the dead body.

Or saw what was left of it splayed in a large puddle near the corner of the Theology Center. The academic building was a tower so tall that it dwarfed most of the others in the Academy's Eastern District—its walls all poorly set brick, stone, and the buttresses and gables one would expect of a cathedral. Lightning raced across the sky, webbing the clouds around its central spire, and at the peak rested heavenly shadows, the terribly beautiful statues of angels and demons, some grasping flickering lamps. One of the demons even seemed to shift position, though Angela was certain it was an illusion caused by the rain, the mist, and the difficulty of picking out details from such a distance. The corpse, though, rested in a dank corner of the alley opening out near the tower, the stone street eventually slanting toward a cliff that spoke of one of Luz's older, lower levels.

The dead student was a young woman, one missing an arm and a leg.

Surprisingly, what Angela saw disturbed her less than the mangled rat at her bedroom door. Mostly because she was struggling with the disappointment that it hadn't been her lying there, bloodless and ravaged. Dead at last. The crow Kim had chased away must have been picking at the body, warning them away from its meal.

"Aren't you glad you had me for company?" Kim was saying. He sighed, sounding more angry than afraid. Sweat ringed his collar, and he brushed back a few drops from underneath his bangs. "Luz"—his tone was unforgiving—"tends to devour the naive. I hope you'll learn from this."

Actually, you wouldn't believe how disappointed I am.

"Yes," she said instead, very slowly. "I guess you're not a serial killer after all."

Kim grabbed her by the arm, pulling her out of the alleyway and into the stark lamplight near the Center. No one had noticed what street they'd used to enter, and a passing trio of academic officials nodded at them, smiling slightly as they entered the building. Once inside, Kim assumed his usual calm demeanor, the terse professionalism in his voice mixing well with the greetings of the other novices, most of them milling and spilling into various classrooms. A few students glanced at Angela but quickly sped off to their assigned rooms, while others sat beneath an elegantly carved statue—an angel holding up a lamp that resembled the sun.

"Until tomorrow," Kim said to her, briefly touching her hand. His hushed tone was filled with more warnings. His gaze was cool and measured.

Obviously, there would be no discussion about going to the authorities and informing them of murder. With Kim so involved in Stephanie's affairs, he probably couldn't afford to be a suspect. That red splash in his bangs marked him as her property, of course. Besides his reputation, which could always be more lies than truth, it was the only safe thing he could flaunt.

"Until tomorrow," Angela said.

But tonight, she was sure of it, there would be many guilty, bloody dreams.

Five

There are some things worse than death.
Pray you never encounter them.
—Brother Francis, *Encyclopedia of the Realms*

The elevators had fallen into neglect long ago, forcing Kim to take the primitive, circuitous route up through a maze of steep and spiraling stairwells. By now his legs ached, their muscles no better than rubber, his every step more ponderous than the last. He'd been journeying through the upper fourth of the Academy's infamous Bell Tower, its innards a dark, forbidding maze of smudged walls, cracking plaster, and grimy, lead-paned windows. Most of the Tower's lower chambers were used as storage space, but the top three floors had the distinction of possessing three separate chapels, none of them in official use, but all of them used on a regular basis by Kim, by Stephanie, or by anyone who wanted to host a private ritual. Today, though, he was aiming for the Tower's pinnacle, where the Vatican's hundred-year-old brass bell had once rung out the hour on the hour, but fell silent after numerous seasons of harsh weather took their toll, crazing the bell and splitting it down the middle. Now it was a relic, hanging in shadows seething with bats and rats.

And much, much worse.

He dragged himself up the last set of stairs, turning onto a rickety landing. Rain tinkled against a nearby window, dampening the sound of flapping wings.

Shadows flickered.

The crow paused on her newest perch, cocking her head side-ways, peering through the pane. Kim listened to the notes of the falling water, half glancing at the bird, fingering the stolen keys in his pocket. Finding the right one at last, he slipped its metal into the keyhole. The door groaned as he pushed, nudging it open.

Two rats squeezed through the crack, scuttling over his feet and down the stairwell.

The smell was almost overpowering. Rodent urine and bat fe-ces. Decaying meat. But the Bell Attic was in reality more cavern-ous than its outer architecture—and its smell—suggested, most of its vermin hiding in holes chipped out of the stone or nesting near the bell's metal supports. The low, sloping roof was mostly to blame, as it kept the wind from entering and flushing out the stench. Kim picked his way around a mound of bat dung and a selection of hollowed-out bones. "Troy."

Silence.

At least she couldn't fool him. Light outside, no matter how scanty, meant Troy's presence inside, and the sunbeams had at least another half hour before they disappeared completely. But standing exposed in her territory like this, alone, ignorant of where she was roosting, was far more dangerous. No matter how familiar his scent might be, her hunger could always overcome her common sense. Kim stared up into the darkness, barely able to discern the beady eyes of bats staring back at him. If he took a few careful steps, keeping the wall against his shoulders—

A human arm, shredded to the elbow joint, dropped at his feet.

Ten black fingernails reached down from the gloom, pinching into the stone near his head. Troy appeared soon afterward, and their faces were parallel, inches apart.

"It's about time," she said.

Kim bit back the scream in his throat.

Troy's corpse-white skin, her large yellow eyes, those short, sharp teeth. No matter how many times he looked at her, the ter-ror refused to die. And though Troy might have been somewhat typical of the Jinn, her stealthy silence was second to none. She had a horrific way of creeping up on him, on anything, without giving herself away. Often he'd find that she'd stay in the same position for hours, frozen as only a hunter could stay still. Watching him and waiting. Yet she'd chosen to ignore him again for the moment, instead swiveling a pointed ear in the direction of the rain. Water dripped from her chopped black hair, her sickle-shaped wings and layers of rags. One of her chilling hisses broke the silence, and she licked at the blood caking her bluish-white lips. They always seemed bruised to him. Punishing.

"Why so slow?" she said again, shaking the rain away. Her eyes flicked in his direction, cold and terrible.

Troy's games could be infuriating. As could many of her other habits. "Your latest handiwork slowed me down. It took me an hour to cart the body to the sea."

"It's your own fault for interrupting my meal. Besides"—her voice held the hint of laughter—"Fury warned you well enough in advance. Although it was fun to guess how long it would be till you arrived here angry and depressed."

"Stop stalking her," he said. His voice sounded bitterly crisp.

Another hiss, as if in consideration. Troy descended from the wall, her body fluid and lean, her eyes seeming to glow like ghost lights. Cackles from outside announced Fury's arrival before the crow glided inside, aiming for the severed arm lying on the floor. A Vapor, a soul-slave granted the shape and nature of a bird, Fury gave her true identity away through unusual size and eyes similar to her master's. Whenever Troy couldn't bless Kim with her unsettling presence, the Vapor was never too far away to take over the job. He'd already tried bonding with Fury, half hoping that years of tasty tidbits might trick the nuisance into letting her guard down, but to little result. Today, the bird found both his offered hand and its morsel distasteful as ever, choosing instead to hop onto Troy's skinny shoulder. "You're in no position to give orders," Troy said, growling. "Didn't the death of your favorite student teach you that?"

"It doesn't change the fact that you need me, and that your petty snacks are only going to make this harder for everyone involved." Kim grasped one of the prayer wards in his pocket, caressing the paper. He'd use it this time if she pushed him hard enough. "The priests," he said, unable to hold back his triumph, "are on to you, Troy."

She shook Fury away, snapping at him more than speaking. "On to me? Let them try and rid this city of my presence. I'll gut them myself—"

"Although they still suspect the demon over you. She's keeping a low profile, but it's only a matter of time until they exorcise you by mistake, maybe through her instigation. It would be wise to stick to rats for now."

"I see a rat I'd like to stick," she spat back at him.

Kim noted how her ears folded back against her skull and gripped the paper more tightly. Fury continued to listen to their exchange, tugging on sinews near her toes. "Angela is different, striking. But that doesn't mean she's the one we're looking for."

"Oh? And how many times have I heard that?" Troy glanced at Fury, looking annoyed at the continuing loss of her meal. Her teeth bared in a new, but still angry, smile. Blood had stained them to a dull shade of pink. "Sometimes, I think you're toying with me, Sariel—"

It was never a good sign when she used his Jinn-given name.

"—that all of your searching for the Archon and determining that this one isn't suitable, and that one isn't right, is all a ploy to keep my teeth out of your heart." She shifted slightly, the muscles in her wrists bunching together. "That makes me question your usefulness, you see. How many years have you spent, mating with one female after another to find what we're looking for? And meanwhile, the seconds of your life pass away, always moving you closer to my jaws." Troy spread her wings, stretching their tips into the darkness. Bats fluttered out of the tower, escaping into the evening fog. "You can only hold off the inevitable for so long. So do us both a kindness and make up your mind. This dimension is too unstable for us to wait on your instincts, however dull they might be."

Thunder cracked overhead, so close to the Bell Tower that Kim's ears hurt. Lightning blinded him, and Troy must have smelled the electricity in the air, had been hoping for the distraction, because Kim was startled for a single second. And that was all it took.

She pounced at him, all violence and the intention to hurt.

Fury flapped out of the way, cawing in alarm.

Kim threw the prayer ward into a maelstrom of feathers. "*Abnocto*," he whispered, his voice shaking with echoes of his own fear. The Latin hurt Troy even more than the paper. She snarled in frustration but landed on all fours, her eyes glowing from a nook near the rear of the chamber. How could any creature move so fast? Bones crunched beneath her hands and feet as she wandered nearer to him again. "You bitch," he said to her, brushing at the cut on his cheek.

It was shallow, but the blood still wet his fingers.

"The Tongue of Souls." She grinned, excited by their little battle. "But what will you do when your mouth is finally sealed shut? I'd venture a guess . . ."

She crept out into the open again, seemingly unaware that her posture revealed the Grail.

Lucifel's fabled Grail. It was an emerald that looked exactly like the legends said—a great eye with a miniature abyss for a pupil—but of all places it swung from Troy's neck on a crudely hewn chain, perpetually teasing Kim with its mysteries. Usually, she kept the treasure hidden beneath her rags, but their skirmish had temporarily forced it out of hiding. And much like Troy, it gave off an aura of watchfulness that filled him with horror. The sight of its beauty was as nightmarish as it was desirable. Only the Jinn could protect such a gem without going mad.

Would Stephanie react the same way, recoiling with a fractured mind?

Or would she prove herself to be Raziel's worthy vessel and clutch this relic of his to her heart? Kim wanted to try one last test before he took the chance. Angela seemed too softhearted underneath all her recklessness to be the Archon, but her paintings spoke of memories more angelic than she realized. It never hurt to test a theory.

"Like what you see?" Troy wasn't smiling anymore.

"Before I go," Kim said, fighting back the urge to lunge and throttle her, "give me Telissa's arm back. I want her ring."

Fury croaked from a gutter below them, protesting. But Troy reached up into the mess of her hair, untying a knot that held a glistening Academy ring amid specks of teeth and bones. Trophies from her older kills. This gift was her way of declaring a shaky truce. "The ring," she said, "but not the arm. I'm still hungry tonight."

She tossed the metal at his shoes, returning to what was left of his student's remains, disdaining his presence. The ring clattered to a stop, jaundiced in the poor light.

Kim wouldn't cry, but at the sound of the first bite, he turned from the scene and retched.

Six

---

*There is very little difference between angels and demons. Except
that demons have stopped pretending to be perfect.*

—THE DEMON PYTHON, TRANSCRIBED FROM *The Lies of Babylon*

The sun slanted its last rays into the archbishop's office, illuminating the statues, the leather armchairs, even the snuffed candlewicks with a fine outline of gold. The room was cozy, but its enormous double windows spanned most of a wall, offering an impressive view of Luz and the lower tiers of the Academy. Expense, opulence. The perfect choice for a priest with too much money on his hands. For the briefest moment, St. Mary's Cathedral, its steeple rising like a brown spike above the buildings surrounding the lower courtyard, looked like it was on fire. Then the clouds began to take over again, and Westwood's outlying properties dropped back into an ominous grayness.

Stephanie peered toward the west, searching for the tufts of the Tree hidden in Memorial Park, but darkness stole over the world fast, and soon she was perusing the lights blinking into existence throughout the city.

A crow soared toward the window, as if out of nowhere.

She flinched, brought back to reality while its feet scraped across the glass. Ruffling its black feathers, the bird settled on the outer sill and cocked its head toward the sound of the archbishop's voice. Naamah glanced at the crow from the corner of her dark eyes, an agitated twitch tugging at her mouth. She sat at Stephanie's right, squeaking in her seat whenever she shifted position, tapping her chin, suggesting she was dangerously bored.

". . . ah, yes, here we are." The archbishop finished rifling through a stack of papers and set them in front of him on the desk, finally placing his folded hands on top. "But, of course, I can't give you this information without anything in return."

He had a thunderous voice even in such a stuffy room, and a mass of gray hair that seemed overly combed. Stephanie examined the brass nameplate near the candelabra again.

His Eminence Gregory T. Solomon, Archbishop of Luz.

"So what are you suggesting?" she said softly. "Another deal?"

Stephanie set her jaw, tense.

The archbishop stared shortly at Naamah, but flicked his gaze away as she stared back, hard and uncompromising. The demon had her hood up, yet if her fine features and copper skin wouldn't give her away, the Theban tattoo inked alongside her neck and collarbone would. These priests weren't as stupid as they acted sometimes. Luz was a world where the supernatural constantly kissed the mundane, and the archbishop was dealing with a demon sitting in his office surprisingly well.

"These murders," he continued, "taking place in the city. From what I understand, our little truce has been paying out profitably for us both until now. But if the Pentacle Sorority continues its mistakes on a daily basis, we're going to have a major problem on our hands. Already, I have three junior exorcists lined up, itching to test their skills—"

Naamah slammed her hands on the desk, standing abruptly. She loomed over the archbishop, blond braids dangling out of her hood's mouth. The demon's cloak had turned her into a living shadow, swiftly matching the whispers of night that began to overwhelm the room. The glow of the wall sconces wavered, as if her presence oppressed them.

"Your arrogance," she whispered, "annoys me, priest."

"*I thought you had her under your control,*" he hissed at

Stephanie, never taking his eyes off Naamah. His round face was blanching quickly to a pasty white.

Stephanie kept her smile. His reaction was a lot of fun to watch. "The sorority? No. We know enough to keep our messes hidden."

"Then who?" he shot back at her, trying not to tremble under Naamah's scrutiny.

The demon hadn't budged, clenching the wood like a cat eager to display its claws.

How appropriate.

"An irregularity," Naamah said slowly. Her voice was gentler this time, but no less lethal. "A rat in the walls. It's not something you can take care of."

"That hardly answers my question—"

Stephanie adjusted her ponytail and crossed her legs, enjoying the feel of the leather against her thighs. "There are other creatures to fear besides angels and demons, Your Eminence. In-between things."

She raised her eyebrows meaningfully.

The archbishop took a breath, slumping back in his chair. He held a hand to his forehead. "God . . . How could this happen?"

Naamah left him and wandered over to the window, crossing her arms while she gazed out into the evening. The crow strutted below her, its yellow eyes glinting in the candlelight. The first sigh of rain washed against the glass.

"Because the world is in a state of flux. Answering to Her call."

His frown deepened.

"Or haven't you noticed the weather?" Stephanie gestured outside.

Dull lightning flickered to the north.

Archbishop Solomon straightened himself, flipping through the papers with a finger. "What I want to know is, yet again, why do you think this blood head in particular, mentally unbalanced or not, is a threat? And what do you intend to do about it if she is? In other words"—and now it was his turn to lean forward, intending his whispers for Stephanie's ears alone—"why do you go sticking your pretty nose where it doesn't belong?"

She stayed silent, keeping her composure. If only she had Naa-mah's blades, her strength, her utter lack of remorse.

He was really asking for someone to put him in his place.

"Why did you summon a demon into this city, Miss Walsh? To prove that you are indeed a witch? To shove the prophecy in our faces? Because it's a fatal and ignorant game to play. People are dying out there. People will continue to die. And if there's something I learned from my years of theology— it's that their kind," he pointed at Naamah, "don't understand sympathy."

"So you're concerned for me. How encouraging." Stephanie stood from her seat, her hand outstretched. "I think it's time for me to leave." She curled her fingers, beckoning. "But not empty-handed."

"Watch your step," the archbishop muttered. "To humanity, the Archon is the Ruin, not its overlord."

"But there are two who can be the Ruin." Stephanie took the papers from him, reviving her smile. "It simply comes down to the choice She makes."

She scanned the documents briefly, overwhelmed by a sense of satisfaction.

> . . . Angela Marie Mathers. Date of birth, the sixth of Decem-ber . . . schooling, ten years of private home tutoring, intensive counseling at the Forwallis Institution . . . parents, deceased . . .

Normal enough. Stephanie continued scanning, turning through pages, at last reaching confidential psychiatry files.

Here it was. The important information.

> . . . personality, self-destructive with suicidal tendencies, a marked inclination to the imaginative bordering on delusional; patient has suffered from psychotic episodes with vivid halluci-nations—

A startling *crack* sounded throughout the office, its force like a gunshot.

Stephanie dropped some of the papers, swearing to herself. The archbishop was frozen in his chair, gazing at Naamah with a grim expression that suggested he was fast approaching some invisible precipice. She'd punched through the window, her fist making a neat hole in the glass. Blood streamed from her fingers, but she ignored it, instead examining the black feathers stuck to her skin. The demon flung them to the floor, cursing in a language neither of them understood.

"The crow got away?" Stephanie said, shivering slightly.

Naamah smiled and her teeth appeared, shockingly white. She looked to the priest, a warning behind her eyes. "Back to its rat's nest."

Seven

Witches are easy to manipulate.
Because if they are up to no good, they also think
the same of everyone else.

—THE DEMON PYTHON, TRANSCRIBED FROM *The Lies of Babylon*

The dead student must have bothered Angela more than she'd thought. Her nightmares had revolved around the gray angel, and those crimson eyes that both fascinated and repelled her with their suggestion of disease and blood. In their depths, she saw herself reflected blacker than pitch, as if all the dirt in her soul had been brought to light. Unfortunately, when she arrived for her first afternoon of class, the sickness inside of her seemed to spread rather than mitigate. Kim was the student teacher presiding over her Literature session, and the moment she took a seat next to Nina, it was painful not to stare at him, thinking about what the night would hold. Suddenly, the image of that dead girl was all around her, haunting her with unspoken accusations.

"You look suitably pathetic," Nina said, drumming her fingers on the desktop. "Are you seeing the dead in your sleep now too?"

"So that was who they were." Angela allowed her sarcasm to be heard but stared ahead at the chalkboards. "And here I thought you were making it up."

"Just more angels, huh?" Nina laughed and laid her head on her arms, eyes closing. "You might not be happy, but *I'm* glad your latest suicide attempt crapped out. With you here, this class might actually be tolerable for a change."

"*Omnes relinquite spes, o vos intrantes . . .*"

Kim's voice echoed gently from the entryway of the classroom, rolling in that charming monotone he managed so well. He seemed so out of place up there, standing next to the head teacher, both of them better suited to a chapel than a schoolroom. Why was this Academy so contradictory? The chamber was too large for the number of desks—all of them warped with water damage but carved down to their legs with elegant grapevines and scroll-work—yet there were too many students. Many of them sat near the base of the walls, clipboards cocked and ready for notes. Lyrica was one of them, and of course she glanced at Angela now and then, probably trying to catch her glancing at Kim.

Angela smiled thinly at her.

Lyrica returned to her clipboard, scribbling furiously. No, her gesture said, you're mistaken.

Like hell I am.

". . . and we should discuss the meaning of this passage, in terms of Dante's original influences . . . this, the most famous quote from his masterpiece work *The Inferno*. If you would please read the quote for us—"

She knows somehow about Kim and me. Or at least she suspects. Hopefully, he won't do anything to tip her off—

"Angela," Nina hissed.

"What?"

"Recite the translation!" She shoved her in the arm.

Angela looked around. A mosaic of expectant faces had locked on her, waiting for her to stand up at her desk and recite . . .

"The translation, Miss Mathers," Kim said. His lips fondled her name delicately, but his expression was enough to give it all away. Some of his hair hung in front of his eyes, barely hiding the light behind them—searing, and full of expectation for the evening. "Page 102, the second line."

She slid out of her seat, standing in the middle of the class, unable to hide and feeling the pain of it. Lyrica must have caught on to the teasing inflection in Kim's voice. Her face openly displayed all the satisfaction that would blossom once Stephanie found out, and she was tapping her pen against her clipboard, *tsk tsking* Angela's stupidity. Angela lifted the book higher, blocking her out. "Abandon hope, all ye who enter here . . ."

The remainder of the class was even more painful. Kim focused on her with a partiality that would make any of the other women jealous. His way of showing more interest, she supposed, but in the end, it only made her future confrontation with Stephanie more of a problem. Yet Angela had known what she was getting into. And it wouldn't surprise her one bit if Kim was flirting for both Stephanie's and Lyrica's sake, merely to rub salt in their wounds, just like Nina had warned.

Angela let out a sigh when the session ended, bowing with the rest of the students and leaving the room with Nina after most of the others had already fanned out into the hall. A din of voices erupted again, the chatter muffled by the noise of shoes scuffing tile. Gargoyles grinned down from nooks in the hallway's pillars, hunting as they always did, in stony silence.

At least Kim hadn't bothered following her.

Maybe because he didn't want anyone to murder her too soon.

"I'd ask if you're taking drugs, but I know they probably don't help you much," Nina said. She scowled at another student who bumped into her, perhaps deliberately. Nina wasn't the most popular person at the Academy, by far. If anything, her friendship with the creepy blood head girl in tights and arm gloves was helping out her social status. "Or do they just make you spacey? Too bad sleeping pills are meant to conk you out. I have a lot of those."

"Sorry." Angela unbuttoned her blouse collar and tugged it away from her neck. "I'm just kind of out of it today. I have a busy night ahead of me."

"Really?" Nina's tone seethed with suspicion. "How so?"

"You wouldn't be interested." She led them both around a corner, leaving the majority of students behind. The new hallway was darker and less well traveled, but it connected at the far end to one of the glass tunnels linking one tower to the next, the round panes glittering with the reflection of too many candles to count. Standing in the middle of that circle of light, five silhouettes had gathered, carefully surrounding a much more familiar one—a student with fluffy curls and a distinctive way of clasping her hands. Sophia. Angela could make out the silver of her shoes as they walked closer.

Lyrica stood against the wall, watching Angela's steady approach with a coolly innocent face. In the brief time Angela and Nina had lingered behind in the classroom, collecting their books, she must have dashed out and told Stephanie everything she'd seen and heard.

And Stephanie must have believed some of it.

She turned from Sophia, and though it could have been Angela's fear at work, Stephanie appeared more confident than the first time they'd met. Even her expression—while outwardly cheerful—hid an unnameable triumph behind it. But directly beside her, the young woman with the mass of blond braids, Sophia's punisher, outdid her in second impressions, analyzing Angela with eyes that glittered like onyx. Up close they had the unnerving largeness she recognized from her painted angels, though their lids had been brightened to a misty red. She was the only person not wearing even a semblance of the Academy uniform, dressed instead in a coat that hid her clothing and perfect figure down to her ankles. The tattoo on her neck must have been a nonsense design—meaningless letters made of loops, long lines, and miniature pitchforks.

Angela didn't like her then, and she didn't like her now. At all.

What's going on? Stephanie found out I had class today. She knew Kim was the teacher. And she might know by now that we have some kind of interest in each other.

But would she react to that so fast? Somehow she seemed too smart for that.

"What the hell did you do?" Nina whispered in Angela's ear. Yet the second they walked closer to join the other sorority members, Nina slid to a careful distance, hovering in the background, as if Stephanie had drawn an invisible line she couldn't cross. Her loyalty apparently stopped where one territory bordered another, and a short glance from Stephanie was all it took to cement that fact. She mumbled under her breath, receding even farther.

It's weird. Stephanie is a blood head, yet she's treating Nina like a freak.

Maybe she didn't remember what it was like—to be feared more out of disgust than respect.

"Angela." Stephanie regarded her again. "You're in luck. I was about to go back to the Sorority House with some of the other members. I hope you wouldn't mind joining us for the walk."

Her fingers had wrapped like a clamp around Sophia's wrist, but Sophia herself made no attempts at freedom. Instead she stared at Angela with hopeful, yet at the same time, very glassy eyes, looking more than ever like a doll. One that Stephanie was stealing away to a dank basement near the sea.

"That's fine." Angela had to suck back the irritation in her voice. "Although I'll be going back to my dormitory once we reach an intersection."

"Oh? Sorry to hear that." Stephanie tugged Sophia, leading everyone into the glass tunnel. "I was hoping that maybe you and I could get to know each other better. You are Brendan's sister after all. I can't believe I didn't catch on to that sooner." She covered her mouth, sheepish. "Stupid of me, right?"

Lyrica was the first to laugh, also making certain to flank Angela's left while Stephanie flanked her right. The other sorority members followed them, silent except for the occasional murmur or whisper.

She's acting way too nice. And she knows someone told me that she and Brendan are a couple. I don't like this.

Angela glanced back at Nina, who was still standing in a dark corner, watching everyone file out through the tunnel. She gave Angela the slightest wave and trotted away in the opposite direction, her figure fading into the smoke of the evening. Soon Angela was walking on glass, escorted by Westwood Academy's most influential student, and ahead of her Luz continued to glow like a skewed paradise, its lights blurred by the water dripping along the contours in the panes. A shadow passed over them, another. Crows were soaring to their evening roosts. Night seemed to arrive earlier every day.

"Anyway," Stephanie said, as her boots tapped across the transparent floor, "I've been curious about you for a while, Angela. Your brother's told me a lot about you and your family."

"Like what?" Angela conjured up a memory of the flames, racing up and across her old bedroom curtains, burning their satin drapery to ash. Why couldn't the floor just crack, sending all of them to their deaths together? Would that be too easy?

"You make it sound like that's a bad thing," Stephanie said, her grip on Sophia's arm tightening noticeably. "Well, I wouldn't worry. He had only good things to say about you."

"Like *what*?" Angela repeated.

Stephanie paused in front of a door, a hatchway, set into the glass. She was examining Angela's tights and arm gloves with furtive shifts of her eyes, and the skin around Sophia's arms practically puffed around her fingers. Sophia, though, barely had a word for Angela. She would look at her once in a while, but otherwise, she was acting like they'd never met.

"By the way," Stephanie continued, a hand on her hip, "have you seen my boyfriend lately, Angela?"

A trick question. It had to be. Was she referring to Brendan or Kim?

"I haven't talked to Brendan since I've arrived."

"Really?"

"He's nowhere to be found. Like he never even existed."

"Have you asked any of the other novices?"

An even worse trick question. Sophia's breath caught in her throat, like she'd planned on saying something. Would she get in trouble too if Stephanie found out? Angela took the hint and diverted the topic. "I've been considering it. Is there anyone in particular I should ask?"

Stephanie sighed, rubbed a hand on the glass. A channel to the ocean roared beneath them, dampening a rumble of thunder. "You're not a bad liar."

"I don't know what you're talking about."

She gestured toward the blonde with the braids, holding out Sophia to her. "Just for a minute," Stephanie whispered.

The blonde sighed in annoyance.

Then she opened the hatch, grabbed Sophia by the back of her blouse, and before Angela could completely understand what was happening, shoved her forward so that she leaned dangerously into the night. If it weren't for the blonde's hand, twisted inside her shirt fabric, Sophia would have already plummeted into the channel. Wind whipped through the hole, blasting Angela's long hair from her face, flapping it behind her like a red banner. The sea crashed beneath them, almost more deafening than the thunder. Churning. Merciless.

If Sophia didn't plummet, it would be a miracle.

Angela cried out, dropping her book satchel. Her clipboard flipped into the wind.

She's going to lose her. Any second.

There wasn't any way that blonde would have the strength to hold Sophia for long. Her blouse was straining, one of the buttons popping off and falling into the water.

"Do you understand how things work here, Angela?" Stephanie's voice was loud, and yet too calm for what was taking place. She watched Sophia's skirt bluster against her knees, entertained, but with all the sophistication of a cruel child. "You might have made a few friends here and there, but I'm the only friend that's going to count. And you shouldn't hide things from your best friend. Right?"

Sophia's going to die.

She's GOING TO DIE.

For a second, Angela saw the corpse in the alley near the Theology Center. But just as quickly, she saw Sophia again and ran to yank both her and the blonde back into the tunnel—if she could.

She'd barely moved before the blonde jerked Sophia back inside, tossing her into Angela's chest, both of them collapsing in each other's arms. Sophia still refused to speak. But her lips trembled, and tears streaked down her face, wetting Angela's blouse. Her fingers curled with rage, grasping at anything, as if she could suffocate the sorority members inside her palms.

"*What the hell's wrong with you?*" Angela hissed at the blonde. "*She could have died.*"

"Don't be an infant."

Incredibly, Stephanie sounded annoyed. The students behind her, excluding the blonde, glared at Angela, equally exasperated. Their blank faces said everything: this kind of craziness was normal, expected, routine. At last, Nina's strange wariness of Stephanie held a lot more weight, and Stephanie's pretty calm seemed much more like the serenity of a coiled snake. "We weren't going to kill her. I just wanted to get the message across. About what can happen when you have a lot to lose and no one to look out for you."

Her voice was too soft. Too normal. Angela fought with a wave of dizziness that must have been her fear. "I could tell the Vatican authorities what you're doing, Stephanie. This is—it's sick."

How could she just stand there and watch?

And the senselessness of it made the question that much more terrible.

"Go ahead," Stephanie said, "but I don't think they'll care. Much worse goes on here day to day. Besides, I have connections. Connections you could share, if you'd only listen to common sense. If you knew the rules, you'd also understand there are certain novices you can talk to, and others that are off-limits. Are we clear on that?"

Angela couldn't even answer her.

She was biting her lip so hard it might have been bleeding.

Sophia pushed off her at last, standing to rearrange her uniform. What could she have possibly done to merit punishments like these? Her curls were soaked through with rain, and her eyes were bloodshot from crying and terror. She stared at her slippers, her face taking on the vacant emptiness that could be terrible in the right kind of light and atmosphere. When Stephanie spoke again, Sophia looked at her with a revolted expression.

"Try to do what's smart from now on," Stephanie was saying to Angela, "so that you won't run into problems like these. Like I said to you before, sorority members are exempt from the sufferings ordinary students have to endure—"

Sophia was a sorority member, and she was suffering.

But this wasn't the moment for sarcasm anymore.

"—and make sure that next time, you tell me the truth. That way, we won't have to go through this again."

"It will *NOT* happen again," Sophia said. In front of her fellow sorority members, she marched up to Stephanie, her eyes like vacant holes.

Stephanie stepped away from her, an uneasy frown washing out her face.

The blonde grabbed Sophia instantly, slapping her across the mouth with a sound that resembled a gunshot. Sophia took the blow, her face twisted by the pain, yet she was gritting her teeth, holding back more of God only knew what kind of curses, revenge, and pure hatred. She clenched her fists so hard, blood that looked black in the poor light spattered from her palms onto the glass.

"Remember why you're here, Sophia," the blonde with the braids said. Her voice was absolute poison. "Don't make this more difficult than it has to be."

"She's not the One," Sophia said, pointing at Stephanie. "She will *NEVER* be the One."

"Well, don't worry . . ." The blonde looked at Angela as she responded, and her gaze almost hurt in its utter lack of sympathy. Her face seemed to meld with the gray angel's, yet with the poorest imitation of her pride, and elegance, and dark, deadly beauty. This woman was like a scorpion, merely waiting for the moment to strike. ". . . we'll find out soon enough."

Eight

---

*Is such a being capable of love? Because I firmly believe She will
find it impossible to love anyone but Herself.*
—St. Imwald, Letters to the Holy Father

Angela had asked Sophia why she allowed that kind of abuse.

She'd begged her to leave the sorority and tell Stephanie to get
a life.

But according to Sophia, no one really understood her situation. She'd earned her punishment and there were no other options
left. Angela would do best to forget everything she'd seen.

That, though, was the problem. She couldn't forget a single detail.

"You seem distracted."

Angela blinked, returning to the gray darkness of the dormitory room. She and Kim were alone, sitting side by side on her bed,
his musty-smelling book spread across her lap while he flipped
occasionally through the pages. The book's leather cover had a
significant heaviness to it, and her legs were close to falling asleep.
She glanced at the image of what appeared to be an angel—very
tall, very fine featured, with the characteristic large eyes. Though
it had two wings, not four, and lacked another pair near its ears.
This was a generic picture, probably the equivalent of a child's
scribbles meant to emulate the real thing.

"I'm sorry," Angela said, handing the book back to him. "There's
just a lot on my mind. That's been my excuse every day lately."

She groaned, stretching her legs.

Out of the corner of her eye, her beautiful angel stared back at her, his own features painted to a soft perfection. Kim was a novice. He was as close as she could get to any kind of real heaven. But he didn't have gorgeous mats of feathers, or four pairs of beautiful wings that trailed behind him like a prince's robe. If his waist were more slender, his skin more like fine pearl, his eyes a fascinating, teasing blue—

But that wasn't exactly fair. Kim was attractive in his own way, and though that way might have been the opposite of her angel's, he was no less fascinating. Maybe she'd been cut off from affection for too long. A priest in training flirted with her once, and she instantly lost her head.

Angela shut her eyes, alarmed at the warmth in her face.

I guess I'm never satisfied. This might not have been a good idea after all.

"Is this frightening you?" Kim touched her leg, right where a band of scars hid beneath her tights. His hand felt strong, reassuring.

"You'd be surprised to find out what actually scares me."

She was seeing Stephanie again and the coldness in her eyes. Sophia, weeping and reaching out to strike her.

And that blonde . . .

Did Kim know about the kind of people Stephanie called friends?

"Honestly, I'm more worried about you." Angela settled back on her elbows. "Stephanie warned me in her not so subtle way to keep out of your business."

Kim lost his smile, his eyes hardening slightly.

"But it's my own fault. I know what I'm doing. I just never meant for Sophia to take my punishment for me."

"Sophia," Kim said. He closed the book and stood over her, taking a moment to gather in some more of her paintings, her dolls. His gaze lingered on the gray angel, but soon turned back to Angela, golden and searching. His stare felt more penetrating and grim than before. "She was the one glaring at me yesterday in the church. Is she your roommate?"

"She's a member of the Pentacle Sorority. That's what's important."

"I see." Kim sighed, rubbing back the red in his bangs. "And she's not in Stephanie's good graces?"

"Don't you know about any of this? I can't believe Stephanie wouldn't tell you."

He sat back on the bed, not leaning into the pillows with her, but staring at the scars on her exposed arms, his attention then flitting like hers to more dolls, and the paintings, and the barely perceptible tremors of candlelight. He was analyzing her, of course, probably quietly judging her qualifications to be the Ruin according to her personality, past, interests, and desires. Unfortunately, his fingers strayed back to her face, and she almost forgot to keep her guard up as he cupped her cheek, bringing her in close.

"If Stephanie made you so angry, if your friend will pay for it, why are we doing this right now? I can leave if this makes you too uncomfortable."

"No," Angela said shortly. "Otherwise, you won't tell me anything about finding angels. You said so yourself."

"That's right." Kim leaned forward on an elbow, bending over her with his shadow. "I did say that. Well, what do you want to know, Miss Mathers? I brought one of my best books and you're too flighty to read it. That's not really my fault."

"I don't need a book. I need someone who has experience. How do I find an angel? Where are they?"

"First things first. What kind of angel are we talking about?" He pointed at the paintings on her wall, his voice cooling to a murmur. "Are they dead or alive?"

Angela sucked in a breath, overwhelmed by the sudden sense of her own ignorance. The question had taken her completely off guard, and without a second thought, she knew he was referring to how much she believed in what she painted and obviously saw. *Were* the angels alive? *Were* they real? Angela had always firmly felt that to be the case, yet she didn't truly know a single fact about angels at all—besides that they existed—even after years of watching them interact in her dreams. Her own name was like some kind of joke. Dead?

Death? It was everywhere she turned anymore, but never helping anyone out.

Last night, as Angela and Sophia stood before each other, still reeling over everything that had taken place, Sophia had mentioned what it would mean for Angela to join the Pentacle Sorority.

If you do join, you'll have to treat me like I'm no better than dead. You'll have to watch me suffer, just like the others do.

Angela said she wouldn't.

That she'd make sure Stephanie—and her friends—never touched Sophia again.

The ridiculousness of her reply hit them both at once. Sophia's gray eyes had widened. She'd turned from the window, clearly astonished that anyone in their right mind would risk everything to protect her, especially when that anyone was a girl she barely knew. And Angela couldn't justify it either, even if she was crazy, until that sudden ache seized hold of her and she realized why.

If Sophia was destined to be a doll, then she was at least going to be Angela's.

Sophia wasn't dead. Angela's angels couldn't be dead. But she knew one thing absolutely.

"They're mine," Angela said, reaching out as if she could caress the beautiful angel. Kim's eyes never left her for a moment, but a muscle in his jaw tightened slightly. Was he nervous? Jealous? But it passed, and he took her hand, settling it back on her lap. "That's . . . all I know. Not if they're dead or alive. Only that they're mine, in the sense that they've been with me for a while. Like they've been existing for me all along."

Kim unbuttoned his collar, taking a deep breath. "Then that leaves you with a quandary." Black hair tickled the side of her cheek, and he whispered into her ear, like it was important to keep even a ghost from hearing them. "A deceased angel can be summoned, but not controlled," he said, staring back at her in the reflection of her bedroom mirror.

His white face seemed so strangely perfect and balanced, it could have been chiseled from ceramic. Completely unlike hers, especially when all she could see was her scars and how worthless that fire had been. She'd been failing in her search for too long.

"A live angel," he said as his hand turned her back to him, "can be controlled depending on its age and authority. But to do so requires a sacrifice most humans aren't willing to give."

"What's that?"

"Their lives."

"As in death?"

"More than that." Kim's voice was almost nonexistent. "Their souls. Although there are ways you can protect yourself from making too harsh of a bargain. Your only trouble would be finding the right angel, and hoping that they happen to like you. In other words, the odds of finding the angels you're looking for would be slim indeed."

"But there's a chance," Angela said, as hushed as he was.

Kim held her closer, forcing her to stare right back at him. "Hold on, I'm not quite finished." Then he paused, waiting for the wind to stop whistling through the eaves before he began again. "You're forgetting that angels have minds of their own. They can choose to protect, even love, a human. And in extremely rare cases, there are angels that have died only to reincarnate themselves in a mortal state. It would be safe to assume that their past memories stay with them for some time. Or so we think."

She'd never considered that. Reincarnation.

Could that actually happen with angels? And how could an angel die if it was already in Heaven or Hell? Then again, their world might be too alien to understand. Rather than spirits, the angels in her dreams did seem made of a flesh and blood that was different from hers but also very solid, even though she still couldn't imagine them becoming ill or growing old. Often, the beautiful angel brushed his hair, or sang, or drank from a delicate crystal glass—very physical things. The gray angel was more vaporous, but she too had her moments of cold reality. Yet, even though Angela sensed that she knew them or was linked to them, she had never felt like one of them.

"Your paintings, Angela"—Kim's words fell hard and certain—"seem like memories to me."

But that didn't explain Sophia recently entering her dreams where the others danced, moved, flew, and ate. Sophia wasn't an angel. She was—

Hurting.

It amazed her to think anyone could keep so much pain locked up inside for so long. Angela knew what it was like to suffer, but she'd learned over time to dissociate from her torture in one way or another. When they had finished talking last night, Sophia had dropped the velvet headband she'd been wearing, and as Angela handed it back to her, the act of accepting it had felt like a silent agreement between them that Angela would keep her promise.

But tonight, when Sophia had left the mansion to give Angela her alone time, that silent peace between them had cracked. Sophia had been clasping her umbrella in hand, ready to leave the dormitory, but she was moving too slow, hedging, as if she didn't trust Angela's plans for the night and would have liked to supervise. But they weren't that close. Not by far.

I don't keep anything locked up, she'd said unexpectedly. *I simply find a better way to express what I feel. Don't get the wrong idea. My outburst last night was an accident . . . it was pathetic.*

And the vacant, resigned look in her eyes had returned.

When Sophia shut the door behind her, the sound seemed to continue forever.

Angela should have known better than to encourage someone who didn't know what hope was anymore. That, though, was one of her flaws. She never could just give up on things.

"If I wanted to summon an angel," Angela said, "how would I go about it?" This wasn't good. She was starting to care about too many people in this place, and the more she cared, the harder it would be to die when she had the chance. Why couldn't this all be over with already?

Kim's answer sounded too easy. "I'd say you should attend the Pentacle Sorority gathering tomorrow night. In fact, Stephanie is banking on it. She wants to humiliate you and prove that you're not the One."

Sophia's term. "The One?"

"The Ruin. Although, that's not so much who she is, as it is one of her possible futures. In higher circles, she goes by another name."

Then Angela was right about why Kim was probably sleeping with Stephanie, or with any blood head female that showed supernatural promise. "And what's that name?"

"The Archon."

The rafters creaked overhead, harming the silence of the night. It was too quiet outside now that the rain had ended.

Kim listened for the creaking to stop, that strange nervousness tensing his grip on her arm. He was behaving like they were being watched, though by what was anybody's guess. Angela's pulse quickened, her temples throbbing in the dull quiet. "The term refers to an angel reincarnated as a human. In this case, a vengeful angel. Let's just say that from what we've learned, he died tragically and wants to right some wrongs in the universe. Unfortunately, there are a lot of people, angels and demons alike, standing in the way of that."

Demons. Angela had forgotten all about them. She'd never even stopped to consider what the real differences between angels and demons were, whether she was infatuated with someone who wasn't exactly good for her, or whether a truly evil angel could even exist. The gray angel was frightening, but Angela felt too familiar with her to call her evil. "So why does Stephanie suspect that I'm this Archon?" Angela said. "Because I paint pictures of angels and dream about them?"

"Of course. You're a threat. Until now, she's been grooming herself for the position."

Stephanie was a real fool then. Just like Angela and Nina, she could just be suffering from the birth pangs of the true Archon making herself known in the world.

"But why? Why would anyone *want* to be such a horrible person? Doesn't she realize the Vatican will exterminate her the second they determine she's the one they're looking for?"

Kim smiled at her, amused at her cleverness. "The answer is power. Don't make the mistake of so many others and let her soft appearance fool you. Stephanie is ambitious, relentless, unsympathetic, and power hungry. What I'm telling you is arcane knowledge, but—the angel left behind an artifact when he died, one that—once opened—has the power to fulfill the prophecy of Ruin. But only the Archon can actually open it without suffering terribly." Kim's grimmer expression returned. "Stephanie's playing a dangerous game. Actually, more than one. If she's wrong, and she tries to open this artifact without truly being the Archon, she'll go absolutely insane."

The roof creaked again, and footsteps pattered across the shingles.

Angela glanced at the chandelier, quaking a little. There was still some light. Enough to last them another hour or so. The previous evening with Sophia and Nina was coming back to her in all its disturbing detail. "This artifact is—"

"No one knows its true form—they say that those who've seen it by accident have gone mad. But it does have a name." Kim spoke the words half under his breath. "The Book of Raziel."

The first angel name that could hold any meaning for her.

But not for the reasons she'd been hoping.

Kim registered the blank look on her face and grasped her by the hand, pulling her to her feet.

"What is it?" she said.

He opened the door to the hallway. "Come with me."

Angela had been in the library once since moving into the dormitory mansion.

She hadn't found a reason to return yet.

Every other room in the building had a distinct sense of old elegance to it. Lamps were tarnished, wood needed polishing, and upholstered furniture sat overloaded with dust, but otherwise her new living quarters had retained at least a speck of understated dignity. The library, though, was almost as dreary as that private apartment Sophia had been calling home, only much more forbidding. The ceiling, high as it was, escaped into the darkness like there was no ceiling to be found. Paintings of landscapes from the days when the Academy was in its planning stages graced the walls, though years of dirt had grimed their sunny imagery into shadows. But besides a heavy table with six even heavier chairs surrounding it, the room was wall-to-wall books. Angela had stopped at one shelf, rifled through volumes of theological discourse texts, and finally left when it became clear she wouldn't find anything of interest.

She let out a sigh of relief when Kim walked by that particular shelf and stopped at the next, his candelabra raised high.

Gold-embossed text glimmered on the spine of a particularly giant book. *The Lies of Babylon.*

He heaved it off the shelf and dropped it onto the table, gesturing for her to take a seat.

"I told you I'm not that interested in books," she said, sliding out a chair. "How often do you come here, by the way?"

"What do you mean?" Kim set the candelabra on the table and swiftly opened to a set of pages heavily illustrated in deep shades of red and gray. The first symbol Angela noticed was the pentagram, its design almost identical to the Pentacle Sorority's.

"You seemed to know exactly where to find this book. That implies some kind of familiarity, right?"

"There's a copy in every mansion belonging to the Vatican."

Angela stared at him, watching the candlelight play off the strange hue of his eyes. "Why? It doesn't look very holy."

Kim didn't answer, but he let her flip through the pages as he observed, and the more she flipped, the more uneasy she felt. Whatever chapter she was in, there were no angels to be found, just a lot of strange quotations, formulas that resembled spells, and most disturbingly of all, prayers written in red ink that could just as easily have been blood. When his hand touched hers, suggesting that she stop, the heat from it seemed to jolt her back into reality. "Do you understand anything that you see?" he said, hardly bothering to hide the interest on his face anymore.

He was gazing back at her carefully, and she knew something mysterious depended on her answer.

"Not really," she said, watching his reaction.

But that was before she turned to the last set of pages, a mess of symbols that she certainly recognized from somewhere. The sharp lines, the forked scripting, tugged at her memories, and then she read the translation on the opposite page.

I was stamped with the seal of perfection, complete wisdom and perfect beauty. In Eden the Garden of God, I was, and every precious stone was my covering . . .

"Hold on," Angela whispered, almost more to herself than to Kim. "I do know this."

She continued reading but the light dimmed and the walls could have been closing in on her. Before another minute had passed, she slammed the book shut. The moment the cover glimmered back at her, the candles seemed to gutter back to their former brightness.

"It's talking about the Devil."

Kim nodded. "And how do you feel about what you read?"

"Feel? I don't see how any of this can help me—"

"We're starting at the beginning, Angela. You know nothing about angels so I'm testing your knowledge with one of the most . . . infamous." For the first time she noticed he was tugging at an iron cross necklace that hung against his chest. A gem had been set in the cross's center, its surface smooth and red. "Remember, the Devil was once an angel, and even if no one else remembers that—she does."

"The Devil is a woman?"

"And perhaps a misunderstood one."

"You can't be serious." Angela left her seat, but only to lean against the table, trying to think.

"I can't be serious about what?" he said, standing with her. "The idea of her being a woman or—"

"Both."

"Angela," he said, gently turning her head by the chin, "look at me."

The moment she did, it felt like a mistake. He was obviously attracted to her, she was attracted to him, even if for the most selfish and superficial reasons, and now that they were acknowledging that without a sound, she also knew there was no use ignoring it. Usually, this kind of desire came and left her just as fast, dissipating whenever she stole a glance at one of her paintings. But with Kim, there was both excitement and a sense of safety. They barely knew each other, but Angela felt they had more in common than she realized, and she was curious to find out what those mysterious things were.

That, though, implied more time. And they had very little to spare.

He brushed strands of hair from her shoulders, fondling the tendrils left to him. "Have you ever thought about history, about how stories can be skewed one way or the other depending on who wins the war?"

"Maybe," she said, allowing him to play with her tresses, remembering their moment together in that grimy alleyway. Would it be wrong to wish for more, even if it was just to spite Stephanie? *It's not like she doesn't deserve this.*

"Then you can imagine how a story like this one has transformed over time. There are many versions of it, and I've read them all. But then I found out the truth that every version was based on, and the ideas I once had about angels, demons, and everything in between changed forever. Until that moment, I'd been lost, searching for a reason to go on with life. I was a lot like you, Angela. Reckless. Because there was no reason to be anything else."

"It sounds like you have me figured out," she said, only slightly peevish.

"I'm just calling it as I see it." Kim took a deep breath, looking more melancholy than before. A strange dullness had washed out the light in his eyes again, much as it had while he sang hymns at the introductory ceremony. "So do you want to know why she fell from grace? Why she instigated her rebellion to begin with?"

This was easy. There was no way this element of the Devil's story could have changed.

"Pride," Angela said, also proud of herself for knowing the answer.

He turned to her and there was a soft smile spreading across his face. "Disillusionment."

Angela had nothing to say. That one word implied so many things, the least of them being that Heaven hadn't been what she'd hoped. Otherwise, what could make an angel disillusioned at all?

It almost changed everything, exactly as he'd said.

"So you have sympathy for the Devil." Though she didn't feel half as afraid of him for it as she should have, probably because she understood exactly how he felt. Angela's life had been one grand series of tragedies from the very beginning. That would be enough for anyone to question the meaning behind life in the first place, or even the point of forging ahead. But that was where she also differed from everyone else, apparently, the Devil included. She attempted suicide because she *had* a hope.

But what did that mean for Kim? He'd said that had changed the course of his life. The next question was, of course, How?

"Sympathy isn't something they understand very well," he was saying. "That also includes the ability to cry."

He was touching the cross necklace, absentminded.

"It's pretty," Angela said, pointing at it. "I hope it wasn't a gift from Stephanie."

Kim stared at her, his smile erasing the strange haunted look on his face. "It was from my father, actually."

"That's nice. You must have a good relationship with him."

"And you?" His voice softened. "Stephanie told me about your past."

She let the silence grow between them, unaware of how much it would hurt to speak again until she decided to make herself heard. And that wasn't until they were far from the library, returned to the relative coziness of her bedroom and the dolls, paintings, clothes, and bedsheets that defined her. At least, she thought they did.

"Do you think I'm the Archon?" she whispered, almost afraid of what the answer might be.

"I think that there are better reasons Stephanie should be nervous right now."

Kim took her by the hand.

Then, with a cautious slowness, he covered her mouth with his own, gently relinquishing his kiss only so that the next one met her even more softly.

Angela's breath sucked away, her head swam. Soon she'd allowed him to hold her by the chin and take her lips with tender persistence, melting beneath the thin, pleasing lines of his mouth, the sculpted strength of his face. When she broke away from him, hoping to stop the problem they were creating, her body instantly grew hot along with the warmth in his hands, and she found herself sinking beneath Kim's skillful touches, unable to quell the eagerness to keep enjoying him. His skin tasted like salt and sour wine, and it wasn't until he pressed her hand against his face that she felt it, disrupting the smoothness of his cheek. There was a cut on his cheekbone, below his eye. In the poor light, she must not have noticed. Kim pulled away, and she blinked back at the room, strangely bewildered by what had passed between them.

"Did you cut yourself?" she finally said.

Kim made a wry face, annoyed, but apparently not by her.

Creak. Snap.

The roof groaned again, and—silence. Angela glanced out the window, shivering. The blackness was dimly lit by two spots of yellow, and then they blinked back at her, shutting off into pure darkness. Kim watched with her, cursing under his breath. She barely restrained him as he slipped off the bed, hastily rebuttoning his collar.

He leaned in for the good-bye kiss, and she jumped a little, startled, smelling his sweat and her own peculiar scent in his hair. Whatever they'd both seen, he'd taken it as a bad sign. "If you go to the gathering tomorrow night, I'll be there," he said.

"Wait—your book—"

"I don't mind lending it out for a day or so."

He escaped the room, shutting the door with a soft *click,* and his footsteps clattered down the hallway, the stairs.

Angela glanced around, unsettled for the first time by the idea of being alone.

At least Sophia would be home soon.

It was probably a good thing she wouldn't see Angela like this, staring wide-eyed around the room, acting like a scared mouse. Worse yet, Sophia's parting words for the night almost wouldn't allow it. *You're brave,* she'd said. *Brave enough to stand up to Stephanie Walsh. But if you knew what she knows, you'd think twice about trying to protect me.*

Angela had asked why, too defiant to be frightened at the time.

Now, she stared at the book, her breath catching. It had flopped open to a page Kim must have deliberately skipped over, the illustration depicting some kind of angel with sharp black wings and long ears. It was familiar somehow, and the strange writing on the page had a harsh, upsetting look to it. Angela looked out the window again, feeling so small, dwarfed once more by everything that surrounded her. The dolls. The walls. The world.

Sophia's warning sounded ominously all over again.

Some people have the courage to be cruel.

Angela kept her finger beneath the small print of the page, careful not to lose her spot in the paragraph. The illustrations had become stranger and stranger the more she perused them. Long gone were the chapters on angels and demons. What information there was seemed half guesswork and half anecdotal experience, not to mention the repetitive scripture passages and commentary from people with names she could barely pronounce. But this chapter, "Of the Jinn," had struck her immediately. Kim had never mentioned anything called a Jinn since they'd started talking about angels. In fact, she was certain he'd purposely avoided the entire chapter.

Angela stopped at a picture of the same angel with black wings and long ears. Unlike the real angels, its eyes were larger and its feet and hands had horrible-looking nails.

It was eating a human.

She skimmed the sentences below the gruesome image.

It has been learned through consistent and most excellent sources that these creatures are perhaps the most dangerous of the angelic races. Violent and prone to bloodlust, they have been cited in many cultures as the devourers of human souls, though how this is possible is not entirely known.

Angela turned the page, fearful of what might show up next.

This time the Jinn in the illustration hovered possessively over a human woman. Below, a black cat inked with yellow eyes stared back at her above a new caption.

Regrettably, it has been proven through various instances in history that the children of such unions exist, despite the majority being killed in their infancy. To prevent such a misdeed, often the witch will use a Binding contract to control her lover's actions, ignoring the fact that this usually leads to tragic circumstances. It has been well said that Jinn, in all their promises, are never to be completely trusted.

She proceeded to read the formula for the Binding, thinking of the gargoyles she'd seen on the mansion rooftops, and how similar they looked to these mysterious Jinn. It made sense. If angels and demons could be depicted with a fair measure of accuracy, then it was entirely possible an artist could chisel out these horrors with a nasty—if much cruder—kind of detail.

No wonder Kim had skipped over this section.

The more Angela browsed, the more the silence seemed to weigh on her, darkness wrapping around her like a thick quilt.

Without warning, there was a loud knock on the door.

Angela's heart could have shot out of her chest. She gasped, slapping the book closed on her lap. "Who—who is it?"

"It's me. Sophia. Is it all right if I come in?"

Thank God.

"Yeah. Go ahead."

The door popped open and Sophia stepped inside, gently shutting it behind her again. She was carrying a small plate of crackers and cheese.

"You scared me," Angela said, sinking into the bed, her face burning. She pointed at the dresser. "Set it over there. I'm not really that hungry right now."

"If only I'd known." Before setting the plate down, Sophia took a cracker for herself and nibbled on its corners. She then made her way to the window seat, passing a picture of the beautiful angel Angela had put on display for Kim. It was an oil portrait with darker colors than she commonly used, most of the image focusing on the angel's heavy-lidded eyes and enticing smile.

Sophia paused in front of it, suddenly somber.

"I really didn't think your visitor would be gone so soon," she said, still examining the picture.

Angela slid the book off her lap, setting it on the floor. That last sensation of Kim's lips on hers tingled inside of her, forbidden and unmentionable. Somehow, it felt like he'd left only a second ago. "I was tired. Really, I just had a few questions about things, and after that—"

"Questions," Sophia said, adjusting the ribbon at the end of her braid. "About what?"

"Well . . ." Angela flipped back the covers from her legs. "What did you mean when you said that Stephanie couldn't be 'the One'?"

Sophia froze, her fingers still on her hair. "It was nothing."

"Don't lie to me," Angela whispered back. "You were talking about *Her,* weren't you? The Ruin. *The Archon.*"

Sophia whirled on her. "Who mentioned that name?"

But she was too delicate to be intimidating, and Angela continued, vaguely aware that she was treading in even more forbidden territory. "Why do you know it? I've just learned that the Archon is supposedly the reincarnation of a pissed-off, *dead* angel. And no matter how ridiculous that might sound, I can't help but wonder what Stephanie's power trip and my dreams have to do with all that."

The quiet lingered, and for once, Sophia seemed genuinely upset with her. She was trembling. "I told you earlier that it's not a good idea to toy around with Stephanie. Whoever's toying with you"—and her face suggested she already knew Kim had his hands all over Angela's face—"I hope they'll show how much they really care and let the matter rest."

"Why don't you want me to help you?"

"That has nothing to do with it," Sophia said gently.

She wavered, reluctant to leave the room. But when it became clear Angela would ask more questions, she took the plate away and whisked out into the hallway, leaving for her own room. Angela listened to her soft footsteps and the creak of the mattress, the click of the lamp. Then it fell silent, and Angela cursed under her breath, angry for them both. This was all Stephanie's fault.

The doll that resembled Sophia seemed disjointed in the shadows. Shy and pained.

I'm actually afraid of losing her. I actually want another human being around, and I've already made her mad.

She should have known Kim's visit would have more than one downside.

Angela cursed again, finding his book on the hardwood. She flipped pages aside randomly, still angry, searching for answers that always eluded her. When she stopped to glance at the pictures of her angels, her temper softened a little, but it couldn't stop that gnawing sense of failure from laughing at her inside her head. Then she paused at a paragraph, appalled at the idea that, according to this old monk, humans were nothing to angels, little more than toys that could become possessed and infatuated by them in the blink of a proverbial eye.

No wonder she felt guilty about Kim's kiss.

In a sense, her angel had been watching her the entire time. Once she entered her dreams, she'd find nothing but regrets.

But at least that was better than nothing at all.

Nine

Surprisingly, he was happier than she'd ever seen him before.

But it wasn't the kind of happiness born from love or joy. Instead, his face shone with triumph. Angela had suspected for a long time her angels didn't like each other. If they were in a portion of her dreams together, they either argued or ignored each other.

This time, the beautiful angel could have been emitting his own light.

His victorious smile was that brilliant.

His slender body and high, arching wing bones had been covered in an armor more like fabric than silver, terrible splotches of crimson staining his beautiful hands. Feathers framed him in a bronze aurora, and his pink lips curled around teeth whiter than pearls. His hair had been gathered into a tight topknot, and glass formed into the shape of snakes wrapped around his winged ears.

Far from lovely and delicate, he was the picture of beautiful terror.

Below him, the gray angel waited, tensed for the blow from the magnificent spear in his hands, her figure more vaporous than usual.

Tension and violence permeated the air.

Then the bronze angel turned to Angela, much as he had when Sophia had entered her dreams.

Only his face betrayed horror instead of triumph, and behind *him, the sky revealed itself, its ether hazed over with a snow of bloody feathers, falling and falling to an invisible ground. She only had a second to scream back at him, silently as always, before she felt a piece of herself rip away, and all of her mind die in a void that consumed the world.*

Ten

Those She interacts with are destined for darkness.
It will only be logical.
—IMWALD'S PRIVATE LETTERS

"I'm kind of insulted that you won't talk to me about last night." Nina flicked ash into the plate on their table, and then took a long drag from her cigarette. The smoke had a way of bringing back bad memories for Angela, but Nina wasn't stopping the habit for anyone, even someone who associated smoke with grotesque burns and failed suicide attempts. "I'm not as stupid as I look, you know. Stephanie grilled you about Kim, didn't she? Sophia's a spy, Angela. You've got to throw her to the curb—"

"Shut up," Angela hissed back. "She's not a spy. She hates Stephanie, okay? You don't know the half of it."

Sophia was still heading back to their cafeteria table, her tray loaded with the most sugary drinks on Earth and a dish of crisped potato skins. Most of the nearby students ignored her when she stood next to them or asked a question, but a few gave her nasty looks. They were obviously people sympathetic to Stephanie's cause—whatever that happened to be. Apparently, part of Sophia's punishment involved others shunning her.

"Whatever you say," Nina said, setting the stub of her cigarette down, "but I smell a rat. You don't know Stephanie like I do. She has this magical way of making you think you have her all fig-

ured out and then BANG"—she slammed her fist on the table—
"suddenly you're drowning in a social cesspool."

"Just keep it to yourself for now," Angela said. She poked at the
pudding in her bowl, swirling its insides with her spoon. Sophia's
shadow had fallen on them, and now she spread her skirt to sit,
sliding into the chair next to Angela. No "good morning." No
"hello."

Why is she still mad at me? Because of last night?

Maybe it was more than that. Sophia had a knight in shining
armor in Angela, whether she wanted it or not. For various reasons, that could be a blow to her pride.

"I didn't hear you leave the dorm this morning," Angela said
to her.

Nina raised an eyebrow, glancing up at them as she returned
to her peanut butter on bread. She was perusing the newspaper
despite the gloom, squinting every so often beneath the reddish
glare of the stained-glass storm lamp on the table. The cafeteria
was cavernous and resembled an actual cave in many ways besides
size, its walls set with huge blocks of crudely hewn stone. The
tables—if you were lucky enough to get one—were mostly twisted
by water, and the chairs were equally ravaged, their plush cushions
worn down almost to their stuffing. Tapestries of the Academy's
history covered the high windows, blocking out the gray sky and
replacing it with clumps of blacks, reds, and sickly yellows. The
tapestry near their table was easy to understand: the Academy had
formerly been centered around the massive tree in its Western District. From what Angela had learned, that area had been off-limits
to students for at least sixty years.

"I hope you weren't upset that I slept in," Angela ventured,
watching the light glance off of Sophia's sorority ring. "I was too
tired to get out of bed on time."

"Don't worry about it," Sophia said. She nibbled on a potato
crisp and placed it daintily back on her plate. "I tend to be a light
sleeper. When I'm upset, I often awaken hours before my alarm."

Nina dropped the paper, her voice barely audible over the chatter at the table next to them. "Don't worry about sleeping tonight. It's Halloween."

"And?"

"And?" Nina laughed, crossing her arms. "When the Vatican outlaws a holiday, everyone does their best to observe it. There are going to be a lot of parties tonight, some of them pretty wild. I'm not invited to any of them, of course, but we could sneak into a few, grab a drink here and there. I purchased"—she ducked down, rummaging through her bag, reappearing with a headband topped by triangular, fuzzy ears—"these cat ears after all. I have devil horns you could borrow, if you'd like."

Or I could just go as myself. Without the tights.

"Actually," Angela said, picking her words carefully, "I heard that Stephanie's having a party tonight."

Nina's eyes seemed more bloodshot than yesterday. "Oh, God—and you want to go? How did she blackmail you into that?"

"She didn't. I'm just curious about what they do there."

Sophia sighed, pushing her tray aside. "I'll be right back."

She left her chair and walked into a crowd blocking the bathroom.

Nina rested her cheek against her hand, grunting. "What perfect timing. Off to tell Stephanie you're interested, I'm sure."

"You talk as if you know her, Nina. You don't know a goddamn thing."

"I know enough. She's a member of the Pentacle Sorority, and she wants to get back into their good graces. But I'm telling you, of all nights, tonight isn't the time to get interested in what goes on in Stephanie's inner circle." Her voice lowered conspiratorially. "Because it's Halloween night, she's having the sorority gathering in the Bell Tower, in the unused chapel that has the veranda porch to the outside. She's a witch, Angela; you're forgetting that. It's no coincidence that she wants you there, if that's what you're driving at. For all you know, she'll curse you to vomit up nails or something. That spot has a reputation—"

Noise rippled through the cafeteria. Chair legs screeched

against wood. Students of all ages murmured to one another, some standing to get a better look at the sudden commotion on the other side of the room.

Nina stood up with them, straining to see. "You're not going to believe this."

"What is it?" Angela felt her insides seize up. This wasn't going to be pleasant.

"Your brother's chewing out Stephanie and Kim, right in front of three other novices and a superintendent priest."

"My brother—" Angela bolted out of her chair, scanning heads.

There he was, with those curled hairs below his ears, and that face that could have been a clone of her father's, all soft jaw and sloping nose. But Brendan's usually calm demeanor had cracked. His acidic tone could be heard even from where they sat, angry to the point where one of the novices reached out a hand to restrain him. Stephanie glared at him in shock, her green eyes narrow, her arms crossed above her hip as she dared him to keep speaking. And all the while Kim stood next to her, impassive, unreadable.

"Where are you going?" Nina said, grabbing for Angela's arm. "Angela—"

"Wait here."

Angela pushed through the crowds of students, weaving her way through tables and chairs, until she broke out directly in front of Kim. His eyes brightened as they caught sight of her, but he showed a wry smile, turning away as Stephanie did the opposite, staring at Angela with genuine surprise. Brendan's voice died, and he looked at her too, slowly blinking as if he couldn't believe she was standing almost right next to him. He was a mess, his long coat stained and torn in odd places, his hair greasy, like he hadn't washed it for a week. A strange, sour odor, like a mix of flowers and old meat, clung to him in a cloud. What was wrong with him?

"Brendan, I—"

He ignored her, rounding back on Stephanie. "You thought I wouldn't find out? Is that it? Well, here's news for you." He thrust an accusing finger at Kim. "I knew for months, that the two of you were in bed, Stephanie. IN BED. At least four times a week—"

The superintendent priest shot an angry questioning look at Kim, but Kim merely shrugged off the matter, shaking his head like Brendan had gone crazy, which certainly seemed to be the case. The other novices continued to stare at the proceedings, pale-faced.

"It is over, Brendan Mathers." Stephanie's voice was too soft.

"You're damned right it is." Brendan laughed, pushing back his hair. "After all, I don't need this charade anymore." He tore off his novice's coat, throwing it onto the floor and shoving it with his foot toward the superintendent priest. "I'm done. No more vows, and no more of your occult bullshit, Stephanie. God, you're going to get what's coming to you."

"You're such an idiot."

There was a hint of childish desperation in Stephanie's voice, and her cheeks were turning bright red, and then redder and redder as the news began to spread farther back into the cafeteria. Yet she bit her lip, obviously seething. Maybe planning revenge.

"Am I?" He smiled wickedly. "But you're the one who's ignorant, Stephanie. And it's going to kill you. I promise."

"Too bad *you* didn't die while you were gone," she spat back at him. "It looks like I shouldn't have bothered caring."

"We all know you didn't. You're a self-serving bitch, and you think you're the best thing to walk on this planet. Well, I've found someone who makes you look like a pig in the mud, in bed and out of it." Nearby students gasped, Brendan's comments ricocheting back and forth from one ear and mouth to the next. "Soon, your fancy witchcraft's going to backfire on you, and then I'll be there to watch and say I told you so."

Kim's smile tactfully faded the second it appeared. He was enjoying this.

Stephanie trembled, her fingers digging into her own skin, the nails leaving horrid crescent-shaped marks. "You have it backward." Her voice was too low for anyone but a few bystanders to hear. But the promise within it sounded much more inevitable than Brendan's spastic outburst. Her expression cooled to that terrible apathy as she turned, her ponytail swirling around her. "It was fun while it lasted, little boy."

She glanced at Angela once more before she left the room.

Her face was normal enough, but the emotions behind her eyes spoke volumes.

"Brendan," Angela said as she shuffled closer to him, reaching for his shoulder, "you have to calm down. This is insane—"

He spun around, shocking her into silence. Who was this person? Definitely not the same Brendan who arranged candies by color and stuck to a curfew like it was law. He seemed to peer right through her, into a world invisible to everyone else. One completely hollow inside. "What do you want, Angela? Why are you even here?"

This really wasn't the time or place, but—

"To apologize," she whispered. She didn't need any more explanation than that.

His tone had hurt her, like a punch to the gut.

"You're talking about Mom and Dad?" He laughed again, almost as cruel as she'd imagined in her nightmares. "Why are you bothering now? Why apologize? Everyone excuses you anyway, so why not just assume I'm going to do the same?" Brendan widened the collar away from his neck, revealing a line of red bruises. "I can't believe you even got into this Academy, but I'm sure it had nothing to do with your hair, with those mental diarrheas you call paintings—"

Kim stepped forward, grabbing him by the shirt. "I think that's enough for today."

Angela felt the tears gathering, but she wouldn't let them go. Not in front of so many people. "Forget it, Brendan," she heard herself saying. "You're right. From now on, we should go our separate ways."

His face glazed over, regretful. Before she could even ask why, he shoved Kim away, following Stephanie's path out the double doors, and normal cafeteria life resumed.

"Are you all right?" Kim said. His eyes seemed to caress Angela, feeling her pain. Beside him, the priest snapped at each of the novices in turn, his face crimson with embarrassment. Brendan and Stephanie's affair might turn their order upside-down for weeks. "Perhaps you don't feel like going to the gathering tonight . . ."

All that anticipation for nothing. Brendan's changed . . .

"Stephanie didn't invite me."

"That's because I'm doing it for her." Lyrica Pengold strutted out of the crowd to meet them, her thigh-high tights seeming to absorb all the red light in the room. Her hair was pale for a blood head, more like a delicate strawberry shade, but still enough to qualify. She drew close to Angela, whispering excitedly. "She'd meant to ask you before your brother made a scene in front of a hundred students. So are you coming?"

"I'll think about it." A solid lie. Angela was coming, and she was going to summon an angel—participating in the very rituals that made other students shudder in fear. Nina would be very, very disappointed in her. But it was the only way to find the angels that haunted her dreams. "What time does it start? Just so I know?"

"Midnight. Of course." Lyrica nodded at Kim, knowing not to display any further familiarity. Then a shadow darkened her face, and she frowned. "What's this all about? I didn't walk all the way here to look at *you*."

"Save it, Lyrica." Nina's voice, shaky. She stepped forward next to Angela, Sophia's delicate figure observing in the background. One sight of Kim, and Sophia's polite, pretty face froze over with the withering glare she'd reserved for him in the church. Only this time, it was worse. "Tell Stephanie," Nina continued, "that Angela won't come unless I do."

"Why?" Lyrica's tone bordered on saccharine. "So you can botch the whole thing like last time? Face it, Nina Willis, you're not a blood head. Whether you dye your hair or not."

Botched? How and what did she botch last time? Is this the real reason why she talks to dead people in her sleep?

Then, things could go wrong. Like Kim had said. *Very, very wrong.*

"Give me a chance," Nina begged.

The shadows grew around them. Glass rattled. Sharp wind began to bluster against the hidden windowpanes.

Then the rain started, roaring.

"Give me a chance . . ."

Eleven

I loved him, but he never turned to me again.
I ached for him, and he laughed at my humanity.
This desire would be my certain destruction.
—Unknown author, *A Collection of Angelic Lore*

The doors to the church slammed open with a *bang*.

Brendan stood at the threshold, his teeth gritted and his hair sopping, lightning splitting through the sky behind him. He'd discarded his coat somewhere, leaving his black clothes to soak through with the torrential rain. Israfel peered at him through sporadic waves of droplets, safe and dry on the large chair at the head of the altar. Rakir and Nunkir had been resting at his feet, sleeping side by side. Now their wings tensed, and Rakir sat up, his chiseled features masking over with distaste. Nunkir remained lying down, her eyes open, watchful.

"This is unexpected," Israfel said, hoping the message would get across.

It didn't.

"She's playing with fire," Brendan said, not bothering to mention who. "And she's going to burn. And I'm going to enjoy every second of it."

He stormed inside the church, forgetting to shut the doors, letting the wind enter and toy with loose strands of Israfel's hair. Israfel tucked them behind his ears and returned to his lyre, plucking at the strings, timing the rhythm to the relentless pounding in his head. Tonight he'd been free of the usual cramps and nausea, but the headaches had been searing, torturous. The Father's blood had stopped the worst of the pain, instead leaving him with the world tilting, and his speech slurring at odd intervals. Still, though, he could feel the fluttering movements of the unborn chick inside him, threatening to abort itself at any second in the quickest, bloodiest way possible. Obviously, he wasn't numb enough.

"What is that?" Brendan stopped short of the altar stairs, ignoring Rakir's new, threatening stance. Nunkir remained by Israfel's side. Moisture glistened on her feathers, shellacking them with liquid crystal. "What is that smell?"

Israfel returned to his lyre. "What do you need, Brendan? We were about to retire for the night."

The human's mouth slackened, and he stared at Israfel. Hungry. "It's like blood," he said, whispering. "And flowers."

He glanced at Rakir with a sudden wariness, like the scent was a trap.

But the angel kept still, examining him, finally turning to Israfel.

They were in complete agreement.

Brendan's possession had made him more beautiful than ever—even if he didn't know it—his broad shoulders and soft face hardened beneath the weight of starvation and thirst. The poor thing wouldn't last much longer at this rate. He'd fallen to Rakir's curiosity for hours the other day, every breath he'd remembered to take simply draining more of his scant life. If anything, the fear the Throne caused acted like a stimulant, making him taste that much more addictive. Yet out of the three angels at his disposal, Brendan continually submitted to the one who cared for him least, maybe as a penance for his perceived sins, or perhaps because he simply welcomed the pain.

Either way it had made an excellent amusement for the night.

"Go ahead," Brendan said, almost hopeful. "Get it over with."

Rakir licked his lips but turned away, disgusted again.

Brendan inched closer to Israfel, no longer disguising the longing on his face. Nunkir sat up now, her braids dangling from her head like silver chains, their weight swinging beneath the rain. Her jealousy, frosty even under the best of circumstances, always made the night interesting, and she looked to Israfel much as her brother had done, her face mean with the longing to snap Brendan's neck once and for all.

Israfel gestured for submission, cutting off any more thoughts of revenge.

"You are perfect," Brendan said, his lips trembling with the words. "All of you. Just like in the pictures, the paintings . . . but"— he regarded Rakir again, careful—"these angels are different from you—I can sense it."

Rakir closed his eyes, opened them, battling with his opposing lust and anger. He beseeched Israfel one more time, and much like his sister, received no permission to end his torment.

"Rakir and Nunkir," Israfel said, "have been my guardians since their days as chicks. Although what you see isn't even close to their true form. It's merely a derivative, made to be more pleasing to the eye."

And they were exceedingly pleasing, especially considering their rank and station. Though most Thrones were cursed with deformities of one kind or another, Rakir and his sister had been created with a flaw that merely made them more appealing—almost complete silence. Israfel could settle for no less than the best of the litter, deliberately choosing a brother and sister whose bond made them ten times more lethal. If pressed, he would admit Rakir was probably his favorite. Strong, but also abnormally tall and lean, his face was cut with perfect angles, his green eyes painfully endearing.

"Patience," he mouthed to him gently.

Rakir's wing bones began to tremor, but he remained obedient, gazing into nothing, barely repressed.

"Now tell me why you're here," Israfel repeated, setting down his instrument, swinging his legs so that they hung over the chair rail. "Especially after I told you I wished to be alone. You mentioned another human . . ."

Brendan fixated on the scales covering Israfel's feet and at last tempted fate, clasping him by the ankles, imprisoning him with his hands. Nunkir watched with murder behind her eyes, her lips pressing together so tightly they began to turn blue. "I need your help." His face paled slightly. "There's a witch in Luz and I want her burned at the stake."

"A witch?" Israfel observed the storm through the holes near the ceiling, watching black tufts appear and disappear amid a haze of water. "Whatever does that mean?"

"She's threatened to kill me, and I believe her. Stephanie pretends to be a normal woman, but in reality she's capable of anything."

"She was your lover?"

"Not just mine." Brendan kissed the side of Israfel's foot, begging the worst. "She was also with another man in my seminarian group. He's untouchable. But I'd be doing everyone a favor getting rid of her and that damned sorority. She thought my words today were just a show, for spite, but finally she's going to suffer like she's made other people suffer."

Israfel allowed the quiet to enfold them, listening to Rakir's occasional sigh of protest as Brendan continued his caresses. The Throne's fingers twitched, straining to hurt.

"Your kind," Israfel finally said, "aren't so different from us, in the end. I had a sister, you know. And she treated me much like your lover treated you. Cruelly and indifferently."

"What did you do?" Brendan said, catching his breath as Rakir turned back to him.

Israfel swung his legs to the ground and stood from his chair, reeling for a second as the world spun. Colorful specks dotted his vision, and he sensed himself beginning to dream, slipping away into the sweet drunkenness of the drug. He blinked, and Raziel seemed to appear in front of him, so beautiful and perfect that he put Rakir to shame, his figure all blood-red feathers, blue eyes, and gentleness. "I sent her to Hell," Israfel said, sighing out his illusion. "And she's been there ever since, chained, rotting. Chained and rotting just like me. How much I hated her—*hate* her—for what she did."

"And what did she do?" Brendan tugged at the buttons closing off his shirt. Rakir whimpered at Israfel, pleading now, but his salvation wasn't about to appear just yet. The Throne panted, desperate to restrain himself. "Something that deserved Hell, I'm sure."

"She took from me what I loved most—" Israfel said, feeling Raziel's hand cup his cheek.

No. It was only Nunkir, concerned.

"—and violated him right in front of me. And she laughed the entire time, like it was a game to take my heart and crush it underfoot. *My heart.* I never thought she'd dare . . ."

"What was her name?" Brendan absently touched his own skin, playing with his neck and collarbone. With or without his sister, Rakir would murder him, or at least that much was obvious from the way his lower jaw shivered. If the obsession growing inside of Brendan didn't destroy him from the inside out, then in a day or so, the Throne would rip him in half.

Israfel's lips trembled. "Lucifel."

Brendan froze, his eyes widening, too shocked to remember his caution anymore. "He's—a woman . . . but that can't be—"

"Yes, a woman."

Lucifel was a woman. One who had forced her subjects to call her "Prince" out of envy. But she wasn't—and couldn't be—like Israfel no matter how she dressed or spoke or cut her feathered hair. Because Israfel was a natural enigma, his true self known to a very privileged few, most of whom had never lived to tell about it. They'd exchanged an evening of intimacy for their lives. "A woman who gave birth to two abominations that resemble her, and with the very person I loved most."

"Then, she's the Ruin." Brendan sounded triumphant. "You said she's in Hell. But we believe that she's coming to Earth for revenge. The public aren't allowed to read the official prophecies; they're told about the red hair she possesses so that they send qualifying children to the Academy."

Nunkir was shaking, so deeply had Lucifel's name upset her. Yes, it brought back terrible memories for them all. Israfel knelt down, dizzy, but took her head against his lap, letting her hear the hope moving inside of his slender stomach.

She relaxed, though her concern for Rakir continued. Her eyes had narrowed to green slits, and still, Brendan continued to gaze openly at Israfel, teasing her brother until it bordered on cruelty. The crimson stripes flaring on Rakir's wrists and hands said that he was aroused, but the feeling was far from deliberate. Red stripes of rage blushed across his cheekbones as well.

"The Archon," Israfel's words began to slur again, "whom you ignorantly call the Ruin is not Lucifel."

Brendan was too enamored to be aware of his company anymore. He barely noticed Rakir step nearer to him, the angel's tall shadow darkening their faces. "Well, thank God."

"The Father has nothing to do with it." He couldn't even if he tried.

Israfel had seen to *that*.

He slipped away from Nunkir, stroking her shoulders and hair. Slowly, he approached her twin, distracting Rakir with a soft touch until the Throne's eyes closed once more, and he relaxed into the tenderness of Israfel's gesture, grateful. He had certainly suffered enough. Israfel took his hand and brought him nearer to Brendan. "Come," he said, hot with the fire of the Father's blood in his veins.

Brendan groaned, turning to escape this sudden temptation.

Israfel lifted a finger, and the human froze, invisible chains of ether locking him into place.

"Poor thing," Israfel said, clutching Rakir close so that they stood tightly together. "I should reward you for your self-control."

Nunkir smiled at Brendan, gloating over his lesson for the day. It was one she'd learned long ago: possessiveness had its price.

"Please," Brendan said, his slightly muscled arms already shaking underneath the tension. "I can't stop thinking about it."

"You mean punishing your ex-girlfriend?" Israfel said, teasing. He pulled Rakir down for a kiss.

Brendan gasped. "God . . ."

"Oh, but he would punish *you*."

"Israfel," Brendan pushed, hardly understanding the situation in which he was entangling himself, "come with me tomorrow, to the All Saints' Day ceremony. Stephanie will be at the ceremony with the other members of the sorority. They have to attend in order to keep up appearances. Once you show up, the priests will listen to you—they'll have to—and then she'll be officially tried as a witch and"—his voice lowered, softer—"burned."

Israfel broke away from the honey of Rakir's mouth. "How barbaric."

"It's justice," Brendan said, lunging forward violently. "It's what she deserves."

"But what will I receive in return for such an immense favor?" Israfel said, slipping off his coat, savoring the breeze. His slim, androgynous lines seemed to make Brendan's mouth water. "What could you possibly give me in exchange for that kind of generosity?"

Brendan looked from him to Rakir, possibly imagining all sorts of wonders that could take place between them. And as they waited, Rakir's wings rustling as they folded tightly against his back, Brendan decided on the choice of fools and hedonists. "My soul."

Nunkir's smile was perhaps even deadlier than before.

"If you need it, I'll sign a contract—"

"I am no demon," Israfel whispered. "The desire is enough."

"Then—it's official?" Brendan's voice was low and full of manhood, but his choices were anything but. He wanted to be a slave, for all Israfel's remaining eons—and there would be very many if all went according to plan—merely to satiate his appetite for another human's destruction. Oh, the possibilities. The endless entertainment of forcing him into one body after the next, using him until he perished only to begin the process anew. "You will have me? Because I want"—he stopped hiding the lust in his voice—"to be yours. I think I've been dreaming of you since I entered the seminary. My angel."

That was highly doubtful. He'd been dreaming of sin.

"Then so be it. Now—" Israfel pulled Rakir down, murmuring in his ear. He couldn't help relishing the words. "Satisfy yourself."

Rakir smiled, kissing the glove on Israfel's hand. Israfel smiled back at him, hallucinating someone else. Like Lucifel, Brendan would learn about possessiveness the hard way.

The human would have no chance at freedom.

Israfel had bound him tight, and he would keep him bound until long after the night was over. He left Rakir, returning to his seat with slow, drunken steps, settling into his temporary throne like he had once, long ago, in the pride and beauty of Heaven. Rakir would be absolutely brutal tonight, and Israfel's oversight would be necessary to keep Brendan alive. The bruises on his arms would look like scratches in comparison to what was coming. The human was already shuddering, his broad shoulders tensed as Rakir came closer, treading with doom.

Israfel closed his eyes, imagining the Archon held tight in his arms—there was a strong possibility she might be at the feast day rituals. Then he began to sing, miring himself in memory and passion, all his self poured into each verse.

How long it had been since he and Raziel's duet?

Brendan's screams mixed with the refrain.

Twelve

If they desire something of us, rest assured,
it is never in our best interests.
—Brother Francis, *Encyclopedia of the Realms*

Stephanie paused outside the door, her hand on the knob.

Turn it. She had to turn it.

But no matter how often she welcomed this hour, whenever it arrived, she always second-guessed herself—like she was entering a nightmare where something could go wrong any second—and the more Stephanie broke the holy laws that kept certain creatures apart, the more she feared doing it again. At least here, in the middle of the sweat, the alcohol, and the haze of drugs, she fully understood what she faced, despite how bad for her it might be. Humans had a comforting kind of predictability to them.

Music continued to throb inside the Bell Chapel, shivering into her like one tiny earthquake after another, nearly drowning out the suggestive laughter to her right.

She glanced toward it, peering through the shadows.

Two people were making out next to a private dressing room, their bodies tangled and sweaty beneath a painted pentagram. Through the door behind them, the sounds of other people enjoying themselves erupted, muffled and somehow awkward. They were probably in a group. Stephanie could handle the drunkenness, but the sex still bothered her, and she turned away quickly, knowing not to show it on her face. Her candle flickered, spitting more of its pathetic gold into the darkness.

"All right. You're going to keep an eye on things for a little while."

Lyrica's mouth settled into a line, her face pale. She'd kept her cloak's hood up for disguise, probably hoping to avoid a student who'd taken advantage of her during the last sorority party. Luckily, she'd been smart enough to stay away from the drinks this time. They were for the idiot worshippers, not real sorority members who knew better. "Are you going to be very long?" she whispered, wide-eyed. "Is she upset?"

"Make sure it doesn't get too loud out here."

"I can make them play something different—"

"The party has to continue until shortly before I get out. When it's over, I want anyone who's not a member gone, even the drunks."

Lyrica gestured at the other door, unable to express herself audibly.

"They can finish screwing each other somewhere else."

The girl regarded her with horror. "Why does it have to be me who goes in there and—"

"Because . . ." Stephanie yanked her in close enough for a kiss. But her mouth was on her cheek, and her voice was thick with warnings and nothing else. Just enough intimacy to keep down suspicion. Just enough forcefulness to keep up appearances. "You spoke out of turn yesterday, and we both know how bad that looks to the other members. Besides, I shouldn't have to remind you, *she* can hear you whine. So if you can't handle what's coming next, close your eyes. That's what I've learned to do." She let Lyrica go. "Otherwise, she'll break you in the hard way."

Lyrica stumbled backward, brushing the spit off her chin.

Then she dashed away, her shoes tapping through spilled wine, her fists clenched at her sides.

The couple at Stephanie's right paused as she finally opened the door, stepping beyond the threshold. Before the latch clicked, she caught a final glimpse of a trashed university girl, bending down to lick the wine off the stone.

Inside, the music faded to a dull pulse. Stephanie stood alone with her nervous stomach, the stale smell of alcohol, and the fumes of illegal weed clinging to her clothes. Her ears rang, tormented by the sudden silence.

She turned the lock, forcing herself to relax.

Naamah sat in the middle of what used to be an office connected to the chapel, her chair little more than a sad piece of furniture sewn and patched to a mockery. Most of the room was a chaotic mess, overloaded with collapsed brick, stone, and shards of broken stained glass. Wooden boards had been nailed over the open windows, but grimy curtains still suffered from whatever wind entered, snapping their fabric like miniature whips. Thunder rumbled from the sea as the storm moved swiftly inland.

"That girl is more annoying than a cockroach," Naamah said. "You'd think she'd have adjusted to this boring shit by now."

Blood fanned out from her bare toes, leaking from a pigeon whose upturned feet snatched at the air. The walls were covered in crimson pentagrams, all of them remnants of portals Naamah used to communicate with demons Stephanie wasn't important enough to meet. Strangely, though, there was no cloying smell; solid evidence that Naamah often sucked out whatever life remained in that blood, forcing the odor to vanish with it.

Everywhere Stephanie looked the repeating star pattern burned at her eyes. "Did the report go well for you tonight?" she said quietly.

She set the candleholder on a mound of broken stone, its flame licking at the gloom.

The blackness was like an aura. Alive. Listening. Absorbing the light.

Something was wrong. Usually, all of Stephanie's worries melted away once she and Naamah were face-to-face. That included the fear of being in the demon's presence, of making her angry, and of asking for services that always required a higher and higher price.

Yet this time the heavy feeling in her stomach hadn't gone away.

Naamah kicked at the pigeon, still examining her nails. "No." She looked up through her braids, her eyes like dark stars. "We need some results tonight. I can't keep making excuses for *you*."

Stephanie stepped closer, half in a daze, her mind turning in circles.

That last word sounded too harsh to be real.

"I can handle this. From what I read about Angela Mathers, she's gifted, but nothing special. Tonight will be the end of it all."

"She sees angels in her dreams." Naamah cradled her own chin with a hand, leaning on an elbow. "That's hard to ignore."

"You're losing faith in me. Just say it." Her voice cracked, and all of a sudden her blinding confidence shattered and revealed her frustration. "You think I've wasted your time. Don't you?" God, she sounded so stupid, so needy. Like a child begging Mommy to kiss her wounds. She wandered closer, barely aware of the blood on the floor as she knelt beneath the demon, laying her head on her lap. Naamah had her own smell: like ash and vinegar, harsh but somehow infinitely familiar and consoling. Unlike so many details in Stephanie's life, it had always been there when she needed it. Or had the bravery to want it. "But I know I'm the Archon. I—I—"

Naamah waited, eyebrows raised.

"Mother." Stephanie turned to her. "I'm worried about that Jinn-rat ruining tonight's ceremony. I thought we'd have found it by now, taken care of things."

"No. You're worried about that priest's feelings for you. Like a typical, weak, human female."

Stephanie caught the tears before they fell. Outbursts of emotion were never welcome, and when she looked up again, Naamah's face remained hard and impassive. Stephanie's vision had glazed over, yet she could still see there was no real sympathy to be found, just like the archbishop had warned. Until Naamah gently brushed back some of Stephanie's bangs, and she found the courage to hold on to the demon's hand, rubbing the bloodied fingertips against her cheek.

No, that arrogant priest was wrong.

Naamah thought of her as a daughter, not a cockroach.

The muscles in Naamah's palm tensed. "I knew I should have killed the novice when I had the chance. He's using you, you little fool. And it's infuriating to watch."

Stephanie choked on her words, holding on desperately. "No, Mother. I'll be the one to do it, if that's the case. To kill him. If he chooses Angela over me, *it's his loss*."

"Of course." Naamah sighed, briefly petting her on the head.

"Most people deserve to die anyway." Stephanie's tone hardened, hurtful. "Even Brendan. *Especially* a weak moron like him. You told me the whole world needs a new finger on its pulse, but I've been thinking, why not just stop it for good? How much easier that would be."

"True." The demon's own voice lowered to a whisper. "It's the same world that abandoned you, after all. My little Stephanie. Your witch mother sold you to me like a piece of meat, orphaned you, leaving her little cursed blood head for dead—and I thanked her for you by draining her like a pigeon. But then—I have the means for that, don't I?" Naamah laughed, and the rolling muscles of her hand hinted at the blades buried beneath her skin. "You should take pride in the fact that you've been mine at all. I taught you everything you know, even the ideals of the Prince herself. If you happen to be the Archon, well, that's a deserved bonus on my part. But—"

Stephanie stiffened. "But?"

Naamah's reminders were just like her blades. The demon had mentioned Stephanie's birth mother to make a point: Stephanie's bitterness was a part of her now, important to them both, the reason for so much of her happiness and the spur toward her future.

She could barely remember the facts of her past, mostly relying on Naamah's word. But all she'd ever held on to was the idea that her mother had sold her to a demon in exchange for one night of meaningless sex. Unfortunately for her mother, even demons sometimes delivered justice where it was due.

Stephanie had been all of three years old. Filthy, starving, and utterly alone.

Naamah had been the angel who'd saved her, or so she'd thought.

"Story time." Naamah lifted Stephanie's head by the chin, forcing them to look at each other, much like she had when Stephanie was small. Her adoptive mother's black eyes were large and mesmerizing, hypnotic. But her red eye shadow resembled the blood on the walls, and it was difficult to stare at that contrast for long without withering beneath it. "When I was a chick, I had a brother."

"A brother."

Why did that sound so awkward when Naamah said it?

"Yes. And I guess you could say, I loved him. However, the Second War arrived when we were still young, and my mother was obligated to make a sacrifice in Lucifel's service. You see, our Prince has always survived on the essence of others, but those sources must be replenished. Her only"—Naamah lifted a finger—"weakness. At the time, we were low on hostages, prisoners of war, and criminals. That left children—chicks. Unlike adults, we were relatively useless, and when it came down to it, my brother possessed none of my admittedly meager talents or accomplishments. And so my mother readily offered him as the sacrifice, consoled by the simple fact she could always bring another chick into the world to take his place."

Naamah smiled down at her, teeth blazingly white.

"In the end, he was of more use to us dead than alive. Though that never changed my feelings for him. Or my mother's."

Stephanie's breath felt like it had stopped. Terror pounded inside of her, aching to burst out. "Are you—are you saying that if I'm not the Archon—you'll kill me?"

The demon only stared back at her.

Beneath Stephanie, the pigeon twitched in the mess of its own feathers, aching for someone to put it out of its misery.

"Think carefully about what you want," Naamah continued at last, her tone abnormally soft. "You want to be the Archon. And if you are the Archon, and you take the path of Ruin, I will stand by your side, of course. Yet there are many demons loyal to Lucifel who will also try to kill you—and in the most certain and painful way possible—long before you ever set a toe on her Throne. And that's only if you manage to open the Book without risking your sanity. Ask yourself if the sacrifice is worth the cost, daughter of mine. Ask yourself if you can stare into the eyes of death and not regret your desires. Before it's too late for us both."

"Regrets," Stephanie said in a numb echo. She slid out of Naamah's embrace and picked up the dying pigeon. The bird was gasping for air like a little fish. Exactly like she had felt seconds ago. "You just want to protect me from being disappointed."

"That's one way of seeing it."

Naamah allowed her words to sink in heavily.

"*The human way.*"

But Stephanie *was* the Archon. In all of history, no blood head had shown Stephanie's supernatural promise, her ability to learn and grow in the ways of the other Realms, and none could compete with her either. Why would Angela Mathers be any different? The best thing that girl could hope for would be for Kim to use her and throw her to the side. Something he'd never tried with Stephanie, tellingly enough, even if sex alone held them together.

Fate always had a reason for working out one way or another.

There was a reason she and Kim were so much alike. There was a reason Naamah had become her mother. And there was a reason Stephanie had taught herself to kill so easily. Now, it was time to upgrade—the Archon had to be as ruthless as the Devil herself. To choose the path of Ruin, you needed the conscience of a killer.

None at all.

Naamah had made that clear from the beginning. Perhaps the moment was now. Otherwise, even her mother might not find her useful anymore, and Stephanie wanted her love as a living, breathing person—not a corpse.

"You knew from the start what kind of person I was," Stephanie hissed at Naamah. "Well, if you need proof that I'm the Archon, you'll have it soon enough. There's no way some scarred bitch is going to take that Throne away from me."

One twist of her hands snapped the bird's neck.

She tossed the body back onto the floor, breathing hard.

Naamah smiled in her terrifying way, gathering Stephanie close for a surprisingly affectionate embrace, her voice cool and comforting. "There, there. Don't feel guilty for being ambitious, dearest."

The demon's cold lips met her cheek.

Stephanie fought with her shivers again, unable to stop when the tears reappeared. Soon, deep sobs followed, her anguish increasing whenever she glanced up and saw only darkness. There was still a shred of conscience in her. It was stupid and pathetic, but for the first time in a long time, she wished the bird was still alive, flying free. She knew she probably could have staked her claim some other way, and it made her sick enough to die.

To imprison herself in the blackest pit imaginable.

"As they say . . ." Naamah actually sounded proud. "Like mother, like daughter."

Thirteen

Witches are defined by blindness.
—THE DEMON PYTHON, TRANSCRIBED FROM *The Lies of Babylon*

Kim lifted his hood, letting the rain stream onto his cheeks.

The weather had never looked so foul. It was as if all the darkness in the universe had gathered around Luz, intending to swallow it whole. From his spot on the veranda porch, the city spread out to the west, glimmering with decay and a dampness that never seemed to disappear. Lights from thousands of candles flickered dimly, struggling to brighten a world that could no longer tolerate it, and the towers twisted around him, some leaning so precariously it was a miracle they hadn't tipped into the abyss below. Many poor souls would be swept into the ocean tonight. Even within the Academy grounds, poverty equaled death, the most needy students forced into dormitories that would put a wet jail cell to shame. If the water rushed in—an accident no matter how much the Vatican was at fault—then the will of God would certainly determine the survivors.

"Enough of patience . . ." Troy said. Her hiss sounded faintly above him, erupting from a sagging gable. She herself was lost amid the silhouettes of other statues, some of them perched with the same predatory talent. "Your newest mate had better come."

"She will come," Kim whispered back, unable to stop seeing Telissa's arm. Her ring. He struggled with the bile in the back of his throat.

". . . or I will break her open myself . . ."

Then Troy was gone. Like a shadow.

Kim scanned the second level of the Bell Tower, unable to find her yellow eyes boring into him. Fury stood alone, preening her black feathers near a saintly carving, her occasional croaks almost imperceptible below the storm.

"You're nervous." Stephanie appeared by his side without warning, her ponytail streaming behind her in the wind. Now that the Halloween party had ended, she'd slipped back into her sorority overcoat, its red pentacle glittering beneath the lights of the chapel. More so than ever, he noticed her skirt, too short and flapping in the breeze. Her legs were long, soft. That—and her demonic friend—was all she had in the end, when he really thought about it. "Don't be. I have everything under control."

"You weren't under control this afternoon."

She'd been crying again, and deservedly so.

"This won't be like last year. I'll allow Nina Willis to be present—for Angela's sake—but she won't perform the actual summoning."

"You're going to use her as the Sacrament?" He shook his head, chuckling softly. "No matter what you do, this time there's going to be a real challenge. The demon is using you, Stephanie."

She glared directly at him, calm and dangerous. They both knew his words were also a challenge. "And I'm using you. But I don't see you complaining."

Touché. But that warning would be his last kindness. She was repeating his mother's mistakes all over again, and though it would be fascinating to watch her go down the same path, his lingering feelings justified a red flag of some kind. Even if Stephanie, like all ambitious witches, was too power hungry to notice it.

"You know, I never asked you," she said, her eye shadow running with the rain. "Why did you get involved with me to begin with? Was there any reason beyond the obvious benefits?"

She was mistaken if she thought his loyalties went deeper than her usefulness.

But with Stephanie, there was also that hidden question, and this time it centered around her desire to be the Ruin—a perverse desire that had attracted him along with her attributes in the very beginning, but had died considerably even before his night with Angela Mathers. Now, Angela's paintings haunted him most of all, perhaps more than his latest glimpse of Troy's blood-encrusted mouth. The gray angel especially clung to his nightmares, screaming the obvious. Somehow, in some way, Angela had seen Lucifel. The Black Prince herself.

And if Stephanie was asking whether that really mattered, then, yes.

Yes. It did.

"There was no other reason," Kim whispered. "Besides the thrill of putting you in your place, tell me, Stephanie, how does it feel to be on the other side of a lie?"

Stephanie stared at him. She lifted her hand as if to smack him violently across the face.

Then she lowered it, trembling with the effort. "Whatever you say, the truth remains. I own this school. I own you." She spoke in the same monotone she often used after visiting her demon. Like all the brightness in her life had been stamped flat. "And I allow you to sleep with other women and smirk about it because it's fun—knowing that I could crush you, and them, like flies at any second."

"Flies. How ironic. They are her symbol, you know."

"Whose?"

He smiled. "Lucifel's."

Stephanie's courage evaporated, but for a mere second. "She has no power anymore. She's caged, and when I prove myself to be the Archon, I'm going to go to Hell, slaughter her, and take her goddamned place."

An insane idea. Maybe Stephanie had already tried to open the Book after all. It wouldn't surprise him if the demon had brainwashed her into such foolishness, half hoping the wish would come true. Kim understood better than anyone else what it meant to be schooled in shadows.

"And if she escapes that cage? How will you deal with her then?"

Silence.

"Because she will find you." Kim ran fingers through the wet mess of his hair. "And then she will extract the information she needs out of you, and suck your life away without a touch. By all accounts, it will be a painful way to go."

"Why do you care?" Such a soft whisper. For the second instance since Kim had met her, Stephanie sounded truly anguished. The first was when she'd slept with him and then sat up all night crying, like a little girl who'd had her candy taken away. As if he'd forced her into bed at gunpoint. But whatever had taken place with the demon this Halloween night, something had changed. She was blatantly hurt and failing miserably at hiding the scars. "You never tried before. Why start now?"

Kim grabbed her hand before she could leave the balustrade. "What will you do if Angela is the Archon?"

Stephanie ripped her arm away. Her lips quivered. And then her jealousy finally won out over her pain. "I'll kill her. But it doesn't even matter. She's not the One. And we'll prove it tonight. And then she'll have no choice but to serve me for four long, miserable years. Now make sure everything is ready, *priest*," she said, her tone so soft, but so fatal. "It's time to teach your newest girlfriend a lesson."

Westwood's leading blood head marched back inside of the chapel, dignified.

Yet, despite her confidence, the night could turn out to be a disaster in many ways.

If Stephanie misplaced even one of her carefully planned steps . . .

Kim lifted his hood again, its edges flapping in front of his face. Above him, Fury screeched into the incoming storm, lifting into the air and spiraling up, up, up into the black and gray clouds.

Human evil could be terrifying, but also so petty compared to the real thing.

Fourteen

This is the night of spirits.
This is the hour when veils are thin.
Far be it from me to make demands on
what I cannot understand.

—Archbishop Gregory T. Solomon, Unofficial Correspondence

"Someone might die tonight," Nina said, muttering to Angela under her breath. Her eyes looked even more bloodshot than usual, practically crimson, and her hair stuck out from its bun in a hundred messy tangles. "Or so I've been told. I had the worst dreams you can imagine early this morning. There were so many people talking to me. Young. Old. Ugly. Pretty. And they all looked the same as when they died—frozen in time. The worst are the people who've drowned. Their skin has this nasty bluish color to it."

Angela kept her fingers wrapped around the doorknob. Soft light emerged from below it in a strip, like the orange hue of a dying fire. She'd chosen to be deliberately late, missing the dancing, the drinks, and the music.

Now the silence suggested she'd missed a little too much.

They stood on the creaking stairwell, two young women surrounded by a vertical shaft of stones, as if they were two Rapunzels locked away in their tower. Rain seeped through little chinks in the rock, sliming the interior. It was cold, almost chillingly so, but that could have had more to do with Stephanie summoning spirits than the actual weather. Above them, lost to the murky shadows, the stairwell continued to a third chapel and the Bell Attic. Below, there was little but cobwebs and the occasional window.

"Did you happen to see any angels?" Angela said, careful about what she might be insinuating. "Any that died? Maybe— tragically?"

It sounded even crazier out loud than in her head. And she felt a little guilty, aware of how she shouldn't keep shoving her own much happier dreams in Nina's face. Last night, she'd seen the bronze-haired angel and had been fascinated by his strange anger and the petulant smile on his lips. The black makeup around his eyes was even more intricate than she remembered, precise circles of shade and ink that brought out the unbelievable sea of his irises. His wings were so perfect, and she'd awakened wondering at their softness; the way that down would feel, caressed between her fingers. It was probably heaven compared to the ghostly visitations that haunted Nina.

"Angels," Nina said, taking one last drag of her cigarette before they entered the room. Her hands shook, peppering her boots with ash. "No, sorry. I don't even think they *can* die." She raised her eyebrows. "Can they?"

"Apparently so." Angela grabbed the cigarette and pitched it down into the darkness.

Nina watched it tumble away, sucking in her bottom lip. "You really do hate those things, don't you?"

"Smoke. It brings back bad memories." She turned the knob.

"Like of the fire that didn't kill you?"

Exactly. And if Stephanie pisses me off enough, maybe I'll try another.

Angela sighed, pushing the door open. "Let's get this over with already."

She'd expected more of a dungeon atmosphere, but the deconsecrated chapel glowed cozily with the light of hundreds upon hundreds of candles. They had been set in ritualistic semicircles throughout the room, framing a pathway that led to an even larger, closed circle, complete with a pentacle carved deep into the floor.

There were no signs of a party. Not even a broken bottle or two. Just the faint odor of herbs and alcohol.

"Angela. And here I was afraid you'd chickened out again."

Stephanie stood in the middle of the candles, robed, her porcelain hands on her hips, smiling at Angela and Nina like she'd been waiting for them all her life. The other members of the sorority, at least thirty strong, had adopted regular spots near a porch that opened to the storm. Behind the shallow veranda, the storm bubbled smoky gray and violent.

"So what do you think?" Stephanie spread her arms, indicating the decorations around them.

Angela stared at the peeling paintings, the worn frescoes, the marble altarpiece completely split in the middle. Yet the chapel was strangely cavernous, and most of its outer reaches extended into unreadable darkness. Besides the leftover junk, everything was too clean. Too orderly. Like someone had been sacrificing so many animals here, they'd decided to make it home.

"Luckily, it didn't take as long as it looks to set up." Then Stephanie lost some of the soft sweetness in her voice. "I'm glad you came, Angela. Tonight is an important one to the sorority." She paced inside the pentacle. "Or didn't you know that? You are somewhat out of the loop, I think. Just like your brother. Who, by the way, will not be here with us."

Why the hell is she bringing him into this again?

"Why not?" Angela said, keeping a firm grip on Nina's arm. Nina's teeth were chattering, and she was tensed and ready to bolt. Any kind of proximity to Stephanie seemed to terrify her.

"Because as you saw this afternoon, he insulted me." Stephanie made a visible effort to smile. "And because he's lost it. Don't you think I'm right? And now that he's also lost my favor, he's going to lose a lot more. At least with the sorority, you can always count on your sisters."

There was a rustle from a corner of the room.

Angela caught a glimpse of Sophia, huddled in the darkness near the veranda, far enough away from the candles that her soft curls blended in with the shadows. Her eyes shimmered, like two black pools of oil, and her lips had parted, like she was astonished by something. But soon her mouth sealed into a grim line, and before anyone else noticed, she quickly turned away and stared out into the night.

That left one more missing person. Kim.

He'd promised to be here, but Angela couldn't make out any of the other hooded people in the room.

"So are you finally interested in joining us?" Stephanie sounded triumphant, like she knew Angela's decision already.

"Yes."

Nina gasped. "Angela, you don't know what you're—"

Angela tugged on her arm, shutting her up. It was all an act, but Nina didn't need to know any of that. Only Kim would know, and if he was there at all, she could imagine him grinning at her boldness. "So what do I do? How do I join?"

Stephanie was smiling genuinely now. "You prove yourself. If you're a true blood head, you should be able to summon a spirit."

"You mean an angel?" Angela said, scanning each robed figure for the foreign blonde with the braids. She was there, somewhere, maybe hoping for Stephanie to accidentally plummet off a cliff. The chapel suddenly felt heavy with evil intentions. "Or do you mean a demon?"

"Lucky you if that happens." Stephanie resumed pacing. "But you could give it a try. Realistically, I'm sure you'll end up with something subpar. Like most blood heads and"—she glanced at Nina—"gifted people. Maybe a dead human who can pinch people who tick you off. That kind of superficial stuff happens more often than you'd think. Nina Willis could tell you all about it, I'm sure. Which reminds me, Nina, I didn't welcome you back properly."

Stephanie's eyes narrowed almost imperceptibly.

"Welcome back."

Nina breathed hard, her skin beneath Angela's palm clammy and moist. "I'm not here to summon a spirit, Stephanie," she said, her words shivering with her. "All I want is to get rid of them."

"Get rid of what?"

"The voices and visions in my head. You know what I mean."

"Good luck with that," Stephanie said. Her voice lowered, suddenly dangerous. "But you're not here to be cured. You're here to be a *Sacrament,* Nina. You don't think we'd let you back without good reason?"

"What?" Nina's face became paper white. "A Sacrament? *But I'll become possessed—*"

"You knew what the price was, to come back here, to interfere. So make the choice. Take your place as Angela's Sacrament or prepare for your next year to be hairless, voiceless, miserable, and wretched. Either will do. I'm not in the most compassionate mood tonight."

"Enough," Angela said, forcing them both to pay attention to her again.

God. She's crazy. Why would anyone join this sorority at all? Unless they're masochists—

Or social pariahs like Nina, aching for a reason to be accepted by anyone. It might have been the first time in her life, but now Angela was on the other side looking in, and something about that seemed wrong. She wasn't meant to be a witch, or anything like Stephanie at all. Instead, she was meant to crush her. For a brief second, Kim's hope that Angela was indeed the Archon held so much gratifying weight, her whole self burned with it. If Hell really had any demons, and they needed company, she'd be sure to send Stephanie home to roast with them.

But I'm not the Archon. I'm just a psycho with a sense of morality.

"If you want to get started," she said, horribly aware of the echo to her voice, "I'm ready."

"Oh, of course." Stephanie blinked away her previous comments, as if Nina's presence had been nothing more than a fly on her shoulder. The storm continued rumbling inland behind her, and without warning, a fierce wind suddenly rushed into the room, blowing out the candles and throwing the chapel into blackness. "Time to see what you're made of."

The pentacle relit itself, beckoning.

Fifteen

Every Summoning has the potential for disaster.
I myself once summoned a demon who was not what she seemed.
Since then, each morning I live has been paid for in blood.
—Monsignor Joseph Mauss, unofficial correspondence

Two hours and—nothing.

Angela had taken her place at the northern tip of the star that made up the pentacle, chanting according to Stephanie's instructions, Nina taking the opposite position near the outside balustrade, both of them flanked on right and left by robed people who could have been absolutely anyone. But in all that time, very little had changed except the weather, and the occasional flash of Lyrica's stocking-covered feet from under her robe.

Stephanie refused to revel brazenly, yet the more Angela failed, the more she smiled, and the more the new sorority ring on Angela's finger began to feel like a manacle, binding her to the earth. It was like she'd made a contract with the Devil, only this devil would torment you for at least four years and finally dangle you over a cliff. The wind and rain had died down, the new silence signifying that this was the eye of the intense storm hammering the coast. Angela continued to chant as a steady drizzle rolled off her hair.

Stephanie continued to circle her, like a shadow that never completely disappeared.

"This isn't going very well."

Unlike everyone else, Sophia hadn't moved since Angela arrived, still staring at some far, dark corner of the room that held only inky blackness. Since the eerie quiet had arrived she looked absolutely riveted.

Something wasn't right. In so many ways.

"Not very well at all." Stephanie slid by again.

Angela paused, glaring at her. "Then tell me what I'm doing wrong. What kind of gibberish am I saying, anyway?"

"You don't know Latin?" Stephanie shook her head, turning away. "You must have been homeschooled—before your parents died in that suspicious fire, of course."

If that was meant to be nasty, it was a sad attempt. Angela's sense of justice wasn't about to change. Accident or not, for various reasons, her parents had deserved their untimely end, and she refused to sob over it. Even in her particular version of Hell, Erianna was probably drinking herself stupid, and Marcus was likely having sex with an underage girl. He'd do that often, especially if he knew Angela could hear him in the other room. Often, she'd tune him out by trying to suffocate herself with pillows, never managing to die, but at least waking up to a wonderful silence.

"A sacrifice," a cool, male voice murmured in her ear.

Kim had revealed himself at last, his musky breath reminding her of kisses in the dark. If only they could be together alone again instead of wet and miserable. If only Angela didn't adore her beautiful angel so much, she was willing to trample on anyone and anything to find him, even crushing what was left of her pride by muttering a dead language in a hurricane.

"Tell the spirits," he continued, "that you'll give them what is most important to you . . ."

All this time, he'd been standing right behind her, hiding beneath his robe. Now he took the two short steps back to his spot, seconds before Stephanie turned back around. The moment she did, it became clear to her that something had changed. Stephanie bit her lip, glancing around at the other sorority members suspiciously, marching with that light step of hers along a path of candles. "You've given up already?"

"No." Angela's heartbeat quickened. "I'm going to offer them something."

Stephanie peered at her, too interested, her green eyes too cold in the flickering light. "It can't just be something—"

"It's going to be what I hold the most dear. That's the way this works, isn't it?"

"Who *told* you?"

Angela didn't answer. Instead, her heart raced, faster and faster. If she wanted to see her angels at all, the sacrifice would literally be gut-wrenching. The only important thing left to her was her dreams, and no more dreams also meant no more inspiration for her paintings. It meant no more reasons to fall asleep, or even wake up in the morning so that she could simply fall asleep again, which was the nearest thing to death she'd ever experienced. But if she didn't follow Kim's suggestions, the night might end on worse than a sour note. This was a different kind of suicide, one even more painful because it would kill her spirit.

But this was her last gasp, after all.

Kim can't lead me in the invocation. And just saying what I'm offering won't be enough.

Her heart continued to hammer, like an insistent drum. Angela looked to Nina—wet and miserable too, but pale, shivery, ready to faint—and then to Sophia. For the first instance since Angela entered the chapel, their glances connected and held. Sophia's soulless expression had returned. Angela began fading away with her, entering a silent, mindless void. Oddly enough there were words in that void, or inside of Sophia, somehow passing between them, because Angela heard herself speaking.

"By Blood, by Fire, by Air, by Earth—"

Stephanie's face blanked over. "I said, '*Who told you*'?"

The candles began to dance on the floor. Lightning flashed nearby, followed by terrible thunder. Kim's breaths nearby sounded ragged. *Afraid.*

Eager.

"—by Water, by Life, by Death, by Birth—"

A disgusting sound filled the chapel. Flesh, or reality, tearing. Blood began dripping from the broken altarpiece, the walls. It surrounded Sophia, splotching the wall behind her in pentagrams that began to ooze in every other direction. Stephanie's beautiful face cracked. She took a step backward, as if Sophia were ready to throttle her again. "Stop. *Now. You don't know what you're doing*—"

But there was no way Angela could stop. The power was a part of her, *coming from her.* In a single, blinding moment, she felt like the universe had connected to her fingers by a trillion strings, and she could now break them all whenever she chose.

"—by Sun, by Moon, by Sky, by Sea—"

All the candlewicks snuffed into smoke.

Nina's eyes were wide and wild, unfocused.

"Stop it, you stupid bitc—"

Angela screamed. *"I offer what is precious to me, my Dreams, that portion of Death I see, and now—your Spirit—bound by the leash of my Will, shall be—"*

An unbelievable flash of light, a thunderous crack so loud it could break the eardrums, struck the chapel. Lightning. A direct bolt that in a cruel instant silvered the world. And when Angela's mind returned, it was in time to see Nina holding her ears and screaming, her wide eyes the most horrible crimson color imaginable.

What happened next made no sense. At first.

The blonde with the braids threw off her robe, advancing on Nina while almost everyone but Angela lay on the floor, stunned or unconscious. She was wearing that strange coat underneath, and her black eyes had all the sympathy of a wasp's. Then she flicked her wrist and nightmarish, needle-thin blades slid out of her fingers. She lifted her hand, ready to strike.

God. She's really going to kill someone this time. It's not just a threat anymore.

It wasn't just a dream anymore.

"*Nina*," Angela screamed. "*Nina*—"

She said someone might die. And it's going to be her.

"*Nina!*"

There was no time to care about whether the invocation had sent Angela her angels or not. There was no time to look for them. There was only time to keep Nina's throat from tearing open and mixing its blood with the chapel's, splattered across the walls.

Angela ran to tear the blonde down—

The blonde spun around and smiled directly at her. Then she picked up Nina by the robe and tossed her over the balustrade.

Sixteen

They hide in darkness, as their eyes cannot bear even the light
of a few candles. But I speak from grim experience—there
is never enough light to keep them out.

—BROTHER FRANCIS, *Encyclopedia of the Realms*

Troy had the foresight to close her eyes moments before the lightning strike that could have shocked her into a coma. When she opened them again, it was to see Angela Mathers running for the demon, plunging in an act of suicide over the balcony to drop after her friend.

One thing stood in Troy's way.

A female with her hood thrown back by the wind had wobbled shakily to her feet. She stared out into the storm, her short red hair blustering around her ears.

Troy shot from the ceiling, cutting her down with her nails.

The human shrieked, collapsing beneath the gash across her back. Blood spattered across the floor, wetting the slippers of the one huddled next to the porch, her vacant eyes wide with horror. Troy raced past her, her hands slipping across fallen candlesticks.

The demon had spread her wings, intending to follow Angela.

Naamah. It was Naamah, the Fourth Great Demon of Hell. Though it had been ages, Troy would know her scent anywhere. Sariel's witch had allied with one of the worst crows Hell had to offer, and now Troy had a full view of her undignified wings, smelling of acid and rot, their feathers sparse, blond, and bloody, their skin stretched into tight webs between exposed bone and artificial supports. The metal in them creaked angrily as Naamah spread her pinions wide, preparing to dive into the maelstrom.

The demon turned at the last second, her black eyes cold with surprise.

"You didn't forget me, did you?" Troy said, pouncing for her, nails ready to snag into Naamah's neck. Her sickle-shaped wings snapped open, rolling thunder. "Looks like I'm back for more."

The demon cursed, her voice more poisonous than her finger-blades. She swiped at Troy.

Too little, too late. Troy landed near to her feet, snapping her jaws. A second later she followed Naamah into the storm, both of them vaulting over the edge of the stone. Large droplets needled Troy's back and arms, stinging like miniature teeth. Both Angela and the newly possessed human were still falling.

She could hear the screams.

Naamah was gaining on them fast. She wouldn't let Angela's friend survive if she could help it.

But she couldn't.

Troy caught an updraft and ascended, enough to let her take aim.

Then she smacked into Naamah, flipping them both into an opposing tower.

Metal screeched across brick. Stone cracked, ripping from the building in chunks. Blades whistled past her ears. Naamah's shriek was as desperate as the human's Troy had cut down. "*Having fun, rat?*"

She thrust out her hand, probably to knock Troy down with an ether current.

"Forgetting again." Troy shook her head, rattling the bones tied to her hair. "You're a part of me now, bitch."

She bit into Naamah's flesh, and they fell again.

The wind screamed around them, the world passing by in a blur of fog and weak light. A set of windows seemed to shoot upward as they plummeted, lost to the sky. Another. Another. Below, the turbid sea took shape, half of its waves bleached by lightning. Troy's eyes smarted from the glare, and she closed them momentarily, using her nose and ears to assess the danger. The demon was anything but quiet.

Naamah screamed out curses, and water cascaded down the curves of Troy's wings, soaking into their feathers and slicking them to an oily sheen. The air buffeted them violently.

Finally, Troy shoved Naamah away.

In moments, the rain fell too thick to see.

Angela's scent reemerged, emanating from a flooded channel near the base of the Bell Tower. The demon would never catch it in time.

Troy arched her wings into sharp crescents and dived, eventually hovering above a choppy mess of icy black water, peering through the night. Angela was treading the channel, somehow still alive with her arms wrapped around the human she'd nearly killed herself to save. Her friend looked like she had a broken leg, maybe an arm, but she smelled like her brain was reasonably intact. Not that it would matter otherwise, but even Troy couldn't let a human who might be the Archon perish. She flapped above Angela, snatching for her, and Angela glanced up at her through the rain, sputtering seawater and hair from her mouth.

Her face whitened to Sariel's shade, and her eyes rolled back in her head.

Luckily, the water was too shallow for her to sink like a rock.

Seventeen

---

*We have determined that the Archon will suffer through
the greatest personal torments. And I would be lying if
I said I felt sorry for what She must endure.*

—St. Imwald, Letters to the Holy Father

There were no more dreams.

Angela, though, remembered so little of what had happened
before that. The last thing she'd seen clearly had been Nina falling
over the veranda porch. She'd sprinted after her, hoping to save her,
because whenever Angela tried to drown herself, it hadn't worked
and she'd lost every bit of fear that it would. Just as she'd expected,
a searing pain had shot through her head, and her clothes flooded
with icy water. In a daze, she'd found Nina and wrapped her arms
around her, keeping them both afloat. Then, of all possible rescu-
ers for them, she'd hallucinated the devil on her dormitory roof,
fluttering overhead.

But after she'd fainted, there had been no dreams. Nothing. No
hint of her beautiful angel. Not a wisp of his gray companion. Not
even a trace of Sophia and her pretty silver slippers.

From the first day Angela could understand what a dream was,
she had one every time she blacked out of reality. That meant at
least one dream every night of her life, not even counting the times
she fainted.

Now—nothing.

The invocation must have worked.

The hard, astonishing realization pounded through her head as she cracked open her eyelids, amazed to find herself back in the chapel where so much had gone so wrong. Stephanie and the other sorority members had fled, leaving one of their own in a bloody pool close to the balustrade, the student's breathing painfully intermittent. Kim and Sophia knelt by Angela's side, Nina's twisted but twitching arm peeking through a gap between Sophia's bloody slippers. And the devil who'd saved her . . . must have disappeared like the vision it had been.

There was no sign of an angel with bronze hair and wings—for all she knew, Angela had summoned a monster—but they'd never find out until Nina opened her eyes again, and that didn't look like it was going to happen any time soon.

Angela blinked up at the murky ceiling, so high and cavernous, just taking in air.

A horrid shudder moved up through her chest, and she turned her head, hacking up salt water. It spat out of her throat, burning. She swore out loud.

Kim laughed, sounding relieved. "She's here with us. Thank God. You shouldn't be alive, you know." He leaned over her, his amber eyes gleaming before the meager circle of light. Sophia held a candle in her hand, her other palm cupped around the flame to protect it from the breeze. The worst of the storm was over, its tail edges rumbling out to the west. "Would you like to explain yourself, Miss Mathers?"

Angela took a second to breathe again. Her chest hurt and her ears were ringing a little. "Wouldn't you . . . have done the same?"

"No," Kim said, his face reappearing, "because I would have known it meant certain death. So either you don't have any sense of self-preservation, or you know that killing yourself isn't a possibility." His warm mouth tickled the rim of her ear. "You were holding out on me, Angela. There's more to you than those paintings and dreams." His finger brushed the tights near her thigh. Ugly purple scars peeked through a hole in the fabric. "Where did these scars come from, by the way? Would it be an insult to call them self-inflicted?"

"The first day we met—" Sophia's face was still out of sight, but her voice sounded too content. Like a child who'd found her mother at last. "The first day we met, I caught her trying to jump off the roof. She's reckless. Suicidal."

Crazy, you mean.

Sophia knelt down and brushed the hair from Angela's cheeks. Her curls had frizzed over in the humidity, but her face remained lovely and chinalike. Perfect, especially with that smile. "I'm glad you're all right."

And I do feel crazy. When she says things like that, it makes me wish it had all been for her.

"What happened?" Angela moved to sit up, but her muscles felt like string, the sorority ring around her finger heavy as a gold boulder. "Where did Stephanie and the others go?"

"Back to where it's safe. Probably to the Pentacle House, where she can plan how to deal with you best."

"How to deal with me . . ."

"You weren't supposed to succeed at anything tonight, Angela. Or was my ex-girlfriend's envy lost on you? She was hoping you'd fail and end up Lyrica's clone for the next few years of your life." Kim lifted her gently by the shoulders, his hands as warm as the night they'd kissed. "Although I doubt that kind of mercy will remain in her much longer."

Ex-girlfriend, he'd said. Angela slumped against his chest, trying to ingest the enormity of what had happened. Kim's heart beat steadily, all his fear during the invocation replaced by a certainty that calmed her and made her taste his skin, his flesh, all over again.

Sophia's interruption was more than a coincidence. Her words had a short clip to them, jealous almost. "Maribel is dying. I'm going to at least make her comfortable—"

"Don't take another step . . ."

Angela froze instinctively.

The new voice had a cruel rasp to it, and a soft hiss trailed at the edge of each word, honing their preciseness. She stared into the darkness surrounding the outer edges of the candlelight. Two large, yellow eyes flashed in the shadows, narrowing at Sophia in warning. They held their own light, glowing, phosphorescent, mind-numbing.

"Are you planning to keep her for yourself?" Sophia asked.

There was the slightest hint of a growl. "What do you think?" *It has a female voice.*

Kim clasped Angela's arm, as if he knew she might try to escape. As if he knew what her reaction was going to be when she saw what crouched beside Maribel. "Don't show your fear," he murmured softly. "It will work against you. I promise. Troy"—his voice grew louder—"you know this one is going to die."

"Of course I do." The eyes flashed open again, their pupils huge. Whatever she was, she began to pace softly beyond the reach of Sophia's candle. "And she's mine. I brought her down, and I'll be the one to finish the job."

"Then please do," Sophia said, moving away so that the light barely touched Maribel. "Before it becomes too painful. She was always . . . kind to me."

Angela could barely breathe again, but this had nothing to do with being waterlogged. Her shivers had started, the symptoms of a hypothermia that wouldn't kill her, but would ruin her night. Nina had a robe wrapped around her legs and waist, and now Kim opened the folds of his own robe, tucking Angela inside where she could lean fast to the warmth of his hard chest. Yet the world continued to fade, everything else lost beyond the spotlight that glimmered faintly on Maribel.

Then, without any more warning, *she* emerged.

An angel? A demon? But in the end, there was nothing to adequately compare her to. Troy—if that was really her name—had a pixie-pretty face, but one holding a mouthful of tiny knives, blood-stained, hiding behind lips the bluish shade of a corpse. Luminous eyes, savage and hungry, scrutinized Sophia with an air of cruelty only a hunter could express, and lengthy, batlike ears swiveled, catching the terrible sound of Maribel's breathing. Troy's skin was whiter than Kim's—whiter than chalk—and yet her hair, her sharply curved wings, and her nails were a black too deep and dark to name.

She was breathtaking, with a horrifying, predatory kind of beauty.

It was hard to look. And it was even harder to look away.

Troy sniffed Maribel's neck, frightening her into a rigid catatonia.

"What is she?" Angela whispered, already knowing the answer. This was the devil she'd seen on the dormitory roof and hovering above her in the channel below the Bell Tower, *and it was real*. Of course, it didn't make her feel any better that Troy was her rescuer. Nina's real savior.

In her mind, Kim's book lay wide open again, and she stared at those horrible illustrations of a creature that seemed more nightmare than flesh and blood.

"You know this thing?"

"Troy," Kim said, whispering back, "is a Jinn. They're immortal, like angels and demons, but scavengers, cave dwellers that survive in the upper reaches of the Underworld." He stopped talking as Troy glared at him, suspicious, eventually resuming in an even lower voice. "They claim to be descended from angelic offspring that were rejected and thrown into the lower Realms. The result of eons of interbreeding in the harshest environment that exists . . ."

He made Hell sound like a land as real as Luz, or the Earth, or any other planet in the universe. Not just a place where spirits and untouchable ghosts wandered, punished and burning for all eternity. No, Hell was a place in the most material sense of the word.

And that meant Heaven was too.

"How do you know her?" Angela said, shivering.

There was a pause, and Kim's tone dipped into tangible anguish. "She's my cousin."

His cousin. His father's or mother's niece. That means at least one of his parents is a Jinn. A devil. A monster that murders people like a cat hunts mice.

Angela didn't have to ask. Luz's infamous serial killer stalked around Maribel, right in front of her, a mere foot from Sophia and the candle cradled in her hand. Suddenly, the dead rat, the dead student near the Theology Center, and the lights Sophia had maintained in their bedroom—suddenly all those instances combined to make this deadly picture. Troy had been spying on Angela all along and eating other people in the meantime.

No wonder Kim had avoided the key chapter of his book.

He'd wanted to forget about his terror of a cousin, even for just one night.

A long screech filled the chapel. The crow that had warned Angela away from the dead student landed on Troy's shoulder, wings adjusting for balance. Its beak clacked as it cocked an eye at Maribel.

"Fury." Kim's whisper was softer than a breath. "That's the bird's name. But the crow's body is merely her shell."

"A shell for what?"

"A human soul. She's a Vapor. A familiar bound to Troy. But her human memories are gone by now. Now . . . she's nothing but an extension of her master."

Fury chattered her beak and flapped her wings. Anxious about something, it seemed. Troy regarded her with a low growl and leaned down over Maribel, her skinny hands reaching for her like a lover. She and Fury must have silently agreed on a course of action that would satisfy each other, if not everyone else. Maribel had been bleeding so slowly and for so long, her skin had just begun to shade off into gray, and her eyelids were growing heavy. She moved her lips, trying to speak. Angela thought she could make out a strained whisper of thanks, each word painfully drawn.

Then Troy snapped her neck.

That, at least, was mercifully brief.

When they arrived at Angela's dormitory mansion, Nina was muttering in her sleep, shivering like a leaf and frighteningly feverish. Troy chose to remain at the Bell Tower for the time being, choosing to dispose of, or more likely devour, Maribel's corpse.

Nina's prediction of death had been spot-on after all.

Over and over, Angela's mind replayed the events of the night, and when she, and Sophia, and Kim—who had volunteered to carry Nina the entire way—walked into the mansion, the first thing she did was dash into the kitchen, throw open the refrigerator, and suck down all of the water in a glass pitcher. Afterward, she promptly ran to the bathroom and vomited for at least half an hour, seeing more sticky pentagrams on the walls, and more blood everywhere she looked, even if it was only in her imagination. By the time Kim knocked on the door, she lay next to the toilet, curled up on the cracked tiles so that their chill leeched through her tights and arm gloves.

Her hypothermia, much like her other aches and pains, had disappeared even earlier than usual, and the bathroom smelled strangely comforting and clean. It was too old, though, even for the mansion that surrounded it, and a crack ran through the mirror's middle. The light was meager, coming more from the space beneath the door than the candle next to the sink.

"Can I come in?" Kim said. His voice sounded sultry as always. Angela rolled onto her side, fighting off dry heaves. "Ye—yeah."

This isn't me. Running like that.

But it also wasn't her to suck a lightning bolt down from the sky.

Everything was changing. Everything. She stared at the coiled radiator next to the toilet, hardly knowing what to ask first or how to ask it. She was just lucky that Kim must have sensed her distress and decided to take the initiative for a change. "Are you ever going to leave this room?" His fingers found her hair and lifted some strands, rubbing them. He sat on the toilet, bent over her, his black coat sweeping the tile. "Or should I carry you to bed like I did your friend?"

"No," Angela said, getting to her knees and pushing onto her feet. "I can go myself."

"When you're ready."

He watched her brush her teeth and lean down to drink more water from the tap, probably trying to make sure she didn't pass out again without being there to help. Then he followed her silently out of the bathroom and up the stairs to her own apartment, standing politely outside the door until she waved him in. Angela grabbed a brush and tugged through the knots in her hair, but she didn't feel like changing her clothes anymore. She was too tired and dazed to care, and once her hair was more civilized-looking, she collapsed onto the bed without even taking off her boots, the world still spinning.

Kim's weight settled on the bed beside her.

"I'm sorry," she whispered, feeling stupid. Under ordinary circumstances, she would have wanted to be alone. But after seeing Troy, any company was better than none. She was just relieved it was Kim. Sophia would have been hovering all over her, worried. "I'm just—not myself right now."

"True. You haven't been from the start. I think it's time to be more honest with me."

She closed her eyes, taking in a long breath. "My dreams are gone."

Kim gazed back at her, silent.

"Every time I fell unconscious, I dreamed about my angels. *Every time.* Now . . . I guess my offer was acceptable after all." Angela rolled onto her back, staring up at the ceiling. "So—I want to understand. Both Stephanie and that blond woman with the braids—the way she threw Nina over the side of the building. *Why?*"

"Because that woman is a flesh-and-blood demon, and Stephanie summoned her to Earth. To Luz." There was another pause, filled with telling silence. "Whoever you called into your friend is a threat to them. The red eyes"—his words slowed considerably—"gave that away rather quickly. Naamah wants Nina dead now, and she'll finish the job eventually. The only question is when."

Nina was going to live. It was probably the only good thing that had come out of her being possessed—her new spirit friend wanted her to stick around. But if the demon found her, sniffed her out—

A demon. *Naamah.*

Unbelievably, Stephanie was that dangerous. It was hard to digest that a human being could go so wrong, so young. Had she offered her soul in exchange for Naamah's services? When and how could that kind of relationship even begin? It was almost beyond comprehension. But in one night, every legend or rumor about Luz had revealed itself to be horrendously true. "What about me? Now she knows that I have power of some kind, whatever it might be. Now I'm a real threat . . . a solid candidate to be the Archon. That has to piss Stephanie off."

"And it does." Kim rested with his hand against his chin. "From this point on, she won't play nice, Angela. Your bolt of lightning was equivalent to a declaration of war, and Stephanie won't let you call yourself the Archon whether or not it turns out to be the reality of things." His expression was flat and grim. "Didn't I say not to let her superficial act fool you? Stephanie has killed before, and she'd kill again. In ways that could turn even the hardest stomachs."

"But I don't get it. Why does she want to be the Archon so badly?"

"We've already discussed that. It all comes down to power, and perhaps bitterness. But think about what you've learned of the Archon, Angela. She will have a choice to make, and most believe it will be one of Ruin. Who is the Ruin? The real Ruin?"

Angela thought hard.

"The Devil?" she said, her breath almost stopping.

"Exactly. In other words, some of the demons want the Archon on the Throne of Hell. This means challenging Lucifel, the Devil herself, for the position. The risks are terrifyingly vast, but the rewards would equal them. Stephanie is a typical witch who only thinks about the latter half."

So her name is Lucifel. Just like he said, it's different from the name everyone knows.

Her heart began to pound like it had in the Bell Chapel, skittish with fear and shock. Kim's voice was low and earnest, but he could have been screaming, her nerves were fraying so badly.

"You and Nina can't stay here anymore, Angela. It's not safe."

The final nail in the coffin. Her throat went dry.

"Then where?"

"Anywhere but here."

So I'm officially homeless again . . . and this time, because someone actually wants me dead.

Angela sat up, her arms wobbly. Kim helped her, steadying her by the shoulder—until she accidentally pulled him down, and they ended up pressed together, his handsome features blurred by their closeness. Angela's mouth was right against the curve of his neck, and without even thinking, she pressed a light kiss to it. Her whole self was succumbing to their proximity, and she could sense his own desire in the firm grip of his hands, and the hungry light of his eyes.

He was more like Troy than he realized.

"No," she said, angry at herself. "We shouldn't."

Kim leaned over her a second longer, but the instant he pulled away, she guided him back.

Why can't I make up my mind?

Part of her wanted to forget everything, but the other half couldn't stop remembering that Nina was unconscious in Sophia's bed, that they were both waiting for her, and that Kim's cousin was a devil from Hell, eating one of his students like a midnight snack.

Her beautiful angel gazed back at her from one of his portraits, smiling in his ambiguous way, like a celestial Mona Lisa.

Angela tried to shut out the idea that he didn't approve.

She glanced at the door, noticing with gratefulness that it was shut and locked, and that Kim wasn't stupid enough to let someone walk in on them alone.

Without a word, Angela put his hands on the buttons of her blouse, telling him with her eyes to begin. Just as silently, he worked at the shirt from the bottom up, relaxing her more with his warmth and a gentle kiss here and there. When it came to what they were about to do, it seemed understood that discussion wasn't necessary. And Angela had more important questions anyway. "Why is Naamah working for Stephanie?" she said when he'd undone the last button. "Stephanie couldn't have forced her into it."

Yet it was difficult to believe she'd summoned a demon to Luz and that was that.

There was more to their relationship than a working one. It only made sense.

So why Stephanie, out of all the blood heads in Luz?

"Oh, a demon's definition of loyalty is nothing like ours," Kim said. He kissed her bare shoulder, starting to work on her skirt. "In the end, she's here to answer other kinds of questions, and she's hoping Stephanie has the answers. Or that you do," he said ominously, "if Stephanie proves to be a waste of time. The demons want the Book of Raziel opened, but as I said before, only the Archon can do that. So Naamah's biding her time, going along with Stephanie's games . . . waiting for the second to decide when she'll have outlived her usefulness."

Angela opened her mouth to ask another question, but Kim covered it with his own quickly. Immediately, it began. A repeat of all the fire she'd felt the other night, though even more intense, because there was nothing to keep them in check anymore.

Kim kissed her until it was a pleasure to be exposed, to feel the coolness in the air. So often—too often—she was head to toe in tights, fabric, anything to hide the scars.

With Kim, things were different.

With him, in a strange way, she was free to be whatever she liked, and she had the peace of knowing that he didn't care one way or the other.

She stared up at him, aching with the sight of his angular face and strong body, enamored by the thin line of his lips. Locked together like this, the rest of the world swiftly melting away, Angela wasn't aware of how much losing her dreams had hurt, until she lay against his chest again, and by listening to the rapid beat of his heart, felt how empty her soul had suddenly become.

There was nothing left to live for right now.

"What is it?" he whispered, even gentler than before.

Angela buried her face in his neck.

But she knew he could feel her tears.

After that, she instinctively understood the urgency in them both was partly from guilt and partly from loneliness. She had to bite her lip so hard that it bled, desperate to keep Sophia from hearing them, and when it was all over, and his telltale shudders began, she collapsed against him, letting him kiss the sweat off her skin.

Kim ran fingers through the red stripe in his bangs, sitting up on the bed. He was so pale and unearthly. Yet he was also too human for her to fear the hunger hidden behind his smile.

"You keep mentioning the Book of Raziel," she said, reluctant to leave the heat of his body. Not until her guilt about leaving Sophia and Nina—and her angel—became too much to bear. "But you haven't said anything about where it is."

"That's because I don't know."

"Does anyone know?"

He laughed. "Naamah. But she won't tell you anytime in the near future." Kim massaged her neck possessively. "But it's nearby. That's a given. She won't risk letting the Book wander too far if the opportunity arises to open it."

Wander?

"Are you always so distracted?" he said, holding her crushingly tight.

His teeth had just found the rim of her ear when someone knocked on the door.

"Angela? Angela, are you all right?"

Sophia.

Angela sat still.

Kim's teeth held her, seeming reluctant to let go. Uncomfortably, she thought of the illustration of the Jinn hovering over the human woman, ready to snatch her off to the Underworld with his fangs.

She pushed off him with all the strength she had, hastily tugging up her tights and throwing on her uniform. Kim watched her with a cool smile on his face.

"Yeah, I'm all right," she shouted. "I'll be out in a minute."

It took another for Sophia's footsteps to trail slowly down the hallway, with all the speed of molasses. Either she knew what had just taken place, or she was worried that it might. Her distrust of Kim was getting stronger by the hour. Maybe she hated him because he was Stephanie's lover. Or maybe there was a lot more going on than Angela had seen on the surface. All of a sudden, it troubled her: the calm way Sophia had been dealing with Troy, the strange coincidence that she and Angela were living together, and Naamah's crisp exchange with Sophia after she'd scared her into a rage.

Remember why you're here, Sophia . . .

. . . she's not the One . . .

Sophia had actually been frightening that night. In a less definable way than Troy, but frightening nevertheless.

. . . she will never be the One . . .

Angela laced her boots, watching Kim work the buttons of his coat and reconnect his white collar, the sharp cuffs of his sleeves. He was glancing at her from the corner of his eye, still smiling, his thin lips soft and hungry all over again.

Sophia knows Naamah. She knows what's going on here. And I have to face her now and lie about—this.

The situation wasn't black and white anymore.

Instead, it was turning a terrible shade of gray.

Angela stood back and caught sight of herself in the mirror, her face carrying angles almost sharper than Kim's and her blue eyes wide and overly large. Her hair was too straight, too long, and red as blood. For the briefest moment she saw a woman who could crush the world if she had to.

Yet that moment always passed as soon as it arrived.

Eighteen

The sacred number of Three, the pedestal on which so much rests.
—Unknown author

"Tell her the truth." Sophia's tone was polite, but Kim also heard the million unspoken threats hidden behind it. She sat next to Nina, her uniform skirt spread across the sheets, her bloody slippers neatly set near the footboard. "Tell Angela the truth, or I will say it for you."

Angela halted at the doorway, pale. She looked even sicker than in the bathroom.

Rain slung itself against the windows, glazing over the impressive view. Wrapped inside one of Sophia's bedsheets, her red eyes blinking slowly, Nina lay like a woman who'd just spoken to death and returned to tell about it, gazing out into Luz with an expressionless haze over her features. A candle flickered on a table near the bed, bringing out the tired, ghastly thinness of her face, and perhaps even more disturbingly, the gleam of perfectly mended limbs. Her broken bones had already healed.

Had the "something" inside of Nina who'd fused her bone marrow together also told Sophia his secret? Sophia had been suspicious from the start—and now, Kim felt himself getting angry. He should have begged Troy to kill her and be done with it.

One less person to worry about. She was Stephanie's slave after all.

"The truth?" he said, entering the room despite her threats. His voice came out sharp as a knife. "Which truth, and relating to what?"

"Oh, you know precisely what I'm referring to, Kim. Or should I say, Sariel of the Sixth Clan?"

She knew his Jinn name.

Angela turned on him, instantly accusing. "*You're still hiding things from me.*" She was angry now too, a picture of indignation that mirrored the gray angel of her paintings, and she walked closer to him, bold because of their intimacy and how much power she thought it had gained her. Her beautiful face was all angles and frightening eyes. "You said that Troy is your cousin. What does that mean? *Who is your mother? Your father? What are you?*"

The charade was officially over, then, but only by half. Kim dropped into a nearby chair with his hands clasped atop the rails, adopting the same bored attitude he took in the confessional. Except right now, Sophia would be the soul on trial. If she wanted to play this game, he wasn't going to hold back. "I'll tell you, but only if Sophia explains her demonic friend. Fair is fair."

Angela gasped. She'd forgotten all about that, hadn't she?

"How do you know Naamah, Sophia?" he said, hardly in the mood for mercy.

She pursed her lips, so tightly that they looked bloodless.

"Sophia," Angela said, demanding. "Answer him. I don't have time to learn who I can trust and who I can't."

"She is—" Sophia took in the sight of Angela and Kim, almost side by side, and refused to hide the bitterness in her voice. "—she is my master."

"God," Nina said, swearing in Angela's place. Whether she truly remembered what had thrown her over the balustrade, though, was another matter. It could just as easily have been her possessor speaking, praying for them to suffer.

"Your master," Angela repeated for her. She crossed her arms, imperious. "Where are you from, Sophia?"

Silence.

"*Where?*"

Sophia stared at Kim, her pretty face white with resentment. Her words, usually so sweet, could have been dipped in acid. "Hell. I'm dead—and this is my punishment. Naamah oversees it and with the Prince's permission torments me however she pleases." She was like a beautiful, life-size doll, but overflowing with hatred. No wonder Angela felt a certain affection for her. In a world of dolls with curls and ribbons, hats and petticoats, some dressed in kimonos and others in contemporary fashions—Sophia had become the capstone to Angela's collection. Naamah clearly had planned putting Sophia here as the perfect spy. There was no question in Kim's mind. What that demon hadn't counted on was Sophia's fondness for her blood head roommate, or Angela's for her. "Stephanie's control over me is temporary. Her pact with Naamah makes her think she has some kind of say in what I do and how I do it. But she's been overstepping her bounds lately and getting bolder. The incident in the tunnel—"

She and Angela exchanged a glance filled with understanding.

"—was a perfect example of that."

So Sophia was a Revenant. A human who had been given her body back, but only so that it could be tortured along with her soul, mind, and heart. Even physically die again. That, of course, was the cruelest part of the punishment—never knowing when you would be killed, but knowing that it would be soon, and perhaps more painful than last time, leaving the cycle to perpetuate itself into eternity.

Only Lucifel could devise such an exquisite torture.

Angela opened her mouth, full of questions, but must have decided to focus instead on what fascinated her most, sitting down next to Sophia and looking at her in wonder like she'd never seen her before. Sophia's face twisted with pain. She was holding back tears, and she set Angela's hand aside. "Day after day, nothing changes. Day after day, I wait for her, and she doesn't come. I was starting to worry that Stephanie would be the One after all."

"You mean the Archon," Angela whispered.

Sophia nodded, one hand against her forehead. "She can set me free. If She wants to."

"But what could you have done? Why are you, out of all the humans who've ever died——why are you being punished like this?"

Then, Kim saw it. A brief and horrible glimpse of something unimaginable appeared behind Sophia's gray eyes, and for that single, long second, they became so deep and hollow, they could have sucked in the universe. Whatever she had done, it had been a sin far beyond simple explanations. He allowed her to speak, overly aware that what was being said would be little more than a half-truth. The whole truth would be too incomprehensible for Angela's ears.

"I died in childbirth."

"You have children?" Angela said, shocked into a murmur. "How many? How long have you been living like this?"

Silence again.

It was clear Sophia wouldn't explain further. Instead, she brought everyone's attention back to where it had first centered, on Kim, her face whipping around to meet his gaze, all her meticulous curls fluffing around her shoulders. Her soft mouth was all smile and no tenderness. Sophia and he were on equal footing now, and she was letting him know it. "I'm not a spy," she said, back to her old calm and confidence, "and I'm not on Stephanie's side. If anything, you're the questionable element, Kim, Sariel. You and your cousin."

"I'm a half-breed," Kim said to Angela, desperate to gain her trust, smart enough to know it could escape at any moment. He was on perilous ground now. "My mother was a human witch— just like Stephanie. My father was a Jinn—just like Troy. He died when I was an adolescent. My given Jinn name is Sariel, but my mother named me Kim. Kimberly." He shrugged, accustomed to the question in her eyes. "It was a common name for boys at the time."

Angela glanced at Nina, worried, but her possessed friend

wasn't saying anything at all, only blinking, listening, and breathing. She turned back to him reluctantly. "How did your father die?"

"I killed him." No point in being evasive, unfortunately . . .

Angela's lower lip trembled. She put her head in her hands.

"He was abusive, Angela. Like only a Jinn can be abusive. Father or not, I think you can understand why I had to put an end to that."

He held the cross at his breast, regretting his inability to tell her more than his own half-truths about its origins the first time she'd questioned him. Her words had unintentionally wounded him that night.

"How long ago was this?" She wasn't looking at him anymore.

"Long. I don't age like you."

A lengthier pause. "Are you really a Vatican novice?"

"I've been part of the Vatican for five hundred years. Emerging onto the scene, disappearing, reappearing later to become a novice all over again, and in that time I've gained a mastery of Latin, and I now know more about angels, demons, Jinn, and the dimensions of Hell than is probably good for me." He ran fingers through the hair in his eyes, shrugging it back. "That knowledge saved my life. The Jinn have been waiting for the Archon for eons ever since Raziel died. And because I knew what to look for and how to find it, Troy had no choice but to let me live until I did."

"She's going to kill you," Angela spoke certainly, "for murdering her uncle . . . but that doesn't seem right. She doesn't seem like the kind of creature that would care what happens to anyone—"

"Not so fast." Kim lifted a finger. "Troy might look savage, she might behave savage, murderous, and evil—but the Jinn are known for two things: determination and loyalty. Both of these combined equal my death sentence." He continued, encouraged by the calm seriousness in Angela's expression. She was listening very carefully, picking apart his every word. "The Jinn have a clan system, and the members of a particular clan—of a family—are expected to adhere to one another like glue. It doesn't matter what the circumstances are. Directly killing a family member is their cardinal sin, punishable by death. Making matters worse, I'm a half-breed. Usually, we're exterminated at birth. In Troy's eyes, I'm an abomination, flawed from the start."

Another sorrow they could both understand. Angela lowered her gaze, pensive.

Nina coughed in the background, suddenly lively. She wasn't shivering anymore and her fever looked like it had faded. Now, she stared at Kim along with everyone else, wide-eyed and grim.

"Why are you and Troy involved in this?" Angela stood up, stalking far enough away so that no one could touch her. "I thought you were looking for the Ruin, the Archon—to kill Her."

"Hardly." He gave Sophia his finest smile, enjoying her silent anger. "I'm on your side," he said to Angela. "If you turn out to be the Archon, of course."

"And if not?"

"Then I suppose you know too much."

The unspoken implications of that hung between them, crushing. Kim didn't want to kill Angela. She was a beautiful young woman, smart, interesting, and talented; and her personality— with all of its raw recklessness—tormented him with curiosity, the desire to delve deeper and deeper. But he'd been disappointed before, and Stephanie was probably the worst disappointment yet; not because she wasn't a candidate, but mostly because her mind was unhinging itself. There would be no cooperation there.

"Well, I changed my mind. I'm not ready to die anytime soon."

Sophia regarded her with surprise. "Is that the truth? You're going to stay?"

Angela shared a brief glance with Kim, as if she either regretted their intimacy or ached for it again, and then walked over to a window, pressing her forehead against the glass. Her voice was almost inaudible. "I can't be responsible for what happens to Nina. Her possession is all my fault."

"No," Nina said. "Not entirely."

Her eyes were such a stark shade of crimson, it almost hurt to look at them. Bloody as the eyes of Lucifel herself. Kim slid out of his chair, strolling closer to the bed until he was leaning over her. Nina turned her face up to follow him, her arms lying peacefully at her sides, her features too content. Then she smiled at him. "Don't try, priest."

"I knew it. Who are you?"

"That's none of your concern."

"Are you working for the Black Prince?"

Nina's smile faded. "I'm not working for anyone."

"You were the one who told the demons that the Archon could be found in this human city, am I right? You told them that Her time was arriving." His tone sounded cooler than even he meant it to be. "That's why they want you out of the picture. You'll complicate their agenda."

"You have no proof."

"Your eyes are proof enough. What do you want? You could have left by now and gone back to the Netherworld."

"*I was never in the Netherworld to begin with.*"

"You're saying you've always been a spirit?"

"Yes."

"Impossible." He leaned in even nearer, but she didn't back away, her face strangely alien and disquieting, as if she didn't quite know how to use it. "Every angel, demon, and human is made of both body and soul. You're no different—unless you're dead, and just a soul."

"I never had a body until recently. And I left it when I found my opportunity." She and Sophia measured each other, and a brightness lit Nina's eyes, as if they'd come to some silent agreement. She then turned back to Kim, oddly dignified. "It is the end, priest. The dead are yearning for release, and only *She* can give it to them. As a spirit, I've wandered all the dimensions and seen the horror that can be ended by Her coming. If I help Her, She will free them, and they will serve Her like no other master. She will take the place of the Supernals and lead like they were never able to."

Angela seemed to step in out of nowhere, her presence breaking the small hold Kim had on the situation. "The Supernals. They are—"

"Israfel, Raziel, and Lucifel. The Angelic Trinity. The pegs on which the universe rests."

"And"—Angela's entire self seemed to be yearning, and her voice shook—"what do you know about them?"

"That one is alive, the other dead, and the last—caged."

Kim had been slowly pulling out the prayer ward in his pocket. Now he unveiled it, waving the paper in front of Nina's possessor. Nina narrowed her red eyes, stung to the core, reading the Latin scribbled on the ward like it was visual poison. Kim brought it closer, forcing her to squirm in the sheets. "Why not just say that you're Lucifel's chick? That the Demon herself is your mother, and that you're rather upset she abandoned you? But it's not very nice to use other people just to slap Mama's hands—"

The angel inside of Nina hissed at him, her frustration eerily similar to Troy's hunger tantrums. "I am no *demon*," she said, her words childishly spiteful.

"I never said that. But I did say that Lucifel is your mother."

Nina turned away, breathing hard.

"Isn't she?" Kim moved the paper closer. "Those red eyes. You can't hide what you are, dear. And here everyone thought you were executed, aborted. I wonder how long you've been floating around, possessing creature after creature, all so that you can see and hear and speak like us? Pathetic—"

"Kim," Angela said, grabbing for his prayer ward. She actually sounded upset, afraid of what his interrogation might do to Nina, to them.

He spread an arm, blocking her from coming any closer. Nina's chest rose and fell, her voice clipped by desperation. This was the dangerous part. "Stop it," she whispered. "You don't know what you're doing . . ."

"What's your name?"

"Never . . ."

He put the prayer ward on her head, eliciting a shriek. Her red eyes flashed, pained. "What is your name?"

"No," she shouted as she twisted, sliding closer to the headboard, "I won't. I won't let you—"

"*Now.*"

The walls shook, vibrating. Crystal vases slid from their shelves and clattered to the floor, some breaking. The candle sputtered, threatening to snuff out. Angela barely flinched, completely absorbed by the spectacle of Nina, her eyes red as a rabbit's, her face still hers and yet not her own, twisting her mouth open and spitting out the name that would free her from Kim's power. "*Mikel. My name is Mikel.*"

He ripped the prayer ward away.

It spun from him, disintegrating into hundreds of tiny pieces. Paper flakes drifted to the floor like snow, snagged in Sophia's hair, and dusted the laces of Angela's boots. Slowly, reluctant to take her eyes off Nina, Angela stooped and began to pick up the broken glass, piece by piece. Her expression was utterly flabbergasted and unsettlingly resigned. Almost against her will, she was becoming used to this.

"Mikel," Kim pressed. "Let Nina go."

"I told you not to try," the angel said, petulant but oppressed by the use of its name. "It's ridiculous to try. You can't evict me. Nina Willis was willing, and now we share a bond."

"Then bring her back, so she can tell us that herself."

"Not yet. Not until you speak to Tileaf."

Tileaf. The world's last surviving Fae Queen. Her tree was the symbol and namesake of Westwood Academy, but it was also cut off from students, novices, and citizens of Luz who weren't in the know and didn't want the burden of living with the knowledge. Tileaf's powers had provided prosperity and power to the Vatican officials at the Academy for a century, and lately they'd been tapping her like a maple, draining all the sap of her energy with the most menial requests or demands. Perhaps exulting in humanity's imminent sufferings, she'd triumphantly revealed to the priests that the Archon would indeed be a woman, and that when the time came, they would be under Her heel like the insects they were.

But to speak with her . . .

It was almost out of the question. Tileaf had no consideration for anything now but death. Actually dying but unable to speed up the process, she hated anything that couldn't grant her the release her heart desired. That, of course, meant most living things.

"Who is Tileaf?" Angela said, and the name rolled off her tongue with reverence. Wonder.

Kim turned from her, missing their tryst, half wishing for all the world to implode. He hadn't counted on one of Lucifel's legendary children to burst out of the past and into his life, and he couldn't understand why it was happening now and not five years ago, ten years ago. Why had Mikel waited until this moment? "Tileaf is a defector from the angelic realm," he said to Angela, trying to bite away his fear. "But you would be more familiar with the term faerie. And she doesn't have any affection for humans. We'll have to take Troy with us."

From the look on Angela's face, that was not what she had in mind.

"I'll stay here," Sophia said, folding her hands on her lap, gazing out at the night. "Naamah and Stephanie won't bother me, but—I'm sure Kim agrees—you and Nina need to leave, Angela."

"Admirable," Kim muttered. "The sacrifice in you."

Sophia sucked in a breath that was more likely her next comment.

Kim walked over and grabbed Angela's hand, kissing it. He couldn't help himself. Not with Sophia so infuriated and Angela standing in front of him, accepting his reverence like she was the true Archon and not merely a human who'd be staring Lucifel's Grail in the literal eye, wobbling on the edge of a terrifying darkness. "Remember," he said to her softly, "that I can protect you. But not against Troy. If you show any signs of weakness, I can't promise your safety. To stand with her, you must think like her."

"And how is that?" Angela said, her face fiercer than she realized. Her hair was like a waterfall of blood, cascading past her shoulders. Long, needle straight, and portentous.

"Hunt hard. Kill swiftly. Waste nothing. And—"

He let her go. It was never good to grow too attached.

"—offer no apologies."

Nineteen

They had a great city, the terror and beauty of the Underworld before a single War crushed it mercilessly. Its name is a prayer to these beings; the distillation of their hopes for vengeance, given only to the most excellent and skilled of their kind. But human language is a poor filter for their alien speech, and so, we must make do with approximations of dreadful things.

—CARDINAL DEMIAN YATES, *A Brief Compendium of Hell and Its Realms*

Troy. The High Assassin of the Jinn.

Thanks to Kim's hasty, half-whispered explanations, Angela had learned before stepping into his cousin's lair that she was the product of a world where compassion equaled death, and hunger steered the soul. Where any weak links weeded themselves out in a vast and intricate darkness. In essence, she was the personification of survival of the fittest.

Through the prism with which Troy saw the world, Angela would show her true colors— either as a help, or a hindrance destined to bleed beneath her nails.

Unfortunately, it was impossible to say which one the Jinn was deciding on at the moment, and Angela's breath stopped, and her heart nearly seized up inside of her as they stood perilously near to one another. Kim had taken Angela up into the Bell Attic at the top of the Tower, where Troy had kept her larder since coming to Luz, stashing her half-eaten bones and body pieces in a space that stank of bat dung and rotten flesh. Up close, she was perhaps even more terrifying and beautiful than in the shadows, the blue veins of her skin taking on the appearance of intricate lacework, her large eyes such a brilliant yellow that they bordered on fluorescent. Every other second, her left ear flicked, swinging a chain earring with a metal crow's foot at its end. Her hair was a short, choppy mess, knotted with tiny bones and teeth, and they rattled softly as she turned her head aside, considering.

"Why did you bring her here?" she said to Kim, her teeth bared.

"We need your help." He actually sounded nervous, and his voice took on that shaky quality it had possessed in the cathedral. Troy must have been spying on them that day. How horrible. "Angela's friend is possessed, Troy."

The Jinn snorted, looking amused. She was reclining like a cat, her wings folded crisply against her back, bones crunching beneath her feet as she shifted position. "Bring her to me. I'll put an end to that quickly enough."

"It's not that simple. She wants us to speak with Tileaf."

Troy's ears flipped back against her skull. An irritated growl rumbled in her throat.

Oh, God. She's not happy. Why did we come here? Why?

The Jinn rocked onto her feet and stood with surprising grace, revealing the flash of a metal chain beneath her rags. There was a glint of an unbelievable green, but it vanished just as quickly. Kim was keeping the light purposefully poor, perhaps to hide much of the carnage around them, and perhaps for Troy's sensitive eyes. But even this wasn't enough, and whenever the candle flickered, she hissed as if it were a flame pressed to her skin. "The Fae will murder you the second you step within her reach," she snapped at Angela, "and then Sariel can mop up your blood with his priestly coat. Perhaps he hasn't told you, but for years he's used her leaves to make exorcism wards."

"What a bitch you are tonight." Kim's eyes brightened with spite.

Now the cut on his cheek explained itself. Judging by the little snarl in his voice, Angela suspected these arguments were day-to-day affairs. Kim wasn't a full-blooded Jinn, and he could hide whatever nastiness he'd inherited from them, but Angela was smart enough to know he'd certainly slipped every now and then. Hopefully she wouldn't be there the next time his confident and calm demeanor collapsed.

"Oh, the truth hurts, doesn't it?" Troy spat, laughing. "But the fact remains, if you weren't such an abusive bastard, things wouldn't be so hard now, would they? Remind you of anyone, Sariel? Those old tales of your father come to mind."

Angela stepped forward, eager to make her presence better known.

She thought otherwise almost instantly.

Troy leaped for him, her wings beating so powerfully that bats spiraled out of the tower, shrieking in alarm. Fury burst through their black cloud, landing beside Angela to cheer on her master to victory, croaking with dark excitement.

She's going to tear his throat open.

Her nails were inches from his neck.

Kim thrust out his hand, muttering a Latin phrase that sounded more like a wish than a prayer.

Troy swerved, landing so that her left pinions rubbed like sandpaper against Angela's tights. Despite the feathers, her wing felt hard and overly muscular, probably painful if it hit you the wrong way.

Troy laughed again, her teeth catching the candlelight. Kim must have worked some kind of magic, because miraculously, the wick had stayed lit.

"You're such a weak coward," the Jinn hissed, regaining her old anger. "Why not fight me like the man you claim to be for a change? Give me something to do other than eat your girlfriends."

Troy rounded on Angela, sniffing, her teeth wet with saliva. Her eyes narrowed, maybe fatally. "You smell wrong," she said, ears cocking forward.

Kim's face said it all. *Don't move.*

Angela's knees shook, and she locked them together, conscious of her beating heart, her breath, the all-too-sudden silence. Fury strutted away into the dark corners of the Bell Attic, tugging at something hidden behind the actual bell. They were so high up above Luz that when the wind whistled again, gusting through the openings and back out into the night, it came with a blast of unbelievable coldness. How tired she was. Aching for sleep, selfishly disappointed that Nina was possessed by the Devil's spawn rather than the beautiful angel she loved.

"What are you?" Troy said softly. She seemed amazed by something.

"I'm a human."

"I mean *you*," the Jinn shot back, instantly annoyed. She circled Angela like a prowling lion. "*You. Your inner self.*"

"The Archon?" Kim said.

Troy glared at him, her hair standing on end. "She smells wrong, Sariel. She's wrong inside."

Tell me something I don't know already.

"And how is that?" Angela dared to say. Her exhaustion was overriding her common sense.

Troy hissed, ignoring her. "Angels don't smell like this."

"Well, then your nose is wrong for once," Kim said, his tone cool. "You saved her from the water—and yet you wait until now—"

"The water hid the scent," Troy snarled at him, equally cool. "Did you ever consider, cousin, that maybe *you're* wrong? That your *human prophecy* is wrong. Maybe Raziel is the spirit protecting the Archon. Maybe the Archon itself is something else entirely."

"Like what?" He crossed his arms, waiting.

Troy let out a long sigh, flexing her wings. Then she turned from Angela, obviously thinking, but in a Jinn way that dropped her back onto the floor, sitting on her haunches to lick her nails. If she could also smell Nina waiting for them on the lower stairs, she barely showed a sign of it. Instead she lifted her head, catching the next breeze and its various scents, as if they could help her with whatever new decision she was trying to make. Kim watched her cautiously, waving Angela off from approaching any closer. Finally, Troy spoke again, and she actually sounded tired. "She can't stay. We must get rid of her."

Angela's throat went dry. She turned to Kim, trying to get the message across without saying a word. Death wasn't part of her plans anymore.

He stared at her, apologetic, but inched closer to Troy than was probably wise. Her nails scraped into the stone, like she was holding back her desire to rip out his spine.

"That's too drastic."

Troy spun back around, her wings beating the air violently. "Too drastic? And so says the man who would be smart to prolong his search. I'm wondering—what tricks do you have up your sleeve? Why not kill her and wait a thousand more years? This is your Earth, not mine." Her expression was chillingly indifferent. "And I could care less if it cracks like a hollow bone."

"I'm not saying that she's special—"

That's not what he said the other night. My dreams . . .

"—but it would be stupid to kill her just because she smells different, Troy. One of Lucifel's chicks has found her—" He stepped nearer. "There has to be a reason—"

Troy's hair bristled even more frighteningly. "Don't say that name in my presence—"

"Try this, and I'll make sure they exorcise you." His pale face became cold, unreadable.

"Oh, the priests?" Troy was a terrible spectacle now, all sleek rage and beautiful anger. Like a nightmare Angela never wanted to end. Maybe it was those glowing eyes, the way they sucked you into themselves and dismissed you just as easily. "And what then? The minute they send me back, I'll begin my return, and there will be no second chances for you that time, cousin." Her tone of voice was promising and hungry. "First, I'll take them down, one by one—send them to the second death where my relatives await—and then I'll come after you, and I swear by all the hunger inside of me that my retribution will hurt."

Silence. Kim breathed heavily, but he said nothing.

"The last thing we need," Troy whispered, "is a problem on our hands, and no time to fix it. We do the smart thing. She dies. Now." She composed herself, settling her wings against her back, turning back to Angela at last. "Any final requests? This is going to be quick."

"Yes, actually I'd like you to change your mind."

"Not about to happen." Troy's upper lip quivered. "You have five minutes to hide somewhere if you want. It would be more entertaining than just walking up and slitting your throat."

"You're not doing this."

Troy's eyes brightened, her smile deadly. "No? And how do you propose to stop me?"

"I don't know, but I'm going to."

"Ah, the reluctant victim," the Jinn said, slipping into the shadows like smoke. "But I doubt you'll even know what hit you . . ."

Kim's anger was out in the open now. "You should never have opened your mouth—"

Scrabbling. The soft sound of laughter amid the wind. Troy was above them somewhere.

"What do I do?" Angela said, frantic. "How do I fight her off?"

"You can't. You can't do a goddamned thing."

"Can't you?" she screamed back at him.

"Do you think it will make a difference?" He gestured wildly at the darkness around them, but made no move to come any closer. When she realized why, it felt like all the life had already drained out of her. He was resigning himself to her death. She could see it in the new and shockingly distant expression on his face. "She'll just murder you the next second I close my eyes," he whispered. "It will either end here, or somewhere worse."

Feathers rustled overhead. Angela looked up, only to see Fury gazing at her sympathetically.

"At least hide," Kim said, despair in his voice. It was obvious he couldn't help her without paying for his actions later anyway—and Angela understood his reasoning. Her death would be a blow, but not as terrible as one from Troy. He must have gone through this enough times that hoping for the best was no longer an option. "What the hell are you doing—"

"Time's up." The Jinn dropped from the darkness, a maelstrom of feathers and incredible menace, leaving Angela less than a breath to dodge her. But Troy was enjoying the chase, and she let her escape, toying with her like a cat.

Angela backed into the corner where Fury had been tugging at her prize.

Maribel's corpse knocked into her boots. She was half eaten, her rib cage exposed, and such a mess of blood that it was impossible to stare without throwing up. Angela choked down the bile rising into her mouth, desperately trying to regain her sanity. Troy continued to pace nearer and nearer, her expression now more business than games. For all her nasty sarcasm, she took murder seriously. Like Kim said, there would be no apologies.

She's just like any other predator. Beautiful and a hundred times smarter, but still a predator. Even if she's immortal, she can die. She has weaknesses, limitations.

The problem would be figuring them out in the space of a few seconds.

She remembered Kim's own attempt to save himself.

Latin. It hurts her.

But Angela didn't know any Latin. Except . . .

Anything. Anything is better than nothing.

"*Omnes relinquite spes,*" Angela shouted.

Troy shuddered like she'd been rapped on the knuckles. Her lip quivered up again, revealing her glistening teeth. "That was uncalled for," she said, still advancing, though slower than before.

Bind her. You can Bind her to yourself.

But how?

You know how . . . you made the Rules, after all.

These thoughts. They had her voice, her inflections—yet—

Angela gasped. It took less than a moment, but in that blinding flash of time she held Kim's book again, gazing into the pages where the illustration of the Jinn gazed back at her, dark and terrible. The Binding. Its every word and intricate detail hovered before her anew, completely and mysteriously understandable, as if she'd known the ritual forever, merely forgetting for a convenient length of time.

As if she'd written the words herself.

A hideous growl interrupted her vision.

Troy bounded across the gap between them and lifted into the air, descending with her wings wide and her hand pulled back, ready to strike. One blow would be enough to push Angela out of the picture permanently.

But now Angela was ready.

She grabbed a bone shard lying on the floor, lifting it just in time to collapse beneath Troy's fury, her strong, relentless wing beats. Angela was almost crushed, given no space to breathe, the Jinn's sharp nails biting through the thin fabric of her blouse. Blood welled beneath them, soaking into the cloth and warming her skin, but she'd made her mark. Troy's hand had been sliced wickedly along the palm.

The Jinn wrenched the makeshift knife from her hand. It clattered across the floor, unreachable.

Then the world was feathers, shadows, and pain. The worst Angela had ever felt.

She fought off her dizziness and pressed the Jinn's bony hand tighter to the blood on her chest.

"You are Bound," she hissed back at Troy.

They were face-to-face, and the Jinn's eyes narrowed in rage. She attempted to free herself, but Angela held her tight, as if they were lovers. She was literally embracing Death, and Death would either be hers or rip her heart out if she made a single mistake.

"You are Bound, and I am the one Binding you. We are One now in blood, according to the Law."

This sounds right. It's right.

"The Creature is under my command. To assist when I ask in my need, to destroy when I demand to be avenged—"

"*You're done, you bitch,*" Troy screamed at her, nightmarish with rage.

Yet her strength wasn't what it had been before. Angela's words were draining her.

Angela wrestled her tighter, locking her violently like she was a dog beneath a chokehold. Troy's voice was weaker now, but just as deadly. "I told you," she screeched to Kim, "that she should *die*. She's a danger—"

"To be released," Angela murmured into her long ear, "when I request death at last."

Troy stiffened, frozen by her words. A deep quiet filled the Bell Attic, and they gazed into each other's eyes, both of them overwhelmed by the invisible tethers connecting their souls. Then Angela let her go, and Troy backed away, injured within and without. Her expression was that of a person violated. If Angela ever did release her, they both knew she'd be destined to die just as the Binding had warned. She now had a guardian, but one tied to her by force rather than affection—and she could barely explain how it had happened.

Kim's wide eyes were like golden pools, reflecting every bit of light.

He must have certainly thought of Binding his cousin, but he'd also never been stupid enough to try. Now it was hard to tell who he feared more.

Angela stood and brushed the bat feces off her skirt, her tights, her arm gloves. She was a real mess now, her shirt torn and bloody and her hair tangled all over again by the wind. She kicked some of Troy's bones away, pointing at the Jinn. "And now, you're going to take me to Tileaf," she said, still gasping for breath, "and you're going to make sure that Fae doesn't strike me dead."

Troy's wings snapped shut, echoing her anger. Surprisingly, a terrible smile crept across her face.

She reached beneath the rags covering her chest.

What is she doing? She can't hurt me with weapons now.

That was the Law, both according to Kim's book and Angela's own instincts.

Yet Troy was acting like whatever she was about to reveal would hurt Angela even more than death. "Looks like you're going to release me sooner than you expected," Troy said, her words escaping her like evil steam.

Then it appeared, swinging at the end of the crude chain around her neck.

It was a gemstone more like a living eye than a crystal, its surface all emerald green iris and a pupil so dark it seemed fathomless. Kim was shouting something, but his voice grew fainter and fainter, while Angela's mind sank deeper and deeper, falling into this cold Eye that watched her and the universe with an unnameable intelligence. All her wishes, dreams, and hopes seemed to swirl inside of it, and they flashed back at her, teasing and threatening to drive her mad under the power that they held. Had her soul ever felt so dark? Had anything ever held meaning other than this? Her brain felt like mush, and she was going mad for a single unbearable second, every element of existence suffocating her in a boundless ring.

She was as astonished as everyone else when she strode up to Troy and ripped the Eye from her hand.

It glazed over, returning to a blind rock.

Troy went rigid as a cadaver. She slowly turned to Kim, but his face was almost the same shade of white.

Angela slipped the chain around her neck. She and Troy were eye to eye once again. "It looks like this is mine."

No one said a word the entire journey to Memorial Park.

Nina—or Mikel—shuffled quietly behind everyone, gazing at the bridges and the rickety buildings, tiptoeing through puddles like she'd never encountered water before, taking the strangest pleasure in a rumble of thunder or the drone of the rain. Deeper and deeper, they descended into the lowest levels of Luz, tapping down slick stairways and taking side routes through stone tunnels only Kim seemed to know, the rats and roaches skittering away from their shoes and his light. Tileaf's tree was the centerpiece of the Academy, yet it couldn't be more hidden from the public, stuffed away in a crumbling, gated courtyard on the western outskirts of the school. When Kim stopped to open that gate—an enormous fence of iron with a tree engraved on the center lock—Angela was greeted with a grove even more dismal than the overgrown flower beds behind her parents' mansion. Weeds and bushes tangled in and out of each other, their branches scraggly with neglect, scratching against the high stone of the walls. Poison ivy crawled up trunks of ancient maple and oak. The wind barely had a chance to filter down or toss foliage onto the moldy earth, and trees stood in clumps of unbearable, stuffy darkness, their leaves either bloody or black in the terrible light. Straight ahead, a tunnel made of embracing tree branches bored to the center of the grotto.

The path to Tileaf's oak was more inhospitable and gray than gravel; nothing but dirt, puddles, chunks of old cobblestones, and the fog curling beneath a steady haze of rain. Kim started down the pathway with a sigh, pushing Angela back when she tried to step ahead of him.

Without warning, Troy peered from a spot in the trees, glowering at her.

Shortly after, the Jinn scampered away into the darkness, twigs popping beneath the weight of her feet and hands.

Kim's next sigh was heavier than ever. "You should never have Bound her to you."

Jealous. He might actually be jealous.

"What is this thing?" Angela plucked at the Eye lying against her chest. The chain felt like a rope of ice around her neck. "She thought it would kill me, or make me crazy."

"You're already crazy," Kim said softly, "just like you warned."

Or maybe he feels guilty about giving me up for dead. I know I certainly would.

"Does it have something to do with the Archon?"

"We never said you're the Archon, Angela."

"Then explain how I Bound Troy and stayed sane when she waved this in front of my face."

Kim unbuttoned his white collar. His sculpted cheekbones seemed to glow, full of moonlight that didn't exist, a trait he'd probably inherited from his father. It seemed the corpselike pallor of a Jinn's skin had its own special beauty. "It doesn't make sense," he said, but as quietly as if he were talking to himself. "The Archon is a reincarnation of Raziel, an angel. And you have his blood-red hair, his blue eyes, his memories, but—"

"You could be wrong."

He examined her sharply. "What?"

"You could be wrong, just like Troy said. Maybe the Archon has Raziel's features and memories because he's possessing her, but she's actually a reincarnation of someone else. Maybe he gave the Archon his features so that she'd be recognized as someone important—so that everyone would think she's Raziel—because that was the person they remembered. Because they'd never seen the other one."

Kim shook his head. He shivered a little. "There is no one else. Mikel said it herself. Israfel is alive and Lucifel is caged. That leaves us with Raziel."

"Is there someone more powerful than them?"

He laughed. "God."

He must be right then. There is no one else. But I know I'm not Raziel, even though he must be protecting me from killing myself.

"Kim."

"What is it?" He continued to pace ahead of her, tall and blurred by the fog. The tone of his voice wasn't encouraging, but Angela couldn't stop herself anymore. Some secrets had to come out in the open.

"I never really thought about this. I mean, it happened only once that I can remember—"

He stopped, turning around to face her. Branches framed his strong figure, groping like skeletal arms. He appeared tense again, waiting for anything.

But could he even be surprised at this point?

"When I was eleven years old," Angela said, "I tried to kill myself with a gun. It didn't work, like always, but the pistol kicked back, and I knocked myself unconscious. Like I explained to you before, whenever I was unconscious, I would dream. And almost always I dreamed of the angels you saw in my paintings. But that time—was different from all the rest."

Angela wrapped her arms around her shoulders.

She could still hear the gun firing, the sound of it almost bursting her eardrums.

"Go on," Kim said gently. The park could have been waiting with him, its silence suggesting that even the trees listened and considered.

"It was only for a minute, but I thought I saw another angel. He said something to me, which was strange, because the others never spoke to me at all. But it's been so long—and I was so disappointed with surviving . . . I can't remember what it was, or if he really said anything in the first place. If that makes any sense."

"So you've seen three angels?" The way Kim stared at her, she felt like Troy was crushing her all over again.

"I guess."

"But you can't remember a single detail of what he said? Even the feelings he tried to communicate to you?"

"Maybe . . . that I had to stay alive." Angela examined her hands, and it seemed impossible that she'd ever held a gun at all. "Because people needed me."

"Then why did you keep trying to kill yourself?"

She turned from him and faced the gate to the park, its iron bars faintly discernible in the mist. Nina approached them slowly, still keeping a safe distance from Kim, her eyes glowing like crimson dots. "If you had been in my position, you'd have known it was a lie."

So an angel didn't want her to die. But now Angela knew there was much more behind that than kindness. From what she'd seen of Troy and Naamah, and even Mikel, real angels didn't care about you. Not as much as they cared about what you could do for them. The situation was searingly ironic. And even more ironic, the closer Angela crept toward being the Archon, the more Kim had started to disbelieve. Either he was afraid the search might be over, perhaps because it meant Troy's teeth in his neck, or he didn't want anything bad to happen to her.

His kiss met the top of her hair, followed by the warmth of his arms, embracing her from behind. "Don't take my actions in the chapel the wrong way. I didn't want you to die. I just try not to get attached anymore."

"Then why do you look at me like that?"

But the more he looked, the more it felt right. And the more Angela learned about angels, the more it felt foolish to love an elegant, dazzling creature who would probably never love her in return.

Angela had given up suicide, dreams, and family. Now she was even giving up on her angels despite being closer to them than ever.

She barely knew herself anymore.

Kim sighed in her hair. "I thought I had everything figured out, and you're changing that for me yet again." His thin lips touched her cheek. "Don't mistake me—I want you to be the Archon, Angela. You and I work well together. In fact, we're a lot alike."

"How?" she said, truly desperate to know.

"Well—" Kim tugged her by the hand, urging her to keep walking. "Both of us have suffered from prejudice and abuse because of how different we look. My mother and I"—his tone became grim—"we were cast out of village after village because of me. They said I was a child of the Devil—which wasn't so far off. But my mother deserved a little better than that."

Village after village. A child of the Devil.

Kim was conjuring a world of superstition and witchcraft that had only recently returned. How old was he? Hundreds of years . . . and yet he hadn't grown tired of living yet. That fact was almost as incomprehensible as his paternity.

"—and then there is the matter of your parents. You were so appalled that I killed my father, yet you've done exactly the same—"

"It wasn't the same." Angela let go of his hand. Tileaf's oak loomed ahead, its massive trunk seeming to grow the closer they came until it was thicker than seven people could hug with their arms touching finger to finger. Branches grew from it in a gnarled mess that spread almost as far as the roots, their thick bark coiling and curling through the strong-smelling earth like sea serpents. The tree was dying, but sparse tufts of brown and green leaves still clung to it, rustling in the slightest breeze. There was a silence here that hinted of death and sickness. Every spoken word felt like a sin. "It wasn't the same at all."

"You mean they didn't deserve to die for how they treated you? I *know* they abused you."

His cool face questioned her, wondering.

Angela stopped to let Mikel walk ahead of them, the angel's red eyes gathering in the tree with awe. "But that's where you and I differ, Kim. They didn't deserve to die." Angela slipped the Eye beneath her blouse, letting its chill touch her heart. For once, her bitterness felt like it belonged. "They deserved worse."

Her lips said it like a prayer.

"They deserved to suffer."

Twenty

From the highest of heights they fell;
Stars longing to clothe themselves in Nature's garb.
Fairest of creatures who dance on mortal Earth,
Are those Untamable Ones who sing of the trees.
—Various authors, *Songs of the Fair Folk*

"When Tileaf appears don't act frightened . . . or show that you're
upset . . ."

". . . is she in pain, dying like this . . ."

"Torture . . . would be the better word . . ."

Troy etched the Blood Circle into the dirt, directly in front of
the Fae Queen's tree, trying her damnedest not to run over and rip
Sariel's mouth out of his head. His every word annoyed her, her
palm twitched from the cut Angela had dared to inflict on her, and
her pride wasn't doing so well either. She traced lines through the
soil, finger shaking, drawing the sigils that would protect the bitch
from the harm she deserved.

Angela might have been possessed by an angel. But she wasn't
an angel herself.

Sariel didn't understand, partly because he didn't have the nose
of a full-blooded Jinn. Angela was all wrong, twisted and warped,
and her soul's scent resembled both the freshness of a spring-fed
pool and the most oppressive darkness Troy could remember.
Worst of all, she'd known how to consummate a Binding, which

wouldn't have been such a miracle if it were on any other Jinn. But Troy, as the Underworld's most skilled hunter, its High Assassin, had more than enough power to ward off such a trick. Angela might as well have clipped her ears and caged her—which was absolutely unthinkable. Yet she'd been forced into a bond she'd never wanted, leaving her in a numb state that would turn into a rage hell-bent on killing for killing's sake.

If she couldn't snap Angela's neck, someone else would have to die. That was for damned sure.

Troy tucked away her next angry hiss, feigning indifference.

Angela sat next to Kim on top of one of Tileaf's roots, her possessed friend resting behind them in the leaf litter. Often, she would stare at Troy, intensely interested in what she was writing, and then Troy would merely spread her wings, turning them into a mantle that blocked her view.

This was more than spite.

The bitch had also taken Lucifel's Grail.

It had been a miracle more heartstopping than surviving Troy's attack. But it also left unsettling questions lingering in its wake. If Angela wasn't the Archon, then why could she stare into the Eye without disaster? Troy wanted answers now as badly as Sariel and the angel who'd possessed that frazzled human, Nina Willis. Troy now remembered hunting her once, but turning away in disgust when she saw how broken her prey was inside. Depression was the worst seasoning for any meal.

"Done," she snapped, lifting off from the ground to recline on a nearby tree limb. She settled her wings back into place, ruffling them slightly beneath the cool rain.

Sariel stood beneath her tree, gazing up at Troy and her hand dangling over the bark. Her left leg had bent beneath her a little—a cushion.

She couldn't stand the sight of him. "*Now what do you want?*"

"Aren't you forgetting something?"

"Whatever do you mean? I don't quite follow," she said. His danger would be obvious from her tone of voice.

"The sigils mean nothing without blood, Troy."

The muscles in her ears and wings tensed. "Then tell Angela to use her own. She seems competent to me. Full of shit and water. So, likely full of blood."

His teeth set. "You and your foul mouth."

"Oh, I have plenty of reasons to curse." She bounded from the branch, landing beside him, spraying leaves in every direction. How empty she felt without the Grail around her neck. For the Jinn it was a privilege even to look upon it, and yet despite their race's legendary toughness, there were few who could tolerate its watchful presence. Troy had been one of those few. Her sister, the other. "If I had known you'd brought that meat sack to Bind me, I would have killed you both the moment you entered the room."

"I didn't bring her to Bind you. I brought her to look at the Grail, Troy."

"Yes," she spat back at him, "and now she's stolen it."

"Taken it."

"*She's not the Archon.*"

"We don't know what in hell she is right now, and if you don't awaken Tileaf before Naamah weeds this garden, we might never know. That Circle would bleed us dry. So why can't you just cooperate and slit your damned wrist, and then, by all means crawl back beneath the rock you slid out of." His smile was intended to infuriate her. "Back to your real Hell."

"And yet," she clicked her teeth at him, "mine is only temporary."

Now Sariel's smile wavered.

Troy shoved him out of the way, stomping over to the Circle and the carefully arranged patterns in the dirt. Once she was standing in their center, she reached for the obsidian dagger strapped to her thigh, slid it from its sheath of rags, and cut a long but clean wound up to her elbow. Her blood dribbled into the circle, outlining her furrows with a red that bordered on black.

She cleaned the injury, licking her teeth for Angela's sake.

". . . why the blood?" Angela whispered to Sariel, doing her best to avoid eye contact with Troy, probably hoping she couldn't hear.

Oh, but she could hear.

"You have to think of the Fae as carnivorous plants . . ."

Nina closed her eyes, coughing like the smell of the blood stifled her. More likely it stifled the angel.

"Blood provides nutrients they must otherwise live without . . ."

It began.

Twigs snapped, scratching against rough bark. Wood creaked. The trees were coming to life under a strong, supernatural breeze, waving and dancing, and Troy raced up the nearest trunk for a safer view, clinging to a thick branch while it groaned beneath her. A dim green glow flashed throughout the great clearing around Tileaf's tree, highlighting every crumpled leaf.

Shortly afterward, the Fae materialized. She was a ravaged mess with a leash of light wrapped around her slender neck, her spring green wings and voluminous hair disheveled from constant pain. Like all angels she had been imposing once, perfect as only they could be perfect. But now, blood streaked her spider-silk train, most of it her own, and her feathers either drifted into the dirt like her leaves or quivered pitifully, twisted from the priests' ritualistic cruelty.

"*You*," she said, her words thick with hatred.

She'd spotted Sariel almost immediately.

"You have your leaves, *priest*. What do you want from me now?" She swayed, dizzy from awakening, but energy snapped around her body nevertheless.

Miniature lightning bolts rocketed in his direction.

They crackled against the barrier Troy had set up, dissipating into harmless tendrils, the force behind them fanning Sariel's longer hair behind his neck. Troy opened her eyes wider, no longer pained by the light, happily gloating at the sight of Angela, aghast. This was not the type of faerie she'd obviously expected. Not a bird with its wings broken by her cage, lashing out at them desperately. Tileaf groaned, as if the barrier had wounded her more than Sariel's survival, and she slumped against the trunk of her tree, heaving for breath.

Nina stood up, more anguished than Angela. "Vevaliah," she said sorrowfully.

Tileaf regarded her with agony, gasping. Then she noticed Nina's red eyes and stiffened with dawning comprehension. "Who are you?"

"Mikel. One of Raziel and Lucifel's chicks."

There was a long and strange silence.

"That . . ." The Fae whitened in her face, seeming afraid. ". . . that cannot be."

Mikel lowered her head, shaking it. "What have they done to you? Were you not Israfel's favored one? Why did you defect?"

"That heaven was a hell," Tileaf whispered shakily. "You of all angels should know that . . ."

"More than here?"

The Fae shut her eyes. Her mouth twisted with anger. "If you can't kill me, then leave. I have so little time left. So little of everything. They're gone. All of my children. I am the *last*."

Mikel stepped forward, her hands uplifted in supplication. "Then, please, show them! Show them what you remember of the Supernals. There must be others to remember for you, Vevaliah, when you have passed on. The moment is a crucial one, you know this."

Tileaf closed her eyes again, behaving like the merest mention of the past crushed her. When she reopened them, she gazed intently at Angela, almost hopeful. "Are you Her?"

Her tone left hardly any room for a no.

"The Ruin . . ." Angela turned aside, growing more and more upset by the sight of the shattered faerie standing in front of her. "I—I don't know. But I have memories of these Supernals . . . Two of them. And"—she lifted the Grail into the open—"this—"

Troy cursed under her breath. The stone was not for the curiosity of others.

"—whatever it is."

The Fae's eyes widened, reflecting the green of the more watchful Eye in all its terrible beauty. It spun in front of her, glinting and almost intelligent. "Lucifel's Grail." Her words were heavy things, escaping her with a visible effort. "She gave it to Raziel as a gift, shortly before the Celestial Revolution in Heaven. It is a dreaded object . . . cursed from spilling the blood of countless angels. Put it away, *now*. It should never be out in the open for long."

Angela tucked the Eye under her shirt, troubled. "Spilling blood?"

Tileaf nodded and leaned her head back against the tree trunk. "Using the Grail, Lucifel would conjure the Glaive. Her most terrible weapon, though she probably had no need of it. It was rumored to have the power of cutting through anything . . . anything in the universe, even substances that could not otherwise be cut." The Fae's expression became more distant and haunted. "Why she gave such an object to Raziel was beyond our understanding, though many said it was a lover's gift. He then handed it to the Jinn shortly before his . . . death. It can only be used by those who carry the spirit of the Supernals—"

Making Angela's strangeness all the more discouraging—as there were only three.

"Raziel," Tileaf continued, "Israfel, and Lucifel."

"What is it though? A stone?"

Tileaf shivered all over. "Perhaps. But I am glad it is no longer before me."

Angela stood with Kim, her face bland, but her stance firm. "Show me. I need to see them for myself. The Supernals." She edged nearer to Tileaf, fascinated by her beauty, but with all the foolishness of any other human, her fingers aching to touch or stroke. "I'm sorry about what happened to you here. I am—"

Tileaf swallowed, pained. She could barely disguise her disgust. Angela was human, a member of the race responsible for more than half of the Fae's earthly torments, and she had less than little to offer for this kind of service. But the spirit inside of Nina was right. This was also Tileaf's last chance to pass on memories that few angels had survived to record, and perhaps to the person who could help her most. So she eventually looked at Angela again, making it clear that Angela and Angela alone had a place in her consideration. "You will not understand all that you see." Her words were like a dire warning. "You will be entering *my* memories and thoughts, and because I am not human . . . this experience will be very unlike what you're probably expecting. It might affect you for quite a while."

"That's fine," Angela said.

"Yet, before we continue," Tileaf said as her fine brow creased, "you must promise me something in exchange."

"All right."

"If you are truly the Archon, as soon as you are granted the opportunity—you must kill me without any hesitation."

Silence.

Angela covered her face with her hands and took a deep breath. Another. Time passed and Sariel began to move nearer to her, perhaps fearing she'd fainted from shock. But then, with all the suddenness of a sparking flame, her face reappeared between the screen of her fingers, and her expression was one of steely resolve. "If that's what you want, I'll do it. It's only fair."

Troy flicked her ears, unable to hide her interest in where the conversation had turned.

Sariel had wisely stepped back into the background for the time being, but now he glanced at Troy with an eyebrow raised, echoing her surprise, both of them putting aside their mutual hatred long enough to quietly concur that whatever Angela might be, she was more than either of them could have hoped for or suspected. It couldn't make up for the indignity of a Binding, but it was at least enough to earn the tiniest measure of respect.

Tileaf's expression was eagerly keen as she beckoned to Angela. "Then we are agreed. Now come here, as close as you can. We must be touching . . . for this to work."

Her disgust, it seemed, would have to rest for now.

Angela reached out, stretching her hand toward the Fae, Troy's barrier shimmering like water as her arm passed through it. They were inches apart. Less than a breath.

Then their fingertips met, and she dropped to the ground, senseless.

Twenty-one

I am a demon. I have willingly gone down into darkness.
Yet there is an Abyss that even I have not dared peer into.
—THE DEMON PYTHON, TRANSCRIBED FROM *The Lies of Babylon*

First there was a void.

Then there were three thrones. And three Angels sat upon them.

The first and highest, seated above the others and above all the stars that spread into the sky, was Angela's beautiful angel. He was more dazzling than in any dream she could remember, though right now she could remember none, and his hair and wings gleamed with a bronze that put the purest of metals to shame. His large sapphire eyes, like pools bluer than the richest seawater, considered everything below him with delicate pride, and his lips, pink and thin, filled her with want and endless desire. On top of his head, he wore a crown that resembled a vertical halo of crystal, its spindles likened to silvery rays, and below, near his winged ears, glass serpents dangled tongues of ruby.

He was dressed in crimson, the fabric hiding his body from ankles to neck to wrist, and yet all was revealed, because she wanted all.

For the briefest second, he opened his mouth and sang, and Angela sensed things around her connecting and reshaping themselves into other, more perfect things. He was the Creator

Supernal, that was what Tileaf's memories were saying, and he ruled because all who loved him wanted him to rule. And they were the majority.

This, she understood, was Israfel.

"In the ancient days of angelic history—"

Tileaf's voice seemed to echo from an impossible distance, her words more like images that explained themselves through infusion.

"—God created three great children called the Supernals. Israfel, Raziel, and Lucifel. Creator, Preserver . . . and Destroyer. While all three shared equal power and influence, Israfel gradually rose to great favor . . . and was named Heaven's first ruling Archangel. But although we refused to acknowledge a problem then, it soon became clear that a confrontation between him and Lucifel was inevitable. She had always been a solitary creature, but after Israfel's coronation, an even greater and more impassable rift formed between them . . ."

But, like she had first seen, he was not alone.

Below him sat a shadow.

This shadow gazed up at him with open scorn and contempt, more disgusted than jealous, as if she could see flaws that no one else bothered to pick apart. This was Lucifel, the Devil herself before she threw down a third of the stars from Heaven, and she sat with a languid callousness that emptied the heart and the soul and spit it back into the void. Where Israfel was softness and sensual perfection, she was hard lines, her skin paler than fog, and her eyes redder than blood.

Gray.

Dust. She was ash, smoke, and vapor. The Destroyer Supernal's wings and hair gathered about her like a mist, and her clothing was the opposite of Israfel's, a careless swathe of fabric barely hiding her bloodless white limbs and shining feet. Around her neck, she wore the Grail, and the Eye seemed more alive than ever, blinking at the universe and sucking away its life.

Lucifel was living death.

There was a vacancy inside of her that was growing and no one knew when it would stop, and Angela could sense millions flocking to her because she had the power to take away life as if that were ecstasy, and they exulted in that darkness . . .

". . . Raziel, who cared for them both, found himself acting as an intermediary. And so, the first step toward disaster occurred after his brief but unexpected absence. With Raziel gone, the civility he'd nurtured disintegrated rapidly. And by the time he reappeared, Heaven's loyalties had been split in two. To be honest . . . a great many of us found Lucifel unapproachable, her ideas too heretical—and against Israfel's powerful charisma she might have stood little chance. But he had changed after Raziel's return . . . And when Israfel's confident behavior faltered, so did the trust of thousands . . ."

One alone gazed at Lucifel with pity.

Angela herself.

Or rather, an angel with Angela's large blue eyes and deep red hair. He was dressed in a coat of midnight blue, its silver embroidery seeming to be made of light plucked from the heavens, and jewels that resembled stars swept beneath his brow line and up onto the mysterious wings that were also his ears. His pinions were larger than Israfel's and Lucifel's, a beautiful blood red, and the stiff feathers over his wing bones drooped heavily beneath silver cuffs.

Gentleness shone in his expression, and he glanced from Israfel to Lucifel and back again with a sad premonition in his smile. Wiser than either of them, he seemed to know that his affection could never mend the hatred that was darkening Heaven.

This was the Preserver Supernal, and Angela felt all his stability and reassurance, relaxed in the blessing of his presence.

Until he did the unthinkable and flew from his throne, diving into the abyss . . .

"The situation only grew worse from there . . . for very soon afterward, Lucifel was found pregnant with Raziel's chicks, and mating is forbidden between male and female angels, let alone siblings, unless the union has been approved. As you can imagine,

Israfel did not take the news well. Not only had Lucifel betrayed his crown, she'd taken a brother away from him. And Raziel, by all appearances, had picked his ultimate side . . ."

Then a great horror appeared in Heaven: Lucifel, sweeping her Glaive—a dreadful weapon that seemed made more of blood than iron—and the stars blinking away into darkness beneath her lack of compassion. She walked among angels of all descriptions and genders, perfect or deformed, and those who refused to bow to her blade were cut down ruthlessly. Behind her, amid a sky that was green with evil storms and also black with their clouds, great serpents twisted through the ether, clearing vast flocks of angels with their fearsome jaws.

The vision was familiar and yet terribly alien, as Tileaf had warned, and Angela found relief again only when the scene changed to that of the Destroyer Supernal, gazing down at the blood she had so wantonly spilled. Completely unsympathetic . . .

Utterly vanquished inside.

"It was the Celestial Revolution. The chicks—it was long said—had been torn from Lucifel's body and aborted, and rather than suffer any more punishment or humiliation, she'd summoned the cult that worshipped her to rebellion. An infamous rebellion . . . and also the beginning of Raziel's final hours. The battle was reaching its climax when he crossed the bridge to Ialdaboth, the highest dimension of Heaven, to speak with God, presumably about an end to what Raziel termed a useless battle . . .

The verdict must have driven him mad . . ."

Now, a scene of almost unimaginable bloodshed.

Angels tearing down other angels with energy and ether and weapons that glittered like crystal but cut with the cruelty of ice. They tumbled and screamed in agony, feathers falling throughout Heaven like snow, and behind them, plummeting from a bridge that rose to the spire of the material universe, its gables made of pearlescent glass—Raziel, his face blank with terror and pain.

His wings were shredded. They were no more than rags spewing blood.

And that meant the end.

It was over, as if someone had flipped a switch, as every combatant paused to watch one of the Supernals die . . .

It was over.

"Lucifel had lost the war. And Raziel, it was commonly agreed, had committed suicide rather than subject himself to the punishment of God . . ."

Darkness came over all of Heaven. Lucifel and her flock of dissenters, descending like a living smoke, down and down and down . . .

"For with her lover dead and the war decided, she fled to Hell . . . piercing it all the way to the Abyss, where the demonic regime continues to this very day. Her name is hateful to the angels, and every one of her supporters, including Raziel, shares that legacy. All his belongings and writings were destroyed, and among them was his greatest work—"

The Book of Raziel.

Reality shifted and Angela was suddenly out of Tileaf's memories, standing in a space where she could walk, talk, and breathe, her consciousness now separated from the Fae's by a renewed sense of individuality. In this place, she had will and sensation, but for a short time, the strangeness of what she had just seen, that sense of the alien, curled her into a ball of terror and pain. She merely lay there, in the blackness that was enough to give her existence, seeing nothing but Lucifel's face and Israfel's beauty, and the immense starlit perfection of Heaven spattered with their red blood.

She was a grain of dust before all of it. Ignorant and terrifyingly weak.

The shock refused to leave her, the terror would never end, this hell would never end—

And then, *it* was lying next to her. A book made of pure sapphire, its cover emblazoned with an Eye that nearly matched the Grail around her neck in size. But this Eye was gray in color, more sad than terrible, and without thinking, Angela stretched out a hand and brushed it with her fingertips, causing the eyelid to shut.

"Yes," Tileaf's voice continued like a whisper, "there are rumors that the Book still exists. That it was not destroyed, as was commonly thought, but, that of its own free will it followed Lucifel . . . to Hell."

Angela leaned closer, trying to pick up the Book. But the sapphire was far too heavy, leaving her with the option of opening the cover or walking away.

She touched it, rubbing her hand across the blue rock.

It had a heartbeat. It was alive.

"Do not be fooled. What you are seeing is only a representation, a symbol, of the Book passed down in legend and myth . . . There are perhaps none living besides Lucifel herself who have seen its true form. And, of course, opening it is impossible.

"Those who try to do so, but do not possess even one of the Supernals' spirits, are stricken with insanity.

"Besides . . . the Key and its Lock have yet to be found . . ."

The Book vanished, curls of blue ether wrapping around Angela's fingers before disappearing. Light illuminated the darkness, and she rocked back to her feet, still standing on a void that seemed solid as real earth but glassy smooth. Perhaps this was the foundation of Tileaf's mind, firm despite so much torture. Angela stared out into the space she'd been granted on it, and a wind sighed from the nothingness, blowing through her hair, full of voices that sounded like a million souls speaking at once. Beseeching her.

The light continued to brighten.

"The Archon, known mistakenly to humankind as the Ruin, is said to be the reincarnation of Raziel's soul. The Supernal's Book, which contains both a power and a knowledge beyond the comprehension of most creatures, must be opened, and only by Her, because with Israfel vanished into the highest reaches of Heaven, there is no other able or willing to do so without suffering severe consequences.

"Lucifel is *not* an option . . ."

There was a sun peeping over the unnameable horizon, but it gave off a sallow glow that barely revealed the rifts and valleys of Tileaf's mind. Angela now stood on a cliff with a jagged edge, her boots scraping it precariously, and within the barren valley below her, human beings stood in rows of silence, their souls gray as the sun was gray, looking up at her with a sense of need and longing. Angela gazed out at them, overcome by their numbers, their misery.

"Even the dead are aware of the looming threat of the Great Satan. Lucifel, she who was prophesied as the one who would confront God in order to become a god herself, is now crazed to the point of utter darkness. Seeking to open the Book of Raziel, she would only use its power to end the universe she believes has wronged her . . . and her cult, which makes up half of Hell, wishes for the fulfillment of her ideals.

"The omens are there, and her most fanatical believers now move to assist her . . . to open her cage . . ."

Storm clouds gathered in the far distance, echoes of Tileaf's pain and her warning. Lightning sliced the sky like a pitchfork of crimson.

"For there is only one Archon . . . but there are two who can be the Ruin."

The clouds boiled, saturating the atmosphere with a new and painful blackness, taking the life that remained to the souls below her and turning their spirit bodies to ash. A violent wind gusted through the valley, and their symbolic selves dissipated, disintegrating in the new breeze blowing through Tileaf's mind. Little by little, the terrible image stripped away into tatters, tearing off to reveal the same space where the Book had lain next to Angela, alone.

But now Tileaf stood before her, beautiful and untouched by the priests' greed.

Her lovely face held the bleakest expression, and she stepped softly toward Angela, holding out her hand.

She didn't have to ask.

Angela slipped the chain over her neck and handed her the Grail, now more an Eye than a stone. Green, and horribly alive.

"This," Tileaf said, cradling the Grail in her palm, "must never find its way back to Lucifel. Whether or not it was a lover's gift, Raziel eventually gave it to the Jinn, and thus to the true Archon, for a reason, and once it finds Her hands, it must never leave them. It is cursed, certainly, but also important, though only he might have known why or how . . ."

Angela nodded, accepting the Eye as it was passed back to her.

"If you yourself are the Archon, when the time comes to use the Grail, remember that it cannot be handled without consequences."

"And what about Israfel?"

Angela's heart ached, almost to the point where she could cry. Seeing her beautiful angel so clearly, she'd wanted him more than ever, and more than ever, the possibility seemed nonexistent. The danger was obvious. If she didn't ignore this corner of her heart, the thirst would eventually kill her on its own. Israfel took up her world; he always had. Only for a few days had someone stood before or beside him in the space of her affections. Kim had enough pleasure to offer, enough beauty and charm, but could a relationship built on danger last? Besides, if Angela proved to be nothing more than what so many had suspected—insane—then he'd kill her.

How alone she was. Unable to trust even her own feelings.

"Israfel . . ." Tileaf sighed deeply. "As I said, he vanished into the highest dimensions of Heaven. Raziel's death affected him powerfully. And no one has seen him since that fateful day. He may no longer even be alive."

That couldn't be. It simply could not. Besides, Mikel had *said* he was alive.

Though she could have been lying from the start.

"How can I find him? I was hoping that maybe I could summon him to Earth like other angels, but—"

"No." The Fae's voice hardened. "He is a Supernal. They are angels. But they are also on a much higher plane of existence. Israfel is not the type of being who entertains demands."

"Then what do I do?"

"You can hope. It is what we've all been doing since Raziel died and took most of what little hope remained with him . . ."

"And that's all?"

Tileaf lifted her hand, thrusting with it as if she were pushing Angela away. They began to separate with the same slow intensity with which they'd first come together, and a grim knowledge entered into Angela's awareness. This was the last time she and Tileaf would speak on equal terms. The next instance they'd encounter each other, Angela would have to be the Archon to survive it, and she would have to keep her promise and kill someone who otherwise wished her dead.

"Yes," Tileaf said, sounding more resigned than ever. "That's all."

Twenty-two

His voice is unlike any other. A music that torments the soul.
—UNKNOWN AUTHOR, *A Collection of Angelic Lore*

Were you there in the Garden of Shadows?
Were you near when the Father took wing?
Did you sigh when the starlight outpoured us?
When the silver bright water could sing . . .

Angela rolled over onto her side, sighing, trying to wake up, though her brain was crawling from sleep with infuriating sluggishness. Someone was singing to her, such a haunting, incredible song. She recognized this voice—she'd heard this melody before . . .

Have you drunk from a river of amber?
Or eaten the nectar of dreams,
Where thoughts linger determining eons,
And time stretches apart at the seams . . .

Who? Who was this?

The voice was like pure birdsong and the gentle ring of a chime, yet with all the force of a rushing tidal wave. Angela moaned out loud, half awake, turning aside in a mound of what felt like dead leaves. They crackled underneath her, her back hit an iron-hard root—and her eyes popped open, revealing the unearthly decay of Tileaf's grotto.

She sat up, groggy and unusually tired.

Kim lay beside her, his arm flopped across her skirt. He looked so different, fast asleep like this. Innocent, his hair thrown back from his face and neck, completely unlike the cold, professional persona he projected, his lips gently parting as he breathed and mumbled what sounded like Latin. Troy, though, was gone, perhaps because dawn was almost upon them. She'd either escaped deep into the undergrowth or had left entirely, unwilling to watch over the two people she hated most as they curled beside each other.

Luckily for Kim, she also must have had an aversion to murdering anyone unconscious. Jinn must have had the morality peculiar to hunters. Twisted morals, but still, morals.

Thump.

What was that?

Angela turned around, her heart pounding.

A branch had fallen from Tileaf's tree into the dirt. She too was gone, silent, back to dying alone—just as she seemed to prefer it.

> *Now the coffin of spirits awaits us.*
> *Now the sliver of life it escapes us . . .*

"Hello?" Angela stood up and crunched through the leaves, stepping over another large root. She was still wobbly and tired and her head felt foggy. It was hard to see, though that was thankfully improving. The trees caged the entire grotto in darkness, but between their black limbs the slate-colored sky was appearing in the early morning light. And it was an uncommonly pallid and dirty light. Clouds scudded by with the wind, their tufts boiling with a menace peculiar to Luz, threatening another deadly storm. Strangely enough, it had only been last night when Angela, Nina, and Kim—when they'd survived lightning bolts, and rain that could cut into your skin. "Hello?" she whispered.

Nothing. Just the scraping of twigs and leaves.

It's in my head. The voice is in my head. No one else can hear it.

Kim continued to sleep, rolling over and resting his arm against his forehead. If the voice truly came from an outside source, it was certainly loud enough to have awakened him by now.

If we tarry in this place.
If we take not the chance to taste . . .

Whoever was singing, was calling *her.*

Angela left Kim behind, slowly walking through the same tunnel of foliage that had led her to Tileaf and a thousand dreadful images, most of which lingered in her mind. Her boots crackled through leaves and dry twigs, splashed through mud, and tapped against old stone. The weeds on either side of the path shivered, as if saying farewell; Angela patted the Grail resting in its cold lump beneath her blouse and slipped her fingers through a space between the buttons, stroking its smooth surface. Without warning, it struck her—perhaps Angela had never heard this song or this voice before. Perhaps it had been tailor-made to seduce her. As if whoever was singing knew exactly what she wanted to hear, offering it to her along with all her dreams and hopes, if she would simply—

Come to me.

Bushes rustled nearby.

Angela froze, frightened, then relaxed in relief.

Revealed by the moving bushes, Nina shifted her sleeping position against a tree trunk. Her blouse had been torn by a patch of thorns. Otherwise, she looked too peaceful for someone possessed. But if Angela tried to wake her up, she might only end up speaking to Mikel.

Angela shuffled past her, slowly following the path out of the park and up to the immense wrought-iron gate. As always, the return journey seemed shorter than the arrival, and she stepped out onto the cobblestones tentatively, like someone might catch her, hear her, and force the trees to snag her back inside.

Now where do I go?

A long wet street escaped into the fog ahead, and on either side stretched the avenues and tunnels Kim had used to get them to the Park in the first place.

Instead, Angela chose the route the song—or her heart—suggested. A narrow alley directly to her left. The verses repeated themselves, throbbing inside of her like a heartbeat, and soon she was obeying, entering the most dilapidated section of the Academy's Western District, its buildings more like vacant shacks hoisted too tightly against one another. A rat skittered across the street and over her boot.

Come to me.

Luz passed her by, little more than a blur of black and gray.

Grates that covered the ocean began to line both sides of the street, water churning beneath them, frothy and ice cold. But the melody pounding through her head drowned out both the sea and the threat of its unusually high waves, their tips licking the grate's lower edges. And somehow, she knew where to go, despite distractions, despite guilt—

> *You were there in the Garden of Shadows.*
> *You were there when the Father took wing.*
> *And my words will remind you of pleasure . . .*

She paused, backpedaling to a stone church, its perimeter surrounded by barbed wire. Whoever owned the incredible voice was inside the building, waiting, and the instinct carried her like a dream, one foot after the other pushing her up the stairs, and then hand by hand over the fence and the barbs that tore into her skirt and her tights. The Vatican had closed off this church to the public and to students for good, for forever, perhaps because it stood too near Tileaf's tree, and so, too close to secrets. Time and acid rain had both done their share, and once-impressive stone reliefs had been worn away to featureless lumps. Most of the stained-glass windows had been cracked or shattered, and the wooden doors had warped from constant rain. Locked or unlocked, a hard push would snap them open, but Angela tried the handles anyway.

Cool, tarnished brass met her hand.

She turned her wrist.

The door gave way, creaking open.

And imprison your soul in a ring.

Gray haze veiled the altar.

Numerous puddles surrounded the pews like moats, reflecting the brick of the nearest towers in a collage of brown and russet. Ragged holes had been torn in the walls near the ceiling, leaving most of the floor naked to the rain, but Angela followed the central aisle, picking her away around the water, wondering at the moldy tapestries and the stench of mildew. Then the mist receded, revealing one window still intact. Angela stopped to examine the stained glass, dulled beneath its film of grime. Its image was barely discernible: an angel handing a lily to a frightened young woman.

"She carried a treasure in her body."

A soft voice. A real voice. Just like the one that had been singing to her.

"That's the legend, or so I've heard . . ."

The pitch sounded gentle but too deep to be female. She forced herself to turn around, heart working overtime, everything seeming to happen in slow motion, as if time were in the very process of freezing—

To come face-to-face with absolute Beauty.

She could only stare, drinking in the ivory of his skin, the pink of his lips; losing herself in his lined, sea blue eyes, so large and so bright. Even his star-white hair seemed to shine, dispersing the gloom with an ethereal brilliance, with the scarlet ribbons woven through the tresses near his shoulders and graceful neck. His perfection was overwhelming, staggering. It erased the memory of Kim's face in an instant. It made Tileaf look like an ugly duckling desperate to be a swan.

This was Israfel. Her beautiful, beautiful angel.

But he was no longer a dream or a vision or a memory. He was now a solid, flesh-and-blood reality, standing in front of her, his embroidered coat dazzling her eyes with its silver thread, his own shock looking supremely out of place. Israfel backed away from her, actually seeming afraid. His smile hardened the same as in her dreams, whenever he was upset. "You—"

His voice cut off.

Perfect. It's perfect even when he isn't singing.

Neither of them moved.

"You," he said the words reluctantly, as if she'd pulled them out of his mouth herself, "you look like the—"

Like what? Like Raziel?

She shouldn't let him touch her—not yet—but he was already doing so, fascinated like she was fascinated, losing all his caution to melt any trace of fear with his slim fingers. The longing inside of her grew like a living thing, threatening to burst out in all the wrong ways. How many times had she kissed his portrait, painted another picture, or sketched a scene from one of those ephemeral dreams, aching and sighing and pining away inside? How many scars had she inflicted on herself in the insane suicide attempts, all so that she could rest in the circle of his bronze wings?

They had yet to appear, though. Even more troubling, his hair and eyebrows were pearlescent white, not the bronze she'd seen in Tileaf's memories and her own detailed visions. But his face, his slender figure, his graceful movements, even the soul gazing back at her through those languid blue irises—those were all the same.

It wasn't until he leaned in closer, and the soft light from the towers grazed his features again, that she saw how heavily the kohl circled his eyes. How thickly he'd painted his eyelashes a deep shade of black.

Their roots were white as his hair.

"You heard my song," he whispered to her.

"Yes." Anything she said sounded foolish compared to the way he spoke.

"Is it you? Have you come back to me?"

He means Raziel.

"I don't know." That sounded even stupider.

But more than anything she wanted it to be the truth. When he cupped her face and drew her in close, she gave in with a delicate sigh, returning the pressure of his soft, insistent mouth, overwhelmed by a warmth that burned every other thought away. She sensed him testing her, tasting the deepest part of her soul and liking what he found, whether or not it was what he truly wanted. So much emotion, so fast. Insanity. Danger. This angel, a creature of such power, could crack her spine with a snap of his fingers, and yet Angela had fallen into his embrace brainless and lovesick, an idiot without equal, just like she had imagined over and over and over again. Kim's face reappeared in the depths of her mind, protesting, but then he sank back into an abyss where she could no longer see him.

There would be no salvation. Because these feelings began somewhere else, long, long ago.

They broke apart, and Israfel licked his lips, as if still savoring the taste of her.

He stroked her hair, running its blood-red strands through his fingers, just as Kim had done. How right this felt, though. So impossibly right, yet in a way so different from the rightness Kim made her feel. He'd been passionate enough for her, but the sensation was ultimately far from the same.

"But how did you find me . . ." Angela gazed at him adoringly, unable to help herself. "How long have you been singing?"

Israfel smiled, and for the second time, sunshine seemed to break over Luz. But just as quickly a strange coldness came over him, and he let her go, and that sunshine turned to a ray that could burn whatever displeased him. Painfully, it became clear to Angela that her worst fears had been realized: her humanity was a factor almost too lowly for Israfel to consider. That made his next comment hurt all the more.

"You are not Raziel."

"Why not?"

"Your taste," and he looked so achingly hungry when he said it, "is entirely different."

"I'm a different person."

No one ever seemed to bother considering that. Well, now that she had her angel in the flesh, she was going to *make* him consider it. Anything to keep him from flying out of Angela's life and back to Heaven, where it might take forever to reach him. For a second, the Grail beneath her blouse felt heavier, tempting her to bring it out into the open, to show him that she possessed something only the Archon could hold without eventually suffering for it. But the little voice in the back of her head cautioned against it, and for once, Angela listened. So much could go sour if she said or did the wrong thing.

"Yes, you're right," Israfel said. "You are a different person." He examined her further, but with a tact Troy was too savage to possess. How could any angel evolve into a Jinn? Hell must be more terrible than Angela had imagined. "So am I. For some reason," he said, caressing her cheek, "I haven't killed you yet."

I take it back.

"You are not him," Israfel continued, gentle, "and it would be unwise to let you live now that you've seen me. That is—unless you are willing to pay the price." His body swayed, like a slender lily, and the answer was of course, yes, absolutely. Though he might have been a Supernal, Israfel suddenly appeared so delicate and broken, he might crack asunder if Angela didn't protect him. "Because all happiness," he said softly, "has a price."

Words meant nothing at this point.

She clasped his gloved fingers, noting how he held his palm facing up—not down like most humans when they formally extended a hand.

"You choose wisely." He shook from her grip, biting his lip. "For the short time you have left, you will be content, I'm sure." His expression softened, lovely once more. "But, if you'll excuse me, I must leave and do a favor for a plaything of mine. He's paid handsomely for my service, and it would be rude to disappoint him, don't you think?"

That teasing smile. But he sounds more like he's going to punish this person rather than help them. I should have known. I should remember. Tileaf warned me without saying anything— angels don't think like us.

"Where are you going?"

As if she could follow or stop him.

Israfel laughed, his voice like a bell. "To a feast for God's underappreciated servants. Apparently, it's being held in a church on the Academy grounds you attend." He glanced at her skirt, her blouse, the dirt and holes in both of them, noting her utter filthiness. "You might want to come. It will be a rather interesting morning for everyone."

Wind gusted. A flurry of feathers hid his beauty.

Down puffed against Angela's cheeks and tumbled like snow to the floor.

Israfel had finally opened his wings, but they shone with a damp film, like water had been sprayed on them when she wasn't looking. There were four of them, two that resembled thick but expansive mats of down smothered in stiffer feathers, and another thinner pair, settled between them and trailing onto the floor. Considering his size, they were slender, elegant, and unable to carry even half of Israfel's weight. She reached out to touch those pinions, to imprison herself inside of their walls of white and never escape.

He stretched them, flapping, rolling a furious breeze throughout the church, and then he was soaring up through the largest hole in the roof, like his body was made of air rather than flesh. Angela watched him leave without a sound, amazed to see that he was already a white speck fading into the mist and the clouds.

Mine. You're mine. And I'll make sure it stays that way. This dream—if it is a dream—can't end.

No. This wasn't a dream. She'd given them all away.

What was happening to her? Inside, she felt a terrible possessiveness. Something that scared her almost more than Naamah, Troy, and the thought of possibly battling the Devil herself.

It's like I'm starving, and the whole world isn't enough.

Angela clutched her head, still groggy and suddenly sick to

her stomach. The shock that had burned between her and her angel, Tileaf's Creator Supernal, the Devil's own brother, Heaven's highest angel, was fading and her thoughts raced and her body weakened all over. She trembled, running fingers through the hair tangled near her neck, glancing around wildly at the church and its decay, like she could bring him back or make him even more real than he was. But why had he changed so drastically from what she'd seen in her visions, in Tileaf's memories?

He was now white as snow—and yet dark. Like he'd painted over his soul as much as his eyelashes.

A plaything, he'd said. That didn't sound right. Who could it be, anyway?

Israfel had been referring to the All Saints' Day feast, scheduled for late morning at the same cathedral where she'd spoken to Kim. All the university grades would be there, celebrating Mass with at least one hundred priests and novices, and worst of all, Stephanie Walsh.

As head of one of the Academy's sorority houses, she would be expected to show her face—if she was still alive. And if she was alive, Stephanie had definitely been planning some kind of evil in the hours that passed. Maybe she'd even murdered Sophia out of spite.

Sophia.

I almost forgot all about her.

If she started running, Angela could make it in time for the homily. So without a second thought, she spun on her heel and dashed out of the church, clutching at the Grail like it was her heart.

The real one might never stop racing.

Twenty-three

What is this hope but a dead Bird's dream?
Where is the truth of the Ruin foreseen?
—CARDINAL DEMIAN YATES, *Translations of the Prophecy*

"That rotten little *rat*," Naamah muttered between her teeth. "I'll slice her in half. I'll make her blood rain all over this hell of a city."

She ripped her wrist away from Stephanie, causing them both to flinch.

"Let me do this, or it will get even more infected," Stephanie said, grabbing for it again, her eyes tearing up pathetically. This was the first time she'd ever seen her adoptive mother injured, and the sight made her sick inside, overwhelmingly angry. That horrific creature—it could only have been the Jinn—had done this. The lightning bolt that hit the Bell Tower had knocked Stephanie unconscious for a short time, but not before she'd seen a living shadow streak in Naamah's direction. The unnamed menace had been lurking in the chapel all along, waiting and watching, just in time for Naamah to show herself and make a move.

"Why didn't you kill her sooner?" Stephanie hissed, trembling. "Then they would both be dead."

Naamah's blood slicked her hands like oil. She slopped old bandages onto the floor and fully exposed the wound, terrible with its torn flesh and underlying bone. Naamah cursed under her breath, her alien words giving neither of them any comfort while she pushed Stephanie aside to lick the injury.

"It will heal in time," the demon whispered. "Don't worry about that annoying rat. I'll make certain she and her vermin relatives pay for this soon—"

"How did she even get close enough?" Stephanie lifted the candle higher, illuminating the sharp beauty of Naamah's face. Her mother's copper skin took on a burnt shade of red in the darkness, fascinating, but only reminding her of more blood and more death. Lyrica stood behind her, pale and silent, so frightened by their closeness she seemed more a statue than a person. She glanced at Stephanie, wide-eyed and terrified, probably still seeing Maribel's death over and over again, her grasp on sanity lessening the more her palms curled around the clean bandages in her hand. "I thought you can use ether to bring them down," Stephanie said, wiping away more tears with a fist. When she yelled, it sounded more desperate than angry. "*How did she hide in that room without us knowing?*"

"Because she's the High Assassin," Naamah snapped.

A door slammed shut.

Lyrica had locked herself in the bathroom. In seconds, she began to throw up, her gasps like shuddering cries for help.

Stephanie's room was almost pitch-black, but the candle gave off a meager light that sharpened every object. Anything was now a menace. The chandelier, the half-open wardrobe, the curtains that hung so still in the heavy air. The Jinn could be hiding behind blankets and bookshelves, dressers and unlocked doors.

Naamah shrugged off a suspicious noise near the window, sucking more blood from her wrist until it was dry enough to rewrap. Stephanie helped her, unable to think properly, her mind lost in a faraway void until Naamah spoke again.

"She's a rat who climbed up the Jinn hierarchy by murdering and murdering well. The Jinn Queen's sister, or so I've been told. Dangerous and highly skilled, an expert at ambush attacks. We met once before—in my younger days—and I suffered well enough for my lack of caution. She tore a bone from my wing. Not enough to kill, of course, but enough to protect herself from me in the future." The demon shook a hand through her hair, tugging at her braids. "Scrawny bitch."

"I warned you." An overly gentle voice spoke.

She stepped into the light, hands folded calmly, her face completely expressionless. Sophia's hair was still wet from the rain, twisted in frizzy ringlets below her shoulders. But the emptiness behind her eyes was back, worse than ever, and of all inhuman things, it was the horror Stephanie feared most of all.

"I warned you about overstepping your bounds," she was saying. "And now look where it's getting you. If you don't stop before it's too—"

"Shut your damn mouth." Stephanie turned on her, screaming.

Sophia's face blanked.

There was a long and awkward silence.

"What is it? Why are you looking at me like that?"

Naamah blocked her from view, holding Stephanie by the shoulders. The demon's hands wrapped into her skin like steel clamps. "Why are you shivering?"

"I'm shivering?" Stephanie whispered. She looked down at her body, all her limbs vibrating, her knees knocking together. "It's so cold in here," she said, her voice echoing from a distance.

Naamah spoke to Sophia, more alien words.

The girl stared at Stephanie, a morbid look on her face, but obeyed with a silent huff and stepped out of the room. When she reappeared, she held two more candles, their flames like tiny spots of light in the deep and miserable gloom. But the room didn't brighten for Stephanie, not even a shade. Instead, her vision swirled, and she cradled her head in her hands, hoping she wouldn't end up like Lyrica, vomiting on her knees.

The world felt like it was collapsing, unhinging beneath her feet. Sensation ceased.

A greater darkness loomed before her, and she glanced up, astonished to see that Sophia gazed back, the same punishing expression on her face.

Naamah was gone, the bathroom silent.

Near her bed, the clock chimed out the hour. Eight in the morning. Strangely, an hour had passed without her even noticing.

"Did I fall asleep?" Stephanie said, glancing furtively around the bedroom.

Sophia continued to stand in front of her, still and silent.

"Where is Naamah?"

No response.

"The demon. My *mother*—"

"Is waiting to meet you at St. Mary's," Sophia said, her voice little more than a breath of air. Another clock chimed in a lower room, the sound somehow jarring. As illogical as the sudden leap in time. "Today is the All Saints' Day feast, Stephanie. You wouldn't want to miss it. I'm sure you have all kinds of . . . plans."

Stephanie stood up, her knees still weak, and shambled over to the mirror to rearrange her hair, closing her eyes and opening them to a brighter room. Of course. She must have imagined all the darkness. All of those gray and black shadows. Now, her room appeared more normal, and a million times less ominous, even cheerful with its white crown molding and royal purple curtains. Sophia was just a harmless doll standing in a much more harmless doll house. Her fingers, though, were bloody. Probably from the pentagrams in the chapel.

There had been so many.

"Not that I blame you. I'd be nervous too."

The tone in her voice was alarming.

Stephanie turned around, finding her old sense of confidence the more Sophia revealed herself; mousy, waiflike, and ignorant. How could she be so afraid of her? What she mistook for an unworldly horror was really just Sophia's empty mind shining through. Surely there had to be consequences when you brought the dead back to life, especially more than once. Every time it happened, more and more of Sophia's brain probably disintegrated.

"It seems like everyone has friendly advice for me lately." Stephanie picked up her overcoat from the bed, slipping it over her shoulders. "If you want to help, you can start by telling me what happened to Angela Mathers after the ceremony." Stephanie spun on her heel. "She was with Kim, right?"

Sophia turned aside, visibly holding something back.

"I guess that's one thing you and I have in common. We both don't want them together. Though—not for the same reasons, of course. Did you think I wouldn't notice how you stare at her when she isn't looking?"

"Stephanie, this is the only instance you and I will speak as equals. Now listen to me for once. You need to stop this, while there's still a chance for you to turn back. Has Naamah told you about the Supernals?"

"Of course she has." Stephanie regarded her carefully.

"Then you know the danger that you're in."

"Raziel's dead," Stephanie said, welcoming the certainty of it. "And he's inside of me. That's one bird down. Lucifel's not a threat either."

"Do you realize how ridiculous that sounds?" Sophia was back to her gentle, measured tone of voice. For a moment, she could barely look Stephanie in the eye. "And what about Israfel?"

"Naamah said he's dead too. They're all either dead or on their way out. Where are you going with this?"

Sophia leaned in close, all whispers and mystery, like her words erupted from some deep and invisible well. "Israfel has many names, Stephanie. 'Israfel' itself is just one translation among many, the most accurate in human terms. But he has others that are better known." Her face looked gaunt in the gray light. Tired. "You don't know him like I do. He's older than Naamah. Smarter. Infinitely more beautiful and cruel, and if you can't understand that paradox, you will not be able to withstand him if the moment arrives."

Withstand him? But Naamah had said time and again that even if Israfel was alive, he would have no interest in Earth. Angels of his rank simply didn't care, too lofty beyond the human imagination to bother with irritations like Sophia or the Archon. Raziel was dead and had shown his true colors as Lucifel's lover. What reason could Israfel find to bother with his brother's human shell?

Yet the idea of him, the sound of his name, crawled inside of her and wrenched at her insides.

"Oh . . ." Stephanie clutched her head, sick all over without warning.

The room faded. A dull ringing filled her ears.

"You . . . think . . . so much of him, don't you?"

What little sense that made. But . . .

A deep, irrational envy had taken sudden hold of her. She laughed quietly, seeing Angela's fierce face, the possessed glaze over Nina's eyes, and Kim, standing beside Naamah with the strangest kind of boredom, like they were both so well acquainted with each other. In a flash, she saw dead pigeons and rats drained of blood. The pentagrams appeared everywhere, ringing her like crimson planets. But behind it all was the conviction that she was spinning out of control, until she grabbed Sophia by the chin, forcing her to stare straight into her eyes.

Sophia's face paled. She recognized who was talking to her.

"But remember," Stephanie heard herself say, "it's our little secret."

Twenty-four

*Jinn have fallen in love with humans on occasion. However,
the offspring of such unions are often killed outright by
either parent; an act committed in cold blood, but one
where instinct has rightly reigned over affection.*

—BROTHER FRANCIS, *Encyclopedia of the Realms*

"Mama, what are you doing? Mama?"

Kim knelt beside her in front of the fire, watching as she tossed
baubles into the grate. His mother was beautiful. The most beautiful person in the world. Her hair was more lustrous than a ra-
ven's wing, full of curls, and her eyes were a mix of earth and
green grass. He'd never seen a woman with skin so white, and
whenever her arms wrapped around him, hugging him close, he
had to touch and pinch them as much as he could, because there
was always the chance it might never happen again.

Lately it was harder and harder to get her attention.

She knelt in front of the fire a lot, throwing her rocks and jewels
into the ash, whispering in a strange language he couldn't figure
out. Calling for someone. Begging. And their cottage walls had
become covered, floor to ceiling, in symbols she never bothered
explaining: circles, sharp lines, pictures that resembled flowers,
and another picture of a face with horns on its head.

He never liked that one.

"Mama?"

"Hush," she said, clapping a hand over his mouth.

Kim squirmed, resisting her. Then he grew still and she let go, continuing her soft mumbling. She grabbed some of the earth piled in a fold on her dress near her lap, tossed it into the fire, and the flames roared, bursting into a dazzle of orange and yellow. Mice crawled up and down the wood pile to his right, squeaking, relishing the warmth. Kim cleared a patch of rushes on the floor and sat next to them, hoping to catch one. They were always too fast.

"Kim," his mother whispered. Her pretty eyes seemed larger.

"Yes, Mama?"

"Don't you think it's time to go to sleep? It's very late, and the village master will be upset if you're not tending the fields—"

"But I want to stay with you! What are you doing?"

"Papa's coming tonight, Kim. You should know that by now."

He shivered; always hating the way she said "papa," and the idea that for days she'd be gone as if she'd never existed at all. Then he'd be holed up in his tiny room, rocking on the lice-covered bed, wishing and hoping her back until it became reality. Papa's visits were always like that. Kim never saw him or spoke with him, and often he'd just press his ears to the door, listening to them talk about places that sounded strange and far away, and then the noises would begin, suggesting that his mother was in pain. He was convinced Papa hurt her all the time. Mother's arms and legs and feet were covered in long, thin, scars that looked like cuts. Sometimes, when she finally unlocked the door and let him out, she would still be bleeding.

The rushes would be sticky for days, mice covering the floor and licking up what they could.

Tonight, though, was different.

He was going to see Papa. He was going to make sure he was noticed.

"All right," he said, "I guess I can go to bed."

"Good boy." His mother hoisted herself up and stretched out her hand.

Kim took it and allowed her to lead him to his room, a dank

little space with the bed on the floor and a few rags for blankets. The walls were bare stone, and the thatch over the roof usually dribbled insects for most of the night, but it was autumn, and many of them were dying or in the process of dying. His only regret was how alone that would make him. Mama never said she'd leave him in here for days, but they both knew that was the case. Kim stared at her nervously, stripping off his shirt and pants, dropping them near a mound of potatoes she'd set next to the door.

The water would arrive in a pan come morning.

"Mama, will you be gone long this time?"

"I don't know, Kim."

"Why do you lock me up in here?"

Wrong question. She slapped him across the face, and the tears sprang to his eyes immediately. He wouldn't cry, though. She hated when he cried.

"Don't make me angry. Get in bed. NOW."

Kim ran and hugged her instead.

"Get off me, Kim." She said it like he was a cockroach. Like she was afraid of him and disgusted and ashamed, all at the same time. Mama could be so pretty and kind. But when Papa came, she changed. This was the mama he feared. The one who would curse at him and call him a devil. He found the key before she realized what he was doing and took it out of her pocket, hiding it inside his fist. When she moved to hit him again, he scampered to his bed and crawled below the rags, already feeling the fleas nip at his ankles. "Don't leave this room. Promise me."

"I promise." The lie was easier than he'd hoped.

She shut the door, playing with the outer lock until it latched.

His candle eventually guttered out. The room stayed pitch-black for a while, until the moon rose over the cottage, and its silver light slipped through slats in the shutters. The noises were starting already. A hiss like the whisper of a snake. The low growl of a dog and the snarl of an angry fox. Kim gathered the rags below his chin, listening intently, amazed as always to hear the noises become words he could understand. They were talking about leaving. Papa wanted Mama to go somewhere with him, and she was protesting, but then her gasps and pained screams began, and she must have changed her mind, because she said Papa's name over and over, like she was desperate to make him believe it.

His name was alien, sounding like the harshest mix of vowels and consonants.

The more Mama said it, the more unhappy she sounded.

Kim slipped out of his covers, gripping the key. Softly, he tiptoed to the door, lifted the key to the lock.

He pushed it inside, turning.

There was a click—and the knob rolled beneath his fingers.

Mama was silent.

Kim opened the door slower than anything he'd ever opened before, peeking through the slit at the hearth. The fire had burned down to cinders, smoldering a dirty orange. Next to them, her back and waist white as a cloud, his mother rested in the arms of someone with skin paler than hers, and his thin arm was tracing a nail along the skin near her neck, up and over the scars already there. Another cut opened beneath it, and the blood oozed down her back, red as garnet. Then Papa bent over her, slightly revealed by the moonlight, his great eyes shining like two yellow stars. Ribbed horns curved upward from a headdress that wrapped below his hair, and two shadows billowed behind them, making a breeze whenever they moved.

His mother turned her head and looked up at Papa, all longing and passion.

Then he scraped the side of her neck with his teeth, and while Mama shuddered, Papa stared back at Kim with those terrible yellow eyes. And all he could do was scream, scream, scream—

"Sariel—"

Kim's eyes snapped open. He shot up from the leaves, sweating, gasping.

He was soaked from head to toe, his coat soggy with rain and probably his own fear. A gurgle of thunder broke overhead, and Nina appeared in front of him, peering into his eyes with a mirror image of Lucifel's. Mikel either hadn't released her, or Nina didn't want the angel to leave after all.

"Where's Angela?" he said, fighting the sudden instinct to smack her aside and begin his search. "Did she leave?"

Mikel nodded. "You're too late. He's found her."

He stood, brushing twigs and dirt from his back, knees, and shoulders. Then he shook out his hair and pieces of mulch sprayed side to side. Kim gasped, still smelling the hearth and the stuffiness of the rushes on his bedroom floor. "He? Who are you talking about?"

The angel regarded him coolly, probably remembering how he could torture her if he felt like it. "Israfel."

Kim stopped breathing, thinking, almost living. He just stared back at her, his teeth chattering a little from the cold, the rain rolling down both of their faces. An immense crack of thunder resounded overhead and she stole a quick glimpse of the lightning only to meet his gaze again, unnaturally calm. The park roared on every side, leaves dropping like snow as they collapsed beneath the onslaught of water and wind. Branches waved and scratched against each other, and in their midst, Tileaf's tree stood untouched, as if the storm weren't worthy of putting an end to her misery. "How would you know that? You didn't follow her—"

"His song." Mikel held out a hand to catch the rain. "I could hear it. I am a spirit, priest. But it's not my place to say when Nina Willis's body awakens from sleep. I couldn't follow Angela any faster than you."

"Where did she go?"

Or where did *they* go?

"I have no way of knowing that."

Israfel had been alive all this time, living like a hermit in the farthest reaches of Heaven, and suddenly, out of every era he could have chosen, the Supernal decided to visit Earth now? He must have been searching and waiting for the Archon all along—hoping to reunite with his dead brother. But Angela wasn't the Archon. Troy had said so. Or, at least, she wasn't Raziel. So why would the angel bother with her in the first place? Either he was—despite his lofty nature—as ignorant as them, or someone, somewhere, knew something that everybody else didn't.

Mikel blinked at him, glassy-eyed.

Kim grabbed her by the throat, nearly lifting her from the ground.

The angel's teeth gritted and she clutched at his hands, furious at how helpless she was.

"What do you know?" Kim shouted at her. "And how do you know it? It seems odd to me that if Angela isn't the Archon, she still managed to snag your attention."

The trees groaned, turning in on one another, their limbs snapping ominously. Then the wind picked up, mirroring Mikel's fury, and a gale besieged Tileaf's grotto, branches splitting and tumbling from thick trunks, leaves blowing about in a whirlwind, every gust whistling, howling. Rain slanted into Kim's eyes and his mouth, and still he held on, threatening the worst.

"Answer me, angel."

"I don't know what she is either," Mikel said, screaming over the storm, "but she was powerful enough to call me, and so I came—"

"You told Israfel that the Archon was here. Just like you told the demons." He tightened his grip. "You're toying with everyone."

Mikel twisted, kicking at his legs. "I told him *nothing*." She glared at him, equally exasperated. "Israfel was my torturer, priest. He was the one who forced me—the one with no body—into a body made for nothing but pain. And the moment she called me, I left it. He is no more aware of that miracle than you were before this moment."

Kim dropped her, shoving her away from him. "You're saying that the official history—that Lucifel's chicks died—was a lie he made up. There are more of you?"

The wind died down. The rain fell slower.

"One other. My brother."

"And he is like you?"

"No. He is both body and soul, but he collaborates in my torture." Mikel rubbed the skin of Nina's throat, coughing. "You're not listening to what I'm saying to you. I didn't come to Angela Mathers. Angela Mathers called me. I left that prison summoned by her power, and if she is not the Archon, then we are all very mistaken about who the Archon is." Her voice quivered, and she spoke to him sharply, insisting. "I am the offspring of Raziel and Lucifel. I am above the other angels, in case you are forgetting, and the power to break Israfel's prison must be equal or greater than his."

Equal. Or greater.

But there was none greater that they knew of.

Until now, everyone had believed Mikel and her brother to be dead, so what else had Heaven been hiding all these eons? What else lived and existed in its highest spaces? Israfel was more like Lucifel than even Kim had imagined, and perhaps it explained their terrible antipathy a little more logically. Their flavor of cruelty, anyway, was a close match. And if Israfel had the Archon, his sister's possible future opponent, on his side . . .

A harsh screech echoed through the park.

Fury spiraled down amid the rain, her black wings settling clumsily as she landed on Kim's shoulder. She croaked in his ear, persistent. Troy must have known where Angela and Israfel had disappeared to—and it certainly wouldn't be Heaven. Grim and keenly unhappy, he watched silently while the bird glided to the ground and scratched letters in the soil. A flash of lightning highlighted the grotto, and for a brief moment, the Vapor's true form appeared, overlapping her avian body—a little human girl with blond curls, her face as gray as when she'd died.

S-A-N-C-T-U-S

She used her beak, slicing into the earth.

M-A-R-I-A

E-C-C-L-E-S-I-A

Sanctus Maria Ecclesia.

"Saint Mary's," Kim muttered under his breath.

Not good. This morning was the Feast of All Saints, one of the Academy's most important holy days. Priests, novices, visiting bishops, and every Westwood student from the grades of college freshman upward would be required to attend the ceremony. If Israfel showed his face in front of them all, it could mean absolute chaos. And that wasn't counting whatever tricks Stephanie might have up her sleeve.

Kim slid a hand into his pocket, touching his knife. Perhaps it would be murdering another angel, another Jinn, or another demon. And no matter how much it hurt to admit it, Kim and Troy had one thing in common.

Mikel knew enough to dash into the bushes, before he could grab her.

He couldn't wait.

Twenty-five

They look into the soul, they see all sins.
Worst of all, they judge accordingly.

—Venerable Maximina, *Lost Writings and Annotations*

Angela threw open the doors of the cathedral, rain streaming down her face and squishing in the soles of her boots. Thunder split the air behind her, horrendously loud.

Yet the music inside of the church was even louder. Apparently, the feast had been postponed until shortly before she arrived, probably because of the harsh weather. While the church had been a morass of darkness and unholy light only a day or so ago, now it overflowed with life and expectation, every wick lit, every candle burning, every lamp shining brightly.

Angela stood at the end of the aisle, alone. Ahead, and flanking either side of the building, rows upon rows of students stood in their pews, observing the tail end of the procession heading toward the altar.

She couldn't even count the novices. There could have been one hundred, two hundred.

No sign of Israfel. If he'd arrived before her, then he was hiding.

She proceeded down the aisle, scanning heads as she went.

Students turned and stared at her, some angry, most simply perplexed by her dirty blouse and tattered skirt. And in the meantime, the bishops and superintendent priests climbed the short set of stairs to their seats, robes drifting across the gray stone. Angela followed them, growing ever more aware of people examining her like the freak show she must have looked like, unable to find a spot to sit or stand among them, or even a friendly face that was inviting her in. Then the priests turned around to face the assembled students, taking their assigned places at the head of the altar.

Angela shoved her way into the nearest pew on her right, still dripping water everywhere.

Lyrica Pengold stood on the opposite side of the aisle, goggling at Angela like she was a corpse come back from the grave. By sheer bad luck, the entire Pentacle Sorority was gathered next to her, Stephanie standing in the very front row closest to the altar.

Sophia and Naamah flanked Stephanie like bodyguards.

Sophia's all right. But that could change in a minute. I've got to get her out of here.

The organ music stopped, its echo resounding against the walls of the church. Slowly, the head priest of the Academy raised his hands, motioning for complete silence. Students who had been chattering while the music continued now stopped to listen, very few paying any more attention to Angela.

Lyrica, though, trembled. She leaned over and muttered to a sorority member on her right. Instantly, the message began to relay farther up the ranks, heading inexorably for Stephanie Walsh and the demon standing with her.

Shit.

"I want to thank everyone," the priest proclaimed, his voice booming all the way back into the eaves, "who was involved in last night's relief efforts at the lower levels of the Academy. Those who opened their dormitories to shelter students now without possessions, and those who assisted in the brave task of bringing the deceased out of the waters, and into a place where their bodies could be prepared for burial. Despite the intense wind and waves, by the blessing of God, we suffered very few casualties. Three students, two from overseas, and one whom we will greatly mourn, our resident valedictorian, Maribel Heins—"

Some of the students gasped, shifting uncomfortably in their seats.

"—we will be having a funeral Mass for them tomorrow at eight in the morning. All students are asked to attend and pray for the souls of their departed brothers and sisters."

Stephanie turned her head, glancing at Angela.

Then she turned around, an upsetting smile on her lips.

Angela patted the Grail beneath her blouse, wishing Troy still carried it after all. That way, it would be eternally impossible for Stephanie to see or get her hands on it, and that was assuming she could without breaking under its gaze. But she could look into the eyes of a demon without being intimidated—that had to count for something. If she and Naamah had been making plans over the long night, then it was lost on everyone around her, a testament to how well Stephanie could squash her emotions when she felt like it.

When her name was announced by the priest, she barely reacted.

"—and so, as head of the sorority that claimed Maribel as a member, Stephanie Walsh will now address the student body in her stead before we formally begin the Mass—"

Stephanie slipped out of her pew and walked up to the podium where the priest had been standing, her skirt swishing around her hips. She was probably the only person at the Academy who could get away with attending Mass in a soft-porn school-girl uniform. Then, in a gesture of astounding disrespect, she took her maroon hair out of its ponytail, regathered it, and slouched against the podium, staring out at the students arranged in front of her. "Students of Westwood Academy, of the University," she said slowly. "I'm sorry to say that one of the dearest sisters in our sorority died last night—though not in the way you've been led to believe."

Oh, God. This is going to be bad. I know it.

The novices lined behind her murmured back and forth.

Some of the priests went white in the face. Rain lashed the windows of the cathedral, beginning a hammering downpour.

"I'm sure everyone knows by now about the serial killer in Luz. I'm sure you've been wondering what kind of person could commit such horrible crimes. He's probably disturbed, emotionless. Someone with a history of violence against himself and others."

She paused dramatically, everyone else pausing with her.

"I saw Maribel's death firsthand—"

Liar. What's she doing . . .

"—and I'm afraid to tell you, there's a demon loose in the city."

Angela expected laughter, incredulous snorting. Instead, panic shivered through the entire university population, edging some of the students out of their seats and into the aisle. They stopped abruptly as the doors slammed shut, the locks clicking into place. A few spun around, startled by the noise, by the priest's aghast expressions.

This was Luz, and Stephanie was a witch. Anything could happen now.

Angela glanced at Naamah, immediately suspicious.

The demon lowered her hand, smiling cruelly.

"Miss Walsh—" the presiding priest snapped at her from across the altar. The church became worryingly dark again, candles sputtering out, leaving only those on the altar table bright and wavering. "*Miss Walsh—*"

"But every demon summoned to Earth needs a master," Stephanie said louder. She left the podium, marching across the stone, giving her audience a smile meant for Angela more than anyone else. They stared at each other, and Angela made sure her eyes never left Stephanie's, no matter how much it hurt her to look her in the face.

Why, though, did it hurt?

She's different. Something's changed since last night.

One more mystery among many. Even worse, Israfel still hadn't shown himself. Maybe he'd seen Naamah standing there. Maybe he'd rethought helping his plaything on such a soggy morning. Either way, for now, it looked like Angela had no one to rely on but herself.

"Angela Mathers," Stephanie said, pointing at her, making hundreds of heads whip around, horrified. The student next to

Angela backed away like she had the plague. "She tried to join my sorority by summoning a fallen angel to this Academy. It killed Maribel—"

Resounding gasps of horror.

Stephanie lost her smile. "—and escaped into the city during the height of the storm."

"Shut her up," the priest snapped at those to his left and right, gesturing for them to drag her off the altar. "She's gone completely mad. The last thing we need—*shut her up*," his voice thundered, mixing with the thunder outside.

Stephanie spun around, her hair swinging like a rope. "*Not so fast.*"

Her voice was so forceful, everyone froze, hypnotized.

The priest gazed at her with real fear.

"We're just getting started."

She looked to Naamah.

The demon waved her dark hand, forcing the church into almost utter blackness. Students screamed, some dashing toward the doors, only to find them locked. Others sat in a shocked and dead silent horror, unable to do a thing as the novices backed away from Stephanie, afraid of what else could go wrong if they touched her.

Angela alone remained standing.

Stephanie marched up to her, refined and polite. "That was a pretty good stunt you pulled last night," she said, whispering. "But I don't quite feel like playing games anymore. How acquainted are you with Hell, Angela? You're going to be visiting soon, I think."

Statues loomed overhead. The stained glass glazed over beneath Naamah's bloody light.

Angela almost felt like a prophet. "You'll visit long before I do."

"You're not the Archon, Angela Mathers."

Stephanie's eyes were strangely piercing, her words so certain, so confident, Angela almost agreed. Which might have explained why her answer surprised them both.

"*We'll see.*"

Stephanie turned away, her heeled boots clacking imperiously against the tiles. She walked nearer to the priest in charge of the Mass, his white face matching his hair.

No one moved to obey him, too afraid of what Stephanie could do.

"Archbishop Solomon," she said, meeting him eye to eye. "Considering the circumstances, I think we should both agree that our deal is officially null and void. I'm going to have to take over from here."

"You," the priest hissed, sounding distinctly furious, "have had more than enough freedom to act at this Academy, Miss Walsh. But that freedom ends today. The moment you step out of this church, you are expelled from the school—and"—he glared pointedly at the pentacle on her overcoat—"excommunicated."

She's bolder than before. It must have to do with Naamah. She's growing too certain of that demon's power backing her up.

"Excommunicated." Stephanie laughed softly. "Good one. But that won't be going on here at the new and improved Westwood Academy. *My* new and improved Westwood Academy."

"You're insane," the priest said, his mouth twisting in outrage.

"More than that," she muttered back at him, "I'm aching to tear things down. Don't think I never knew why you allowed me to run around this Academy and do what I wanted. Don't think I wasn't aware of why you sent that novice into my bed. But you made yours, didn't you? Because by turning a blind eye to me, it was so much easier. Because who best to help you with your own sins than a witch?"

The archbishop's eyes widened, and he glanced at his colleagues, denying everything already. "What the hell are you—"

"One year ago today, you made your bed with a girl from the freshman class, Claire Benevento. Then Augustina Hamelin, Nicolette Grimwallis, Marietta Sills . . ."

The names continued until Angela felt dizzy, the whole world twisted and sick.

She finally forced herself to listen again, overcoming her nausea beneath the weight of the archbishop's personal transgressions. He was immobile before Stephanie, already before the Judgment Seat because somehow she knew everything there was to know about his taste in schoolgirls. When she came to the end, no one dared to breathe.

"You wanted to sniff the Archon out and stamp Her flat. Before She could make the first move. Well, you waited too long. Today, one more demon is going to drive out the rest. The ones that aren't useful."

"How will you do it?" the archbishop whispered, trembling like Lyrica.

"First? We'll burn our most troublesome witch at the stake." Stephanie pointed at Angela again, perfectly calm. Her smile made Naamah's look like child's play. "Ready to go up in flames?"

A mass of black cloud had settled over St. Mary's, and its torrents of rain continued to spatter onto Kim and his already soaked clothing. If last night's storm had been terrible, then Luz was approaching the verge of catastrophe on this High Holy Day. Circumstances, it was obvious, were worsening by the hour, as if everyone now had to function on borrowed time.

Everything was fast becoming clear to him.

Slowly but surely, the Ruin was revealing herself, and the universe, the creatures in it, both dead and alive, were weeping under the pressure.

Kim splashed through the moats of water near the entrance of the church. The rain had increased to a steady slant, nearly burning into his eyes. Soon, visibility would drop to zero, forcing him to fumble his way into the cathedral.

At least no one was around to watch.

The courtyard in front of St. Mary's was empty, the surrounding towers dark and silent. Everyone had locked themselves indoors, far from the violence of the rain and wind.

Fury croaked to his left, emerging for a second through the sheet of water, her wings flapping frantically. She screeched, the chill sound echoing from stone to stone, and flew back into the downpour like a lost shadow.

An alarm call.

He reached for the knife in his pocket, gripping the handle.

The wind changed, rushing on him from above. Kim slammed to the ground beneath its force, the breath knocking out of his chest, hot pain racing along his torso. A new shadow, like Fury's but so very much larger, descended on him with a falcon's speed and fury. He whipped around, fending off two black wings the length of his own body, their feathers beating against his skin. Screaming, he tore the knife out of his pocket and slashed wildly.

The rain parted, revealing a male face with green eyes.

Then the angel swerved out of his reach, disappearing behind the water, its wings missing the knife again by a hairsbreadth.

Another deep peal of thunder shook the ground, ripples of lightning highlighting the world with silver.

There, to the right.

The angel had landed nearby, standing like a tall, black nightmare behind the curtain of rain—examining him for a weak spot.

He hadn't expected this. A demon, yes. Israfel, maybe. The Supernal must have had bodyguards, servants, or children. But whoever this angel truly was, he didn't want Kim in that building, already seeming to understand how important it was that he eventually get inside. Kim had nothing to save him but his instincts and his skills, and they wouldn't count for much when he could barely see his opponent.

"Is that all, you sneaky bastard?" Kim shouted over the storm.

Silence.

The angel was waiting for him to make the next move.

Fair enough. Kim reached for a prayer ward on the inside of his coat and lifted it into the rain. The ink melted off the paper, its once crisp edges folding over with moisture. He tossed the ward as far as it would go, meaning to give himself that second's worth of protection before it disintegrated. "*Libera me a malo!*"

The angel backed off into the shadows, vanishing amid the towers.

Yes—it was working.

Kim pushed onto his feet, laughing a little. This would be easier than he'd thought.

More wind. He pitched backward onto the street, crushed beneath the fury of two white wings hammering the air above him. This time, a female face broke through the sheets of water between them, her eyes a perfect match for the male's, green with venom. He swiped at her with the knife, cutting the side of her shoulder. "*Libera me a malo! Averto absum!*"

She screamed back at him, more enraged than hurt.

Then, with an infuriated shiver of her wings, she fought through the needle-sharp pain of his words. He aimed his blade at her throat, but before he could touch the angel, her fingers wrapped around his neck. Kim coughed, straining to wrench her hands away, his back arching up from the stones. They struggled, rolling on the ground, but the angel held tight and already the world was fading into a giant swirl of gray, every bit of his pain lifting like a fog before morning. His body began to numb over. He relaxed and stopped clawing at his murderer's perfect face.

Another surprise. He'd never imagined Angela would be his final thought.

The slow, sarcastic clapping from the side entrance of the altar sounded suitably horrific.

Brendan appeared seemingly out of nowhere, marching through a rank of novices who parted like twin waves. Hideous bruises bloomed on his face and neck. Sophia glanced at Angela for the first time since she'd entered the cathedral, biting her lip, visibly nervous. Beside Sophia, Naamah frowned, flexing the knives buried beneath her nails.

Brendan doesn't know about the demon. If nobody does anything—he'll die.

"Oh, it's you," Stephanie said, letting him get close. Too close. "Good timing, Brendan. You can do me a favor and join your sister."

Brendan laughed, the noise abrupt and harsh, ringing against frescoes and stone. "Really, I'm impressed. You've done it this time."

SABRINA BENULIS

"And you sound—and look—as ridiculous as I expected."

"I just find it ironic that you're threatening my sister, when you're the one about to burn." Brendan pushed the greasy curls from his head, appearing unwholesomely careless. The expression on his face was disturbing. Older, more mature, but in the way of a person who'd sunk his teeth into forbidden fruit, losing all his innocence the more he tasted it. The sight was a terrible one, but Angela knew better than to open her mouth. She'd have her chance to act.

Besides—this wasn't her brother anymore.

"Remember when I said, 'nice knowing you'?" Stephanie folded her arms. She beckoned to Naamah, encouraging her nearer. "I lied."

"One of your friends from Hell, I'm guessing?" Brendan's lazy grin hadn't changed.

Naamah stepped up to the altar, unperturbed by the closeness of any holy objects, people, or pictures. But it was fast becoming apparent that only part of what Angela knew about angels was the actual fact. Latin hurt them, yet a holy object seemingly had no effect whatsoever. Darkness oppressed the cathedral as Naamah climbed the stairs, and the priests cringed, some pressing against the walls. They could sense the wrongness of her.

She glared at them, her eyes blacker than two pools of oil.

Then the head priest made his mistake. "*Vade, daemon.*" Despite the thunder, even murmuring the Latin sounded louder than a trumpet blast in the quiet cathedral. "*Anima vestras ad infernum remittite . . .*"

Naamah flinched, like he'd stuck her with a needle.

She rounded on him, teeth gritted. Those nightmarish blades slipped out of her fingers.

The archbishop blanched whiter than death, still mumbling under his breath while she advanced on him. Her braids resembled a coil of miniature snakes attached to her head, and she loomed over the novices, tall and perfect and completely lethal.

He tried to speak, but she snapped her fingers, their metal clanking together.

His mouth sealed shut.

"That's funny." She leaned into him. "You're suddenly speechless."

Stephanie sighed in the background, impatient and unsympathetic. She folded her arms, leaning against a stone column with her ponytail swinging against it, ropelike. "Get on with it."

Naamah's mouth twitched, and she stiffened ever so slightly. Stephanie's tone of voice had bothered her.

There was a tense silence.

The demon swung her arm.

The priest's head rolled down the altar steps, its face staring at her in disbelief. It seemed to take forever for the archbishop's eyes to glaze over, for Angela to catch her breath again.

For the tremendous panic to begin.

Students burst from their pews, stampeding in thunderous chaos to the doors, the windows. The screams were deafening. Glass smashed. People howled, stepped on by others, by friends. Outside, the storm continued, relentless and terrifying, and as the doors held fast and the windowsills sat too high for anyone to climb through them, the pandemonium increased by the second.

Angela dashed from her own pew and snagged Sophia by the arm, holding on with real pain while the novices swept by, screaming with the others. Those brave enough to challenge Naamah had already died, either bleeding or collapsing from an invisible blow to the head, the chest—it was too hard to tell.

Everything was madness.

There's no way to stop her. Even I can't do it. If I try to use Latin, she'll kill me, or at least shut me up.

Then the singing nearly brought her to her knees.

Every person's reaction was instantaneous. Those in a blind panic paused to listen, rapt with amazement. Many of the novices' eyes widened large as saucers, and they picked themselves out of the mayhem, stepping closer to hear. The priests froze like deer sighted by wolves, staring in shocked reverence.

Stephanie looked like her face had been dipped in bleach.

Naamah trembled, her unfurled wings spasming with either rage or wretched fear. More skin than bloody feathers, her wings were riddled with patches of tendon and bone. Metal had been ribbed through them, as if to keep the ragged mess together.

Sophia squeezed Angela's hand, shivering.

Brendan looked ecstatic as Israfel appeared, gliding from the shadows that veiled the altar's side entrance, a white, graceful, lovely perfection that broke apart the darkness, the bloody light, the hell that the cathedral had become. His wings were all white feathers and elegance, trailing behind him like a prince's robe, and his embroidered coat shimmered like a newborn star. Platinum chains, sewn to the fabric, jingled musically whenever he took a step. There was a sudden flowering of scent, like musk and lilies and salt water.

Israfel was so beautiful, he was more an apparition than a reality.

And he's mine.

The second Israfel stopped singing, Stephanie screeched at Naamah, wild-eyed, red in the face.

"You said HE WAS DEAD."

The demon wasn't listening. She stared at Israfel like he'd risen from a grave right in front of her, her fingerblades clenching and unclenching with indecision.

"WHAT ARE YOU WAITING FOR? JUST KILL HIM."

The storm raged over Naamah's first sentence, and barely revealed the next. ". . . a Supernal. If you take one more step closer, I'll cut his throat."

She meant Brendan, of course. He was laughing loudly again, but so close to Naamah that she merely grabbed him by the shoulders and put her fingers to his neck, snapping out her demands.

"Stay back, angel."

Now it all made sense. Israfel's plaything was Brendan, Angela's own brother. She'd probably never know how they'd met—whether it had been coincidence, an honest mistake, or deliberate seduction—but Brendan's nasty comments in the cafeteria suddenly meant so much more. Whatever kind of activities he'd been participating in the last few weeks, they'd either changed his personality, or brought out a darkness inside of it that he'd managed to hide for quite a while.

Stephanie had ironically met her match—she had her demon and Brendan had his angel. Now, they were on frighteningly equal footing.

They never loved each other to begin with. Love can't turn to a hatred this strong.

Then she recalled Tileaf's memories of Lucifel, and that certainty took wings and flew from her, never to return.

"He's mine, crow." Troy's voice echoed from far away, its anger burning the soul like living fire.

A piercing howl tortured Kim's ears.

The Throne's cruel fingers unclenched from around his neck, Angela's ghost disappeared, and he crashed onto the drenched cobblestones, sweet oxygen burning into each lung, his body gasping and boneless with pain. The female angel writhed beside him like a worm on a hook, blood streaming from a wounded wing, the other flapping maniacally, scraping his coat. Troy lunged again from the shadows, snapping her teeth, careful to stay out of arm's reach. Then she connected with the angel—and both of them tumbled to the ground in a flurry of nails and feathers, holding nothing back.

Fury circled overhead, a black silhouette croaking in alarm.

It was another warning, one that Kim would be wise to pay attention to again. He could have been beaten by a club, his muscles felt so sore. But he was also a half-Jinn, and fueled by the blood and the sound of Troy's wrath, he was back on his feet with surprising speed. The rain continued to fall in buckets, and in an instant, his cousin and the angel disappeared, lost to Luz's gray waters.

Wings rolled a thunder greater than the storm's. The male angel was returning.

The knife. He needed the goddamned knife. Kim had lost it while the female had him by the neck.

He dropped to the ground, pawing the stones, barely missing outstretched fingers ready to wrap around his throat again. Kim swore, hissing more curses, finally feeling the familiar curve of the handle settled inside his palm.

He turned, swinging his arm in a wild arc, desperate to fend off the latest shadow.

Troy swooped out of the rain and down to the ground, the female following close behind. The angel was a picture of white rage, almost as frightful as the Jinn who'd torn a gash in her wing. Her cheeks flared with red stripes, like elegant, terrifying war paint.

These angels fought like rabid dogs.

Troy galloped on her hands and feet, closing in on Kim. When they met, she pressed against his back, spreading her wings in a threatening display, gnashing her teeth furiously at the white angel who leaned over them both, tall and furious. Troy's pinions rubbed Kim's shoulders and arms, the feathers on each stiff and unforgiving as razor blades. "Do it," she shrieked. "Before the male returns."

Too late. He was heading straight for them.

Troy fended the female off, spitting like some nightmarish cat.

"Just don't whine that it hurts." Kim tore the buttons from his coat sleeve, rolling it upward.

He set the knife to his skin.

God—the cut felt like a streak of fire.

A long red line appeared, followed by more crimson dripping slowly down his hand. Kim's fingers slipped against each other, soaked with redness despite the rain. He began tracing the pentagram in the air shakily, hurried by panic.

"I said *do it*," Troy shrieked again, hissing so loudly at the angel Kim's ears throbbed in pain. She lunged, the bones in her hair rattling like a snake's tail. "Throne," she spit at the female. "Abomination. Back to your cage and leash, bastard crow. Better that you'd rotted in the depths of the Underworld, a chick without a hope."

The female screamed wordlessly, but Troy's insults kept her

close and vulnerable. She flapped her wings, face-to-face with his cousin, both of them continuing their threat displays.

Troy bit for the angel's throat, her teeth smashing together.

A Throne.

No wonder these angels fought like berserkers. For once, Troy had a challenge on her hands. When it came to fury and relentless murder, they were probably a closer match than even she felt comfortable with. But there was no doubt now that Israfel was nearby, probably right inside St. Mary's, wreaking all kinds of havoc. These were his guardians, and most likely, some of the best that Heaven had ever produced. Thrones were the privilege of the high angels, the powerful personalities. And they were also—unfortunately—the first set of opponents if anyone dared infringe on their master's interests.

Most never survived to tell about it—but Kim was hardly ready to settle for death.

The smile spreading across his face had the joy of hurting more than the angels behind it. "*Defende nos in proelio!*"

Troy stiffened against him, hardly able to bear his voice.

Kim's blood remained in the air, the droplets holding fast to the invisible pentagram. His arm shook, and he glared directly into the male angel's eyes. In a few seconds, they would be on top of each other. Behind him, the female moaned, her wings slowing as Troy's also relaxed, both of them stricken. His cousin's breath was like a ragged whisper.

"*Contra nequitiam et insidias diaboli esto praesidium!*"

The pentagram blazed, its light like a red star.

Troy collapsed to the ground, panting, her nails scraping the stone.

"*Libera nos a malo! A malo!*"

The red light exploded, expanding in a circle of brilliance to the fringes of the courtyard, all the rain seeming to turn into blood. Within it, the Thrones shrieked with a chilling kind of rage, and then their own silver light flashed in front of the church, lightning that mixed with more lightning.

In an instant, they escaped into the next dimension and were gone, wounds still streaming, wings thundering faintly.

Troy's gasps came slower, but the pain on her face was something Kim rarely witnessed.

Her ears flicked water away from her cheeks, and her glowing eyes hid under half-mast lids, dimmed by the spiritual oppression. Gradually, she folded her wings tightly against her back and clambered onto hands and feet, rising to sit on her haunches. Her face was uncharacteristically expressionless. Kim knew better than to talk. He knew better than to listen for a thank you. Instead, he watched the water roll along the white curves of her face.

If only the prayer had the power to kill her.

But Troy was a Jinn, and one of the toughest. His exorcisms could ward her off, temporarily weaken her, even send her back to Hell for a short time. But he'd never be able to kill her. It would take a demon, an angel, or something unimaginable to accomplish that.

"Do you want me to thank you?" she said, snarling coldly.

Fury spiraled down and landed on her shoulder, pecking at the earring near her neck, its metal crow's foot scratching into her skin. Troy batted her away, and even in the wetness, her nails looked lacquered with bright red.

Angel blood.

She licked them clean and spat onto the cobblestones. Her entire body shook. "If—you—*ever* even think of using that ward on me—"

"Consider us even. A life for a life." He stepped around her, eager to get inside the church and keep Angela from killing herself prematurely.

Whump.

Troy landed in front of him, blocking off his escape. She was very close, her yellow eyes almost hypnotizing him with their inner fire, and her breath blew back in his face, pushing the wet hairs from his cheeks. "For now," she said, through lips tinted with the blood from her nails, "you live and speak your mind. But remember that your miracle won't happen more than once. I could have let them kill you, Sariel." She smiled cruelly. "But my pride couldn't stand seeing anyone else's teeth in your spine."

"And if Israfel beats you to it? He is a Supernal."

Troy paused, her ears perking. She'd either heard something he could not, or Israfel's name had a unique way of disgusting her.

Then she regarded him again and laughed. She was beating her wings, ready to enter the cathedral at the moment when she'd be least expected or wanted, which seemed to be every other second of the day. "I'd worry more about your mates tearing each other apart. It will be entertaining, at least."

He gripped his knife, heading for the doors of St. Mary's. It was going to be very entertaining when she saw how mercilessly he could clip a bird's wings.

Kim licked his blade clean, relishing the blood in spite of himself.

Especially a bird of God.

Twenty-six

Most beautiful of all creatures, was the Star of the Morning.
And the eye that gazed upon him already grasped its heart's desire.
—UNKNOWN AUTHOR, *A Collection of Angelic Lore*

Israfel was staring at Brendan like they'd never met before.

His eyes were so large and beguiling, Angela clenched Sophia's hand in a death grip, afraid she would abandon her soul for the sake of another kiss.

Sophia must have sensed the conflict. Breathing heavily, she yanked Angela closer, like they'd belonged to each other for years.

The angel regarded them both with a quick glance, a lovely smile.

Then, for Brendan, his face became unexpectedly apologetic. Thunder and rain erupted through the broken windows, merely highlighting the soft strength of his voice.

"I'm sorry, Brendan."

Angela's brother stopped laughing, and he became so still, Naamah could have killed him already. The demon, too, was in shock, as if Israfel had just told her he was ready to kneel at Lucifel's feet and kiss them.

"What do you mean?" Brendan said, his voice cracking. He was sweating, almost writhing in between words, like Israfel's mere presence was enough to make him lose control. There was an unnerving wantonness to it all. "Israfel—my angel—"

Israfel didn't react.

"Kill her. Do it. Burn her." Brendan pointed at Stephanie. "*The witch! Burn her!*"

Stephanie stood still, blank in the face and silent. Israfel could snap her neck with a blink of his eyes, and yet he was turning on the person who'd brought him there in the first place. Then, a silvery light circled the angel's head in a halo of energy. His ears changed, their upper rims growing, slipping between his hair and lengthening into delicate but feathery sickles. Wings. These were another pair of wings, and he tested their muscles, fanning air through the white tendrils near his cheeks.

When he spoke again, his voice was resigned. "Are you ready to go?"

"You promised." Brendan sank to his knees, but Naamah kept a grip on his hair. She seemed as disturbed as everyone else, her hard eyes never leaving Israfel. "I gave you *MY SOUL. MY SOUL.*"

The echo could have lasted forever.

His *soul*? Kim had warned Angela about that kind of idiocy.

Now she was witnessing it firsthand.

Israfel's loveliness seemed to grow, like he'd calculated it the best way to torture Brendan even further. Angela could see it with a detail that struck her painfully inside. She had envisioned those eyes for so long, the slightest change in them stood out like ink on snow.

"You shouldn't be afraid," Israfel said with a measured gentleness. "Of course, I can always bring you back in a new body, whenever I feel like it. And then another. And another." His pink lips mouthed the words too softly. "So why fear death? You're going to be happy now, Brendan. An eternity of slavery to me, just as you wished. And you'll have a million bodies with which to enjoy it."

Sophia shuddered next to Angela, like her own execution had been pronounced.

Brendan will be just like her. Dying over and over, only to wake up in a new body—all to wait for a different kind of death.

Somehow, Brendan had pissed Israfel off. Now he was going to pay for it dearly. For eternity. "Why?" her brother gasped, almost lunging out of Naamah's lethal grip.

Israfel looked to Angela.

Brendan followed his gaze, horrified.

"No need for two in my confidence," the angel whispered. "It simply wouldn't be fair."

Angela's brother was suddenly a mess, his hair tangled in front of his eyes, his face contorted with anger. "You," he said to Angela. "You!" He pointed at her, shrieking at the top of his lungs. *"It wasn't enough to ruin the family? To ruin my life? And here I scraped and slaved my way into this seminary, and yet you enter Luz simply because you're a blood head—"*

He was raving. Israfel had pushed him completely over the edge.

Angela lunged to grab him, to rescue him from the danger that loomed more menacingly every second. But Sophia yanked her back just as swiftly, her fingers like an unbreakable vise.

"—but you can't have HIM, Angela. He's MINE. MINE—"

"Brendan," she said, trying to say more with her expression than her words—

Shut up. Shut up before it's too late.

"You sound like a crazy person. You sound like—"

Sophia held on tighter. Painfully, impossibly tight.

"You're crazy! You're going to be the ruin of us all! Why didn't they just kill you that night—when we were born—LOOK WHAT YOU DID TO ME—"

Sophia turned away, her eyes squeezed shut.

As if this was her cue, Naamah gave a slight flick of her wrist.

Brendan's throat slit open like a ripe fruit. He gurgled, slipping in the mess of his own blood, flailing out of her reach and onto the floor, clutching at his wound. Angela didn't even realize she was screaming until Sophia twisted her arm, shocking her back into a dreamlike, semiaware state. But no one could save her brother. And Stephanie, his former lover, simply watched, her mouth set in a line and her expression stony. Brendan crawled for the angel, spitting more blood as he tried to talk.

Israfel stood over Brendan, judging him like a god but not saying a word. Her brother grasped the angel's foot, his skin paling to chalky white, his eyes round with shock. An exchange of thoughts seemed to pass between him and Israfel, ones that brought shivers to Brendan's body.

He collapsed a second later. Dead.

Naamah breathed heavily, wiping her dirtied blades in a fold of coat fabric. "He was uncommonly loud for a priest," she said, muttering. Then she laughed at Israfel, certainly overjoyed to see him distressed by her violence. "I wouldn't be too upset. He also wasn't a fitting toy, am I right?"

"Angela," Sophia was saying, as if from very far away. "Angela . . ."

But she was becoming one with the audience trapped inside the church, dazed and overwhelmed. That raving mockery of humanity hadn't been her brother. Yes, he and Angela might have been estranged for years, but even so, the thought was the only support that was keeping her from losing her last precious thread of self-control and collapsing inside for good.

Her reaction, though, was a universal one.

Everyone else who'd been left alive to watch her brother die stood in the same dull kind of silence, as if the bloodshed no longer meant anything. Some of the novices had huddled in the darkest corners they could find, and out past the dim light of the candles there were the reflections of hundreds of eyes, the ragged breaths from hundreds of mouths, the prayers whispered half in fear and half in the hope of escape.

I can't just curl up and cry. It won't change anything.

Despite her resolve, the tears trickled down her face.

No. Angela knew she had to help. She was one of the only people who could.

But how? And without killing herself?

You should have never Bound her to you . . .

Troy. Angela could actually use that terrifying creature and she was nowhere to be found.

But if you are nearby, she said to herself, *you'd better come.*

Members of the Pentacle Sorority had sat still in their pews, protected from the mayhem until Israfel's arrival. Now they rested on the tiles, their knees tucked up within the circle of their arms, watching Stephanie and Angela like they were two gods on the verge of battle.

Perhaps they weren't mistaken. Stephanie shouted at Angela, breaking her trance.

"—and I think it's time we finished this. Naamah—"

The demon wasn't moving. Instead she narrowed her eyes knowingly at Stephanie, dark with concentration as Israfel approached with the same grace he'd used to enter the church. Stephanie backed away from him, screaming, but the angel silenced her with a sharp gesture of his hand.

She clutched at her throat, still spewing words no one could hear.

Turning to Naamah for help, finding none, whatever pride she was holding on to melted with the shattered look on her face. She whimpered, like a child begging for protection.

Sophia grabbed Angela's wrist, squeezing it again. Her voice was fainter than a breeze. "You must not let him see the Grail."

How does she know I have it?

Angela's blouse was loose enough to keep it hidden. But she obeyed without questioning any further, realizing that her instincts had been correct all along.

The Grail would be a reminder of Lucifel.

She clamped her hand over the Eye, almost wishing it could fuse to her body rather than swing from her neck.

"Is it you?" Israfel was saying to Stephanie.

She was calming down, entranced. But her hands remained balled into fists, and she shivered all over, responding to his closeness like the threat that it was. Then Israfel reached down and lifted her chin, leaning in for a familiar kiss. Stephanie struggled with him at first, but soon gave in, and Angela bit her lip, feeling it bleed. In an instant, her grief was forgotten. Instead, it was taking everything in her—and Sophia's fingers clamped into her skin like cold iron—not to repeat Brendan's mistake and start screaming like a maniac.

Israfel broke away from her quickly. "What is this?"

Stephanie shook out of her short possession, panting. Naamah's expression had changed to one of sudden and unexpected anguish. His reaction had told her something important, maybe devastating.

"That taste," Israfel said, practically spitting her out of his mouth. "Like you've crawled out of the Abys—"

Boom.

Thunder resounded through the cathedral.

The rosette window at the front of the church exploded into a million shards of color.

The double doors of the church slammed back open, their locks cracking with a burst of crimson light. Students, teachers, novices, priests, and civilians flooded out of the disaster into the storm, into Luz, as above them, the city's notorious serial killer winged her way through a new rain of glass. Troy seemed to descend in slow motion, every flap of her feathers sounding more forceful than a million growls and hisses. Lightning raced across the open sky above the cathedral, highlighting the little razors that were her teeth, and she landed on all fours with a grace that matched the sleek beauty of her wings and ears.

Then she ripped into a student who stood in her way. He fell with one swipe of her nails. In seconds, she was racing in Naamah's direction.

She came. Why? Because she's Bound to me? Because she heard my thoughts?

Troy passed Angela, giving her a glare that confirmed everything. There was no time for explanations.

Stephanie screamed for the demon, the other sorority members taking their chance at escape. Only Sophia wasn't going anywhere.

Israfel seemed to have materialized out of the air, pulling her out of Angela's reach.

Sophia glared at him with surprising hatred. "Let go of me, Israfel. Or you'll be sorry for it."

She knows him too. Oh, God, why can't I hate him for this? For letting Brendan die? For anything?

Angela grabbed her back, yanking her close.

The church continued falling to pieces around them, glass smashing and plaster cracking. "What are you doing?"

Israfel ran his fingers through Sophia's curls. "That careless demon saved me a week's worth of searching. Who'd have thought they'd leave such a precious item lying around?"

"But that doesn't make sense . . ." Angela's body trembled, her insides freezing over. This was surreal. It simply *didn't* make any sense whatsoever. "Israfel," she forced herself to sound firm, "you're making a mistake. Sophia is just a friend of mine, she—"

She's a person who already died, and you're going to kill her again? Not today . . .

Unlike Brendan and his repressed lack of morals, Sophia hadn't done anything to justify another punishment. Angela felt her first spark of anger, staring at Israfel's kohl-rimmed eyes and stainless perfection. Whatever enchantment he'd used on Brendan, her feelings must have been too genuine for that to matter. She wanted to slap him across the face, like she'd been tossed into the middle of an argument between two lovers and was now forced to pick a side. She actually felt stronger than him, even when he laughed and the noise sounded lighter and farther away than the stars. The wings that were once normal ears flapped and folded again, hiding beneath his hair. "Friend? Excuse me, but someone has put silly ideas into your head."

"No."

"Yes. For the Father's sake, let's get this over with."

He lifted Sophia's left arm and stripped away her skin in one smooth movement.

Sophia never cried out. She barely shed a tear. But her face twisted with a terrible anger, and her gray eyes regressed to those vacant holes Angela feared so much. Israfel let her go, and Sophia stumbled away, clutching her arm while black blood trickled down to her wrist. Israfel dropped the part of Sophia's arm that seemed more glove than skin—and Angela stared at the white muscle, the black veins that had been hiding beneath it—understanding that she was seeing something alien and inhuman, and maybe worse than both.

"Do you know what she is?" Israfel said gently.

In the background, Naamah screamed and Troy hissed like some gigantic snake as they fought. Candlesticks, altar cloths, tapestries, and glass fell, smashed, crashed. But that chaos was nothing compared to the blow Angela was feeling. Her stomach felt like someone had pulled it out with a hook.

Why? First Brendan, now this.

"She said she'd died—"

"A lie." Israfel forced Sophia to turn back to them both, pinching her chin between his fingers. She was frightening to look at, her porcelain complexion contorted by the rage that was showing in her unwholesome eyes and quivering mouth. "Or maybe a half-truth: one can never know when it comes to her. In actuality, she is a golem—an artificial creation."

"Whose creation?" Angela's mouth went dry. She was torn between screaming herself and wrenching Sophia out of Israfel's grasp and shaking her like a rag doll. "*Whose?*"

Israfel leaned down, repeating the question like she was a child. "Whose creation, Sophia?"

Now the tears began. Sophia glanced at Angela, her face streaked by water and misery, half sobbing. "Raziel's."

Raziel's . . .

"*You lied to me.*" For the first time since they'd entered the church, Angela took the chance to yell like everyone else. No one was who she'd thought. Everyone seemed to hide behind masks, secrets, half-truths, and martyrdoms. "You lied . . . you said that you died in childbirth, that you had been brought back to life as a punishment—"

"It's true!" Sophia struggled and squirmed from Israfel's touch.

She held Angela fast, forgetting the horror of her skinless arm. "I did, and I am. Kim was not wrong. I am a *REVENANT*—"

"*Then explain this*!" Angela thrust her away, indicating her inhuman body.

"You weren't supposed to know," Sophia mumbled between her tears. "What I really am. But everything I told you before was the truth."

"Were you ever truly human?"

A wretched sob. "No."

"Oh God." Angela clutched her head. "Then what?"

Sophia fell to her knees, pounding the tiles with her fists and screaming. "The Book! I'm the Book of Raziel! *And I've been in Hell for eons, watching, and waiting for Her to open me—*"

The darkness behind her eyes was terrifying. Angela stepped backward, seeing nothing but the Book from Tileaf's memories and its great Eye, gazing through her. The Fae had said that few creatures, if any, knew what the Book truly looked like. Kim had said that if it was opened by the wrong person, they would go insane from what was hidden in its pages. But there lay the horrendous mystery. How did you open a Book that was a living, walking, talking, intelligent creation, and not a tome or collection of scriptures? Where were the pages, and how could they be read? And if you did manage to pry into Sophia's depths, what terrors would lie in wait for you, sucking away your soul if they couldn't be withstood?

Sophia stood with incredible speed, turning on Israfel, and she was a frightful vision of grace and unearthly anger. Even worse, her arm was already healing, new skin solidifying and hazing over the white muscle beneath. "Child," she hissed at him, "and murderer! But I will let all of Heaven and Hell know what you have done, Israfel. It will be through my mercy alone *that you find any redemption*."

"My sister's words?" he glared at her coolly. "You speak of Hell, but it was your own fault to follow her there . . ."

"Lucifel was not my master. Neither were you."

"Why not say," he smiled delicately, "that your punishment is self-inflicted?"

Sophia's mouth kept moving, but no sound came out. She paused, her cheeks flaming red, her fingers trembling like she would walk up to him and take him by the neck. No one would have ever guessed, but Raziel's portentous Book was a golem in the shape of a human young woman, her features and actions doll-like, aching for protection. No wonder Angela had been tempted to dress her, hold her, simply be with her. That must have been the effect she had on people, and once you made the mistake of trying to open her—free her—it was too late.

You saw the worst, and your mind shattered.

Israfel kissed Angela's hair, wrapping his large wings around her like she'd always dreamed. Sophia's lips pursed in that danger-ous way, her frame shivering. "That's right," Israfel continued, "it's because you can't. It's because, no matter how much you threaten and curse, other people can control you, lock you, seal half of you shut. Because you're nothing more—"

Her gray eyes were full of pain.

"—than a thing."

Twenty-seven

Love is desperation. Always.
—*The Demon Python*, UNKNOWN ORIGIN

"Do you miss this piece of yourself?" Troy snapped at Naamah, and they collided in midair, wings spread wide.

Instantly, both tumbled to the cathedral floor in a ball of feathers and hands, knives and teeth. The demon swiped at Troy desperately, aiming to murder her with the poisoned blades on her fingers. "You—*annoying shit.*"

Troy scampered aside, and they lifted into the air again, two birds locked in combat, their hair windblown and their speed terrible. Naamah stared at her lost wing bone, tied in a knot of hair near Troy's ears, and her eyes glittered like cold obsidian. The bloody residue from her wings already slicked Troy's fingers with the consistency of oil, and more spattered around them as she flew, crazy with rage. She was like all her kind, emotional at the most crucial times. Today it would probably cost her dearly.

Troy waited for her, still aloft and snarling with excitement. "Oh, so now you recognize my little trinket?"

The demon was closing in fast.

"Remember how much it hurt," Troy continued, "when I tore it out of you, *bitch*?"

"*SHUT UP.*" Naamah sliced for Troy's neck, but attempted to shove her away just as quickly.

Troy bit for the wrist yet again, scraping a mess of bloody bandages with her jaws.

A shrill scream echoed above the storm.

Stephanie, the witch, was running for them, her eyes streaked by water and her hair as wild as the demon's. She was hysterical, and it took a second longer for Troy to even realize the human was calling Naamah's name.

"GET AWAY FROM HER—"

"Stay out of this," Naamah screamed back at her, finally disengaging with Troy.

The demon landed on the opposite side of the platform at the head of the church, clutching at her wrist and panting with the pain. Nearby a stone table had been set at the forefront, its surface half draped with a white cloth and rows of brass candlesticks. A few novices lay dead around the table, and temptingly close by lay a severed head capped in white. The church stank of blood, and the hideous scent of the Supernal Israfel, a mixture of flesh and flowers that reminded Troy of a rotten nest. She landed with Naamah, wiped the blood from her mouth, and hunched down on her hands and feet, flipping her ears back against her hair.

Stephanie, though, was far from obedient. Changing direction, she rushed for Troy head-on. She tore off her sleeve, revealing a tattoo above her elbow that matched the demon's. A witch's mark. But before the human could make another move, energy sparked from Naamah's hand and blasted her onto the floor.

Troy hissed, blocking the light from her eyes.

When she glanced up again, Stephanie had crumpled into a ball, cursing. Then she was on all fours like Troy, her face hidden between the mess of her hair, her eyes wild, screening her rage.

"Don't make me break your legs," Naamah said between her teeth.

Troy licked her lips, gazing at Stephanie with new interest. These two shared a bond that went beyond the typical for a witch and her demon. "Perhaps I could do it for you," she said, smiling at Stephanie.

Stephanie opened her mouth to reply, but Naamah gestured sharply at her and turned back to Troy.

The demon's tattoo seemed to twist, dancing in the shadows.

Like all those in service to Hell's Prince, the inked number marked Naamah as Lucifel's property; the Fourth in a ranking system based on ambition and cutthroat policy. Troy had never entertained the pleasure of meeting the other Three, nor did she have the desire to.

This one represented the younger, copper-skinned generation, and she was horror enough.

"Aren't you aware of what's going on down in the Underworld?" Naamah shouted, flexing the blades in her fingers. The pain of having them inserted in the first place must have been considerable. "Your race is merely a step away from extinction. Once the dimensions crumble, where will you go, Jinn? I'm telling you, there will be another alliance between the angels and demons to crush your rats' nest, only this time, the battle will start where it hurts most. Home." Naamah glanced at the human corpses, and her dark eyes brightened. "Don't waste time hunting demons when you have traitors slithering in your caves. You'd be smart to ally yourself with me, as a protection for when the greater battles begin."

What was this? Was she hedging to protect that irritating human?

More likely her own life.

"You knew the rules," Troy said, suddenly on guard. There was more to this than compromise. The demon was dangerous, and she was planning. Of course, Troy's precarious situation was all Angela's fault. If she hadn't been locked into that hellish Binding with her, she could have watched the carnage, not participate. "You freely chose to walk into our territory on that day, and since then your life was forfeit. Bribery won't save it now."

Naamah opened her hand, gathering another crackling mass of energy. "So I suppose that's a no?"

Troy flapped her wings, narrowing her eyes beneath the pain of the light.

"That won't work."

But that also wasn't what the demon had in mind. Instantly, the energy arced out from her hands, searing into the bodies crumpled across the tile. Souls materialized above them, vaporous and gray, whispering words of human revenge and anger. They turned to Naamah, following the soft movements of her lips. Then they raced forward and surrounded Troy in a whirling ring. She swatted at one, and it disintegrated to tatters, moaning hideously. But others followed, and no matter what she did, there always seemed to be more of them, coming out of nowhere to confuse her, suck away at her life force. Troy bit through them, catching a quick glimpse of Angela, Israfel, and the one named Sophia. They were still in their own disgusting little world, debating and shouting and crying while everyone else bled around them or dropped dead.

There was something wrong, though.

As much as it satisfied Troy to watch her suffer, Angela's expression suggested dire things.

"Enough of this."

Troy beat her wings furiously, scattering vestments and cloths, blowing out the last of the painful candlelight. The ghosts dissipated, like part of the wind.

Naamah fled, her wings creaking in the darkness.

"Get ready," Troy growled, clicking her teeth together. "This time, I'm going to tear your throat wide open."

There was a sudden quiet, broken only by Angela's frantic voice, the incessant rain.

Boom. Boom. Boom.

"*LET ME HELP YOU.*" Stephanie was screaming all over again for Naamah, oblivious even to the debris that crashed perilously near to her.

Troy let her ears find the demon first, and then her eyes.

There she was. High in the air, first the ether and now her powerful wings propelling her near the murals painted onto the ceiling. Their details had been hazed over by deep shadows, but Troy could discern a woman and child, various humans gathered inside a pit of roaring flames, and an angel, his weapon pointed at the neck of a demon with a serpent's head—and rotten, bloody wings.

Troy sprinted on all fours and crawled up the nearest stone pillar.

She latched onto the ceiling with her nails, scampering toward the demon with all the speed she had left. Of course, Naamah knew Troy was tired now. She knew that she'd have an advantage. Troy couldn't fly much longer—not with half of her energy drained away—but she also couldn't let Naamah have the upper hand in this battle.

Naamah must have already realized the balance of power had shifted.

She smiled, her golden braids framing her face like a halo.

Then she touched the tattoo on her neck and tore away the skin. "As Naamah, Fourth Great Demon of Hell, I implore all the power of the Black Prince—"

Blood streamed out of the new wounds on her neck and collarbone, but swiftly spiraled up along Naamah's arm, melding with the tattoo clenched between her fingerblades, solidifying into a red sword that was all jagged edges and rigid forks. Naamah wrapped her hands around the bottom of her weapon, whispering so softly that only a Jinn's ears could hear above the thunder, the rain, and the screaming that continued below and around them.

"—and with the offering of my blood and my life, I seek to defend the honor of her wishes and ideals. Come on, rat," she muttered at Troy. "Come and get me." Her expression turned to ice. "If you dare."

Naamah soared for her, the blood sword lifted high.

Troy jumped onto the chain of a chandelier, its brass links hanging from the middle of a painting. The lamp swung wildly beneath her weight, tipping dangerously to the right and tossing her back into the darkness.

The demon screamed, slashing at her.

Her weapon met the chain, scraping into the metal. A second later, the links snapped, and the chandelier fell thundering to the floor.

Boom. Boom.

The noise of the demon's wings was fury itself.

She swooped in close again, slicing clean through the tips of Troy's wing feathers, showering a black snow to the ground. But instead of turning to face her, Troy fought her aching muscles and flew ahead, racing for the platform that she sensed was an altar.

Her toes scraped the long table, and she soared up to perch on the top of two wooden beams, their cross-wise pattern reminding her of Sariel's necklace. A human figure hung from their center, gazing sadly down at the corpses arrayed across the tiles. Naamah was streaking for both the statue and Troy, her sword held out sideways, ready to chop off Troy's head, the statue's hands. Everything. Anything.

Troy grabbed a cloth hanging to the right of the cross and pitched the heavy fabric at Naamah.

"Time to learn a little respect."

". . . because you're nothing more . . . than a thing."

Kim pressed the knife to Israfel's throat.

The blade cut the angel's ivory skin slightly, staining his long neck with a tendril of crimson. His enchanting voice had died to gentle breaths that spoke of many future events—events Kim couldn't handle thinking about—because they had Angela in mind. He didn't want to blame her for the infatuation she'd fallen into—but it was hard. Angela had been the only woman he'd felt any kind of real connection to besides Stephanie, and the feelings between them had to be based on more than chance, even if they'd blossomed under so much danger. They were just starting to learn about each other, to enjoy the process, and he'd be damned if some angel who danced in her dreams was about to change that.

"You're a human priest," Israfel said.

"Good guess, but you're only half correct."

Angela gasped from inside the circle of Israfel's wings.

They'd been so occupied with each other, Israfel's senses hadn't been enough to warn him of the worst. Sophia had been the only person to see Kim encroaching on them, and from the torment burning behind her eyes and all over her face, it had been clear she wasn't going to ruin the surprise. If someone was needed to step on Israfel's toes, better a half-Jinn than no one at all. And, oh, how that half of Kim burned him inside. Right now, he fully understood what it felt like to be Troy, to become so angry and overbearingly upset that you were blind to what you did and why you did it.

Israfel was still, and Kim was still, his hand trembling slightly, the steel of his knife tickling the angel's throat. God, how he wanted to slice open his neck.

But Angela wouldn't ever forgive him.

She burst out of the angel's arms and rounded on Kim, her face haunted, her expression regretful. Well, it seemed he still had a chance. She wouldn't look at him with that kind of emotion if they weren't a possibility. Every time they locked eyes, electricity seemed to snap between them.

"Well, what now, Angela?" Kim said, more softly than he wanted.

The delicate wings along Israfel's ears flapped, expressing his impatience.

He glanced at Troy, deep in the middle of her latest skirmish with Naamah.

They had trashed what was left of the church, avoiding the interior of the altar more because of Troy's fear than out of respect. Jinn had no dread of holy objects or symbols, but they steered clear of them whenever they could, unwilling to bring down what they considered to be the wrath of the Highest. How ironic that Troy was the professional murderer, yet out of the two of them, Kim was the one who feared absolutely nothing, God included.

Only Troy. Only death.

"Are you happy," he said with a smirk, glancing now at Brendan Mathers, dead and messy near the altar, "with how things have turned out?"

Though he was certain the answer eluded her at the moment,

Angela must not have liked his tone of voice. She blushed, and then the anger began to show itself in the set of her mouth, the firm stance of her tights-covered legs. Should she be mad at Kim for putting a blade to Israfel's neck? But like he'd promised Troy, it would have haunted him forever if the Supernal escaped without a flesh wound.

Lucifel, he was sure, would never stand for it.

"Even if you aren't the Archon, I don't like sharing, Angela." Whether he should have said so or not didn't matter anymore. He at least deserved her honesty in return, and he'd make sure to have it. "I hate it when I think I've found a partner and that person turns out to be—*faithless*. Stephanie did that to me, not to mention waste a lot of my time. Whether she's the Archon or isn't, the day I see her on the Throne of Hell is the day it freezes over."

"What do you mean?" Angela said, whispering. "You're not saying that—"

"I'm working for Lucifel?" Kim sighed, tipping his head and shifting his bangs aside. "I'm sure your new friend would tell you so. But can you really believe anything an angel says? In my experience, the word angel denotes place over personality. And angels and demons tend to think alike."

Israfel laughed gently, like he'd heard a secret joke.

Kim turned the blade slightly against Israfel's neck, spiderwebbing more blood across his beautiful skin. "Remember, there is only one Archon, Angela. But there are two who can be the Ruin. I've known this, and Lucifel has known for a long time. Troy might have been right: the Archon doesn't necessarily have to be Raziel himself. Perhaps She is only protected by Raziel. But either way, I want to find out. For your sake."

For both their sakes.

"I want you to make the smart choice, the best choice, and to have me by your side when you make it."

"So . . . you *want* me to take Lucifel's place. You *want* me on the Throne of Hell." Her voice was a murmur, barely audible above the storm.

"Not so much to take it, as to consider it. The option is better than what he"—Kim's hand shivered, the knife scratching more blood out of Israfel—"has to offer you. Either way, life will be a living hell from this point on. The time to be an ordinary girl is over."

At the word *ordinary,* Angela's eyes widened.

"Angela," he pressed further, aware of how vulnerable he sounded. "You have to trust me."

She gazed at him, obviously confused. "Troy will kill you. What reason would she have to keep you alive?"

"She won't know. We'll leave before she knows."

"For where?"

He sighed again, trying to control himself. Was she being deliberately obtuse, or was she just trying to gauge how committed he was? "For Hell."

Her breast heaved gently, and Kim overflowed with the madness of wanting to murder Israfel and kiss it, just as he had the other night. He beckoned her closer, yearning inside. "Come with me, Angela. That pleasure we shared was a real thing. I know you want more of it. I know how much you want to step all over this world, to crush it beneath your heel, like it has crushed you time and again. I see it in your eyes. We'll work this out, together, because you and I are the same."

She closed them, sighing along with the temptation of his voice. "I don't know . . ."

"Angela . . ."

When she opened them again, they were wide, blindingly blue, and utterly fearless.

But it was Israfel who answered for her. "I think I've heard enough."

He snapped his fingers.

Kim's lips sealed shut against his will.

Another snap of his fingers.

The knife whipped out of Kim's hand, clattering pathetically onto the tiles. Then Israfel lifted his hand and curled his palm, freezing Kim into place.

The angel spun around, smiling and lovely, the most beautiful creature that could be imagined. His eyes were so proud, his lips so sensual, his face so perfect that it nearly took Kim's breath away. He was like a delicate swan—but one that hid all the inner stealth of a tiger. It was only through harsh experience that Kim knew the truth, even if Angela couldn't see through Israfel's veneer. The angel didn't have Troy's sharp teeth, but they were far more alike than they first seemed.

Now, he was in real danger.

"For a priest, you seem to be somewhat agitated. I also think you're mistaken. You see, this young woman is no longer your property, *Kim*." He said his name with subtle and deep dislike. "You've also injured me, claimed some kind of backward loyalty to my sister, and made a mess of my coat."

Israfel looked to Angela, his voice honey sweet. "Shall I kill him?"

She stared at Kim, silent. She didn't seem as upset as he'd expected, but it was obvious she was trying to peer through him, as if she could peel back more layers and see how honest he was being.

This was a problem for them both.

Kim couldn't say that he loved Angela. It was too soon for love. But he could say with all sincerity that the thought of her sharing anything with Israfel nearly made him crazy, and that for her to be out of his sight was painful. If he could, he would have forced out the memories of how easily they'd seduced each other, how perfect she felt against his legs, and how powerful their connection had been.

Maybe she was remembering. For a moment, she hesitated, creeping closer to him.

"No," she said, and her face reddened. "Don't kill him."

Angela slipped around Israfel, and except for Sophia's dark presence, she seemed on the same level as the angel, powerful and suddenly intimidating, and not even knowing it. Maybe that was the real reason behind Kim's desire, his infatuation. He was enthralled, absolutely, by the sinister mystery of her soul. Mikel's words continued to echo, reminding him of how ignorant humanity could be: *If she is not the Archon . . . then we are all very mistaken about who the Archon is . . .*

She reached out, touching the side of Kim's face.

He shivered, wishing for more, pathetically unable to say so.

"You're right, Kim—I enjoyed being with you. But you've got it all wrong if you think I'm ready to sit on a throne, in Heaven or Hell." She tossed her blood-red hair over her shoulders. It was as long as a curtain, tangled by the rain. "Don't you get it? I don't know anything but my dreams. I don't know how to trust anything besides them. I never said anything about changing that. I don't think I can."

She didn't even know what she was saying.

The cathedral seemed to be falling apart around them, mirroring Kim's sudden need to break apart everything that stood between them. He could tear that angel limb from limb. Watch the universe collapse for the simple satisfaction of crushing his wings.

"If it's a choice I have to make," Angela whispered, "then I also need to make it on my own."

She leaned forward to kiss him.

Kim turned his head, not wanting her to notice the anger in him, but against his will, her lips caressed his softly and he groaned inside.

Ever since she'd taken the Grail, Angela had changed.

Like she'd found a piece of herself and was fast becoming whole again. Right now, it appeared Kim wasn't one of those pieces, and he was being discarded, set aside.

"I'm sorry," she whispered to him. "Thank you. For everything."

As if it could erase all that had taken place between them.

"I'm sorry," she said one last time.

Oh, yes. So was he.

"Time to learn a little respect."

The demon's wings buckled, snapping and creaking under the force of Troy's ambush, the weight of the cloth. In an instant they plummeted, Naamah's sword cutting through the white satin—just far enough for Troy to wrench it out of her knife-riddled hands.

It smashed against a wall.

The shards of the demon's blood liquefied, raining down to the floor.

"*Why do you bother?*" Troy hissed over the storm, more angry and irritated than afraid. She knew better than to intentionally damage sacred objects, but like all demons, Naamah lived with a curse and enjoyed it. Her race respected nothing and feared nothing, partly because she had nowhere left to go but up. "Why did you let the witch summon you?"

Naamah dropped from underneath her shroud, blasting Troy backward with a burst of crimson light. "Summon? You think and talk like the ignorant rat you are." She hit the floor, steadying herself with a hand, and gazed up at Troy, smiling triumphantly. "As for my reasons—I think you can sympathize. The moment the Archon opens the Book will be the moment of Hell's renaissance, Jinn. Not every demon worships Lucifel with their hearts as well as their words."

Traitorous scum.

"Or do you have a soft spot for our soon-to-be-dethroned Prince?"

Now her presence made much more sense. Naamah, and the demons who mouthed loyalty to Lucifel yet kept her caged, wanted another god. One much more easily manipulated. Troy folded in her wings, preparing to descend and finish what she'd begun, grinding her teeth together in frustration. Naamah's tattoo was reappearing, its swirls of black ink pooling near her shoulder and neck.

A jolt of silvery lightning swept in their direction.

The smell of flowers and flesh pounded Troy in waves, overwhelming her other senses.

Israfel had finally joined the battle.

Twenty-eight

The Eye with which I see myself is the Eye
through which the All sees me.
— Meister Elmhart, *A Delineation of Transcendence*

Stephanie stumbled to her feet, tears washing out her vision.

In so many ways, the hurt couldn't go any deeper. She had proven what a worthy daughter she was, tried to help her mother, and in return had been forced to huddle like a wounded, useless puppy. Naamah no longer understood her little protégé, at least not in the way Stephanie had intended. Maybe the demon couldn't fathom that Stephanie had reached a point where Troy was less of a danger to her than to Naamah. Or perhaps it was Naamah's version of pity, though right now their intimate conversation during Halloween night rang strangely false. Naamah had acted cold, and yet, here she was, screaming for Stephanie to stand back and save herself.

If Stephanie was the Archon, that was only logical.

But it was hard to get past the way Naamah had looked at her ever since the angel's kiss.

She wiped her mouth, spitting some blood into her palm. Glass had cut her lip and her throat burned from the sizzle of energy toying with the air. She'd tried going over in her mind what had taken place between her and Israfel after their embrace, only to realize that another unsettling lapse of time had passed. Stephanie had remembered nothing until the world was collapsing around her, and it was too late to stop it. She was responsible for part of that collapse—wanted it even—but she'd never meant for it to go this far.

She might lose a mother. Maybe her life.

Or Kim.

Stephanie whipped around, listening to the familiar tone of his voice, so smooth and charismatic. Just as it had in her bedroom, the world darkened around her, the single light left to her centering on Angela. The scar-covered freak was touching Kim's face, leaning in to kiss him.

"You . . ."

It was all she could say. It summarized everything.

In the end, this was all Angela's fault. Until she'd arrived at the Academy, everything had been so clear, so right. Then that irritating bitch had to taint Luz with her own cursed existence. Her dreams and failed suicides had somehow ruined all of Stephanie's happiness in one merciless stroke, but even so, Stephanie was far from ready to make it easy for her.

Kim was expendable in the long run, but there was no way she would let go of a toy without a fight.

"You . . ."

The first to catch sight of her, Kim struggled to tell Angela only to meet with more silence for his efforts. The angel must have stopped him from speaking.

Stephanie dodged falling bits of plaster, barely aware of more rock crashing to the ground behind her. The world was like a blur, faded, buzzing with the strangest sounds. Her legs didn't even feel like her own anymore, and by the time Sophia stepped out of the shadows to stop her, it was too late. Stephanie bit her lip, but screamed from the pain anyway, tearing the tattoo off herself as Naamah had done. She could feel the blood like a raw, red river along her arm. It was agony, enough to nearly faint.

"You greedy bitch," she heard herself saying. "I can't stand you."

Everything after that was fast, and completely beyond her.

Israfel. The angel was preparing to swoop down and kill her. He swept around Angela, a perfect terror that no longer looked so dazzling to Stephanie's eyes. What a relic he was. Like an ancient statue that had lost all its luster, more paint than substance. She noted the way his large eyes narrowed at her knowingly, angry at himself for not cutting her down sooner.

There was no anger in her though.

Just a callous, emotionless spite that took pleasure in his pain.

The shield erupted in a second. Less blood than energy, it took all of Stephanie's soul to throw it at him, a red wall that blocked his progress. Israfel fell back, pained by its contact. Kim crumpled onto the floor, grasping to pull himself out of Israfel's reach. The angel's reaction was far from human.

Rage. Never had she seen it expressed so purely in the eyes of any creature.

Then she whispered the fateful invocation, and the blood sword formed, and she leaped for Angela, swinging the weapon wildly.

Angela shouted, dodging by a hairsbreadth.

It wasn't enough to take her out of harm's way.

Stephanie followed her with a twist of the foot, swinging in the opposite direction. She cut through air, but seconds later a chandelier snapped from the ceiling and smashed in front of her, forcing them both to throw themselves to the ground. She tumbled amid the glass and stone, still in agony, but fueled by such a mysterious energy that it no longer mattered. Stephanie clasped the sword tight, nearly losing her grip from the liquefied blood on her hands, breathing in shuddering gasps.

"Come on, you useless witch." Her throat was hoarse from screaming. "Come on. *Come on!*"

There. Behind her.

Stephanie pivoted to her right, slicing cleanly through a chunk of wood Angela had grabbed as a shield. Angela shouted at her, but the words no longer held any meaning for Stephanie. Nothing mattered now besides Angela's head, rolling like the archbishop's had rolled, and the more she thought that, the more she hacked at her, again and again, fended off every time by her escape, or another makeshift shield.

Then Angela ran out of them.

She tried to run one last time, but Stephanie snagged her blouse, tearing it open near the neck.

An Eye hid underneath.

It was unlike any other. Green with life, but piercing, terrible, unfathomable.

Stephanie understood instinctively that she should look away, but she grabbed for the pendant anyway, insanely possessive, hardly astonished when its chain snapped with a violent tug of her hand and Angela fell against a mound of rubble.

The force shoved Stephanie backward.

The Eye on its chain hung, suspended, in the air.

A brilliant flash of white light raced in on her. Naamah shrieked, sounding to be in as much agony as her daughter, and Stephanie forgot all else, turning to the single person who could understand the abyss she had seen and could never forget.

Troy shut her eyes tightly, hissing away the pain.

The light was blinding, excruciating. She collapsed shortly before her toes could brush the tile, curling into a ball, her spine contorting from the impact on her nerves. Naamah shrieked in the background, obviously wounded.

Stephanie's voice echoed with her, equally pained, and a crimson shield exploded into life, blazing like fire behind Troy's eyelids.

Then everything stopped. A gentler pulse of light signaled Naamah's escape deep into the lower Realms, her curses resounding even after she'd left. Stephanie must have escaped with her—the girl's scent had vanished along with the light—but Troy remained curled up like a spider, shivering from the horror of Israfel's attack. Her sore muscles soaked up the chill of the tiles. Her wings twitched, their tendons and ligaments exhausted by the intensity of the battle and the draining power of Naamah's ghosts.

Sariel's voice was an unwelcome addition to the pain.

"You can get up," he said coarsely. "They're gone. All of them."

His shoe scraped the side of her wing and she bit at him, mad with frustration.

He cursed even more savagely than usual, and then did the stupidest thing possible, pushing one of her wings sideways and stooping down to stare directly in her face. Troy would have lunged and chewed his eyes out, but there was a strange look to him that kept her suspicious and docile.

He was crying.

She watched the water slide down Sariel's cheekbones, mesmerized. From what she had learned, humans cried when they were angry, upset, or hurt. Judging from her cousin's face, he was all three at once.

"Gone where?" she muttered.

"I don't know," he said, hissing like a Jinn himself. "But they're gone. Angela, Israfel, and that resurrected bitch Sophia."

"Together?"

"Yes," he said, biting at his lip. "Now get the hell up and help me arrange some of these bodies. Without gnawing on them, if you can even help yourself." He shook his head, the tears continuing to glisten, his teeth bared. "What a goddamned fine mess this is."

"The witch and her demon escaped to the Underworld," Troy said. "I'd call that a victory."

"Of course you would," he whispered. "Chaos amuses you."

He stepped over a corpse, its arm splayed sideways across the floor.

Troy laughed. She was so tired, the noise came out of her cracked and broken, but it was so obvious to her why Sariel was distraught. In the end, he was no different from his father, from any other male Jinn who'd suffered the loss of a mate, especially a faithless one. Angela must have chosen the angel over him.

Her cousin glared at her, his pale face white like his collar, and she continued to laugh, blissfully licking a cut on her hand.

When Troy paused, it was only to state the obvious.

"You are a ridiculous fool."

Twenty-nine

*I have often debated which Supernal is the greatest among the
Three. But perhaps the better question would be:
which is the most dangerous?*
—BROTHER FRANCIS, *An Encyclopedia of the Realms*

It had felt like a dream.

Stephanie, racing for Angela, swiping at her with that hellish
sword of her own blood; a vision more frightful than Troy, if only
because Stephanie was *human.* Thinking about the danger she'd so
narrowly escaped, Angela had only two things to be truly grateful
for. One was that Stephanie had been too distracted by Naamah to
actually steal the Grail. The other was that Israfel had kidnapped
Angela and Sophia far away from everyone and everything else.

Kim's amber eyes haunted her, even more than the Eye suspended near her face.

The Grail swung like a pendulum in front of her nose, beckoning
her to take it back. Instead, Angela stared at Sophia until a breeze
entered the church through the open ceiling, blocking her vision
with thick strands of hair. She pushed them aside, sighing at the
sudden awkwardness, the difficulty of dealing with people—even
things that merely looked like people—and the pain they caused her.

She actually is a doll, and now I'm afraid.

Sophia was Raziel's toy. His walking, talking creation. "It can't
hurt me," she said, indicating the Grail. "Because of what I am."

Her voice sounded horrifically tired.

Angela shook her head, examining a blackened pew. The church seemed so quiet compared to the last time she'd entered, searching for Israfel. But that of course had been because the world felt that much more alive.

Sophia grabbed for Angela's palm, her own skin strangely clammy and moist.

"No." Angela held her at arm's length, wrapping Sophia's slender fingers around the Eye again, blocking its terrible vision. "It's better off with you right now." She took a step backward and fingered the vicious slash in her blouse, cringing at the texture of shredded fabric. A red line, sticky to the touch, swept across her chest at a diagonal; one more scar to mix with the others. "I don't need him to see it. I don't need any more problems. Or anything else to—"

To come between us, she wanted to say.

Thankfully, the words stopped at her lips.

It was almost too much—the enormity of what had happened only an hour ago. Here, in this abandoned shell of a church, the carnage felt as far away as a true dream. Yet it had been all too real, because Angela was still suffering from Israfel's manner of traveling, especially traveling such a distance in a short space of time. He'd grabbed both her and Sophia, and there had been a roar, the intense rush of wind, and a light that could have melted her eyes. Then, nothing. Until she stood in the church at his side, dazed, disoriented, and sick to her stomach. He'd left her alone with Sophia in their little alcove, leaving for some room that connected to the altar, visibly disturbed by how nauseated she looked. Whether it was because he cared or not—that hadn't even entered into her thoughts. Maybe because she'd had none. For what felt like forever, she and Sophia had simply sat side by side in silence.

Leftovers of the storm rumbled overhead.

Faintly, Brendan's voice spoke amid the thunder, still screaming, still accusing her of every ounce of his suffering and every sliver of pain. But Angela knew it was only her imagination. Her brother was dead. Gone. The last person connecting her to the past, he'd been ripped out of her life just as quickly as he'd returned to it.

Yet the tears wouldn't come anymore.

Despite her best efforts otherwise, she was also seeing Brendan's face in his final moments. Without a doubt, it had been the face of a person lucky to be put out of their misery.

"Angela . . ."

Sophia glanced at the broken ceiling, her gesture too human to be anything else.

Then she looked back at Angela, her eyes darker than the sky, grievously vacant, and all her tormented words about Hell and waiting for the Archon sounded clearer than what she said now. "I don't mind. If you have to talk about your brother—"

She cut off abruptly, noticing what Angela knew was an expressionless haze over her face.

The silence seemed to go on and on even longer than before.

"If you need me," Sophia finally whispered, "I'll be here."

There was a terrible loneliness in her voice, but Angela couldn't acknowledge it. The shock was still too fresh. The pain of knowing Sophia's true identity gnawed at her trust like a worm. Suddenly, her new friend seemed so much less helpless and so much more of a nightmare.

Angela needed—*wanted*—space.

"I'll be here for you," Sophia said again, as if she hadn't heard. "I promise you that."

Without another word, she slipped into the shadows, disappearing like a ghost. She hadn't been crying as she left, but a gentle sobbing mixed with the low thunder. A moment later, Israfel stepped beside Angela, and she instantly forgot everything else that existed, frozen by his proximity and the elation of a dream she'd always prayed to come true, now doing so ten times over. He kept silent, but forced her to face him directly, examining the wound on her chest. His fingers were smooth and unspeakably soft, like sculpted pearl touching the skin above her left breast.

"Does it hurt?" he said at last.

The music in his voice was subtle, but the disgusted look had left his face, replaced by what could have been concern.

"No." She nodded at the cut on his neck, remembering how he'd reacted the last instance she'd touched him without permission. "You?"

His lips pursed together. There must have been pain, but not the kind he'd admit to.

Israfel's hair, already feathery, had become windswept and careless, wisping delicately at his shoulders. He took the strands and stroked them to the tips, his distinctly graceful movements somehow more comprehensible than Sophia's. "You should have let me kill him and be done with it. Why did you stop me? Out of affection for him?"

Angela kept silent.

"Although I feel more grateful by the minute. The smell of his half-bred blood would have been less than pleasant on my hands."

No answer would have been a good one. Which was fine, because too many of her own questions took up space in her mind anyway.

Why was perfection like him living in this horror at all? Israfel resembled a star thrown into a puddle of mud, so above everything surrounding him, that even light lost its luster next to his brilliance. Worse yet, he knew he had that effect. Angela strove to conquer her awe, desperate to pick out the real, though barely perceptible flaws, trying to remind herself to keep her head. He was beautiful, and it was very difficult, but . . .

Yes. She'd found it again.

There was that languid decadence in him that unnerved her somehow. Israfel was obviously used to everything in creation kissing the ground he walked upon, and it showed in the teasing way he toyed with her, with anyone, instinctively moving in ways designed to infatuate. It should have been impossible to resist him—but whenever Brendan's face flashed before her—suddenly everything shone a little less divinely.

Israfel had left her to sit in a nearby pew, his wings tucked away to give him room.

Now he glanced at her again, and there was a sharper tone in his voice. "Why was the Jinn present?"

He folded his legs, waiting for her to explain.

Everything he did felt like an unspoken invitation for Angela to throw herself at him. But she'd been given a second chance to make a better, less idiotic impression, and she was definitely taking it. "Troy . . . She's related to—the priest who held the knife."

Kim. God, why did it always have to be like this? It would have been so much easier if—

If what? More people had died?

And whose deaths would have made it all better, Angela?

No one's, of course.

Israfel rubbed the cut on his neck. "How fitting, then, that he was a demon in disguise."

Now it was her turn. She was still in too much shock to cry, but the more she talked with Israfel and remembered, the more terrible those memories became and begged for their own explanations. Angela worked up her courage, trying to hide the growing bitterness in her voice. "Why did you let Brendan die?"

Silence.

She'd either startled him or made him angry.

Angela drew in nearer, eager to close off a new gap before it widened any further. "How did you even know each other?"

"You would question my wisdom? When you're only human?" He spoke softly, and with the slightest hint at her danger. But she already knew there was something keeping him from punishing or hurting her. Whenever Israfel looked at Angela, it was there behind his large eyes: recognition, and maybe by a long stretch, affection. She suspected both had more to do with Raziel than her own miserable self. "But I suppose you deserve that much for the trouble he caused you. He was your brother?"

"Yes. He was."

Israfel smiled. "Well, I'm sure what you thought of him, and what he was, were two very different things. What is your name, girl?"

"Angela," she said, flinching at the irony of it, and at the idea that she was a *girl* to him.

A child.

He invited her to sit, careful to lean far enough away from her touch that she wouldn't become overconfident again. "The universe can be an amusing place, can't it?" He laughed delicately. "Actually, your brother mentioned you the first day we met. He had been eavesdropping on me for hours and hours. Can you guess why, Angela?"

She arranged what was left of her skirt, trying not to feel so uneasy. That laugh always sounded like it hid more behind it.

"Because"—Israfel blinked, the movement oddly majestic—"he wanted something from me."

"What could that have been?" she said, her mouth dry and scratchy.

Already, the answer seemed to reveal itself in the way her heart hammered, her cheeks flushed. Either he hadn't noticed, or he was even more encouraged by her reaction.

Israfel smiled less rigidly and turned his head toward the altar, like a flower twisting in the breeze. "Yes. I gave your brother everything he wanted. But whether that was good for him or not was none of my concern. It was enough that he wanted it, and that I found his desires useful. So if you are smart," he turned back to her, his gaze steady, "you will not mourn his passing. The fact remains that his soul was beyond saving. I simply exposed the darkness in him before he did it himself."

She breathed hard, sick again inside, unwilling to show it a second time.

"I understand, you see. I had a sibling who was much the same. Only I haven't had the satisfaction of seeing justice done. Far from it."

He sighed.

In it, Angela heard the whisper of Lucifel's name echoing throughout the church.

"But that, like all things, is only a matter of time."

Why couldn't she speak anymore?

Was it fear? Infatuation? The staggering power of his presence?

Angela gazed at the kohl around his eyes, wondering at the sloping perfection of his nose. She sensed the honesty, the logic of what he'd said. Angela had never wanted to acknowledge it before, but her brother wasn't nearly the saint her childhood memories made him out to be. Unfortunately, it had required a tragedy for her to believe it. Tonight, Brendan had shown his true colors in the worst manner possible. It was the how and why that bothered her, much like how she was taken aback by the Supernal's self-satisfied pride. This was horrible. Her mind was turning in circles, and she barely noticed that Israfel was leaning in, closer and closer.

Then his fingertips brushed her face.

"Who are you?" he said, gentle as ever. "You have Raziel's hair and eyes, but not his soul? Though I am appreciative that you've chosen to take your brother's place in my service." His breath was rich with a sweetness like honey, and he could have actually been caressing her with slight, but real, desire. Once again, she knew with a kind of stinging pain that he saw someone else. "It is only fitting, considering the torment we have endured tonight. For a few hours at least, we will enjoy ourselves, you and I."

Now she felt too exposed.

Angela clutched at her shirt, shivering both from the breeze and the implications of his words.

She imagined Kim's searing touch and the tickle of his lips on her neck.

And she hated herself for wanting it all without having to choose.

Israfel's wings folded, disappearing with a flash of light. Slowly, he slipped out of his coat and tossed it at her, nodding tersely in a way that demanded she wear it. "Come," he said, and while he left to glide for the altar, he looked over his shoulder to smile at her. "I want to show you something, Angela."

The way he said her name—it was so unlike the way he'd said Kim's.

As if she were the most interesting and precious person in the world.

She slid on the coat, her tall body still not tall enough to keep the cloth from dragging across the floor.

It was heavy, yet Israfel had worn it like he'd been carrying a thought.

She did her best to step around the puddles, feeling like a bride walking down a broken aisle. The windows on either side had no more color to give, all but one smashed and cracked. The pews stank, and the air was heavy with mist. Ahead of it all, though, like a beacon on the stormy wreck that was her life, Israfel waited, his hand gracefully extended. She marched slowly up the steps and took it, surprised by the strength in his fingers.

"What now?" she said, demanding like he had demanded.

He answered with another smile.

She tried to move to the side, but he stopped her, clamping his fingers on her wrist.

"Match my steps," he said, the whisper a soft command.

They began slowly: Israfel swept to the right, and she followed. To the left, and Angela copied him. Then they moved faster, turning in circles, lifting their hands so that their fingertips met high in the air, brushing in close and backpedaling once more to a flirtatious distance.

With a rush of excitement, it hit her.

They were dancing, and Israfel continued to ignore her clumsy attempts, making up for them with his own grace, keeping them in perfect balance and rhythm with his talent alone. Every move he made—was utterly fascinating. Every curve of his figure—was flawless. Soon, all that existed was his voice, singing in words that dropped like diamonds from his lips. The language was unknown to her, but just as in Tileaf's grotto, she knew this song was for her and her alone.

He'd seemed to reach the end, and a flash of familiar light whitened the church.

His wings had reappeared.

Angela gasped at a sharp sensation of weightlessness.

They were aloft, and though he wasn't flapping, they rose higher anyway, lifted by a mysterious force. In moments the dilapidated floor was far below them, and they were at the ceiling, and Angela wanted to scream from sheer exhilaration, from the breeze, and the craziness, and the glory of it all.

Israfel never gave her a chance.

In a final breathtaking move, his two largest wings arched around her and snapped back just as quickly, causing some feathers to blow loose from the force. As if to match a series of lilting notes, the fallen feathers disintegrated into dust.

It fell like a shower of crystals, all around them.

For a second they seemed to condense, taking the shape of a set of glassy stairs. For a brief second, she saw the angel from her dreams who'd spoken to her and told her to live for something . . . or for someone. For a second, Angela wondered if that someone could be Israfel—or Kim. Then she stared back at her angel through the unearthly rain, at the eyes that had defined every choice in her life.

With a shudder, she finally realized why and how her brother had fallen.

Thirty

---

*And he said to them, "I will be alone this long night.
Is there no one who will watch with me?"*
—THE SUPERNAL ISRAFEL, *A Collection of Angelic Lore*

Israfel worked a needle into his arm, blocking out the world with his two largest wings.

The room of the abandoned rectory was dark, and he could barely see the dime-sized scars covering his right arm up to the elbow. His own fault, in the end. Israfel had waited too long between one dose and the next, losing the time that could have opened an old scar rather than make a new one.

He forced a whimper into his mouth, biting back more pain.

A sharp sting—and the needle slipped beneath skin.

Then the comforting fire began to flow through his body, one inch after the next. He gave the needle's plunger a few light taps, intending to lengthen the process. Drop by drop had become his rule when working with a limited supply.

There was a gentle sigh, and the rustle of cloth.

Angela Mathers, Brendan's sister, slept in a drunk and uncomfortable position at Israfel's right, her blouse half open and an arm covering her eyes. A crystal glass rested exactly where she'd dropped it, near to her hips. Now as the soft candlelight wavered and Israfel's body numbed over, he joined her again, staring down at her face, finding himself unable to look away.

She looked so much like Raziel, with the same shade of red to her hair, the same roundness of the eyes, the same ivory skin.

But then—she also looked like *Him*—

A powerful cramp hit Israfel, like a hundred knives slicing at his insides.

"By the Fath—"

Israfel gasped, overcome by a second of intense pain. His fingers contracted, spasming, the needle he'd brought for her contentment wobbling between them. Then the plunger slipped from his hand, and the needle dropped to the floor, its glass vial shattering into hundreds of fragments. Precious blue liquid seeped deeply into a patch of carpeting, wetting the curve of Israfel's knees.

The peace and pleasure of the drug soon softened any disappointment.

"Israfel," Angela said. She sat up groggily, her shirt sliding down to expose her shoulder while he rested beside her, pressing her back down. "What are you doing?"

"So sorry," he said, whispering in her ear, "but I dropped my little gift for you."

He brushed the glass shards aside. Waves of relaxation were already rocking Israfel's mind into a gentle kind of acceptance. It was a pity, but this bare shell of a room had become a sty, and he'd completely given up on trying to keep it clean. A temporary nest like this one wasn't worth the time or energy when he had more important things to do, and tasting this fascinating soul currently topped that list. Israfel slumped deeper against the floor, laughing inside at the rainbow dots floating through his vision, the heightened sensations racing into his wing bones. The drug's fire throbbed with his heartbeat, rushing up the curve of his spine into each nerve of his pinions.

This was the only delight he could find in being sick, forced to medicate himself like an animal.

"It's so strange . . ." Still intoxicated from the nectar, Angela sat up and embraced his slim body, keeping her hands where he demanded, always on his chest, his neck, his face, never lower. She could marvel at his shape, but it was best she not think about it too much. "It doesn't seem real. How I've wanted you," she murmured, almost crying.

"Wanted me?"

She was like an echo of her brother, but so much less ingratiating and arrogant.

His lower wings brushed her thighs, and she collapsed against his chest, sighing.

"You're as beautiful," Angela whispered, "as a woman. The most beautiful woman. The most beautiful man. You're everything. Everything . . ."

He forced her down again and beat his wings gently, fanning the curtain of hair from her face with a cooling breeze, ever eager to examine her more. Too careless to hide herself once the nectar took effect, Angela had accidentally revealed portions of a body covered head to toe in scars, some of the most hideous gathered around her legs and arms. But Israfel had seen much different and much worse many times before. What troubled him most was how different she was on the *inside*. That obnoxious half-breed priest had become obsessed with her, spilling out all his innermost desires like she would actually take the time to listen. If this lovely one was the Archon, Israfel would see to it that she joined him where they belonged, far from Hell, which by then would be little more than a memory anyway.

Why sit on an old throne when you could start over completely?

Oh, he should have killed the priest when he had the chance. The cut on his neck ached, and his beautiful clothes had been permanently stained.

"You're a child, Israfel," Sophia said softly.

The candle flickered, revealing the silvery shine of her slippers. She'd entered shortly after the girl had fallen asleep and had decided to stay ever since, probably satisfied knowing Angela and Israfel wouldn't share too many kisses with another person in the room. But she knew, of course, that they'd share enough before that, and he couldn't help enjoying how much pain it caused her, partly because of all the pain Sophia had caused him. The demon would be searching for her soon, but by then he'd planned on opening her and being done with it already.

The Book's time was short indeed.

"And why am I a child?" He relaxed Angela back into sleep and struggled up from the floor, spreading his wings for balance while carefully straddling the broken syringe. "Because I hurt you by unveiling your true identity?" His speech began to slur, stretching his consonants. "Remember this night for the lesson that it is. Consider what could happen next . . . every time you defy me."

He tried using the wall as a crutch.

No success. A wave of dizziness flung him back to his knees.

That was just fine. He didn't really need to stand anyway.

"Look at you," Sophia said, sounding like a mother scolding an infant, "debauched to the point where you no longer even see your dissipation. For all your hatred of Lucifel, you don't act any nobler. My warning in that cathedral was not said as a joke." She shifted in her seat, her soft curls catching the light. "Perhaps you're not aware that Mikel escaped your prison."

Israfel half walked, half dragged himself to the velvet loveseat and reclined across from her, his hair spilling against his shoulders. The chick inside him kicked, and his nausea surged up and down, a tide barely mitigated by the Father's blood.

He gazed at her, smiling. "Oh? And how did she accomplish that?"

Sophia turned away, her hands folding tightly against her lap. The arm he'd mutilated so brutally was almost pristine again. "You treated that half-breed priest like he was dirt. But you are no different than the Jinn that fathered him."

He touched the fragile wing connected to his ear, still waiting for a real answer. "You know nothing about prisons," he finally whispered.

Sophia laughed, her eyes cold in the shadows. "What an ignorant thing to say."

"Did you ever consider," he continued, "that perhaps *I* was in a prison? The accepted history is that I entered Ialdaboth . . . of my own free will—and I did."

He glanced at Angela and held his breath, envisioning a different face, a different person. Certainly half the thrill of controlling her rested in his newfound sense of power.

She looked like Raziel, but she also resembled much more.

"But getting out of there was a . . . different matter."

"Murder is wrong, Israfel," she said, still not looking at him. "You can justify it all you want. You can tell yourself that there was a reason. But it won't change how your actions have put everyone in mortal peril. Humans, angels, demons, Jinn. Everything. Anything." Her voice took on that whispery gentleness he'd become accustomed to eons ago. "And now the universe will suffer for your lovesickness."

She never turned until his shadow cast her into blackness. Then she glared up at him, the whites of her eyes somehow blinding.

Israfel slapped her across the mouth, half wishing to tear it off.

What kind of a Book needed to talk, after all?

He breathed hard, the blood rushing to his face, flaring the crimson stripes below his eyes. "Don't speak about what you don't know."

Tears trickled down her cheeks. Like a human, she'd been blessed with the ability to cry, and in the golden half-light, her cheek already swelled, marked with a red welt in the shape of his fingers. She must have been weeping because of the pain. Sophia looked at Angela, hid her face behind her hands, and began to sob. Maybe she did know how despairing he felt inside, because suddenly there wasn't a more hopeless cry in all of the dimensions.

"And what *do* you know?" Israfel said, instantly feeling wretched and filthy. "Do you think it was my fault—to fall in love with my own brother? What could you possibly know about pain? You don't even understand what it is to die."

She glared at him again, fierce with unspoken denial.

But they both knew the truth, and how much it had to hurt.

"Tell me," he calmed himself, settling back onto the floor, "who was that other red-haired woman? The one that tasted like—"

He couldn't say the name. Not now, when he already felt so sick. Israfel put a hand on his stomach and took a deep breath, willing his grace and strength to return.

"—like *her*."

"Like who?" Sophia said, her sobs dying to teary whispers.

"Your previous master," he said, his lips curling distastefully.

Sophia gazed at Angela, either like she was thinking, or yet again, hadn't quite heard what he'd asked. "I—are you talking about Stephanie?"

"Stephanie . . ."

"Stephanie Walsh." Sophia's pretty features creased and her voice lost its sweetness. "She's a witch."

"A witch?" The term was reappearing often now.

Sophia sighed. "A female human who summons and makes a contract with a demon, hoping to bring them under her control. The Vatican, the governing body in Luz, believed that she might have been the Archon, and they protected her, allowing her power to grow without realizing the danger, perhaps even benefiting from it. More than anything, she wants to be on the throne of your sister. Though she has more to lose than most." Sophia shook her head, her curls rustling. "The demon is like an adoptive mother to her. Stephanie knows no other life apart from Naamah, and it makes her dangerous—and unpredictable."

Ah, he saw it. The fear behind the Book's eyes.

Both of them, though, had reason for concern. The taste of that girl—it was as if Lucifel had entered her body and festered inside her heart. The shield she'd thrown up merely roused his suspicions more. In a disturbing reversal, Stephanie had abducted the demon back to Hell, not the other way around. "Was she the one who summoned Mikel?"

"No. That was Angela."

Israfel gripped the cushions on the couch, dizzy again. That couldn't be . . .

"You're saying that she," he waved at Angela's sleeping form, "broke my power."

Now that irritating Kim and his irritating words made much more sense. He'd mentioned that Raziel's soul could have been protecting the Archon, possessing her rather than actually *being* her. Israfel had never considered it before, but there was no reason why that couldn't be so. The Mirror Pools had merely showed him a figure and form, not the soul inside.

He glanced at her with a strange fear of his own.

"Who is she?"

Silence on Sophia's part.

Israfel rubbed his head, feeling the hint of a headache upon him. "How I hate your damnable riddles."

Sophia's pretty lips threatened to purse together. "Do you remember the Grail, Israfel?"

What? *Did he remember?* How could he forget? Israfel had never realized how far Raziel's affections had been swaying back then—until he started to wear Lucifel's treasure around his neck. That horrid Eye had been so like the Father's in its poisonous, all-seeing omniscience. How much Israfel had ached to wear that jewel. To conjure the Glaive himself and cut the throat of the sister whom even death couldn't kill.

"Why," he said, his voice trembling, "would you mention that cursed thing?"

"Forget about it," Sophia said, her smile faint but visible. "I was just making sure."

Angela shifted gently in her sleep.

Sophia's hand balled into a fist on top of her knee. Her expression appeared conflicted, like she sensed an approaching menace, but didn't have the means to run away.

Then the footsteps echoed, marching down the outside hallway.

Two jealous lovers had burned their store of patience, tired of waiting for Israfel's beck and call.

The walls shuddered. His door slammed open, wooden splinters spraying onto the carpeting. The human lock had snapped from his guardians' brute strength, and now the twins entered with matching strides, Rakir reaching Israfel first, Nunkir creeping behind with a forlorn expression. The more injured of the two, her newfound hatred of humanity had devolved into an even more pathetic need for affection.

Poor little bird. She'd never handled her emotions well.

She caressed Israfel's stomach, and then touched her brother's hands, their singular voice echoing inside the room. "*Prince Israfel, forgive us, but we are concerned for you.*"

They examined Angela and Sophia, dangerous envy boiling behind their green eyes. Nunkir's bandages swung from her wing, tickling the floor. Israfel gestured for her to lie next to him, and she collapsed, moaning into his lap. He stroked her fine, silver braids, unable to keep from comforting her. Nunkir and her brother probably deserved better than the existence they'd known, their lives before Israfel's presence more suffering than anything else. Brendan, one of the few creatures to acknowledge the treasures that they were, had made the mistake of going too far, allowing that suffering all over again.

But at least his pain had made up for the insult. Rakir, especially, needed that release.

His sister tilted her head, her green eyes locked shyly on Israfel's.

Also recognizing his chance, Rakir wrapped his strong arms around Israfel's chest, and their wings rubbed together, tenderly. His fingers brushed Nunkir's, eliciting their common voice. "*Why do you waste yourself on these creatures? Let us love you. We will always please you more than them. Always.*"

Nunkir brushed her lips over the stripes on Israfel's hands. Then, finding little resistance, the angel pinned him deep within the cushion of Rakir's arms, her wings flapping with a barely disguised urgency. She brushed the hairs from Israfel's neck, biting the skin beneath. These were harsh kisses, raw with eons of frustration; poisoned by a deep, envious pain. But that was all right, because sometimes it felt so good to be helpless and broken in another's embrace. Israfel goaded her on with the teasing touches she hated, a few well-timed sighs. She didn't have the experience of her brother.

"At least let me clean her up," Sophia was saying brokenly. "She'll be confused when she awakens."

She meant Angela.

Israfel said nothing, allowing his eyes to state his pleasure.

Slowly, as if she were afraid of alerting the guard, Sophia gathered Angela's gloves and boots from their spot near the wall, carefully grasping a crudely hewn chain between the spaces of her fingers. In a strange gesture of modesty, Sophia then turned her so that they faced the window and dressed her in her gloves and shoes like a doll, swiftly passing the chain around Angela's neck when she'd finished and rebuttoning what was left of her blouse.

"It seems I'll have to tolerate you," Sophia said to him, "for now. But I would have you remember one thing, Israfel. I alone know the true definition of a prison and pain. Never again try to beat me at a game of words."

He turned to her. The Book appeared to be growing taller, her eyes vacant and fathomless, patterns of indescribable intricacy flowing across her skin.

"And why is that?" he said, laughing at the unexpected vision.

"*Because I contain them all.*"

Thirty-one

In Her heart, Darkness lies.
In Her soul, the dormant Flies.
—CARDINAL DEMIAN YATES, *Translations of the Prophecy*

Angela awakened alone.

She was lying in a sitting room, its space dotted with velvet upholstered couches and all sorts of clutter, everything from musical instruments to fancy end tables covered in strange bottles and hair clips. The candle near the window had melted down to a sorry stump, its wax dribbled and malformed. But no matter what light there might be, it would have been impossible to put a dent in this kind of shadow. The sky outside was horrid, black and purple with clouds that resembled grotesque bubbles. Nearby, towers already dilapidated with age or neglect seemed surreal, vaporous in a greenish tinge hazing the atmosphere. The city looked sick to its stomach, sitting in a stillness that suggested death.

"God." Angela clapped a hand across her forehead. She felt nauseated, still tasting the unearthly dryness of Israfel's nectar.

She'd never had anything like it before. In comparison, wine and beer were too sweet, and fruit juice was too bitter, like those contradictions had been distilled into a liquid and tinted with a gold that reminded her of Kim's eyes. Even when her mind numbed and her heart raced with the terrible pleasure, it had been hard not to picture him there, staring at her like she was a whore or a sinner, judging her to Hell while she kissed Israfel's soft mouth and touched him in all the places she'd dreamed. It turned her stomach even worse than the hangover—the idea of more guilt, that she'd betrayed him—especially after he'd confused her so badly.

He wanted her on the Throne of Hell? What kind of solution was that?

I'm far from perfect, but I'm not the Devil.

She sat up and the Grail kissed her skin, its surface unusually warm. Angela unbuttoned her blouse and looked down at the Eye, touching the emerald iris and deep, dark pupil. Sophia had known that she'd taken it from Troy. Yet Sophia had known because she wasn't just a Revenant—and Angela doubted how true that really was anymore—but because she was the Book. A thing or a monster in the shape of a person, who was also enough of a mystery that those who tried opening her risked going insane.

It was all coming back to her, harsh and clear.

Angela had used that as her justification for drinking herself stupid.

Now that the facts presented themselves again, it simply hurt.

Where is she?

Where were *they*? Israfel's room was empty except for piles of garbage and treasure. Feathers rested in mounds of white near the walls, and the room smelled of sweetness, stickiness, and that unusual perfume of his: flowers and salt. Jewels and barrettes had been carelessly tossed onto tables or fallen to the floor.

Angela rocked onto her knees, steadying herself, and grabbed a silver hair clip resting near her toes. The gems set inside the metal were strange, hollow and red, but with a sheen of blue and black to their facets. She must have been holding some kind of crystal from somewhere up in Heaven, growing in a place that could blow away the imaginations of every priest in Luz.

It was official now. Heaven was a real, material place.

That meant Hell was too, and just like them, Israfel was less a ghost or a spirit than a solid, fleshy, beautiful creature. Her lifetime's dream had finally touched, kissed, and danced with her.

He bled like she bled, and he spoke like she spoke. From the very start, she'd never thought about how Troy and Israfel knew her language, simply preferring not to care, but she was certain their superiority over humanity had a lot to do with it. Remembering the way Israfel's lips curled around words, it didn't seem farfetched to assume he was speaking his own language, and Angela was always hearing hers. In a sense, every syllable was its own song.

Yes, Israfel and Troy and even Tileaf were flesh and blood, but they could manipulate your soul as easily as blowing on smoke.

Angela put a hand over her chest, shuddering a little.

The Eye had gone from warm to unusually hot. In seconds it was almost scalding her.

"What the hell—" She quickly swung the chain over her neck, keeping the stone far away from her skin. Its surface glistened and she held it aloft, peering carefully at its shininess. There seemed to be something moving across the pupil.

An ant, maybe? Or a spider?

No. It was an image.

Instantly, her ears buzzed, her insides swam, and she was sucked inside the Grail itself. Angela was too surprised to scream or even to be frightened. Then the rectory vanished in the blink of an eye, and she stood in what must have been the darkness at the stone's middle, watching Nina walk by her in a dank, cobblestoned alleyway. The buildings on either side were dilapidated—probably close to where she was now—and ahead a tunnel passed beneath a stone bridge.

Just as quickly, the visions vanished, and Angela was back in the rectory with the Eye still swinging in front of her.

She tapped the pupil carefully.

It had gone cold, and its onyx surface was hard as a rock.

There was no doubt, though, that she had seen what the Eye had seen, or perhaps what it merely wanted to show her. Maybe it sensed the terrible predicament she currently faced and had attempted to help in some frightening way of its own.

She was honestly in trouble, and more than ever before. Despite whatever feelings Angela had for him, Kim was a wild card now—impossible to trust one hundred percent after his strange attempt at compromise. Troy was still Bound to her, but by force rather than by choice. Sophia and Israfel had left her for God only knew where—they could return in an hour or a century. And Stephanie and Naamah would be looking for her, either to kill her and be done with it—Stephanie's preferred course of action—or to declare her the Archon, and—

What *would* Naamah do if Angela was the Archon?

Probably force her to open the Book, then either kill her in Lucifel's name or tackle Kim's proposal head-on and put her on the Throne of Hell.

That left Angela with one person she could count on absolutely.

Nina. She was possessed, and yet she was all that Angela had.

I have to find her.

Angela yanked on her arm gloves and tights, but quickly rethought things and discarded them before tightening the laces on her boots. The air was too humid, she was uncomfortably warm, and while the scars made her a freak, they didn't make her a witch like Stephanie and her alabaster legs.

Her hangover was dying off, replaced by a growing anger.

In her shock and grief, Angela had dared to blame Israfel, but Stephanie more than anyone else had killed her brother. Sure, she hadn't cut his throat herself, but she'd asked Naamah to do it for her. But the most horrible detail of all was also the most haunting. Brendan had been out of his mind, and whether he deserved it or not, murdering him so violently had been no more valiant than putting a rabid dog to sleep. Israfel wasn't human, and he saw the world through those superior angelic eyes. But Stephanie at least used to have a human heart, and she should have known better.

Angela cinched her laces, her fingers shaking.

Outside, the storm rolled into Luz silently.

Too silently. Like it mirrored the dreadful pissed-off state of her mind.

Stephanie expects me to run and hide. She expects me to stay out of her games and let her get away with all this bullshit.

The Grail swung beneath her ruined blouse, suddenly heavy and radiating a new heat that felt oddly comforting the more she got used to it. Not that she could hide it properly anymore. Angela's clothes were so torn and tattered, she must have looked like a zombie. Her skirt had at least two holes in it half the size of her hands, and her blouse was smeared with dirt and blood and was ripped halfway across the chest.

I don't care if I'm the Archon or not. I don't have to open that damned Book to put Stephanie where she belongs.

In Hell.

She left the room, clattering down the steep staircase and along a hallway that emptied into the broken church. Angela splashed through the puddles, hardly even giving a damn about her surroundings. Her brain burned like the stone around her neck, and it seemed to her that through that Eye, she could see the whole universe and everything in it, and how much it deserved to be in her hands rather than in those of a greedy, ignorant person like Stephanie.

This is my world.

Where was that thought coming from? It was the voice that had reminded her how to subdue Troy, and its pitch and tone was still like her own, but much more forceful. Briefly, Angela flashed back to that long-ago dream, when she'd stood before the angel who'd spoken to her so mysteriously.

Now she remembered at least a fraction of what he'd said, though she wasn't sure how much sense it made.

For now, though, it seemed right to agree.

This is my world. Time to enforce the rules.

Thirty-two

She is my Prince, but only because I choose it to be so.
And I dare say there will come a time to change my mind.
—THE DEMON PYTHON, TRANSCRIBED FROM *The Lies of Babylon*

Pain returned to Stephanie along with her consciousness. Overwhelming, shattering pain. She merely brushed the skin near her left elbow and it screamed back at her, all the agony erupting through her own mouth.

But that wasn't the worst part.

She was in pain and darkness, but it didn't take much longer to remember she was also in Hell. Her vision began to return, though blurry, and around her the pentagrams reappeared pulsing and red. She lay in some strange tunnel, its floor smooth stone, its upper ceiling carved with a demonic script that pulsed along with the pentagrams. Theban writing, the same harsh symbols as the tattoo that had matched her mother's.

Barely illuminated by the light, eyes and arms, bodies and legs, jutted outward from the rock, their owners melded seamlessly into the walls. They could have been statues, but Stephanie sensed otherwise, and she shut her eyes instinctively when she imagined hundreds more staring back into hers.

"Stephanie. It's me."

She moaned, her eyelids fluttering back open.

Naamah's copper face hovered over her, the demon's mouth set in a tight line. For a second she stood, half disappearing in the darkness, and then she lifted Stephanie into her arms. Together, they moved farther through the tunnel, Stephanie's legs dangling, her head pressed against a wound that had been stitched near Naamah's neck. Israfel must have injured her, though not enough to kill. If it weren't for Stephanie's quick thinking . . .

That was the most unfortunate thing of all.

She couldn't even remember what she'd thought at the time or why.

"Mother . . ." Stephanie tried to lift herself against Naamah's chest.

Her efforts were rewarded by her body sliding lower, terrifyingly weak.

"Stop trying to move," Naamah said. Her voice sounded as fuzzy as the world appeared, though characteristically emotionless. If Stephanie's condition bothered her, she wasn't showing it very well.

But, oh God, the pain. "What happened? Mother . . ."

She gasped, almost seeing stars, screaming until Naamah clamped a hand over her mouth.

"Be quiet," she hissed in Stephanie's ear. "For the Prince's sake, or we'll both be done for."

Stephanie let the tears roll down her face, trying to focus on her breathing. Anything to keep her sanity. Night in this place felt like an eternal night, and for her, it might continue on and on in the long sleep called death.

Naamah's words came gentler now, her voice soft as her footsteps. "You've lost a lot of blood, but I'm going to make sure you're all right."

"How?"

"Just keep silent."

Stephanie obeyed, hiccupping in her agony.

"Just keep silent," Naamah whispered, "and everything will be fine."

If only she'd sounded more certain. Naamah usually held her

worries inside, rarely revealing her true feelings unless they'd finally overwhelmed her. Perhaps this would be one of those times. Her frame shivered, and she paused before what resembled a great gate set in the rock. Stephanie held her own breath, aware that they stood on the threshold of a momentous and alien place.

Soft scrabbling erupted from the tunnel ceiling. A few pebbles clattered to the ground.

Stephanie gazed ahead, terrified by what flickered at the corners of her vision.

Two of the bodies set in the walls were moving.

Naamah tightened her grip, a silent warning.

Stephanie shut her eyes for the second time, allowing ice-cold fingers to poke at her body, two invisible faces to sniff at her hair and her injured arm, and hungry breaths to blow on her neck. The inspection felt like it would last forever, but finally, whatever these guardians had observed must have satisfied them. Silent as before, they settled back into their flanking positions at the gate, two slim bodies slipping back into grooves carved in the stone. They were angels of some kind, their hair tangled and their wings little more than bone and skin.

It was growing more and more difficult to see.

Stephanie's vision was worse than before, and a fine mist fogged the air, smelling faintly of vinegar.

This was the smell she often associated with Naamah. Acidic.

Clank.

A noise of metal on metal rang down the tunnel. The gate was opening, and Naamah stepped through it swiftly, barely reacting as the iron bars slammed shut behind them and they reached a point of no return. Inside, the pentagrams repeated themselves in circular patterns, illuminating the shape of a rounded cave set in the rock. Farther in, an enormous pentagram appeared in the room's center floor, revolving beneath the tall and slender body suspended above it. A figure hung manacled amid a spiderweb of chains, the incredibly shiny metal extending from arms, legs, and neck. Dank odors also emerged through the mist, smelling of sickliness and musk.

Naamah squeezed Stephanie's shoulder again—another warning.

Trembling, she set her down on the floor below the manacled figure, eventually settling nearby on her knees, her wings flat and arched forward in submission.

Stephanie gasped again, unable to stop.

"Naamah."

The new voice was soft, almost a hiss at the edge of her imagination.

It took a moment for Stephanie to notice the shadow coiling in and out of the mist clinging to the floor, and yet the closer it came, the more it lost its strange snakelike shape and the glitter of its scales, its body disappearing again as the darkness seemed to pull in on itself, molding its inky vapors into the figure of a person. Now he stood to their right, half disguised by the gloom, and Stephanie wondered if she was hallucinating.

He seemed to be a tall young man, with a mop of sable hair that might have been streaked through with violet. A shock of purple paint glowed over his eyelids.

His eyes, though, remained hazy.

Maybe that was for the best, because there was something about them that seemed off to her. Unnatural. Maybe even reptilian. They examined her coldly, briefly reflecting the light with a terrible shade of orange.

Stephanie was actually thankful when Naamah spoke again. It gave her something else to concentrate on.

"Python." Naamah greeted him with a marked coldness. "What are you doing here?"

"Touchy as ever." His lips spread into an expressive smile. "I came to pray, of course." He sauntered closer, eyebrows lifted in curiosity. "At least I was before you barged through the Gate. Now what is this little annoyance you brought? A human?" The demon was encroaching on Stephanie, almost close enough for her to make out the delicate scales hidden below his eyepaint. "I'm sure you wouldn't mind if I took a closer look—"

Naamah shot onto her feet, her fingerblades to his throat.

Python lost his smile.

"Not another step," Naamah said, hissing herself between her teeth.

There was a pause, heavy and oppressive.

"Oh," Python whispered, "but I think you might want to play a little more nicely today. We wouldn't want to wake *her*."

He inclined his head at the figure hanging in her web of chains, her silhouette sharp against a background of crimson.

Stephanie's eyes began to water.

"After all," he continued, just as softly, "you haven't exactly been the most well-behaved chick in the nest as of late. Maybe while we're here, we should tell the Prince about your recent string of failures." Python pushed the blades away from his neck. "Or you could simply let me take a look at your little pet. That is, unless you do want help from *her* instead."

Naamah's braids shone with the eerie light, resembling gold dipped in blood.

"She's dying," she said at last, her voice trembling. "From blood loss."

Python stepped to Stephanie's side, glowering down at her. "I don't see why that matters. Humans breed like common rats and die just as easily. I'm sure you'll find a replacement soon. Unless you think she is the Archon, perhaps?"

Naamah was silent for a while, and that was answer enough. Stephanie couldn't control herself. She sobbed, violated by the idea that Naamah never really believed in her. *Never.* Naamah had mentioned replacements when talking about her dead brother, and now it was Stephanie's turn, just as she'd warned.

"She's a human I—adopted."

Python waited, wordless.

"Her mother sold her soul, in exchange for typical human amusements. This one was only a chick, and with her red hair—"

"Then that means," he said coolly, "that you're still looking." The demon's tone hardened, subtly but in a distinct and terrible way. "It's not a good position to be in, Countess. Some would be led to think you're not enthusiastic about our god's cause. Holding back like that. What a shameful thing to do when so many lives are at stake."

But both of them heard the careless laughter in his voice.

"So how shall you keep her alive? With"—and the laughter was real this time—"the power of prayer?"

Naamah's fingers twitched dangerously, but she calmed down again, glancing at him sideways. "Why are you interested? Do you want to help me? Or are you really just that much of a snake?"

Python breathed heavily.

Naamah turned from him, but he grabbed her suddenly, pulling her in as if for an embrace. Her fingerblades reappeared at the same instant the manacled figure sighed in her sleep.

Naamah froze with her hand extended, petrified.

Python whispered into her ear, and Stephanie thought she saw a forked tongue lick at her mother's skin. "We're not that ignorant, Countess. Or, perhaps I should say, I'm not that ignorant." His fingers pinched her arms cruelly, and his other hand clamped against the wound near her collarbone. "Let's be frank with each other. You made a mistake the moment you sidestepped me for this mission. I mean, what did you think? That I wouldn't catch on to where your true allegiance lies?" He whispered even lower now, voice husky. "It's one thing to secretly plan for our Prince's deposition. It's another to let everyone else figure it out. If I were you, it might be time to make your nest elsewhere. In fact, I'd say you showed your idiocy the moment you stepped into this Altar."

Now it was Stephanie's turn to laugh. She couldn't even say what had amused her so much.

Naamah and another demon were at each other's throats. She was dying.

Yet the laughter left her anyway, cold and mirthless.

Python gazed at her once more, and then his eyes burned with fear.

He licked his lips, unclasping Naamah with a shiver to his arms.

Naamah cursed at him in that harsh language of hers and pushed him aside, lifting Stephanie back into her arms and taking her nearer to the chained figure above them. Stephanie stopped laughing, understanding deep down inside that there was nothing to enjoy. Nothing to hope for anymore. Like Naamah's brother, she was now a sacrifice to the one person Kim warned would find and punish her for the murderous promises she'd so hastily made. Over and over in her mind, she saw the blood and the unhappiness, some of it her own, some inflicted on others through her actions. Then she raised her head, steeling herself to gaze back into the face of Ruin, determined to overcome it somehow.

Stephanie saw only herself, hanging there. Until the eyes opened, red as the blood dripping from her arm.

"Now." Stephanie stopped Naamah, digging her nails into the demon's skin.

Her vision swirled with black, the buzzing in her ears like a mass of flies.

But there was no denying this sense of utter satisfaction anymore.

"Go ahead and pray."

Thirty-three

The Devil does one thing well.
She plans.

—MONSIGNOR JOSEPH MAUSS, UNOFFICIAL CORRESPONDENCE

Angela had wandered out of the church and deeper into the western side of the Academy, vaguely aware that she was circling around Memorial Park. She'd recognized some of the stairways Kim had used that night, and without anything else to guide her, felt that it would be best to try what she knew rather than take a chance and get lost. The streets seemed utterly deserted and it wasn't even nighttime. At one point, Angela skirted one of the lowest levels of the city she'd visited yet, and the subtle chop of the ocean water beneath sounded ominously soft. Luz seemed to be waiting for something and had hushed everyone and everything until that something happened.

Her footsteps cracking apart the quiet could have intimidated the city.

Luz reacted like a living thing to the atmosphere and people inside of it, and though that was perhaps more an analogy than fact, Angela had the creeping sense that she made the place darker and less inviting the more she stomped around. Like an aura of fear preceded her, and even the cobblestones bowed to keep her happy.

She turned a corner, startled to see a familiar tunnel, and Nina standing in front of it.

So I did see her. It wasn't just my imagination.

Nina's hair stuck out around her face in a frazzled mess, and her face appeared paler than usual. It was hard to tell if her eyes were still red because of Mikel, or if they were just back to their usual bloodshot mess.

"I knew you'd be back," Nina said. "She told me so. They told me so."

A sharp breeze blustered Nina's hair and skirt, and the tunnel behind her seemed to sing, its dark mouth open wide. She didn't budge as Angela drew closer and closer, until they were almost nose to nose.

"Who am I talking to?" Angela said. "Tell me the truth. I don't have time for anything else."

But Nina's irises were back to their usual dull color. Tiny bits of leaf and twig hung in the frizz of her hair. "It's me, Angela. I'm myself now. Or I should say, I can speak to you again. Mikel and I have reached an agreement about that, thank God."

"Is that why it took you so long to wake up?"

Nina laughed, scuffing her boot across the stone. "You could say that. I don't think I've ever slept so long, but so poorly, my entire life." She arched an eyebrow, scanning Angela up and down. "You look—different."

"Speak for yourself."

"I'm not just talking about your clothes." Nina shivered a little and lowered her head. It wasn't particularly cold outside. She just seemed as oppressed by Angela's presence as the rest of Luz.

"You said that Mikel told you I'd come back here? How much do you know about what happened—"

"Everything. I know about the faerie, and about that creature—Troy. Why does it feel so appropriate for you to make friends with a devil who eats people like candy bars, Angela?"

Angela shook her head. "We're not friends. I Bound her to me. Trust me, she'd eat me too if she had the chance."

Nina raised both eyebrows now, but said nothing.

"It's a long story."

"Yeah, and I know *we don't have time for it*." She sighed, folding her arms. Yep, same old Nina. "So are you ready? To free them?"

"What?" Angela peered at her intently. "Free who?"

"The dead. The human souls in the Netherworld." Nina glanced at the black sky, its clouds swirling inland with the crushing silence of an impending hurricane, though by the looks of it, this was something worse. Something that had more to do with the same dead people who wanted out of limbo, and the Devil rattling her chains down in Hell. If Israfel could step out of history and show his face—then maybe Lucifel could too. "They were speaking to me all night, all day, and the rest of last night into this morning. They're ready, Angela, but time's running out. They're saying that She's coming. That She's almost arrived."

"Who? You're talking about the Ruin again, right?"

Nina shivered again. "What has Stephanie done since I've been out of the picture?"

Angela's voice sounded hard and icy, even for her. "Killed my brother, taken over the Academy, and shown her true colors."

"God. Anything else?"

Israfel and Sophia were gone for now. No need to mention what could only complicate things further. And Kim—that still hurt her too much to explain. Besides, Nina would simply say, I told you so.

"No. Except for the fact that I'm going to make sure Stephanie either suffers or joins Naamah in some lake of fire."

"Naamah?"

"A demon. Stephanie summoned a demon to Luz. That's the person who threw you off the Bell Tower the other night, when I summoned Mikel. They want you dead now, because for some reason, Mikel pisses them off. I think either she knows details that would make life very difficult for them, or she's a threat."

"Let's say a threat," Nina said, laughing. For a second, her irises were blood red. Then they returned to normal and her face became as icy as Angela's. "When it comes down to it, I'd be pretty miffed too if an angel imprisoned me in some body I never wanted and then tortured it. As for the *real* me"—she relaxed her arms and gestured for Angela to follow her through the tunnel—"I don't remember being thrown out of the Tower, but I'd sure like to do the same to Stephanie."

Angela stepped over a miniature moat and entered the tunnel behind her, the blackness around them crushing but rich with the squeaks and scampering of rats and cockroaches. "You broke some bones too."

Nina cursed under her breath. "Assholes."

"If you don't enter the Netherworld and do this yourself," Nina was saying, "Naamah will encourage Stephanie to do it for you. Even if she isn't the Archon, that would play right into Lucifel's plans. Without anyone to protect these souls, she'll simply wipe them out of existence—and the imbalance will be worse than it is now."

"Why would she even bother?" Angela said. She watched Nina scrape over Troy's symbols left in the dirt, her fingers deftly moving the thick twigs, reinforcing the sigils that resembled constellations and strange, alien things. Tileaf's tree hadn't changed, except that its branches might have been more bare than the other night. This felt like déjà vu. "What can Lucifel accomplish killing souls that are already dead? Is that even possible?"

"You heard Tileaf. Lucifel wants to start over, Angela. Just not in a positive way. For her, the end is the beginning, and she intends to keep it an end rather than trying something new. Have you ever heard of the symbols alpha and omega?"

This had to be Mikel talking.

Nina couldn't possibly know what she was saying. Maybe on a distant level, if her mind was connected to the angel's. But not consciously.

"Think of Lucifel as the omega point. But with her, there's no goddamned alpha anymore. Ever sit back and think how horrible it is that some souls suffer for their sins, burning inside, eternally tortured for what they've done?"

That depends on their sins.

What circle of Hell could Erianna and Marcus be in? Maybe the bottom, where it was all ice and darkness. Angela must have learned a thing or two from Dante after all. From what she remembered, that was the special place for traitors, but that didn't mean they couldn't spare some room for two abusive, perverted, deadbeat parents. They'd betrayed their own child—that had to count. "Yeah. I guess. I always wondered why God would do that to people . . . I mean, if He's merciful and just . . ."

"Well, that's just the thing. It *is* a mercy, because otherwise, they simply wouldn't exist. Torture and endless pain are bad. But what would you think about being erased from reality entirely? No pain. Just nothingness. And you'd never know it, because there'd be nothing left for you to know it with."

She's right. That sounds far from ideal too.

"That's how Lucifel thinks. That's what she'll do. Opening Raziel's Book will just be the clincher. If she can start on erasing everything now, she will."

"Why now? Why is everything happening *now*?"

Nina stood up from her handiwork, glancing over the sigils to make sure they were appropriate. "Because she has the freedom now. For some reason, the dimensional layers that make up the material world, and Heaven, and Hell—they're coming apart. Lucifel can't escape her cage just yet—not unless she's physically freed—but I wouldn't be surprised if she finds a way around that and soon. Enough to come after the Archon anyway."

Then, entering the Netherworld was the only way to stop Stephanie from destroying Luz and Angela's life, and perhaps stop Lucifel from erasing every dead human soul from whatever existence it had, however miserable. Angela wasn't the Archon—so said Troy, and for a while, Kim—but apparently that no longer mattered. She wasn't trying to open the Book, so at least she wouldn't go insane. Though it bothered her, that she felt like the world was crumbling beneath the weight of her feet, yet she had very little to prove that was really the case.

No—they were missing something here.

Angela gripped the Grail, surprised again by the Eye's warmth.

"Are you ready?" Nina said, her skirt swaying in the breeze. Tileaf's tree creaked and groaned, like it was protesting over being awakened again. "But there's no going back once you're in there, Angela. You've got to be resolved about this."

Troy's dried blood must have still been good enough to resuscitate the Fae. Before Angela could answer Nina, the eerie wind began, the intense green light flickered throughout the grotto, and the branches and leaves around them glowed with that strange, unearthly color. While it had seemed to take forever for Tileaf to show herself the first time, this was different. Angela had less than a second to adjust her eyes and blink, and the Fae stood before them as groggy and tormented as before, maybe even worse, her eyes shifting wildly until she saw Angela. The collar of light around her neck seemed to choke off her voice.

"Now—you will keep your promise?" Tileaf beckoned Angela near.

"I have to go to the Netherworld."

I sound like such a selfish bitch.

She was still angry. Her heart raced, but with a fire coming from somewhere different than before. Now, people and things that were in her way would have to step aside, and whenever she needed them to.

Tileaf smiled. "I know. Don't worry, you'll do what I asked. You must—if you want to enter Azrael's domain. Luz is connected . . . to the Underworld. My tree rests over the only way inside and out."

That explains so much about this city.

"So I have to kill you just to get in there?"

"Yes," Tileaf sighed, as if a great weight were being lifted from her shoulders.

Angela wrapped her arms around herself, sucking in a deep breath. This was it, then. But promising Tileaf that she would kill her was much easier than actually doing it. Her parents' deaths were an accident, even though they probably got what they deserved. Besides, Angela had a hard time squashing bugs, and suddenly she had to murder a Fae who'd lived for centuries. If Troy was anywhere nearby, she could have commanded her to do it, but there had to be a reason why Tileaf hadn't asked that Jinn to maul her to death. "It has to be me?"

The Fae trembled, and she sank down next to her tree, her spider-silk dress rustling through the leaves. "No."

"Then why me? Or—why the Archon?"

"Because," said the faerie, her anguished eyes shining, "that would be an honor."

"All right." Angela couldn't even look at Nina. Her only friend at the Academy was going to watch her murder Tileaf in cold blood. The bile rose in the back of her throat. "If there's no way around it . . ."

Angela didn't have a weapon. She didn't have a clue. How was this going to happen?

"This is your world," Tileaf was saying.

And I made the rules.

That voice in her head. It was more familiar than ever, speaking in tandem with hers.

"I can't do this."

"You can. It's your right."

It's my right. Because I made the rules . . .

Angela took out the Grail, folding her hand around the Eye. How could she do it?

She and Tileaf were only a few feet apart. Angela clambered over the thick roots at the base of the tree to where Tileaf rested near the oak's trunk, her tattered dress splayed around her bruised knees. The Fae gazed at her intently, motioning for Angela to reveal the Grail. "Take back what's rightfully yours."

I'm taking back what was once mine.

A sharp pain seared into Angela's palm. Troy's chain snapped and flew to the left, landing in the leaves. She opened her hand, amazed and vaguely terrified to find the Eye fusing into her skin. Her flesh opened and enclosed around it like a new kind of eyelid, and yet as it settled there, becoming part of her whether she wished it to or not, her fear faded into a grim resolve that flowed throughout her entire frame. When she looked at Tileaf again, the Fae had closed her eyes, like a child waiting for her mother's good-night kiss.

"I knew it," Tileaf whispered. "It didn't seem possible . . . but you—you—"

You've been suffering for so long.

Angela stood over her, clenching her fingers into the stone. Its surface ruptured under her nails, and she sensed, rather than saw, the blood warming her fingers.

But now I know exactly how to help you.

She felt the blood harden into a knife.

Then, for Tileaf, it was the end.

Thirty-four

Before my eyes, the Abyss.
In my ears, the howl of despair.
My kingdom is now my prison.
—The Supernal Lucifel, *A Collection of Angelic Lore*

Weight.

Kim couldn't breathe, and it felt like his chest was being crushed.

He opened his eyes to the morning grayness, only half surprised to see Stephanie straddling him, one of her thin hands pressed up against his throat. But the moment his eyelids had spread apart, her fingers relaxed, and she pushed back the hairs near his cheeks as if that had been her aim all along.

How in God's name had she come back after what she'd done and where she'd gone?

And the look in her eyes—Stephanie's face was indefinably disturbing, like a mask. She stared back at him in an odd, expressionless way—even for a person who killed like it was routine. Now it seemed entirely plausible for her to attack Israfel and escape unscathed.

Otherwise, she was gorgeous as always, her crimson eye shadow finely powdered beneath her brows, her legs still long and soft. Instead of her own overcoat, she wore one of his long novice coats that fell to the ankles, and its black buttons gleamed beneath the candelabra's flames.

The sight was unusual enough to make him pause.

He spoke slowly, hoping his voice wouldn't reveal anything. She'd seen him with Angela again, and in the world of their sham relationship, that was certainly a good reason for murder. "Shouldn't you be dead?"

Fury chattered at the sound of his voice. The crow bounced below the window frame, peering inside. Quickly, she soared back out into the gathering darkness.

"Good morning to you too." Stephanie leaned down to kiss him.

Oh no. That wasn't right at all.

He pushed her away, sitting up in bed so that she slid closer to his knees.

Stephanie pressed against his bare chest, stroking the skin with her cold fingertips. "Kim, I want to give you another chance. I want you and me to be together in this."

"You mean in this relationship?"

That wasn't right either.

He grabbed her by the thighs, careful not to act too unnerved. She was lethal now, and if Israfel had received a flesh wound, Kim would probably suffer worse. "Get off me."

Stephanie fought to stay put, but then he succeeded in tossing her to the other side of the bed, and her ponytail swung behind her like a rope, smacking into the wall. She breathed hard, but continued analyzing him with her eyes, as if gauging how best to tempt him again. Even the blush on her face could have been a well-thought-out lie.

"How did you even get in here?" Kim could have sworn he'd locked the door before going to sleep.

"Well, let's just say not all the novices think the archbishop's death was a bad idea." Stephanie crawled back to him, her arms wrapping possessively around his neck. "I could have killed you too, you know. But I didn't."

Her fingers trailed down to his stomach, full of suggestion.

Footsteps traveled up and down the hallway outside of his room. Soft whispers followed them, murmurs, the creak of his door as someone listened outside. The seminarian dormitory was far more alive than Kim had thought it would be. Stephanie must have been right—not everyone was against the idea of her lording over a good portion of Luz, especially the novices, priests, and various people who would benefit from her witchcraft. But that still didn't completely explain how she'd found another key to his room.

"So where did murdering me factor into your sudden feelings?"

He left the bed, picking up the clothes he'd folded near the base of his closet. He needed to behave like this, as if nothing could possibly be different about her. Because if Kim betrayed a hint of suspicion or fear, he was certain he'd pay for it. It was a subtle and deadly game to play. Luckily for Kim, Troy had given him plenty of opportunity for practice over the years.

Sensing Stephanie's unnerving stare, he focused on his clothes, buttoning his shirt.

Their black hue matched the clouds bubbling across the skyline. Since yesterday the weather had evolved into something straight from Hell, and the silence that had lingered into the morning meant what had to be the worst—the Academy was cut off from the rest of the mainland. Now, they were all destined to either sink or drown in the attempt to leave Luz alive.

"We're through. But if you're lonely, you always have Naamah for company—"

"*Shut up*," Stephanie said. She jumped from the bed and grabbed Kim by the shoulders, her nails digging into his skin. He winced slightly, aware of the blood trickling to his navel.

"Tell me where Angela is."

"You talk like I keep tabs on her."

She looked at him coolly, her hands shaking, like she couldn't make up her mind about something, or decide on what she felt. "*Where*, Kim?"

"Why does it matter, Stephanie? Your mind is made up, after all. You're the Archon. You're the Ruin Naamah has been waiting for. So does it really matter where Angela is and why? Unless," he said slowly, "you're second-guessing yourself . . ."

Stephanie stared at him, her eyes narrowing slightly. "You're right," she said, though her voice was hushed. The tactic of someone who didn't want to be heard. "*I am the Archon.*"

"But I also warned you about what that means—"

"I'm not afraid of Lucifel." Her face took on a strange, shrewd expression, her green eyes wide and haunted. "Or that angel who just stood there while Brendan bled to death. That relic—*Israfel.*"

She said the name with such hatred, it was startling.

That's right. Brendan was dead. In the sallow normality of morning, Kim had almost forgotten the blander details of the previous night. But if Angela needed any consoling—and Kim doubted she did—he wasn't in the best position to offer it to her anymore. Besides, right now he had an insane ex-girlfriend to deal with. "Oh, you sound afraid, Stephanie."

"I just don't like what he did to me. His kiss—"

"The way he tasted you," he corrected her.

She shivered more visibly. "Naamah told me Israfel was dead. Now I'm sure that everyone just assumed he was."

"Angels have a way of dropping in on you unexpectedly," Kim said, half glancing at the window. "And always at the worst times."

He knew it. Fury had left to tell Troy what was going on. His cousin would probably try to slash open his wrists, blaming him—not her Vapor—for forcing her into a daytime journey to rip out Stephanie's voice box. The storm continued to darken the sky one black inch at a time, but for Troy, this was hardly dark enough.

She'd find happiness when the rain began and Luz shuddered down into the sea.

"What about my questions for a change?" he said, picking his words carefully. "Fair is only fair. That doll named Sophia." Kim wrestled with the irritated bitterness in his tone. They'd always been like this—perfect in bed, at each other's throats out of it. "Who is she? Israfel showed more than passing interest in her. The fact that he abducted her is even worse."

Stephanie went rigid. "He abducted her—"

"That's what I said."

A delicate lick of lightning brightened the room.

Soon, it seemed to say.

Soon, Kim's mahogany frame bed, his religious paintings, his prayer books, his collection of occult paraphernalia—they would all be destroyed.

The storm was whipping deeper into Luz, and he could only imagine the ocean waves, the swells, the forced evacuations to higher levels of the city. And with the Academy in such turmoil, and the sirens unable to sound unless the deceased archbishop said the word . . .

Thunder broke above them, and Stephanie shook her head. Then her eyes glazed over, and she found a grim expression worse than all the others, so strange it didn't even fit her face. "Fine. Let's play your game." Her lips seemed to move in slow motion. "Kim, Sophia is the Book of Raziel."

He could only stare.

This was unbelievable, a complete and absolute disaster. If Israfel opened the Book—which was apparently Sophia of all people or things—then he would have the power to crush Lucifel, to crush Hell, to remake the world however he wished. And in that world, there would be no place for Kim, possibly Angela, and certainly not for the both of them together.

"You—" He heard the murder in his voice. Every last bit of self-control was slipping from him fast. "Why did you take the Book to the cathedral?"

"I wouldn't worry too much. Not yet." Stephanie's expression was even harder than before. "Israfel would have opened her by now, if he could."

Oh, how tempting it was to stab her through the heart and be done with it. The only thing stopping him was the deadly expression on Stephanie's face, one that prickled his instinct to tread as carefully as he still could.

But, oh, it was hard.

"You needed to know," Stephanie said, pouncing on his hesitation. "By the way, Kim, I told the students inside St. Mary's that

Angela was the one responsible for Maribel's death. Even if she tries to enjoy a normal life in Luz, they'll arrest her for witchcraft and homicide. That is, if I or Naamah don't reach her first."

He had nothing to say.

Maybe he had lost this round. Unable to kill Stephanie, especially with her new and lethal abilities. Unable to keep Angela from Naamah's grasp, even if he won the battle.

"I'm not stupid, Kim. Even if you can't protect Angela from me," Stephanie whispered, "I know you're trying in your own pathetic little way. Right now, we both know I could kill you on the spot. Well, since you've rejected your second chance, maybe it's time to put you to sleep at last—like the unfaithful puppy you are."

A faint red glow outlined her hand.

"You see"—and the green of her eyes flickered to a terrible and familiar shade—"I started playing these petty games long before you even had the chance."

More shadows darkened the insides of the room.

Boom. Boom. Boom.

Stephanie turned to the right, frighteningly fast. She stared beyond Kim, out the small space of window left open by his thick drapes. It was the first and possibly only time that sound would equal his salvation.

"Like I said," he said, his heart still racing, "angels tend to drop in unexpectedly."

The bow window smashed, glass spraying into the room. Kim ducked, covering his head while the embroidered draperies crumpled to the floor, the bar that held them in place swinging violently against the wall. The candelabra flames whisked into smoke.

Troy landed right by his side, facing Stephanie.

Her wings, their great sickles tucked tightly to enter through the narrow space, flared out again like a living darkness. Kim rose steadily back to his feet, actually delighted that his cousin had arrived at the right moment. But she hadn't arrived alone. Fury soared in behind her, landing on her shoulder to caw and cackle with greed.

Lyrica Pengold lay dead and bloody in Troy's arms.

It was almost impossible to tell where her red tights ended and the carnage began.

Her chest was torn open, her heart removed. The lower half of Troy's face was sticky with blood, and her teeth dripped with crimson saliva. She tossed the body at Stephanie, laughing in the raspy way that could stick in Kim's nightmares for days. Lyrica rolled to Stephanie's feet, face frozen in openmouthed terror.

"She was looking for you," Troy said. "But I thought she'd get here faster by air."

Stephanie screamed, but quickly choked off into a deadly silence, like another person had snapped her mouth shut.

Troy vanished into the darkness of the room.

The tide had now turned considerably.

There was a sudden noise above them, and Stephanie lifted her faintly glowing hand, ready to blast Kim's cousin like she'd blasted Israfel, but it was impossible to keep track of how Troy scampered between the shadows. She turned to Kim, wordlessly demanding an explanation.

"A Jinn," he said to her, aware that his triumph was impossible to hide. "My other half."

"It will die with you," Stephanie murmured, hardly sounding sure of herself.

She seemed to consider killing him one last time, but after another glance at Lyrica, a trickle of tears appeared.

Surprisingly, Troy allowed her to escape the room screaming as she slammed the door.

Then the shouts began and the hurried voices, and the harsh knocks, demanding that he open up. Stephanie knew what she was doing by escaping instead of fighting. She could have told the novices anything, and none of it would be in Kim's favor. Lyrica's corpse would be hard to explain away, especially with her heart removed. He was now as much an outlaw and fugitive as Angela.

"A fine performance, Troy. It deserves a round of applause."

Troy's eyes blinked open on the far side of the room. "Oh, but this one's my parting gift, Sariel. No more sinewy flesh between my teeth." Her growl was low and thick. "You understand this is your end? I'm finding myself insatiably hungry for the blood of a half-breed. Especially," she snarled, "one who deserves the same death as his father."

His voice shook along with his body. "Not yet."

"I've tolerated you long enough. From this point on, I can smell the difference between the Archon and a heap of meat."

"I know where the Book of Raziel is."

Troy emerged slightly from the darkness, her ears flicking, catching the noise outside of his door. The cruel perception behind her eyes was like a knife, twisting into him. "You lie. More lies."

"No," he said crisply, "I know where she is."

"She." Troy's wings snapped violently. Fury croaked at her shoulder, impatient. "A person? What idiotic nonsense is this?"

"But for me to show you, I'll have to be alive. Of course."

"If you're wasting my time, I'll make death more slow and painful than you've ever thought possible."

Kim glanced at Lyrica's body lying on the floor. Troy had left more of her remains intact than his student Telissa's, yet that only made everything worse.

Troy blinked back at him, her expression suggesting she was supremely disgusted, perhaps nauseated, by his weak stomach. It was one of the reasons that half-breeds were commonly aborted. They were considered weak inside and out. Thanks to his far from blameless mother, Kim was now the only half-Jinn in the world. Like Angela, he belonged neither here nor there. But the more the world had tried to squash him, the sharper his proverbial teeth had become.

Now his bite was as hard as Troy's, if in other ways.

"If we find Israfel, we find the Book."

Troy looked at Fury and the bird vanished through the broken window, gliding effortlessly through the too-calm sky. The Vapor disappeared fast, a black speck mixing into a canvas of deeper black and deadly green. Already, she was off searching for an-other bird, only whiter, smarter, and much more human looking.

Once Fury's telepathic messages began, Troy would discard Kim fast.

He had to hurry.

The pounding on the door was furious now. Someone worked at the hinges, attempting to screw them apart.

But that was his only escape.

Troy noticed the grim clench of his jaw. She smiled at the door, and her ears folded back with anticipation. "By all means," she said, painfully delighted, her nails scraping across the hardwood, "be a man and lead the way."

Thirty-five

Luz's greatest asset, and its greatest curse, are one and the same.
The Fae, dying though she may be, is still strong enough to be of
use to us. But this I stress: she must stay alive.

—Archbishop Gregory T. Solomon, private letter to the Vatican

Angela knelt next to Tileaf's body, sweeping green hair away from
blood and dirt and the Fae's own dead leaves. It had been too easy
to kill her, a sign of just how weak the priests had made this former angel, tormenting her with their constant demands. The moment she died, Memorial Park seemed to shiver, the trees dropping
leftover leaves to the ground, branches and trunks crashing into
the earth in a broken circle around Angela and Nina. For now,
though, there had come a pause—a deep and terrible silence. Angela wiped her fingers on Tileaf's tattered dress, ruining the fabric
with inky blue blood.

The mysterious knife had melted out of Angela's hands into a
puddle all over the Fae's legs and ankles. The wound in her chest
looked so small, so insignificant compared to the damage it had
done.

Blue blood. Not red.

Angela gasped for breath, fighting off a sweeping sickness in the
pit of her stomach. Then she stood, her knees wobbling a little, her
palm aching where the Grail had nestled into the skin. She opened
it, staring back at the stone that was enough of an Eye to contain

a startling amount of liquid. And worst of all, perhaps it also contained a soul. A spirit that cursed all who wore it and wielded it, damning them along with the cries of the angels it had murdered.

Lucifel's Glaive, the weapon she'd used to strike fear into so many hearts, had been made of blood.

But whose?

It doesn't matter. If this Grail belongs to me now, so do the people who've died because of it. Tileaf was just one more.

Her whole body ached inside, like she'd been punched and bruised everywhere. Yet Angela's soul had never felt stronger. The voice that had echoed inside of her, that had given her the courage and resolve to do what she'd never thought possible, had faded back into her memories. But it had also left behind a passionate sense of certainty, and a strange lack of sorrow. Tileaf had wanted this death, and Angela had given her what she wanted. There was nothing deeper to it than that. Like the voice within had said, Angela had simply taken back what belonged to her in the first place, as if she'd rediscovered some precious object she'd originally lost. The new question was whether that object had been the Grail, Tileaf's life, or both.

She said there were consequences for using the Grail. Maybe she was talking about my feelings.

"She looks so peaceful," Nina whispered.

Angela shifted uneasily in front of the oak. The blood was making her sick. Her own thoughts were making her sick. "I'm sorry," she said. "For not doing it when I first met her. She was suffering so much . . . Those priests were such bastards." Angela's fingers curled into fists. The Eye pulsed inside of her palm, throbbing with her heartbeat. " 'I make the rules.' That's the thought I keep hearing and feeling, over and over in my head. But I wonder—does a thought, no matter how convincing it feels, justify this?"

Nina's irises brightened to Mikel's red. Apparently, her agreement with the angel involved them sharing space equally. When one gave way to the other, eventually there would be a reversal. "That depends on who's thinking it."

"Right." Angela sighed, stepping away from Tileaf. "I guess."

"There's no time to mourn, Angela. You must enter the Netherworld or Tileaf will have died in vain."

That's the problem. I'm not mourning at all.

Angela gestured at the trees. "That would be a lot easier if there was a way in."

"Underground." Nina's voice again. She weaved her away around the roots that separated them so they stood side by side, and then grabbed Angela by the arm, tugging her nearer to a large gap at the oak's base. It was a huge hole, gaping from beneath a tangle of roots thick as her body, their surfaces gnarled and knobbed with grotesque whorls. "You have to dig. The tunnel should emerge clearly and then—"

"And then?"

"The door."

"You're saying I crawl through a tunnel of dirt and push through a door?"

"It's the only way for a mortal to access the Underworld from Earth without dying. This is why Luz exists. This is the gateway to the other dimensions, whether higher or lower. To Heaven or Hell. But first, you need to get around Azrael."

Tileaf had mentioned the same name. "Who is that? An angel?"

"You'll see."

Angela wasn't keen on seeing anything at all. This situation was far from what she'd been expecting. A dazzling portal of light, maybe, or a gaping staircase in the earth. Instead she was going to breach the world of the dead through a worm tunnel, and Nina— or more correctly Mikel—acted like they were strolling out to buy bread. Tileaf had said that she needed to die for Angela to enter the Netherworld, but except for the trees' branches and leaves crashing down, nothing had changed. "She lied to me, didn't she?" Angela knelt beside Nina, following her lead and scooping dirt out of the hollow. "Tileaf didn't have to die for us to find this."

Nina glanced at Angela, her irises back to their dull darkness. "That's not true. She was blocking the way in."

Angela sank her fingernails into the dirt, clawing, pulling through fibrous roots and soggy bits of mulch. Worms and wood lice spilled out of the hole, scattering beneath other roots or burrowing down below the leaf litter. Angela slid across a few of the worms, almost certainly squishing them in the grooves of her boots.

"Tileaf herself, not the tree, kept the creatures underneath from emerging above, and vice versa. Now that she's gone . . ."

"The door's just sitting there," Angela finished for her. She wiped some of the mud off her hands and onto her skirt. It was beyond salvation at this point anyway. "So what does that mean? Could creatures from Hell eventually make their way into Luz?"

Nina sighed. "What does it sound like to you? But that's not the issue right now."

"What bothers me is"—Angela reached in with both arms, churning through the dirt, spitting out the mud that crept its way into her mouth—"the idea that angels and demons could just come to Earth in droves. They could stamp us flat."

"But that's the mistake people make. Earth is an important place for humans, but angels couldn't care less about it." Nina rocked back on her heels, letting Angela punch through the last layer of dirt and rocks that had blocked off the tunnel. It was large enough for at least one person to slide inside. The land within dropped at a slow angle into the earth, thousands of roots dangling from its ceiling in webs and tendrils. "To them this planet is only what you're sifting through. Dirt."

Ow. What the—

A sharp sting creased through Angela's palm. She pulled back her hand, examining the Eye. Flesh had closed over it like a lid, protecting it from the humus and the soil. Either it had a mind of its own, or her body was working on some crazy angelic instincts. She sucked back the sour nausea creeping into her head, dizzy. The sky rumbled faintly overhead, but otherwise there was too much quiet. Too much heavy silence.

"Remember what I said," Nina pushed her toward the tunnel. "Be strong about this, Angela."

"Hold on," Angela went down on her stomach, peering into the musty gloom, "I don't see a door."

"You have to crawl."

"How far?"

Nina shrugged, ruffling a hand through her frizzy hair. "God. I don't know."

"Does Mikel?" Angela snapped at her.

"She said she'll meet you inside. Once you pass through the door." Nina's irises began to redden at the corners. She crossed her arms, suddenly glancing at the sky like it was a predator out for the hunt. When she turned back, her smile was more one of farewell than encouragement. "Because from what I've learned, you'll need all the help you can get."

Angela scooted through the tunnel, her fingers curling into mud and mounds of decay. Insects dropped on her back from overhead, and the gloomy light of Memorial Park disappeared fast. This felt too much like being locked in a closet or spending a day in the crawlspace of her parents' basement, both of which she'd experienced as punishment.

But that was the one good thing she'd inherited from her time at the institution—a way to make her brain melt away her most traumatic memories in favor of others.

And when she couldn't do that, Angela simply accepted them and choked down the pain, quarantining it inside the part of her soul that grew angrier by the day. The part of her that found freedom in the arms of Kim—or Israfel, even if she had to imagine the angel's embrace, even if half of his feelings had been a dream.

But he was real. And the time for dreams was officially over.

Angela took ragged breaths, inching on her elbows through the darkness, determined to focus on anything other than the wall of earth surrounding her.

Israfel . . . He has Sophia now. What if he finds out how to open her?

Tileaf had mentioned a Key and a Lock, both missing. Yet that strange detail didn't make Angela feel any better. Israfel was Raziel's brother, a Supernal, and one of the only creatures in the universe who could open the Book without going mad. If Israfel knew where to look and how to use what he found, there was a chance, however slim, that he would act in the best interests of himself and not so much everyone else. Otherwise, why would Raziel go through the trouble of reincarnation to open the Book himself? There must have been a reason—a very good reason—why Sophia couldn't simply blab every little secret inside of her. And also why Raziel wanted as few people as possible to hear those secrets.

That's why the demons want the Archon on Hell's Throne. It has to be.

To manipulate Her. Use Her as a puppet to open Raziel's Book, and then—

Then they'll murder Her. Whoever is in charge under Lucifel will kill the Archon, take the power inside of the Book—inside Sophia—and rule in Her place.

My *place.*

But they couldn't do that if *Lucifel* murdered the Archon first. Or opened the Book first. Because it was rather obvious that if Angela was the Archon—and with every passing second, she felt more strongly that this was the case—then Lucifel would torture her until she found the Key, the Lock, and everything that went with it. When it came down to it, Angela now had two very powerful and very real enemies. The gray angel she'd grown so reluctantly fond of after years of memories and dreams, and the demons who either wanted Lucifel gone or wanted a figurehead they could murder with much greater expediency whenever the time arrived.

Too bad they didn't know who they were dealing with.

Angela hadn't forgotten about punishing Stephanie for Brendan's death. Instead, she now felt vengeance was her absolute right.

Her breath huffed out of her, stifled. The tunnel could have been losing all its air, and now the earth would swallow her like a gigantic snake, its roots and sticky strands of what could have been spiderwebs or moss sliding across her cheeks, hair, and shoulders.

Angela fought with the panic scorching her nerves, the heaviness tugging on her brain, the sweat trickling down her neck. There was no turning back. And this could go on for a long time. Hours, days, a week. And she hadn't brought any food, or water, or even better clothing so that the centipedes didn't crawl across her skin. Why couldn't she have been Troy, just for one brief second? If what Kim had said was true, the spaces Troy scampered through were even narrower.

It was so ironic. For years, Angela had wanted nothing more than to kill herself.

Now, death actually frightened her. Because now, she wasn't trying anymore.

And if it's not deliberate . . .

Then it could very well happen.

She reached out to pull herself forward—and stubbed her fingernails against metal. Angela hissed back the pain, taking a moment for her digits to stop throbbing. Then she searched in the darkness again, soon scraping her fingertips across a cool metal hatch. It had a ring for a handle, and on its surface someone had embossed what felt like a Tree surrounded by flames or clouds. She pulled, hard, groaning with the effort. Eventually realizing her error, she pushed in the opposite direction.

The hatch opened, smoothly and silently.

Angela paused for a moment, letting the sweat dribble into her mouth. Gathering her courage, she bit her lip and stuck her arm through the opening.

Air. Empty space. And a dismal, vacuous smell that came from everywhere at once.

"Nina!" she shouted. "Nina! What do I do now? Just go through this thing?"

No answer. Her voice sounded hollow. Lifeless.

Angela attempted to squirm backward or to turn her head more. "*Nina?*"

A hand wrapped around her wrist, tugging her toward the hatch. Angela screamed, instant fear shooting through her. She jerked backward, almost smacking her head on the dirt ceiling, and struggled fiercely, cursing, digging her heels into the soil and the roots. And then another hand wrapped around her other arm, and its strength was ten times greater than before.

With one swift tug she was sliding, falling. Plummeting in the grasp of a person, or a thing, that she couldn't see.

Down and down into some dark and endless grave.

Thirty-six

*Their brutality, from what I have seen, is far from human
understanding. Worse yet, they believe themselves to be kind.*
—BROTHER FRANCIS, *An Encyclopedia of the Realms*

Troy killed eight novices in less than a minute.

Her savage efficiency, the speed she'd summoned to cut their
throats, bite their faces, and claw their chests, had been a spectacle
of both pure horror and a macabre kind of beauty. Like all Jinn,
Troy's instincts and reflexes were honed to such a fine point that
human beings trailed behind her like amoebas. But unlike most
Jinn, Troy was the High Assassin, the hunter of hunters, answering only to their Queen, and she had the commanding fierceness
and utmost agility to adorn the title.

Maybe she'd performed for Kim's sake more than her own.

He was covered in blood that had spattered onto his shoes and
soaked into his coat sleeves. Blood from men and women who'd
tried to stand in his cousin's way, desperate to save the lives of their
fellow colleagues. He was a murderer eight times over now, having
sacrificed his former friends to her evil.

Troy's mouth and hands were painted with crimson, and she
licked her lips often, probably tasting her satisfaction.

But her eyes were solely for Kim. The second Troy found the
Book, the millisecond she determined the Archon's identity, Kim's
heart would rest between her teeth. It was frustrating when he

stopped to think about it. Humanity always thought small, fearing werewolves, vampires, and ghosts instead of what was truly real, what truly mattered.

Jinn lived off creatures weakened by that kind of ignorance and anxiety. The former they took down swiftly, the latter, slowly and cruelly, like cats playing with their mouse.

They were devils with a perverse code of honor, clannish and vengeful.

Yet, after witnessing Troy's dance of death firsthand, Kim couldn't help but admire what he'd seen. He could hate her, but he could never say she was inefficient or untalented.

Fury screeched overhead, her voice echoing out over the city.

Kim paused at the entrance to a dank tunnel, catching his breath and resting his legs. Troy paused with him, instantly growling and hissing. Her ears had folded back like fleshy daggers against her skull. "If only you'd inherited some useful traits," she snapped at him, nastier than before. She shook her head, and the bones tied to her hair rattled ominously. "I should have left you behind with your dead friends. Who, by the way, tasted like watered-down acid. How fitting that you acquainted yourself with spineless cowards."

"Try not to be too much of a bitch," he said, almost snarling with her.

Troy's eyes narrowed, their light softer. "It's difficult when I'm suddenly the one leading the way. Tell me, Sariel, do you even know where to find the angel?"

"It doesn't matter," he muttered. "We're headed in the right direction, aren't we?"

Kim resumed walking through the tunnel, his shoes clacking against the cobblestones, the sweat trickling down his neck and chest. Troy swept inside after him, latching onto the ceiling, her yellow eyes peering down at him with rabid disgust as she crawled ahead. Her mere presence had an oppressive effect on him now, as if she were constantly shoving a ticking clock in Kim's face to show the hour of his death. Soon they emerged into the open again, and

Fury glided down to the level of her master, both of them vanishing into the shadows of alleys and rooftops until they wandered down a crumbling stairway, squeezing through an alley too tight for three people side by side. Kim entered Memorial Park, somehow half dazed by the odor of the blood on his coat. It took another chilling hiss from Troy to reawaken him.

Silence lay heavily on the trees, the weeds, its thickness invisibly weighing upon the gate's iron bars. Troy climbed a maple near the entryway and stiffened.

Fury stiffened with her, her stick-thin legs splayed firmly in the mud.

They were listening for something.

Then it passed, and Troy ruffled her feathers, clearly irritated. "There's no one here, Sariel. Once again, your pathetic attempt at saving your life is a waste of my time."

He turned on her, unable to hide the fact that her voice was more of a wound than her presence. Kim's teeth gritted, clenched by his own irritation. "I simply followed the leader. If Israfel's not here, he's somewhere else. He won't go far. He can't—"

"*Shut your mouth,*" Troy said, her ears cocking forward.

She was listening more intensely than before. Cautiously, she lifted her head, smelling, and her nails slipped into wood, splitting the branch to mirror her unhappiness. "The angel. Mikel." The name left her lips with the greatest displeasure. "That annoying woman—Nina—she's still here."

"You smelled her?" Kim said, laughing softly. "She would be filthy enough by now."

"No," Troy replied, baring her teeth at him. "I heard her breathing."

He shivered, reaching into his pocket to touch a prayer ward. Whenever her voice took on that rasping, throaty quality, Kim always prepared for violence. But this time, her hunger faded fast, replaced by impatience. Without another word, she scampered into the black branches, disappearing like the hint of a breeze. Kim continued along the pathway, imagining Angela by his side, cursing to himself as Fury took position and strutted confidently near his ankles. Her beak was like her master's existence—a dagger that could end his life too soon.

Unless he ended Troy's first.

Kim dared to smile.

That smile grew the closer he came to Tileaf's tree. Despite the gloom, Nina's figure took shape in the mist rising from the earth, her brown hair a tangle of wisps and knotted ends. Directly to her right, at the foot of the oak's massive trunk, Tileaf lay sprawled in the brown moss, her silken dress as bloody as his coat. She was dead, her skin a mess of red and blue, the smell of her corpse resembling vegetable rot. Interestingly, Troy's nose ignored plant matter of any variety, whether connected to an angel's flesh or not.

Then he spied the open hollow, gaping at him below a lattice-work of roots.

Someone had entered the Netherworld Gate.

Angela. Kim dashed ahead of Fury, ignoring her angry cackles, dropping to his knees in front of the hollow as soon as he reached it, dirt and mulch spraying around his hands. His fingers met cold metal.

He shrank back from the chill, startled to see the Grail's chain resting below his palm. Kim examined the links, glancing at Nina for answers.

She was lost in some kind of trance, her eyes wide and crimson. The same shade as the Devil herself. As that brief and unsettling flicker of Stephanie's irises.

He licked his lips, already tasting the mustiness of the tunnel as much as he smelled it.

If he was quick, Troy wouldn't see him enter the tunnel after Angela. Not that this would be the wisest course of action, or the most logical. But no matter how much it disturbed him that Israfel had suddenly disappeared, the situation begged for him to take advantage of it. He ignored Fury's infuriated screeches, flattening to enter the hole, his shoes squishing into the mud.

The bird descended on him in a mad rage, her wings beating

furiously. Claws scraped at his coat, scratched across his scalp, and sliced his cheek.

He grasped at the wound, fending off the crow with an arm.

Boom.

Boom.

God, not now. More powerful wing beats thundered throughout the grotto. A burst of crimson light dazzled Kim's eyes, and the sound of electricity crackled into him like a shockwave. He grabbed the prayer ward inside his coat and pitched it, spitting out the first Latin phrase that came to mind, barely aware of what he was saying. "*Sanctus domine*—"

His vision cleared.

The ward shredded to a ribbon of ash, its pieces dusting the soil. Above it, Naamah perched on the roots forming the hollow, the scales on her feet gleaming despite the horrendous lack of light. A blond feather fluffed from her bloody wings, dropping to the ground and into the ash pile, like a bit of dirty snow. It was astounding she could fly at all. The thin skin between the metal struts in her wings seemed almost transparent, raw with exposed bone and ooze. Hideous stitches closed up a gaping wound in her neck. So much pain, contrasting with so much perfection. She leaned over him, her blond braids tumbling out of their carefully arranged coil, her copper face bright with recognition.

"Perfect timing, priest." She put a fingerblade to her lips. "I was worried you'd be late."

Thirty-seven

In the Netherworld all are equal, for the
color of death is one alone.
—UNKNOWN AUTHOR, *A Collection of Angelic Lore*

Angela had thought she was falling.

But she was actually flying, her arms outstretched in front of her, wrists gripped tightly by an angel who seemed no older than a teenager, her platinum hair whipping around them both like a blustering curtain. The darkness was absolute, yet Angela could still see her arms and the rest of her body, including most of the angel who guided their descent. She was an albino, her skin so white and transparent each network of veins resembled blue lace. Her wings matched the color of her hair, a silvery white that was duller than Israfel's but somehow more healthy. And her eyes were red, like blood.

Red—like Lucifel's.

They landed together as if in slow motion, feet brushing the invisible ground. A moment later, the angel turned away, staring out into the darkness. Her wings drooped slightly, their tips brushing across Angela's boots.

"Mikel . . ." Angela ventured.

"Yes," the angel said, putting a finger to her lips. They waited in silence a moment longer, and then Mikel regarded her again, her face young and delicate. "I hope," she smiled gently, "that you're not ready to faint."

Angela shook her head. Her fear had simply been replaced by astonishment. Lucifel's dreaded offspring looked to be no older than thirteen and just as harmless.

But when it came to angels, she'd already learned the hard way that appearances could be deceptive. Mikel seemed no stronger than a hospitalized child, yet it was all too telling that Kim had been frightened of her, and Naamah wanted to kill her. For all Angela knew, this frail girl could make Troy look like a toothless dog.

She couldn't afford to let her guard down for a second.

Is this what she actually looks like? But her voice is the same . . .

"How do I know it's really you?"

"You don't," Mikel creased her wings tightly against her back, "but you'll have to trust me anyway. What you're seeing of me now is an illusion, a spirit-projection of Nina's mind." There was a hollow, banging sound out in the distance, and she paused. Angela shivered under the torment of her eyes. They were too much like Lucifel's, and even brighter now that they contrasted with so much whiteness. Kim was right—Mikel could have been on her mother's side from the beginning. There was no way to tell, and now it was too late for Angela to get out of the Netherworld on her own. "The laws of the material world are slightly different in the world of the dead. Since I'm a spirit, I can navigate through this place much easier than you. I've been here many times."

"Why?"

Why would anyone come here of their own free will?

There was no answer.

Angela shut her eyes, and then opened them again, finding such little difference between both states. Or between the physical darkness and her appalling ignorance. "This must be the body they stuffed you into," she whispered, gesturing at Mikel's frail form.

The angel sighed, her robe slipping slightly from a shoulder. "Follow me."

"I don't see how I'm going to release these souls like you want me to. Why are you helping me instead of your mother?"

Mikel continued walking, like a beacon of platinum in the crushing blackness. "I don't know my mother—and no matter how much I might want to know her—she'd like nothing more than to see me gone." Her voice hardened. "The day we meet face-to-face is the day I die. Since I was born a spirit, it takes a special kind of power to end my life. Only Lucifel has that power."

The mention of Lucifel's name elicited an instant chorus of moans and screams, some far, some frighteningly near. Tendrils, maybe more roots or cobwebs, brushed against Angela's hair, face, and arms. She hugged herself, wishing she could shrink to stay away from whatever seemed to grasp for her. If this was the least dimension of Hell, even nothing more than neutral territory, she couldn't begin to imagine Lucifel's home. "Nina told me that I have to meet Azrael. She said he's an angel like you, but wouldn't give me any more details."

Mikel stopped, turning back around. Her face was grim. "He will try to stop you from leaving here alive. It's against the rules, you see, and Azrael is a creature who abides by rules."

Rules. So it's coming down to that again.

Angela glanced around at the shadows, envisioning millions of eyes staring back at her. Whenever she took a step, the earth quaked gently under her feet, groans and sighs erupting nearby. It was obvious—her presence was a disturbance to whomever— whatever—existed in this place. She induced change—at least she sensed that much—and the more she thought about the rules, the more she felt it possible to twist and bend them however she pleased. Like Mikel said, some people, perhaps people like Azrael, wouldn't be too happy with that.

"What is this place?" she said, her tone growing firmer. "Who is that crying?"

"Compared to the other Realms, the Netherworld is a dead zone, literally. Human souls filter here for either rest or torment, their fate depending more on their state of mind at death than human morality. If you live and die in a state of peace, then that is your state here, despite the darkness. If you lived and died in a state of anguish, then . . ." Mikel took a step backward. "Someone is approaching us."

Two pairs of footsteps clacked swiftly in their direction.

Mikel's wings snapped open, and she held out her hand. Her curious expression seemed to stop their attackers faster than the barrier, and her eyes brightened. "They're saying they know you. Should I let them manifest, Angela? But I should warn you, they don't seem happy that you're here. You might"—the angel's tone lowered meaningfully—"have to see unpleasant things."

Silence. The crushing kind, hinging on a momentous decision.

Angela's lips trembled. Her own soul shivered violently. Two pairs of footsteps. Two angry pairs. She already knew who this was. "Yes. Let them manifest."

Erianna and Marcus stepped out from the shadows.

They were covered in burns. Angela clapped a hand over her mouth, struggling to hold back her vomit. Those hate-filled eyes. That charred skin. Her mother's singed hair and her father's tooth-less mouth.

They rushed for her, before she could even try to run.

Angela's body numbed over. Her breath stifled away, oddly painful. It was nearly impossible to move, and when she tried to speak, her lips felt weighted by cement. Mikel was suddenly so far away, a helpless spectator, and with a terrifying jolt, Angela realized that time had slowed. Before her, Erianna and Marcus laughed at her with their eyes, gloating at her helplessness as they'd never dared to when alive. The past began to swirl around them all, one scene after the next. There was the belt her father had used to devastating effect. The mocking voice of her mother, telling all her friends to ignore Angela, to leave her alone. Brendan, bringing her snacks while she hid, locked in her room. Then, the sounds from her parents' bedroom at night. The whispers among the maids.

The closet used for punishment.

Her paintings, thrown into the furnace because of their unspoken evil.

It was too much. Her head felt like it would shatter as much as her heart, and unable to bear any more, Angela screamed.

The images cracked and burst apart like glass, leaving Angela face-to-face with Erianna and Marcus again, gasping, her cheeks wet and her eyes blurred by tears. But now she could talk and move slightly, as if revealing her pain had forced her parents to relent a little. "What do you want?" she shouted. "To kill me?"

Their faces said it all. This was their revenge for an accidental death, and the intent was either for Angela to join them in that death or to go insane. The voices from the past intensified, mocking her from a million invisible mouths. Images hadn't worked, so now her late family was trying noise. Vaguely, she could hear them shouting to join her, their words almost lost beneath the horrendous abuse. If she didn't take control fast, they would win this time.

Yes, that's it. I'm going to take control.

It was something she'd never done in the eighteen years of her miserable existence except when it came to suicide, but now she was a step above her parents, mostly because she was alive, possibly because she was the Archon. She'd be damned if they were going to squash her hopes mercilessly one more time. For once, and for forever, they would have to either serve her interests or vanish along with the rest of the past she'd abandoned.

She glanced back at Mikel.

The angel's eyes were fearsomely bright. She knew what was going to happen, and seemed almost hungry for it.

Angela rounded on her parents again, struggling to move. "Here's your choice. And it's your last chance. You're either on my side—or you're not. Which is it?"

They glared at her, as if thinking about what that could mean.

Then they lunged for Angela's throat, their burned fingers grasping maniacally.

"Fine." She thrust out her hand as Mikel had, shocked at the sudden force behind her words. "*Go back to the darkness.*"

Her parents stopped. The mocking voices ceased. The past that had been so brutally forced upon her crumbled into mental dust. Hideous groans filled the emptiness, and then the horror vanished into a vortex of wind and power. Angela dropped back into time with a sharp rush of air in her lungs, and immediately the funnel centered on Mikel, coalescing into a glowing sphere held in the center of her palm. The angel held it up to her mouth, her eyes brighter than fire, and Angela slumped over with her hands against the cold ground, huffing and shuddering inside. It wasn't long before Mikel stood beside her again, and she took the angel's hand, standing on wobbly legs.

The sphere that was her past, and possibly the essence of her parents' souls, had disappeared. Their brief moment of revenge was over.

"Are you all right . . ."

Angela waved her away, holding her head. "Give me another second. God." She found her voice again. "They almost—"

"Killed you," Mikel said. "You're right. You were lucky to escape."

Maybe. All Angela knew was that her family deserved an even harsher judgment than this hell, and she'd given it to them. Somehow.

It seemed so long ago when Nina had asked her if she mourned her parents' passing. Now, any leftover grief felt like a sin. With her own wounds healed by time and circumstance, Angela had forgotten the horror of her past for what it really was, repressing the worst and sugarcoating the rest. And that made her next question sound sadder than anything else.

"What did you do with them?" she said, unable to keep from asking. "Are their souls still here?"

Mikel looked at the ground, her expression vague. "To explain now would take too much time. We must keep going, Angela. Once you've reached the pinnacle, it will all be over."

"But—"

"Please."

She was right. It hurt—but she was completely right. There

was no time, either for Tileaf, or Brendan, or anyone else. Besides, it was blindingly clear that Angela's parents no longer deserved her consideration. The past was now the past—and only that—forever.

The moment had arrived to let go for good.

"All right," Angela whispered, but more to herself than to Mikel. "Let's keep going."

Her first steps, though, felt weighted with lead.

She followed silently, making certain to stick closer to the angel this time, trying not to look over her shoulder when she heard more footsteps or whispers in the dark. Their breaths escaped together, and Angela began to stare at the back of Mikel's head, afraid she might lose her mind if she got lost and had to wander around in this abyss by herself. Time passed them by, just how much it was impossible to say, and the scenery—that raw and heavy darkness—still never changed. The terrible truth loomed before her: no living human could stay here long and emerge whole, sane. She wanted to scream, if only to hear the sound of her own voice again, and then, right when she couldn't bear it anymore, they ascended, climbing up a hill thick with invisible bracken. It was beyond her how any plant could survive in a place like this, no matter how hellish and unearthly.

Clank.

Angela slowed down, trying to listen above the sound of branches creaking aside.

Clank.

"What is that?" she whispered to Mikel.

They would have been shoulder to shoulder, but the angel was petite, her head barely reaching Angela's neck. Mikel nodded knowingly. "Your brother. He's up ahead."

Angela stopped. A sharp breeze sifted through the length of her hair, tickling the newly bare skin of her arms and legs. "You never met Brendan. How would you even know that this is him?"

Mikel said nothing.

A bluish light broke over the horizon. Angela shaded her eyes, watching a strange sun peek over what looked like hills, their silhouettes smooth with gradual curves.

Clank.

The pitch blackness lightened to a deep shade of gray. Much like her parents, Brendan stepped out of that grayness. But he showed no signs of recognizing Angela at all. Unseeing and insensible, his skin was a terrible bluish color like the Netherworld's sun, his upper throat bloody and gaping. He was still dressed like a priest, but a collar of light much like Tileaf's wrapped above his collarbone, its leash clanking behind him while he walked. On his forehead, a crimson triangle blazed amid the mess of his bangs. "Israfel," he said, groaning softly.

"What happened?" Angela said, panicked, crushed inside by the sight of him.

Despite all that had taken place, the memories of her brother's few kindnesses lingered, newly resurrected by their parents' attempt to drive her mad.

"Why does he look like that? The triangle—"

"Israfel's symbol. The sign of the Creator Supernal." Mikel's voice was thick with disgust. "Your brother sold his soul. Now, he exists solely and eternally as Israfel's property."

Eternally.

That's right, Brendan has a long way to go. This is only the beginning.

But of what, Angela didn't dare imagine. Already those brief moments in their past were escaping her, and she saw him in the cathedral: the twisted expression of his face and the twisted ugliness in his soul, permanently blotting out whatever kindness remained. Israfel said Brendan's enchantment had revealed all his hidden flaws and sins, and then made them a hundred times worse. But was Brendan the first person to suffer because of the angel? Perhaps, much like staring into the Grail or opening the Book, obsessing over Israfel had been the cause of countless suicides, deaths, damnations, and sins.

Angela, though, was far from eager to sell her soul.

If anything, she longed for Israfel to offer his own.

"His senses," Mikel's tone deepened with pity, "are dulled by his obsession. If he ever reincarnates according to Israfel's desires, his mind will return. But he will be far from the brother you knew and loved as a child. Now his single heaven and endless hell is to be separated from Israfel, and yet to still be in his service. For him to anger that Supernal to such a degree—he must have overstepped his bounds in a grievous and personal way. What you are seeing is the result of his human foolishness. Despite appearances, your brother was a deeply troubled individual . . ."

Angela should have cried again or shed at least a single tear.

But all she could do was stare. She had nothing else left.

He threw himself to this place without a second thought.

Brendan gazed through her for a second longer. Even though he wasn't aware of her on a conscious level, he must have still sensed her enter the Netherworld and had been drawn to her presence or aura or whatever had alerted her parents. There were a trillion souls in this place, maybe more, yet he'd managed to find her. Coincidence wasn't enough to explain that kind of miracle. As if agreeing to the end of their relationship, Brendan trudged past her back into the grayness, soon fading like a washed-out dream. If Angela ever saw him again, this was the last time he'd appear with familiar features and probably any semblance of humanity.

She watched him leave and turned back to the sun's lifeless light. Slowly, the landscape emerged through the gray haze, and amazingly a bare cliff's edge took shape beneath her boots. The land below appeared with its barrenness and cracked earth, and out in the immense plain, souls stared up at her, silent and waiting, their hair ruffling in the breeze.

Millions and millions of human souls, gray like their afterlife.

If I'm the Archon, I should know what to do next. But I don't know a thing.

Where was that inner voice when she needed it most?

Angela let her eyes rest on as many individuals as she could, but the more she tried to think of something to say, the more her mouth went dry. This was the same place she had stood in Tileaf's mind, only this was the real thing. Whether she was Raziel or someone else, she now stood in the portentous spot, with a sizable chunk of humanity waiting for her to say something. There were so many souls, they stretched to the very horizon.

She glanced back at the path Mikel had taken, and it remained black and inky—a valley of shadows that no light could pierce. Without asking, she sensed that only those who chose torment for their eternity remained in that oppressive pool of gloom. The things she had thought to be branches were more like congealed darkness, extensions forming a natural barrier between this part of the Netherworld and its other half, both vaster than the human mind could comprehend.

There was no sign of the hatch she'd dropped through.

"In the valley of shadows," Mikel said, "are the souls who do not wish for release from their imprisonment. Unlike these, they will not find freedom in the Nexus, but will stay trapped in this dimension, most likely until it crumbles to nothingness."

"The Nexus . . ." Angela repeated. "And that's where all these other souls will go?"

"In time. Some will first choose to fight for the Archon in the eventual battle. But all will leave through Luz, walking up the Ladder to their new resting place, safe from Lucifel's eternity of silence—unless she succeeds in destroying the Archon herself." Mikel touched her on the shoulder, but pulled away quickly, her small hands strangely wounded by their contact. Maybe she was responding to the change in Angela's body. Her heart raced, and the Eye throbbed inside of her palm, begging to stare out at the dead and the blue sun. "Now, it's time to tell them that you've come. To free them and to lead them where even the Supernals could not. Raziel—my father," Mikel's face saddened, "would have been happy to see this day."

"He is," Angela said, certain.

He has to be.

She looked out at the souls gathered across the expanse of the plain, her stance hardening. This place and these doomed souls were now hers, practically cradled in the cup of her hand.

"I've arrived," she shouted at the top of her lungs, "to free you. It's time for you to leave this place and go somewhere else. Those who choose to stay . . . *have decided their fate.*" On impulse, she lifted her hand, displaying the Grail for their satisfaction. Some souls sighed, others shrieked in fear, running in the opposite direction. They somehow recognized Lucifel's former treasure. "This is your choice. Either join me, recognize me, or stay in the darkness for all eternity."

They were the same words she'd used for her parents.

And they had nearly the same effect.

The sky overhead mirrored the sky over Luz, bubbling and crackling with distant lightning, just like in Tileaf's mind when Lucifel had turned every soul to ash. Summoned somehow by Angela's words or feelings, the storm rumbled in on them with horrific speed, its clouds more like living things than air and vapor.

Mikel grabbed Angela's hand, hissing back pain as she closed it into a fist. "He's here," she said, her feathers fluttering in the growing wind. "He's been waiting."

The earth below split and heaved.

Souls ran to the right and left, some of them tumbling into deep, seemingly endless chasms, screaming as fleshy roots burst upward from the dry rock.

An octopus with skin the color of human flesh could have been crawling out of the ground, but this octopus had a great mass of branches instead of a bulbous head, and upon those branches, a nearly uncountable number of eyes glistening and gazing out over the plain, like leaves in shades of deep green and muddy violet.

The strange tree was growing at tremendous speed, as if Angela's words had germinated some seed planted long ago beneath the rock. She'd never seen anything so terrible, so alien and wrong, and could barely look away from its trunk of throbbing flesh and its hundreds of branchlike arms.

Then the branches grew more, twisting toward her.

Before Angela could blink again, she stared back into at least fifty different eyes, all of them coiled in front of her face. She bit her tongue, desperate not to scream.

The eyes faded, replaced by the image of an angel with ebony hair, the strands draping over half of his face. Like the tree, his wings were covered with eyes, irises of green and violet gleaming against their black feathers like living jewels. He was much more strongly built than Israfel, with a sharp and severe face.

And you would dare—his voice pounded through her like a drum—*to take what belongs to me. These souls are in my domain.*

Angela glanced around wildly.

Mikel was gone. Vanished.

What happened? Why isn't she here anymore?

The Archon. Azrael smiled arrogantly. *Or at least you look like Her. But my loyalty to Raziel ended long ago.*

Angela regarded him with an angry face. "And he died," she said, hardly knowing why she said it or how she knew it, "when you could have helped him. Selfish hedonist. You came here out of greed, to glut yourself."

Help? Azrael swept his hair aside, revealing the other half of his face. His eyes were as mismatched as those on his wings, his tree. *If it were not for me, this remnant of Eden would no longer exist. If it weren't for my so-called selfish hedonism, these souls would have nowhere to rest, however tormented.*

"Either way, they're no longer yours."

Eden. This used to be the Garden of Eden. Paradise. The birthplace of humanity.

Now it was simply a pit for the dead.

Azrael's branches grew more, their fleshy joints bending to snare and choke her. Angela turned and ran back toward the darkness, searching. But Mikel had either abandoned her, or something was happening in Memorial Park. Nina could have been hurt or killed, their connection severed. Now she was alone, and Azrael was gaining on her nightmarishly fast. In seconds the inky black swallowed them, and she was forced to stop, knocked over by a wall of flesh covered in eyes and the shock of him standing in front of her again. The tree must have been his real body, this angelic form a perfect deception.

Now he was going to suffocate her.

Fleshy branches wrapped around her ankles, her legs.

Azrael's voice seemed to resound throughout the entire Netherworld. *To think that Raziel would punish his Throne, ruin my happiness. How I regret the days when I served him, while he served only himself—*

He was almost at her waist and began to squeeze. Angela screamed, her bones close to breaking, her hands pushing at his countless arms while they moved higher.

—as hypocritical and insensitive as the rest of Heaven—

Briefly, his image contorted into Israfel's, bronze winged but horrendously sneering and warped. Was this how he saw his former Archangel?

—unwilling to recognize me for the power, or the person, that I was.

"And out of all the souls you tasted and imprisoned," Angela gasped through her pain, "how many could stifle your appetite for any of it? You're completely deluded," she said, horrendously angry inside, somehow offended by what felt like blasphemy. "And this Realm doesn't belong to you. And—*I NO LONGER SEE A NEED FOR YOU IN IT.*"

Azrael recoiled sharply at her words, like she'd injured him with her voice alone. His perfect face hovered above her, wide-eyed and strangely fearful.

Angela showed him the Grail.

The Eye seemed to scorch through him, judgmental and terrible.

He moaned in agony, his branches collapsing, going instantly limp and slithering away from her back to the chasm they'd erupted from. Angela fell to her knees, resting her head on the cushion of her arms, searching for air and the end of the pain. It came after a short time with her muscles still aching terribly, but not enough to keep her from rocking on her heels and rubbing her legs, groaning softly at their soreness.

The new light broke more slowly than the rays over the distant hills.

Clouds whirled overhead in a giant cauldron of vapor.

Gradually, with a majestic slowness, the light at their center began to mysteriously solidify and descend in a helix, one amazing, crystalline step at a time.

Angela had witnessed rainbows forming in the sky, but this was different. Infinitely more beautiful, dazzling, breathtaking. The brightness was so strong, it forced the shadows in the valley to recede, and Angela's clothes seemed lined with silver, like a cloud in front of the sun. And as the great Stairs continued to descend, each level grew larger and more magnificent than the last, platforms of light that were larger than any building. Below, Azrael's tree appeared small and insignificant, while souls left his nearly comatose grasp one by one, beginning the steady ascension up to the surface of Luz. Millions rose to freedom, not a few gazing back at Angela in happy confusion, their bodies like a line of gray twining with the helix of the stairs.

The way out of the Netherworld was obviously vastly different from the way in.

It was beautiful. Maybe, besides Israfel, the most beautiful thing she'd ever seen.

But I have seen it before.

Her dream of Sophia. Hadn't she been standing in front of a stairway of light?

And it looked exactly like this one.

"Go up," Angela whispered, suddenly overcome by a sense of urgency. The souls seemed to obey instinctively, but not quickly enough. "Higher. Faster."

Screeches of despair rang out from the valley behind her. Faintly, so very faintly, she could hear someone calling her name as if to curse her. Despite the unspeakable beauty of this Ladder, and how swiftly she'd wrenched it from Azrael's grasp, her confidence was wavering. She was alone, and behind her were countless enemies. Now the darkness they'd chosen their entire lives was ready to swallow them in nothingness. They had chosen Lucifel. They had chosen a void. And they hated Angela for having to make that choice.

She would have to confront them. It was now both her duty—and her right.

Angela stood up, turning to command them into silence.

Stephanie was there to greet her, her expression shockingly cold. She looked to the Ladder, her face bathed in its light, but only to bring out ghastly shadows across her face. "This must be a miracle, but I'm still not sure I believe in it . . ."

Thick surprise choked off Angela's voice.

She's here by herself. But how? Did Naamah help her again?

However Stephanie had managed to enter the Netherworld, or whenever she'd chosen to do it, she must have been hiding all along, waiting for Angela to put Azrael in his place. But what a difference a day could make. She'd dressed herself in a long black coat identical to Kim's, but with the upper buttons open to reveal her blouse, and the lower opened to give her legs room to move freely. If it was possible, her skin and hair and makeup were even more perfect than before. Only her eyes had changed.

Their irises were blood red. Lucifel's shade.

Stephanie spotted the Grail and gestured for it, curling a finger. "By the way, I think it's finally time to share your toys."

Thirty-eight

For these Jinn, loyalty rises above all else, and betrayal
is punished by the cruelest of deaths. Yes, I'm afraid
the consequences of your unfaithfulness will be dire.
—REVEREND MATTHIAS GREENE, *Letters of Spiritual Direction*

Master, the half-breed, he's—

Fury's voice cut off sharply, timed to a flicker of crimson light beyond the trees.

Troy skidded to a stop in the leaf litter, her nails ripping through the soil. She'd heard the thunderous beat of Naamah's wings, yet still hadn't been quick enough. This was her punishment for leaving Sariel behind, no matter how briefly. Now the demon was going to finish a mission Troy had started centuries ago, leaving her with nothing but a bone or two to placate the Jinn Queen. Her sister wouldn't humor any kind of excuse. Troy would be the laughingstock of all High Assassins, abysmally stupid for allowing a demon to snatch her prey away.

What a difference minutes could make.

She'd been searching through the shrubs and undergrowth for any sign of Israfel, catching brief traces of him, but losing most of those beneath another overpowering stench. An herb seemed to be growing everywhere, its straight, limp leaves splayed across the ground and giving off a tremendously offensive smell. Troy had torn one of the plants—a heart-shaped white thing no bigger than her eyes—out of the earth, nearly spitting in revulsion from the thick, peppery odor clinging to its bulb. Then she'd scampered back toward Tileaf's tree, deftly dodging fallen trunks and thick branches.

Fury.

No answer.

Troy paced at the grotto's threshold, smelling fresh blood.

So much of it ringed her mouth and crusted beneath her fingernails, the old scents nearly blocked out the new. But she could pick two individuals out of the musk: one had been dead for a few hours, faintly stinking of rotting vegetable matter and moss; the other was in the process of dying. A female human, vaguely familiar. Troy crept softly through the leaves and latched onto the tree trunks again, flicking her ears to catch any sound besides her own feet and palms thudding against the bark. She emerged into the grotto as a body crumpled to the mulch.

Thump.

Sariel turned to regard her, his face paler than she'd ever seen it.

He stood over Nina's limp body, side by side with the demon beneath a leafless canopy. Tileaf was dead, her white corpse propped elegantly against the oak's roots, a perplexing mixture of crimson and blue blood staining her limbs and her clothing. Next to a gaping hollow at the left of the trunk, Fury's wings twitched like a fly's swatted down in midair. The spirit inside of her had been ejected by Naamah's attack, and she shivered in the mud, human eyes glazed over by shock.

She always looked much better as a carrion-eating bird than a blond child.

"You're finally back," Sariel said to Troy, his voice soft as a breath. His Jinn half enjoyed the smell of blood, but his humanity fought the smile, distinctly unhappy that Troy had arrived. He stared back at her with those dull gold eyes, suddenly so wide, either because of what he'd done, what he was about to do, or what Troy would certainly do to him.

Had he killed Nina?

Most likely it had been the demon. But there was blood on the knife in his hand, and he stood beside Naamah as an obvious ally.

It was easy to see why. Sariel would do anything to stay alive.

No wonder Naamah hadn't murdered him earlier. They were working toward a common goal after all.

"*What a traitor you are,*" Troy hissed.

Naamah laughed, folding her wings tightly against her back. Metal creaked, and their bare patches dripped oily fluid onto the dirt. "Now, priest," she whispered, "let's do this. Before I forget my kindness."

The storm overhead thundered, ugly and insistent. Its clouds were the same poisonous hue Troy recognized from her own home, their wisps a sickly green shading away into pitch-black. Then the wind picked up. A whirling vortex began to form. Smoky clouds whipped around an eye of pure night, one without stars or light of any kind. A void was forming above Luz, and around it lightning streaked from heaven to earth in crooked spears. One of them struck Memorial Park, and Troy ducked, screeching beneath the light's brilliance. Thunder cracked powerfully, shivering the ground.

When Troy's vision cleared, Naamah was closing in on her.

She backed against the trees, snarling. "You would join with the demons, Sariel? Even when your execution will already be so painful? What will Angela think, now that her friend is dead?"

Nina's body lay sprawled in the dirt, the soil around her turning to mud as blood gushed from her throat. She was finally lifeless, her eyes wide open and unseeing.

There was no sign of the angel.

With her host deceased, Mikel had been forced to return to wherever she'd been imprisoned.

"She'll cry, and be sad, and then get over it." Sariel's voice had that steady crispness to it she despised so much. He straightened the closer Naamah approached, his fingers clenching around his knife as he found his confidence again. "But once I tell her who's responsible, she'll also become angry. Troy, we both know that if

I told Angela you killed the girl, she'd believe me. Who wouldn't believe me?" He smiled, obviously enjoying the moment. "You are a devil after all."

Naamah flexed the blades in her fingers, her eyes dark with revenge.

She couldn't use any kind of ether or energy on Troy, but all she had to do was slice off her head. The demon wouldn't take any more chances on poison if she wanted fast results.

"You need the Archon on the Throne of your Prince," Troy hissed back at Naamah, "but you forget how easy it will be for your Prince to stop you."

"Words of praise from a Jinn," Naamah muttered. "But Lucifel won't fall for flattery."

"You're a coward, Sariel," Troy said, spitting at her cousin. "A spineless shadow who seeks sympathy and pleasure, all so you can drown away your sins. And then you ally yourself with these rotting crows, beg them to do your evil work."

His golden eyes narrowed spitefully. "*Contra nequitiam—*"

Troy's breath caught painfully in her throat. Her lungs felt like they were being crushed, and she crouched closer to the ground, the mustiness of the leaves rising to her nose. He was using the same exorcism that had punished Israfel's Thrones. The very words she'd warned him never to use on her.

"*—et insidias diaboli . . .*"

His words trailed off as Naamah gestured for silence, passing a fingerblade near her throat. Even she wasn't immune to the Tongue's crushing effects. Her wings drooped and she panted loudly over the thunder, stalking slowly toward Troy.

More lightning streaked to the earth.

There was an earsplitting crack. Tileaf's tree exploded.

Troy shrieked and shut her eyes against the blinding whiteness, still seeing half the trunk split to the base, listening to it rock backward and crash into more trees, knocking them to the earth. Heat, which was undoubtedly fire, jumped from its crown to the foliage, burning through the drier wood with incredible speed, racing through the park in a ring of flames. Almost instantly, the wind picked up, fanning it farther. Cinders and ash flaked down from the sky, their pieces blown about by the fire and the storm, stinging Troy's nose and layering her skin.

She dared to crack open an eyelid, her joints aching horribly. Her insides were almost overturned by the exorcism.

Sariel stood in front of the flames, a black silhouette framed by the most painful orange. She could sense the smile on his face rather than see it.

"*You bastard,*" she said, overcome by rage. "*You traitorous bastard. You're done . . .*"

Troy would kill him. She'd kill him. Oh, yes, their contract was definitely over.

Naamah stepped in front of her, blocking her view. The demon gasped for breath, her teeth displayed along with her triumph. "All that fighting for nothing. You would have been better off dying two days ago."

She lifted her fingerblades, aiming for Troy's head.

"Time to take that wing bone back."

The black rain hissed to the earth without warning, big, oily drops plummeting from the center of the vortex in the sky. They smelled hollow and rank—sick with negativity, poison, and the most unwholesome matter—and then they fell in a sheet thick enough to be layers of ink. Naamah glanced back at Sariel, shouting something over the roar of the water. But they were definitively separated, and his answer was lost in the screech of the wind.

Blades whistled over Troy's head.

She crawled to the left, hardly making a sound. Naamah was searching for her, frantic. Already, the demon had lost all sense of direction.

Master! Fury's voice seemed to come out of nowhere.

It had been the demon's critical error. Fury had the true form of a child, but her avian body hadn't been destroyed, and she'd joyously crawled back inside of it.

Go ahead, Troy said to her, curling near a tree. The fire smoldered beneath the rain, but its heat continued to soak into her, making all her inner wounds a thousand times more terrible. Naamah's blades swept above again, and the demon stumbled to the right, cracking off a tree root. Troy fought the instinctive desire to snap furiously for the demon's ankles, to break them down to the marrow. *Go ahead. Make her suffer.*

The curses were the first sign that Fury had found her mark.

Then there was the incredible light.

Troy caught a brief glimpse of her Vapor's claws raking Naamah's eyes, but shut her own just in time to stay alive. The wind was incredible, ripping feathers from her wings, forcing her to dig her nails into the bark of her tree. Naamah howled, sobbing in a nearly pathetic agony while Fury dug into her flesh. Then the crow must have torn away. Her wing beats grew fainter, disappearing to a safer spot deep inside the park. Neither of them had time to bother with Sariel, if he was even alive anymore. Hopefully, if the fire hadn't finally charred him to death, the black rain would melt the skin from his bones. Troy gritted her teeth, hissing and unable to stop while the water stung at her legs, her hands, her face.

She wrapped her wings around her body, flattening them against the wind—

Everything stopped.

A voice rose cleanly throughout the park, its melody rich and forceful. Notes that reminded Troy of icy waterfalls and cool darkness rang from end to end of the grotto, seeming to freeze out the fire. The heat dissipated, and in its place a deep vacuum spread into the ether. Troy opened her eyes to slits, watching the black rain fall in slow motion. Half the drops had crystallized into something else altogether, fluffing to the ground in chill, ebony layers. Troy focused on one of the black crystals, hissing softly at the glitter of its facets. The thickness of their layers half hid the horrendous light nearby, dulling it enough to keep her brain from searing.

Soft footsteps treaded through the snow, and the song gently died away.

Israfel emerged from the trees, grasping Sophia by the wrist.

His Thrones were right behind him, their wingtips scraping through the chill black crystals. Troy wrapped her own wings tightly around her body, peering through a feathered gap, careful to keep her pained breathing to a minimum. If any of them had seen her or sensed her, they weren't showing signs of it. The Supernal continued to step lightly across the grotto, stopping in front of Tileaf's tree. The mysterious light gleamed off his hair, forcing Troy to shake away her pain.

"So you do have it," Sariel said.

He was still alive, then. Troy snarled between her teeth, aching to sprint past Israfel's Thrones and latch right onto her cousin's throat. But his execution would have to wait for now.

"But I'd like to know why you're waiting to open the Book, to take what you want."

"And what do you think I want?" Israfel's voice was dangerously gentle. If Sariel was smart, he'd soon realize his life hung by a slender thread. Instead he kept talking.

"Revenge. Against your sister." An awkward pause. "I can help you with that."

Where was the demon?

Fury couldn't have killed her . . .

"Help me?" Israfel laughed, and the atmosphere chilled with more ice and waterfalls. Then he coughed alarmingly, and without any warning, thick waves of scent rolled from his body. Heady perfume and the rancid smell of his blood.

Troy recognized this odor. In the cathedral she had dismissed the memory too quickly, because the match made little sense.

"Revenge? No, priest, you're mistaken. I'm just waiting for her to see my hour of triumph. My sister will be walking to destruction whether I help her or not. I'd rather cause her pain along the journey than shorten it. You can't help me, just like you can't help her." His wings whipped a swift breeze through the snow. "A half-breed. How interesting. I was under the impression that most of you were killed in the womb."

Israfel was pregnant. How or why was beyond comprehension.

But he'd pulled a trick common to most female angels and blocked his scent for the shortest time, effectively hiding himself from Troy's nose. Sophia and the Thrones had simply been near enough to benefit from the disguise.

"Then," Sariel's voice had real pain in it, "I guess you were mistaken."

"This is insulting, even for a demon. To align herself with a half-breed priest who's obsessed with murdering my sister. And why, so you can take Lucifel's place?"

Silence.

"Soon there will be a new order to things. My order. I doubt you'll have a position of power in it." Israfel's tone sharpened cruelly. "You did cut my neck, after all. You'd think I'd return the favor."

"You're not going to kill me?" Sariel gasped. He wasn't even bothering with the Latin. The moment he tried, Israfel would sever his windpipe.

"Why soil my hands when your betrayed god will do it for me?"

Naamah moaned nearby, the smell of her blood now tainting the air with its acidic sourness. Fury must have blinded her and escaped before the demon could slice through her wings. Too bad the rain continued to fall as snow. Only the Creator Supernal could mutate one state of matter into another with the mere power of his voice. But the poisonous effects of the water hadn't stopped, and Troy's wings began to shiver from the pain. If Israfel wasn't the cause of the black rain, it was a foreshadowing of another presence soon to arrive.

The angel's voice was like a smile.

"She's coming."

Thirty-nine

And if your will is gone, what do you have left?
—THE DEMON PYTHON, TRANSCRIBED FROM *The Lies of Babylon*

Angela hid her hand behind her back, nauseated.

She took a step backward, hardly realizing her fear until her vision swam and Stephanie continued to advance like a watery blur, all smiles lost. Her expression had changed along with the color of her eyes. A pure and terrible kind of coldness darkened her pupils, contrasting sharply with those crimson irises suggesting fire and blood.

Deep silence spread throughout the Netherworld.

Angela wanted to believe this was Mikel again, returned to help her in Stephanie's body, even despite what that implied for Nina. But Stephanie emitted a strange aura, and invisible though it might have been, it clashed against Angela's as if they were already fighting each other. Reality warped around them, trying desperately to respond to their mental demands for space.

"Mikel?" Angela's voice became a whisper.

Stephanie paused, analyzing her silently with those same cold eyes.

Angela swallowed the spit thickening in her mouth. None of this seemed possible. Stephanie must have entered the Netherworld on her own somehow, but when had she become possessed? If Nina was dead—

She stammered like an idiot. "How did—"

"Surely you remember Halloween night, Angela." Stephanie only half smiled, managing to make that twist of her mouth one of the worst things in the universe.

Angela shivered back to her feet, unable to find any more joy in the stairway of light. In her mind, she was seeing the pentagrams that had torn open the walls of the Bell Chapel shortly before she'd summoned Mikel. She'd been too entranced at the time to think about why they'd appeared and what it might have meant. Now, the memory returned like a crushing wave. Maybe Kim was right. Maybe Mikel *was* the Devil's daughter in every sense of the word. She could have been manipulating Angela all along, hoping to trap her in the Netherworld and finish her off when the Ladder appeared.

How stupid she felt. Fatally stupid.

"Is everything coming back to you now? Making sense?"

"Where's Nina?" Angela spilled out the words, tormented suddenly by her ignorance. The Grail was worthless at the moment. If anything, Mikel would kill her before she could use it, if it had any effect at all. The angel hadn't seemed severely injured by the Grail's contact before this. Merely irritated.

Stephanie pushed a lock of hair from her eyes, amused. "Oh, she'll be just fine, Angela."

The way she said her name—the effect was worse every time. Angela's insides knotted and her breath seized up. The blackness around them seemed to throb, like they stood in the center of the Devil's heart. But Stephanie took as much notice of it as she did the Ladder. Either summoning it had been less momentous than Angela had thought, or it wouldn't make a difference in the end.

"Mikel." Stephanie's eyes flickered back to their usual green. "You call her so, but in reality she has no name you can understand. Because in her state of being, she doesn't need one."

Angela stared at her wordlessly.

"She's her mother's daughter." Tears appeared in the corners of Stephanie's eyes, as if every word were painful to say. They contrasted so sharply with her dead expression that Angela could barely think. "And did you know she is also a copy of one of Lucifel's attributes? And much like that part of her mother, she can move from body to body, sucking away at the life of her host?"

Stephanie's lower lip trembled.

For a brief moment, her own personality emerged, and then just as quickly it disappeared, her expression cold again.

"But," she continued, as softly as before, "at least Mikel can wander. Unlike her caged mother she had the ability to explore the Realms and taste every one of them. Did she bother telling you how she would often come here, feeding off the souls of the dead?"

Angela clutched at her stomach, struggling with another wave of nausea.

Kim had warned that Mikel was dangerous. Angela had done her best to be more cautious. And yet, in a stroke of bad judgment, she'd practically invited her into the Netherworld—barely questioning the disappearance of her parents and her torturous memories. They'd vanished under Mikel's power, leaving absolutely nothing behind. Now it made sense—the eager, almost hungry, shine to Mikel's eyes, her small hand lifting the glowing sphere to her mouth, and why she wouldn't explain where it had gone afterward.

She'd devoured it.

Justice had been served in its own incomprehensible way, yet Angela couldn't find her former satisfaction. Instead her breath hissed out between her teeth, and her lungs shuddered in the new, dense air, echoing her frustration, denying her the release of screaming out her anger. The atmosphere thickened, whirling and choking her with a swirling mass of black dots, their silhouettes glowing strangely against the void. They were like flies, buzzing for her eyes and ears, hazing over Stephanie's figure as she began to advance again.

"It certainly changes things, doesn't it?" Stephanie said. "When you realize that some people are born to be killers, no matter how much they try to fight it. I fought with that destiny myself. And finally, it became clear to me—"

She took a step closer, her hand outstretched for the Grail.

"—that there's no point to it at all. Why be born, why die, when there's no meaning to the process? Isn't silence the true ideal? No memories, thoughts, or pain can be found in a void. Because the pain, you see, is a detail that's always bothered me. I can't fathom the reason behind its existence—and I've pondered that existence for a long, long time."

"You're wrong," Angela snapped. "You've forgotten why people want to be alive. Or maybe you never even knew to begin with. It's so they can be with other people and feel complete." Her thirst for Israfel. Nina's hope to have friends. Kim's need for pleasure and affection. Sophia's longing for the Archon. Yes, they were the desires that kept them alive and moving in a common direction. "Do you really need to do this, Stephanie? I can end your life, if that's what you want. All I need is a chance."

"Oh, the Archon is surprisingly generous."

Adrenaline shot through Angela, burning into her heart.

Yes, that's what she was. At last, the definitive moment had come. But Stephanie, of all people, was not the first person she'd expected to agree. Why wasn't she upset? Or maniacal like last time?

"But stop and think, Angela. Lucifel's own worshippers fear her. They keep her caged, strung up in adamant chains. And with good reason, because she could suck their life away"—Stephanie's eyes glowed gently—"with a single touch. Consider, then, what it would mean for you to take her place. You—a weak human mistake who happens to shelter Raziel's soul."

"So—I'm not Raziel," Angela whispered, hating him for a second.

"That would be an insult to his memory." Stephanie stopped right in front of her, her closeness somehow making every thought and sensation more painful. "Now give me the Grail, and be done with all of this. If you back down, I'll let you live. You're lucky. It's one of my better compromises."

Angela rubbed the surface of the stone, aware of its gentle pulse.

The buzz was growing louder, the black dots cloying, her strength fading the more they swarmed. "Why do you need it?" she murmured. "Lucifel gave it to your father. Maybe he should keep the Grail."

Stephanie's, or Mikel's, smile was brief. "Wrong again. *He stole it from her.*"

Then—it hadn't been a lover's gift. Angela narrowed her eyes, illogically angry again. "Whose was it? Who did she take it from originally?"

Stephanie's hand waved slightly.

Angela's mouth sealed shut, just like Kim's when Israfel had worked his magic. It was one of the worst feelings she'd ever experienced—trying to open her mouth, finding it clamped tight beyond all of her strength. And Mikel loomed over her, gazing down at her through Stephanie's dead eyes. Angela could run away, but what good would that do now? Mikel could snap her neck with a twist of her fingers. She was keeping her alive for a reason.

Just like before.

"Now," Stephanie said without emotion, "how do I open the Book? You never told me before you died."

She's talking to Raziel. Little does she know he never feels like responding.

Angela shook her head.

Mikel struck her violently across the face. "He can answer without you."

Angela collapsed, blood oozing from the space between her lips and filming the inside of her mouth. Indignant anger was swelling inside of her. The Netherworld began to quiver, both below and above, responding to her feelings with a miniature earthquake that somehow gathered the void above them into an invisible swirl of vengeful darkness. Her strength, though, continued to leech away as if all her energy were being sucked out through a straw.

"Not in a talkative mood? What a difference from that last night we were together. Then you had enough words for us both."

Angela's mouth opened, her new masculine voice sounding so

sad, so soft, so painfully tired. *You know that the Key is inconsequential to you.* She touched her lips in fascination, unable to stop them from moving more. *Because what good is a Key when you can't find the Lock?*

This was the voice that had spoken within her for the past few days, questioning as much as it had answered. Raziel's voice. Its pitch and tone was now different from hers, but only, she sensed, because it needed to be.

He'd been with her all along. She'd simply misunderstood how.

"Then just tell me where it is," Mikel said calmly, narrowing her eyes for the first time.

She sounded just as tired.

Even if I did, you wouldn't understand how to open her. There is more to Sophia than physical locks and keys. The Book is not a jewelry box or a treasure chest.

The glow behind Mikel's eyes faded slightly. "Tell me where it is."

How I pity you . . .

His departure brought Angela's own voice back, and it left her with a tremor. "There. Happy now? But I suppose you didn't have time to tell your father you loved him. Ever talk about *that* before he died?"

Mikel stared at her, her face a blank, impassive canvas.

Then she stooped down, cradling Angela's face in her hands. Angela groaned for air, barely seeing Stephanie's features through the black cloud vibrating around them. Her limbs felt weaker than string, and her heartbeat slowed, rumbling with the insistent pulse of the earthquake beneath them. The ground split somewhere off to their right, and screams filled the Netherworld, signifying the descent of so many souls to a deeper and more permanent hell. "You look just like him," Mikel whispered, almost tenderly. "Your hair, your eyes, your features." She rubbed Angela's lips with her thumb. "When I took his Eye—he banished me for all eternity. But for all his genius, Raziel was a sentimental fool. An imitation like you isn't enough to erase that kind of pain."

She leaned in close, her mouth pure with nothingness.

356

SABRINA BENULIS

"So sorry. But there is only one way to do that."

The kiss seemed to split Angela's head apart. The pain was excruciating, resembling fingers pressing into every part of her skull. She sank to her knees, crumpling in an agony that pierced through to her soul, and though the anger inside her exploded—possessive, outraged—she couldn't express it even if she tried. Mikel was draining her energy away, drinking it like water. There was a strange kind of pleasure to the sensation, a weak and familiar kind of bliss. But that was death's way, wasn't it? To lure you into darkness gently.

Mikel broke away abruptly, sounding annoyed. "Wasn't one death enough for you?"

"So you got here first." Nina's voice broke out of the darkness, sending a new rush of adrenaline through Angela's body. "But somehow you're not so frightening in the body of a sorority bitch."

The Grail throbbed in Angela's hand.

Instantly, the earth pitched, cracking and crumbling around them. Souls screamed. She turned her head, astonished as the Ladder of light, its brilliance like a bridge of glory in the distance, began to fade from the bottom up, the humans upon it leaving for Luz at a feverish speed. They were calling for her, for the Archon, their voices all blending together into a powerful roar that was shaking the Netherworld apart. In a rush, her energy began to return, a gift from the souls thanking her for their freedom.

Angela pushed up from the ground, swaying steadily and spreading her legs for balance.

The buzzing, flylike dots, the part of Stephanie glowing against the blackness, shrank in on her.

Nina appeared out of the void, grabbing Angela by the arm.

A deep gash cut her throat from chin to collarbone. Someone had killed her while she'd been standing guard by Tileaf's tree, and Mikel very well might have used Nina's own hand to accomplish the murder. "Angela, I'm going to take your place."

"Take my place?" Angela screamed over more screams. "No! You have to go up the stairway—with the rest of them—"

The tears rolled down her face, surprising and pathetic.

I might as well have killed her myself.

"I can't!" Nina shouted at her. "You have to go back to Luz! This is the only way—you can't leave the Netherworld like the others!"

"Why?"

"Because you're not dead!"

"But where are you going?"

Nina's eyes widened, their whites no longer bloodshot now that she was deceased. In that instant, she looked calmer and more sane than at any time before, all her fear of Stephanie, and Lucifel, and of the absurd importance of Academy life lost in the definition of her fate. Then, the ground opened up. A sky thick with gray clouds appeared below them, a horrendous stench of sulfur and smoke steaming up through the gap.

Nina fell down into the hole, her hand ripping sharply from Angela's arm.

In the same instant, Angela went up, breaking through the whorl of darkness above them and into a brilliant light.

She was crying when she landed in the grotto, its trees smothered in their heaps of ash, Tileaf's oak split viciously down the middle. Black snow drifted to the ground, illuminated by lightning that cracked through the sky in javelins of white and green, and by the great Ladder that suddenly was so much closer and so much brighter. The ashy crystals fell in such thickness it was difficult to see, but Angela didn't need to search for long.

Stephanie strode toward her, her figure emerging through the drifts. Her eyes were back to their normal green shade, overflowing with all the tears Mikel had stifled. Abruptly, she paused, swaying like she'd pitch into the ground. "It's all your fault," she said, her whisper cracked with grief.

Her mind must have returned again.

But Angela was just as ready for it to leave. She wiped away her tears, stumbling from a burned patch of earth. "Don't try it," she said. "I'll fight you this time. Even if it kills me."

"That's fine," Stephanie said, the tears rolling down her face. "It's too late for me anyway."

Angela paused, wary.

"I have to admit it. I'm jealous, Angela. Because it's just not fair. You thought your life was so bad, but look at you. You're the Archon. You have everything now. And I"—her voice trembled— "I have *nothing*. No father, no mother." She choked back more tears. "Naamah won't want me now. Not anymore."

What was going on here? Stephanie's expression was saturated with despair.

There was a gentle, crunching noise from behind.

Angela turned around, peering through the snow.

Sophia padded gently through the blackness, her beautiful face more frozen than the rain. Something was wrong. She'd been with Israfel—and now she'd walked out of nowhere just in time for Stephanie's arrival?

"I am the Ruin," Stephanie was saying, "just not in the way I'd hoped. Now, it's time to prove it to you once and for all. I command you to show me the Book."

Forty

Ruin is an essential element of the universe.
But in the very end, this balance shall tip precariously.
—CARDINAL DEMIAN YATES, *Translations of the Prophecy*

Sophia looked past Angela, deep into an unfathomable nothingness that hovered far beyond Earth. Her eyes were more vacant than the sky, and the light from the stairway cast her features into fierce, powerful angles. Her hair whipped in a breeze that didn't even exist. Never had she seemed so frightening, so bottled up—like an explosion waited to burst out of her, hungry to burn everything that existed to death. "This is your last chance at redemption, Stephanie," she said softly. Too softly. "Turn aside and leave me alone. Even if it means killing yourself. We both know there are worse fates."

Stephanie's face blanched. "You know I can't do that."

"The weakness of your soul," Sophia said, "is no one's fault but yours. But I warned you once before—and I suppose that was enough."

Sophia's polite smile was chilling.

Stephanie blinked back at her, at Angela, at the mysterious snow and the utter stillness of the park, and for a second it looked like she would actually change her mind. But the moment streaked past like a dream, and then she was walking toward Sophia, her eyes watering with pain. Every step seemed forced on her, and she struggled helplessly against it.

Angela shifted away, unnerved and admittedly terrified. "Sophia—"

"No," Sophia said with a mother's crispness, "let her go."

"But she's not—"

"*Let her go.*"

Sophia held out her hands, materializing a familiar Book held safely by her delicate fingers. It was a large tome with a sapphire cover and a gray eye—exactly like her own eyes—staring intently at Stephanie. Stephanie grabbed it with violently shivering hands, her eyes wide and wild. Desperate with fear.

Angela could sense the bated breaths inside the Park. They weren't alone.

"I can't—" Stephanie slid a finger beneath the cover, ready to flip it open.

There should have been explosions. More lightning. A shudder through the universe.

Something.

Instead, Stephanie opened the Book like a normal manual from a library shelf, scattering pages with her fingers. But the more she perused, the more perplexed her expression became, and finally she dashed it into the snow, shrieking. "I can't—it's not there. The Key isn't there," she moaned, explaining herself to someone else. "I can't. There's nothing in there. *Nothing.*"

Sophia folded her hands calmly. "That's because you didn't open the Book."

Stephanie stared at her, as if she sensed what was coming next and why.

"That was simply the illusion of trying. And you knew that from the very start. Before you used this girl to experiment—and to set your spirit free."

There was a silence deeper than the blackness in the Netherworld.

At first, just as when Stephanie had tried to open the Book, nothing out of the ordinary seemed to happen. She and Sophia had locked gazes, and that was all. But gradually, as seconds turned into minutes, her face began to change. She was seeing some-thing—maybe in Sophia's eyes, maybe somewhere else—and her own eyes became even wider, and her mouth moved in soundless whispers. Then she began to shake. All over. Stephanie clutched her head, screaming at the top of her lungs, the noise reaching up into the sky and then back to stab through the heart. She was go-ing insane, babbling almost incoherently.

Because she's not Israfel, or Lucifel—or me.

"The eyes—so many eyes. What are—what is—*GOD, NO. NO.*"

And the denials continued, screeching and horrible.

Then, the world did seem to explode.

Stephanie collapsed into the black snow, a buzzing mass of flies erupting from her body as if they'd escaped through her pores. They gathered into a silhouette, a figure.

Angela thought she might die on the spot.

The Black Prince. The Destroyer Supernal.

The titles cycled inside of her head, screaming themselves into existence.

The Ruin.

Though . . . there can be two . . .

Lucifel—or more like her shadowy semblance—stood in front of Sophia, aloof and satisfied, her crimson eyes piercing. It was impossible to look at her as she truly was, and also even more im-possible to look away. This was her mere shadow, but the shape, the color of her eyes, and the severe, beautiful contours of her face struck Angela dumb. She was Israfel's antithesis in every way, sharp where he was curved, hard where he was sensual, her pres-ence seducing you by force rather than choice. How tall she was. Slim like a man, and with a man's casual stance. Faintly, Angela could distinguish her clothing, a tight black fabric stitched, and stitched again. With her pale skin and that sickly gleam to her eyes, she resembled a body sewn together and brought back to life.

She was the one who had possessed Stephanie all along.

Angela had called her spirit along with Mikel's on the night of the summoning, not even knowing it, hardly registering what those bloody pentagrams had meant. *God.* It was Angela's fault, exactly as Stephanie had said. Unwillingly, unknowingly, she'd released a part of the Devil from her cage, practically begging her to kill her when she had the chance.

And she'd been talking with her the entire time.

Lucifel glanced up at Sophia, her jaw set with disappointment. Apparently, her experiment had proven Raziel correct.

Before Angela could say a word, the wind picked up. Wings beat powerfully above her, thundering away the snow.

She fell beneath the shadows, squeezing her eyes shut.

Two angels descended on Lucifel, one on either side. Israfel's two guardians. Angela had thought they'd been an illusion, or a product of her imagination, but they were real, and they struck their own kind of terror into the heart, their faces blazing with anger.

The angels streaked like dive-bombing eagles.

Lucifel waved her hand.

Electricity snapped around her in a sphere of crimson, and they plummeted. Both angels screamed savagely, rolling in the snow like its touch was poison. But before Lucifel could silence them permanently, Israfel appeared.

Now the contrast was even more striking.

"Angry?" he whispered to her, somehow audible over Stephanie's screeching. She continued to rock on the ground, hair disheveled around her face. "That makes two of us."

Crimson stripes flared to life below his eyes, and his pink lips pursed together.

His wings quivered, spasming away the flakes as they touched his feathers.

Lucifel smiled. Then she zeroed in on the Ladder, its brilliance half veiled by the snow. She didn't run, she didn't fly, but her figure erupted into a buzzing mass again and zoomed with lethal determination toward the golden light.

Israfel followed immediately, graceful despite his anger, his six wings shining through the blackness.

Angela scrabbled up from the ground, racing behind him.

They're fast. I don't stand a chance.

Would Lucifel kill him? She was frightening enough, and this was only her shadow.

The flakes melted where they met Angela's skin, staining it with an oily residue. She was completely soaked when she burst through a burned stand of bracken, skidding to a halt at the base of the impossibly large stairway. Each one of its steps seemed overly enormous up close, and they shimmered with an unearthly pearlescence that had dazzled from a distance but somehow become more tolerable. as if everything Angela understood about light had suddenly changed.

Overhead, the sky rippled, its maw deep and fathomless where the last of the souls were vanishing into another dimension. The spiraling bridge seemed to extend up into nothingness itself, its height impossible and staggering; a testament to how any human perception of distance meant nothing to angels.

That explained it.

The stairway was operating on an entirely different kind of physics—and it had allowed Israfel and his sister to already reach the halfway point.

Lightning arced down from the clouds, hissing where it touched parts of Luz or the ocean.

Angela glanced back down at her feet again. The stairway's steps seemed made of a dazzling gold that had all the clarity of crystal. Carefully, Angela tapped one of them gently with her boot and finding it solid, braved another. Then another.

Good enough.

She dashed after the two Supernals, her heart pounding along with her footsteps.

Shots of electricity seared the air higher on the stairway.

Thunder boomed around them, the air contracting and expanding beneath the onslaught.

Lucifel had taken shape again, and both she and Israfel were two streaks of gray and white, half running and half flying, higher and higher, water from the sea spiraling up around them in a vortex of diamonds. But though Lucifel often turned to answer Israfel's blasts of electricity, she was still ahead, aiming for the hole in the sky. Angela pushed herself harder, biting back the pain in her joints, only mildly shocked by how the earth below was suddenly so small, so inconsequential. She couldn't afford anything more than a glance—both for her sanity and for the sake of time.

Luz sat below her like a plate of buildings, nearly sliding into the sea. Waves churned against its lower levels, some of them seeping deeply into alleyways, streets, homes, and dormitories.

More lightning surrounded the stairway in silver forks.

Lucifel wants to go through that hole.

She was going to escape into the higher dimensions, to wreak whatever havoc suited her hunger for silence. That simply couldn't happen.

Angela wouldn't let it happen.

She clenched her teeth, stabbing her fingernails into the Eye.

It began to bleed, blue liquid warming her hands. Almost—she was almost there.

"Does this part of me hurt you that much, Israfel?" The Devil's voice was as soft as before, yet unbelievably loud, her words echoing throughout the warped space around the stairs. Each word seemed to ricochet like a bullet. "But if you stood still, it would all be over soon. You know you can't defeat me like this."

The light somehow leeched away at Israfel's loveliness, turning the kohl darkening the circles of his eyes into blotches of pain. He wobbled on his feet for a second, clutching at his stomach with a hiss of agony, his wings flapping. Then he flew for Lucifel, meeting with her so that they crashed and tumbled dangerously down the stairs. Her shadow was still solid enough for a physical battle—until it dispersed again, regathering to swarm around Israfel in a buzzing mass.

He used an etheric blast to break up the cloud, but it swirled back, suffocating.

"*I'm eager to learn how you survived all this time.*" Her voice was now disembodied, echoing. "*You and that infant hope of yours.*"

He was on the defensive, using his wings to fend off her attacks, his gorgeous eyes tainted by the vicious pride behind them.

"*But if you'd allow it, I'll forget the past and finish what I started.*"

She *was* going to kill him.

Angela had finally gained on them, only twenty feet away, if that. Her mind was almost numb with rage, and the blood in her hands solidified to match the ice in her heart, lengthening, stretching, until she held a long shaft capped by a scimitar of crystalline blue.

The Glaive.

She'd at last conjured the same weapon that had killed countless angels, the same weapon rumored to have the power to cut through anything, that could terrorize the entire universe, as if she were a newborn god of death, introducing herself to the masses. But this was the Archon's symbol now, not Lucifel's. And Angela wasn't about to use it for the same thing twice.

Israfel spotted her, his eyes hard with a new fear.

He was gasping for breath, too weak to move, maybe to speak.

Lucifel's cloud sucked in on itself, re-forming into her tall body and imposing stance. She turned her head sharply and glared at Angela, eyes narrow with recognition.

According to her expression, Angela shouldn't have been able to climb the stairway.

Lucifel gestured with a finger, and an etheric blast struck Angela hard in the chest. It flung her backward, stunning her in a tremendous burst of pain.

She cried out, grasping frantically for the edge of the stairs as the rest slid away from her, leaving half her body dangling in the air. Angela's muscles felt like jelly, her head like a throbbing drum.

But she held on, knowing that to let go would be the end of everything.

Lucifel was already standing over her, ready to step on her fingers and send her plummeting. Then she must have changed her mind, and she stooped down for the Grail, plucking the blade from where Angela had hitched it into the stairs. The Supernal didn't even seem to notice the black blood streaming from her hand as the Glaive bit into her vaporous flesh.

"Time to share the toy," Lucifel said, her voice thunderously loud.

Oh, but it wasn't hers anymore.

Angela willed the Glaive to collapse, and the blue blade responded, its blood dribbling from Lucifel's fingers. The angel stared at her, not angry, but certainly annoyed.

They both knew what was coming next.

"Sorry to disappoint you," Angela muttered.

She willed the Glaive to re-form.

It congealed instantly around Lucifel's hand, plunging through it straight for her chest.

The Glaive resisted for a single second, straining against Lucifel's considerable power—but soon pierced her back into a buzzing mass, and then sliced through what was left of it, sweeping her away like dust. The Supernal was speaking, but her words contorted along with time and space. Her amused laughter was now the only intelligible exchange between them, and while the Devil's shadow began to disintegrate, and Angela's grip finally slipped, the snow stopped, the lightning ceased to strike. A great shudder took over the atmosphere, like an enormous weight was being lifted.

Air screamed in Angela's ears. Blue blood fell around her like rain. The wind was a torment.

Lucifel had found her anyway, and she gathered her shadow one last time beneath her, taking the shape of a gigantic fly made of a million others.

Its red eyes burned into Angela like bloody flames.

A horrendous buzzing sound overwhelmed her.

There was a final round of laughter, painfully triumphant. Seconds later the dark cloud exploded, taking the Ladder with it.

Forty-one

And the first words in Creation were a song.
—Unknown author

> *Were you there in the Garden of Shadows?*
> *Were you there when the Father took wing . . .*

Angela had given up her dreams.

That made this hallucination all the more precious. Her vision had blurred, and her body felt like its energy had drained through her wrists, her legs, her feet, her brain. She could very well have been dying. Yet in a resurrection of her old reckless self, she didn't care. If dying meant that Israfel would always hold her like this, if it meant that she would always be cupped by the softness of his wings and stare into his sapphire eyes, she would welcome it with all her heart. They were falling together, the white clouds of his pinions slowing their descent, his song warming and seducing her back to life every time she threatened to close her eyes and sleep forever.

> *Did you sigh when the starlight outpoured us?*
> *When the silver bright water could sing . . .*

He rubbed something in the palm of her hand.

For a split second, his fingers dug at it painfully, eager to tear that part of Angela away.

Then he simply stared back at her, still blurry, but with a gentle twist to his lips suggesting pensiveness. He was trying to figure something out, perhaps thinking the answer hid in the curves of her hand. The wings that were his ears folded back in an elegant sweeping motion, vanishing inside pockets impossible for her to see. Then Israfel leaned in close, and his beautiful face drowned out all her other thoughts, all the agony trying desperately to end her life. He never had looked so much like a woman, with those long lashes, and that feathery hair.

Their kiss was hesitant but searching.

He was looking for a mystery inside of her and trying to figure it out simultaneously.

She barely felt him pull away as the world closed around her, his voice breaking through this new blackness and peace.

It sounded as petulant as he often looked.

"How . . . when you were never enchanted at all . . ."

Enchanted? No. She'd loved him too long for that. And she tried to tell him so before every sensation stopped.

Forty-two

The gun had misfired.

Angela tossed it onto the floor, cursing in the way her parents often cursed. Her head throbbed where the muzzle had jolted against her skull, but that was all she had to prove she'd even tried. That and the acrid smell filling her bedroom.

Once again, she'd been disappointed. Thwarted.

She crashed back into her bed, sobbing uncontrollably for half an hour, thoroughly wetting her ratty pillow sham. It wasn't until the room had darkened and the moon gazed sympathetically through her window that she noticed a weight at the end of her bed.

She hadn't heard a door open.

Angela lifted her head from her arms, astonished to see an angel with blood-red hair and blue eyes just like her own sitting down at the edge of her bed near her feet. Half his body was hidden in the shadows, but she could see the great red wings folded against his back, and the others topping his delicate ears, their arching curves lined with tiny white jewels.

They were like miniature stars, matching the stones set into his dark blue coat.

His face, at least what she could see of it, was gentle. Wise. But he had all the presence of a ghost.

"Why do you always stop me?" she whispered.

Somehow, she knew he was the One, and her bitterness felt like poison.

His voice was softer than she'd thought it would be. "Because I need you, Angela."

"No one needs me."

More bitterness.

"Oh," the angel said as he smiled down at her, "but that's not true. He needs you. That's why you're running from everything, isn't it? To find him." When she stared back at him, his voice became gentler. "This is your world, and you make the rules. Anything can be yours if you want it badly enough."

"Are you talking about the angel with the bronze wings?"

He said nothing at first, and Angela realized he could have been talking about someone she hadn't even met yet. Then the angel stood from her bed and he was tall and infinitely sad. "You must stay alive, Angela, whether you want to or not. And even if you forget this moment, remember this: a heart can bleed long after it's been broken. I will be counting on you to mend that heart."

She knew he was referring to the same person, but she could only stare more, confused and in pain.

At last Angela found her words again. "So you think I'll forget about this?"

It seemed impossible. How could she forget this pain in her head, and this angel in her room? How could she ever forget, or think it was only a dream, when his red wings took up the world?

"Yes," he answered her gently, "you will forget."

A cloud covered the moon and he vanished. Now there was only her reflection in the cracked dresser mirror.

"But not for forever."

Forty-three

All angels can regret or forgive. Very few do so gracefully.
—Venerable Maximina, *Lost Writings and Annotations*

Kim found Naamah near the tree line.

She cradled Stephanie as they lay together on the ground, her wings shivering, her dark eyes scratched into pools of blood. The pain was affecting her strength, leaving her weak and gasping, and when his shoes stopped next to her head, there was no etheric blast, no flick of her fingerblades. She merely flinched.

The black rain that had welcomed Lucifel had scorched through the demon's remaining feathers like fire. Their leftovers twisted from her wing skin, half melted. Much of her neck and chest was redder than usual, coppery with burns.

The tattoo on her neck had faded to a faint tracery.

She could have hidden and kept herself from suffering like this. But it was obvious that Stephanie's deranged moaning had called her, and Naamah had dragged herself toward the sound of her daughter, wrapping what was left of her wings around their suffering.

A sharp sob cracked through the silence. Stephanie—crying out in her pitiful, fetuslike position. She hadn't stopped shaking since she went insane.

Kim could only stare, empty inside even as he looked at her.

Feelings lingered, despite his disgust. That must have been why he'd risked hovering over them.

"You ignorant . . . half-breed," Naamah said.

She must have recognized him by the sound of his footsteps. His breaths.

"All your promises and oaths of loyalty . . . for what?" She spat at his feet. "The Book unopened—Israfel returned . . . you should have died in your mother's womb. Better that than ruin my happiness."

He stooped down and whispered in her ear. "Should I have taken a wild guess about the Archon then? Yes, Israfel is gone. Back to the upper Realms."

"And . . . the Book?" Her fingers twitched pathetically.

"Here. He won't carry baggage that can't help him. Not when it's officially Angela's job to open it."

But Kim knew there was more to it than that.

Israfel must have tried to open Sophia—and failed. Otherwise, why would he have allowed his sister to try for herself? They were polar opposites, and yet frighteningly alike, using anyone and everyone to accomplish their goals without batting a proverbial eyelash, taking a maddening amusement in whatever obstacles they encountered, like toddlers solving riddles.

How true it was that mortals were toys for the gods.

Even if those gods had only the illusion of being divine.

Kim glanced back at Angela sleeping nearly comatose next to the ruins of Tileaf's tree, her scarred legs and arms splayed pitifully around her body. Israfel had done his part to keep her alive, seeming to consider it some sort of favor on his brother's behalf without even saying so, leaving with his disfigured Thrones after blessing Kim with advice.

It's only a matter of time until she puts you in your place.

Whether Israfel had been referring to Angela or Lucifel was beside the point. All Kim had cared about was that the Supernal's last concern seemed to be killing him. Israfel was like the legends said, true to his word, confident that the Black Prince would eventually murder what he didn't feel like touching. Like anyone else with delusions of godhood, he wouldn't soil his hands with a half-breed's unnatural blood—especially when that could displease the Archon and sway her from his influence. For a Supernal like Israfel, the insult was an ironic one. Killing Kim was actually quite beneath him. And Angela's feelings wouldn't allow it.

The stalemate continued.

"Now . . ." Naamah's voice was soft with her pain. "Let me at least die in peace."

"You won't return to Lucifel?"

She laughed at the sarcasm in his voice. "Return? No, priest. There is no return for me. I've failed her, and she is well aware of it." Naamah groaned, her wings flapping into snow, their metal struts creaking with her despair, insistent on moving when she could not be moved. "In her, there is no longer any pity or sympathy. Demons have some. She has none. She," Naamah said, sighing painfully, "feels nothing."

Her voice trailed off into soft whispers.

"But even so," Kim said. "I'm going to let the blackbird out of her cage."

Naamah didn't respond, maybe no longer even heard. Instead she squeezed Stephanie one last time, whispering what sounded like a demonic prayer.

"Mother," Stephanie whispered back, sobbing gently. "Did I do well? Are you happy?"

She could have been lucid for that brief moment, but Kim suspected otherwise.

The demon hushed her anyway, sweeping back the red hair from her face with a shaking hand. "Don't worry," she said, smiling so that her teeth appeared, blindingly white. "You did very . . . very well . . ."

"And you'll stay with me?"

"Always . . ."

Naamah stopped breathing.

The snow, of all things, had finally killed her.

The demon's eyes would have actually grown back if given the chance. But the poison she'd used on so many souls, keeping it safe from her own veins inside the wicked blades overlapping her nails, had been in Lucifel's deadly rain, its potency alarmingly high. The Prince's venom had entered Naamah through the mess of her eyes, and from there to her brain. After that, she probably knew there wasn't much time left.

So she'd decided to spend it with the human she'd grown to love.

Kim waited a few more minutes, and it began.

Slowly, her wings crumbled into fragments of bone and ash, framing her with their metal pieces still connected to skin. Now she was merely another young woman, exotic-looking, but singed and dead. He'd make certain to contact his foster father, Mastema, and send others for her body quickly. Lilith, her mentor, would have many questions that needed answering.

"*Requiescat in pace,*" Kim said, more out of habit than a desire to answer her request.

Stephanie must have recognized his voice somewhere in the tangle that had been her mind. She cried out his name, and then she resumed calling for Naamah, as if the demon could still answer.

Kim left her in her temporary coffin of branches and snow, walking past Angela to gloat over his other conquest. He deserved this one more than all the others, and he ached to glory in it with as much delight as the idea that Angela would speak to him long before she saw Israfel again.

Troy. Dead. Because of the same, miraculous black rain. All these years, and he'd never gotten close to killing her. His cousin was an object of hatred for both angels and demons, feared for being the hungry monster that she was. Jinn of the lower clans spoke her name with reverence bordering on dread. And yet, a fluke of nature had brought her down like a crow with an arrow through its breast.

She'd covered herself with both wings, half their feathers severely damaged by the snow, portions of her feet burned to a crimson red.

But she was frozen like the water.

Unresponsive.

He slid the obsidian knife out of his coat, already tasting his cousin's blood on the blade. He had to finalize this himself. Drain the rest of her life out before it reanimated her like the nightmare she was.

He reached out, his hand shaking, and flipped her heavy wings open.

Her large eyes were closed. He'd never seen Troy asleep, or resting in any position that resembled it, and he stared down at her, as if seeing her paper-white skin, and bruised lips, and sharp, evil nails for the first time. Blood still touched her features here and there, and she could have been beautiful like her ancestors if it weren't for those long ears and that wiry frame. Jinn were made for hunting even more than for breeding, and Troy's more feminine attributes were characteristically undeveloped.

"I win," he whispered, holding the knife above her heart.

It was like murdering his father twice.

She opened her eyes, letting out an eerie gleam of phosphorescence.

Her pupils riveted on him, hard and horrifically cold. "You spoke too soon."

Rage, like always, propelled her in a frenzy of speed. She lunged for his face, raking him mercilessly across the chin, and then latched onto his chest with her toenails, her fingernails, slipping as he was slipping on the sudden stream of blood. They tumbled to the earth, Troy crushing him, Kim gasping for breath as her teeth aimed right for his jugular.

He swore, screaming, lodging his knife deep into one of her wings.

She howled, contorting off him with more hisses and deep-throated growls.

Kim turned and ran.

His shoes slid through the snow, and his lungs felt like they would burst, but Troy was nearly on top of him already. He was pulling ahead, out of range for a death grip, yet her nails sliced with evil suddenness into the skin of his back. A fluid warmth dripped down to his ankles.

There would be no running after all.

Kim wiped his palm across the blood dripping down his chin and spun around, flinging it in her face along with his words. "*Exorcizo te, spiritus immunde!*"

It was the best he could do. The droplets converged on her, glowing with a pain he only recently dared to inflict. She smacked into the crimson shield like it was a wall, her yellow eyes slits that barely opened in the brightness of the light. He'd never seen her so angry, enraged to the point where even the ache of the light meant nothing. Troy was a picture of absolute fury, her nails scrabbling across the shield's illusory solid surface, spit slathering from her mouth and splattering off her teeth, dotting the inside of her prison with diamonds of saliva. The shield of energy and blood had become a bubble, but it also wouldn't last for long.

"You *coward*," Troy snarled at him, rabid.

Her voice was like the hiss of acid, and she spat at him again, a cobra with wings, teeth, and nails both sharper and stronger than steel.

"*You coward. I'll find you.*" Troy's pitch was as close to a roar as he'd ever heard it. "*Sariel. Not even the Archon can save you from this. I'll put you in your place, demon spawn.*"

Israfel's prophecy, it appeared, might have had another meaning entirely.

Kim's entire body trembled, but he scratched Mastema's blood crystal from the center of his cross, aware of Troy's eyes narrowing even more evilly with recognition. He could only use the Call once, but it would be worth the sacrifice to hide from Troy in the abyssal depths of Hell. There, she could never find him. Never reach him. He stole a final glimpse of Angela, pining inside for her heat on his skin, and her lips touching his chest. The next time he found her, there would be a space just for them, a promise for him, and maybe a throne for her.

Whether she understood his reasons no longer mattered.

He smashed the crystal against an exposed rock, actually baring his teeth back at Troy, hardly ashamed at his slip. She'd understand the gesture better than words, and better than him explaining that the worst part of all this failure was leaving Angela behind.

Troy began to gnaw through the barrier, ripping through it with wet, fleshy noises.

Kim escaped in a dazzling burst of crimson. Mere seconds before she crawled through the hole for his soul.

Omega

And now we are at the End.
Though some would call it a Beginning.
—CARDINAL DEMIAN YATES, *Translations of the Prophecy*

"There is no greater sorrow than to be mindful of the happy time in misery." The novice paused, waiting for the class to ingest the quote and contemplate it. She was slight, and looked too young to be teaching university freshmen. Unlike Kim, her mannerisms were all nerves and a complete lack of charisma that matched her mousy brown hair. "Today we're going to discuss exactly what Dante was trying to say in that famous quote . . . now if you'd copy the phrase exactly as it appears in the Italian . . ."

Angela shifted in her seat, glancing at Sophia out of the corner of her eye.

She was obeying the student teacher, copying the Italian in her elegant handwriting, her pen swirling deftly across the paper. Sophia had started wearing an overcoat that matched Angela's—black, brass buttons and an emerald eye stitched on the breast pocket—its sharp lines strangely suiting her neat sense of fashion. With Stephanie permanently absent, and most of the other members gone, Angela had inherited the position of head of the Pentacle Sorority, assuming her role mostly out of spite toward the priests who'd fawned over Stephanie so sickeningly.

Now they would pander to her rules. Ones that would be a lot healthier for all of them.

The novice meandered to the other side of the room, coming to rest under a whitewashed wall, its surface repainted after Stephanie's insane spree of territorial marking. In the brief span of time Lucifel had possessed her, pentagrams had replaced every sign, religious statue, and crucifix in sight. This room's crucifix was back in place, gleaming down from its spot above the door frame.

"Miss Mathers."

Angela lifted her head from its resting place on her hand.

The class quieted, waiting, silently afraid. Most of them remembered Stephanie's accusations in the cathedral, that Angela had summoned a demon to Luz and murdered Maribel. Ironically, the part about the demon had turned out to be the truth, though almost everyone was disregarding it, nervous yet unable to ignore the fact that Stephanie was now clinically insane.

According to Sophia, Stephanie lived in an institution on the south sea cliff of Luz. Often, she would rave about eyes, darkness, blood, and books.

No one paid attention to a single word she said.

"Yes," Angela said, standing. Wind whipped through the poorly patched hole in the ceiling, spraying briny rain onto her hair. The sky peered down into the classroom, blacker than ever before. Most of Luz had been so damaged in the worst of the storm, people no longer cared to hide from more of them.

"Miss Mathers, I'd like you to lead the class in discussion of the quote as it pertains to the chapter as a whole."

Angela tugged at her arm gloves and picked up her book.

She spoke aloud the first question on the discussion page, but her mind was entirely elsewhere. Not that it could be helped.

There was too much to ponder, to fear, to worry over.

It had been three weeks since Nina had died, since Kim had left, and since every angel and demon in her life had disappeared after the short interval she'd known them. In that time, Luz had already changed, its ordinances and Academy life becoming stricter, more secretive, and if possible, even more cut off from the mainland, probably the Vatican's chosen method to keep the sensational a rumor. But what had taken place was no hallucination or trick of the weather. Angela, too, had almost died, though from the power of the Grail rather than a battle between two angels. Using it to its maximum potential had somehow brought her to the brink of mortality, and when she'd awakened in that new bedroom of the Pentacle House, Sophia's first comment to her had actually been a soft reprimand.

And now you know the consequences.

Angela was a mystery, a vessel that contained Raziel's spirit dwelling side by side with her unidentifiable soul. But she was still human, and she could not conjure Lucifel's infamous Glaive without suffering for it. Yet, though she'd eventually emerged unscathed, the deaths that the Supernal's treasure had brought about were almost too many to count. Among them now were the people in Luz who'd drowned, been struck by lightning, or blown over the sea cliffs and off bridges.

"Can anyone explain the symbolism found on page three hundred . . ."

The Eye's curse seemed determined to continue, as if it had exacted hundreds of lives as the price for its use.

Free to consider the pain of those losses, Angela had taken her time to mourn Nina, and even Brendan, crying at every spare moment. But like all things, eventually her tears ran out, and she'd learned to deal with her unusual situation like she'd learned to deal with her previous one: always waiting for that next chance to escape from it.

This was her first class in a long while.

Angela spent most of her hours painting Israfel's picture, sobbing when she couldn't get his face right. The talent that had gotten her into the Academy was, like her dreams, a thing of the past.

She needed the real Israfel.

She'd find the real Israfel again.

". . . or make an outline of the stages Dante passes through before arriving in Heaven . . ."

Though they both knew death wouldn't come soon enough to satisfy her.

Sophia sat in front of the window, absorbed in the swirl of water on glass.

Two days of meager sunshine had at last given way to a chain of sour storm clouds, and Angela realized Sophia seemed to like nothing more than staring at the different downpours through every new window the Academy had to offer. Considering the extent of the damage, that was quite a lot. The Pentacle House, now renamed the Emerald House, had a set of bay and bow windows on every other floor, marking its status as a grand mansion. Most of these were now covered with plywood, turning the building into a match for its neighboring buildings, which most definitely weren't. Stephanie's influence must have been the culprit.

She'd demanded privacy, but not crappy real estate.

"I'm surprised," Angela said, sitting on the velvet chair next to Sophia, the candles flickering, highlighting the darker red strands of her hair. She crossed her legs, still not used to the skin on her thighs rubbing together. During the past week, Angela had discarded her tights permanently, taking pride in being a freak for the first time. "Every time I turn around, you're there, watching and waiting. I thought you'd be gone like the rest of them."

Sophia smiled, her expression amused and lovely. "Well, I am your property now. Why would they bother with a Book they can't even read?"

"You know what I'm saying. It could take a long time to find the Key. The Lock. Maybe I'll never find it, and Raziel will have to try all over again. Maybe you'll always be waiting."

Sophia shook her head, her curls swaying. "Not for as long as you might think."

Gentle thunder rolled above the dormitory, rumbling across the roof shingles.

"Did you see the paper this morning?" She plucked the newspaper from her lap and handed it to Angela.

Angela unfolded the front page, her fingers already shaking. The headline was all too familiar.

FEAR IN LUZ: KILLER'S REIGN OF TERROR BEGINS ANEW

Center City, Luz—With massive death tolls on every side of the island, Luz city officials as well as Academy authorities have been quick to put the deceased to rest, establishing their Memorial Cemetery in a park formerly at the epicenter of Academy life more than sixty years ago. Dedicated to the memory of Archbishop Gregory T. Solomon, often known for his annual celebration of the All Saints' Day feast . . .

Angela glanced at the picture: a priest with white hair and an authoritative face.

The last she'd seen him, his head had been rolling across the floor of St. Mary's, severed by Naamah's overgrown nails.

. . . it has been planned to be a haven for family and friends to mourn their loved ones and erect impressive headstones, their cost benefiting the Academy's slow recovery of buildings, academic materials, and communication lines to the mainland. The disturbing presence of a murdered woman just three days ago, however, has put a halt to one of the most generous outpourings of sympathy in recent years. The killer's habits are familiar, as is the method of dismemberment and the pattern of animalistic cuts on the right . . .

Angela didn't need to read anymore. She set the paper down, hollow inside.

Sophia stared at her, her gray eyes saying everything without her mouth speaking a word. Then she gently took the headband from her hair, setting it on the end table to their right, fluffing out her river of curls. Her lips were set in that line she'd adopted almost constantly since Stephanie's insanity, like any moment she might have to think of an excuse to defend her actions that night.

Clack. Clack, clack.

Sophia didn't even jump as the crow tapped its beak against the window, begging to be let in. "Shall I?" she said to Angela, voice strangely sweet.

Should she?

If Angela said no, Troy would find another way in and be even angrier.

But she ended up saying nothing, watching the bird pace anxiously outside the sill, its croaks rasping between whispers of thunder. Of course, she'd been naive, believing this moment would never arrive. Angela had tried to stay optimistic, hoping Troy would just go home and forget her humiliation in the Bell Tower. How could she have been that stupid? Now that all was finished, Israfel gone and Kim probably dead, Troy was starving for her next taste of revenge.

The confrontation's inevitable. She'll find me, just like she found Kim. I'll tell her not to kill me, hurt me, and just like when she shoved the Grail in my face, she'll find someone or something else to do it for her.

Best to end the problem right now.

Angela stood, sliding off the glove covering her right hand.

She readied to part her lips and say the words Sophia was waiting to hear.

Too late.

The crow flapped out into the gray rain, swallowed quickly by the water. Angela walked up to the window and touched the pane, letting winter leech into her fingertips. Luz was both too warm for snow, white or black, and too cold for anything but a bone-chilling, dreary soaking. She examined the porch roof, vaguely discerning a shape scamper across the shingles. It was the same size as Troy, but a little more wiry, its hair longer and wild.

Thump.

She shouted, stumbling away from the bay seats, grabbing for anything steady.

"You saw him then," Sophia said gently. "He's bold, isn't he? But he's also intimidated by my presence. As long as we're together . . ."

What *had* she seen? A face like Troy's, but with wider eyes and a mane of wild hair, those terrible Jinn features even more sharp and defined. His teeth were a little longer, and the brief glimpse of his wings had startled her more than his curiosity, their typical soot glossy with the sheen of blue and purple, like a blackbird's feathers.

That's right. There's an entrance to Hell now in Memorial Park.

No—Memorial Cemetery.

Angela shuddered, slipping Kim's note out of her breast pocket. She'd recognized his handwriting from the brief class or two they'd spent together, his letters cruder than she'd expected from a centuries-old priest. She hated looking at the thing. Its words reminded her of too many evils, like her selfishness, her iron grip on Sophia, her childish sense of clamping on to the universe—and the unnerving idea that she'd throw everything away for Israfel's touch. The irrational fear took hold of her once in a while, that she would make everything and everyone eventually suffer.

And that was something only Kim understood. Too often, she found herself longing for his warm hands and his cool voice, missing him more than she'd expected.

Whenever she squashed the temptation, it only returned worse than before.

Today, it had been the Jinn's turn to bring it back.

"Let me see." Sophia touched Angela's trembling arm, slipping the note from her fingers.

She perused it with a wry smile, and then returned it, sighing. "Don't read into it too much. Demons have a way with words, but they don't understand them at all." Her whisper was like a lover's kiss. "I'll always be right by your side to explain."

Angela smiled, crumpling the note and pitching it into a trash bin. "You're right. Let them come."

Sophia grabbed her bag, obviously eager to head out for dinner.

"I'll be ready," Angela said, trying to convince herself. To erase the words. But they stayed in her head, and as she turned for a quick glimpse in the mirror, she saw something even more terrifying than any Jinn, blinking back at her, its eyes blue and its hair blood red, its lips gently whispering the new song.

> *Blackbird escapes hungry*
> *The Fly of doom*
> *Her hellfire smoke eager*
> *To scorch, consume*
> *All but the One seeing*
> *Who will assume*
> *The mantle and title of Covenant,*
> *Ruin.*

To Be Continued

Glossary of Terms, Places, People, and Things

Abyss: the lowest dimension of Hell

Angels: intelligent beings that reside in the upper dimensions of the universe known as Heaven; beautiful and powerful, they are thought of as the pinnacle of creation

Angel of Death: legendary angel who guards human souls trapped in the Netherworld; his name is Azrael

Angelic Trinity: collective name for the Supernals Israfel, Raziel, and Lucifel

Archangel: formal name for the angel whose authority is below God alone

Archon: arcane name for the human reincarnation of the angel Raziel; a messiah figure with the ability to ultimately save or destroy the universe

Azrael: name of the Angel of Death

Babylon: a dimension of Hell; the city of the demons

Bell Tower: a building near West Wood Academy known for the enormous bell in its attic; the bell and the chapels beneath it are no longer officially in use

Binding: contract binding a human soul with a Jinn's; ends only with death

Blood head: derogatory name for any human with red hair, thought to be one of the Archon's distinguishing features

Book of Raziel: mythical book created by the angel Raziel that contains all the secrets of the universe and an immense power; can be opened only by the Archon with a special Key; those who try otherwise are fated to go insane

Celestial Revolution: Lucifel's failed rebellion against Heaven; the end result was that a third of the angels followed her to Hell to start their own regime

Chick: an infant angel, demon, or Jinn

Cherubim: an order of angels that guards the highest dimension of Heaven

Clan: in the realm of the Jinn there are six tribes or clans; the Sixth Clan is the most powerful

Covenant: refers to Raziel's ancient promises to the Jinn

Crow: derogatory term for an angel, demon, or Jinn; often used among their kind as an insult; also, many Jinn familiars take the shape of a black crow

Demon: intelligent beings that reside in the lower dimensions of the universe known as Hell; beautiful and powerful, they are either former angels or direct descendants of those who have fallen

Devil: formal name for Lucifel among most humans; in its plural form it refers to the Jinn

Ether: substance that composes much of the universe, it can be manipulated by angels and demons; it is believed that angels and demons use etheric currents to fly, even without the use of their wings

Exorcism: method that can be used to injure or banish an angel, demon, or Jinn to another dimension

Eye: another name for Lucifel's Grail, as it resembles a large emerald eye

Fae: former angels who left Heaven to dwell on Earth and live in symbiosis with host plants; most Fae are believed to be extinct

Father: angelic name for God

Feathered serpents: intelligent, serpentine dragons that live in the high dimensions of Heaven; the most infamous of these creatures became the demon Leviathan

Glaive: Lucifel's fabled weapon used in the Celestial Revolution

Grail: see "Lucifel's Grail"

Great Satan: demonic name for Lucifel as a dark god who will bring an end to the universe

Half-breed: derogatory name for half-human, half-Jinn offspring; most are killed at birth

Heaven: the highest dimensions of the Universe; home of the angels

Hell: the lowest dimensions of the Universe; home of the Jinn and demons

High Assassin: Jinn term for their most illustrious and deadly hunter, second only to their Queen

Hounds: feared predators of Hell; they are thought to be fallen Cherubim

Ialdaboth: the highest dimension of Heaven, accessible only to the ruling Archangel

Israfel: the Creator Supernal and Heaven's first ruling Archangel, legendary for his beauty and charisma; disappeared into Ialdaboth at the end of the Celestial Revolution

Jinn: intelligent beings who live in the dimensions of Hell known collectively as the Underworld; they are descendants of angelic offspring thrown into Hell to die; beautiful but savage, they are known by humans as devils

Key: the object that can open Raziel's Book; its identity and whereabouts are a mystery

Lilith: the most powerful female demon in Hell after Lucifel

Lock: the seal on the Book of Raziel; it can be opened only by the Archon

Lucifel: the Destroyer Supernal responsible for the Celestial Revolution at the dawn of time; Lucifel fled to Hell with the demons, but rules her regime as a god imprisoned by her own worshippers; her ultimate goal is to use Raziel's Book to silence the universe, but why she wishes to do so remains a mystery

Lucifel's Grail: mysterious eyelike pendant in the possession of the Jinn, it was first worn by Lucifel and has fearsome powers; most who look into its depths go mad

Luz: island-city off the American Continent, officially under the jurisdiction of the Vatican; Luz's most well-known feature is West Wood Academy; it has been besieged by increasingly foul weather for at least one hundred years

Malakhim: a dimension of Heaven: the city of the angels

Mastema: the most powerful male demon in Hell and Archdemon under Lucifel

Memorial Park: a large grove near Luz's western coast; Memorial Park is famous for the enormous oak tree at its center

Merkebah: the angelic tongue; in its written form it resembles hieroglyphs in the form of constellations

Mikel: a female angel who claims to be Lucifel and Raziel's daughter; has been presumed dead for millennia; has no real body, so she must possess a host in order to communicate

Netherworld: a dark and forgotten dimension where human souls gather after death

Nexus: the highest existing dimension, known to be the dwelling place of God and where all souls must eventually return after death

Python: one of the most feared demons in Hell; the son of Lilith and Leviathan

Raziel: the Preserver Supernal and creator of the Book of Raziel; he was thought to have committed suicide after his lover Lucifel failed in her rebellion against Heaven; is fabled to be reincarnated as a human who will determine the universe's ultimate fate

Realms: angelic term for the dimensions that make up the universe

Ruin: the most common term for the dark messiah known more secretly as the Archon; many prophecies predict the Archon will choose the side of evil and destroy humanity

St. Mary's Cathedral: enormous church in Luz where West Wood Academy holds most of its important religious feasts and services

Supernals: the highest-ranking angels of all, known collectively as the Angelic Trinity

Theban: the demonic tongue; in its written form it resembles a scripting of curves and sharp lines

Thrones: angelic rank acting as bodyguards for higher-ranking angels; most Thrones have a deformity of one kind or another

Tongue of Souls: otherwise known as Latin, it has the power to harm or bind angels, demons, and Jinn

Troy: the greatest Jinn city in the Underworld, destroyed millennia ago by an alliance between the angels and demons; often used among the Jinn as a given name; the name of the current High Assassin of the Jinn

Underworld: name for the dimensions in Hell that are home to the Jinn

Vapor: term for a Jinn familiar; they are a human soul within an animal body, usually that of a crow, cat, or dog

West Wood Academy: illustrious school that is the only haven for "blood heads" in the world; maintained and run by Vatican officials; West Wood derives its name from the enormous oak tree that can be found in Memorial Park, near the western coast of Luz

Witch: a female human who can conjure angels or demons